Phillip A Young is married and has three adult children; he resides in the lovely Georgian town of Bewdley in Worcestershire, UK. He had a very successful career in IT before retiring, which gave him time to spend redeveloping homes. However, in 2015, he was diagnosed with cancer, and the repercussions from the therapy caught up with him in later years, forcing him to take life easier.

His health has been getting better over the past few years, which has allowed him to pursue his love of writing. His favourite books are fast-paced criminal dramas and thrillers, particularly those written by authors such as Lee Child and James Patterson. In 2007, Phil penned and self-published his autobiography, "*2 Much 2 Young*", after winning a major award for his work in the IT industry. More recently Phil has been working on a trilogy of books based around the character Donovan Temple; 'County Lines' is the first of these books. Phil is very excited to see his characters come to life and for readers to enjoy them.

Firstly, to my wife and family who have put up with my foibles over the years
And secondly, the people who live in or around the Severn Valley, and have loaned me the backdrop to write this novel.

Philip A Young

Temple – County Lines

Austin Macauley Publishers

LONDON * CAMBRIDGE * NEW YORK * SHARJAH

Copyright © Philip A Young 2025

The right of Philip A Young to be identified as the author of this work has been asserted by the author in accordance with sections 77 and 78 of the Copyright, Designs and Patents Act 1988.

All rights reserved. No part of this publication may be reproduced, stored in a retrieval system, or transmitted in any form or by any means, electronic, mechanical, photocopying, recording, or otherwise, without the prior permission of the publishers.

Any person who commits any unauthorised act in relation to this publication may be liable to criminal prosecution and civil claims for damages.

This is a work of fiction. Names, characters, businesses, places, events, locales, and incidents are either the products of the author's imagination or used in a fictitious manner. Any resemblance to actual persons, living or dead, or actual events is purely coincidental.

A CIP catalogue record for this title is available from the British Library.

ISBN 9781035897513 (Paperback)
ISBN 9781035897520 (Hardback)
ISBN 9781035897537 (ePub e-book)

www.austinmacauley.com

First Published 2025
Austin Macauley Publishers Ltd®
1 Canada Square
Canary Wharf
London
E14 5AA

A special acknowledgement to my son George, who has helped design the book's cover.

Table of Contents

Introduction	13
Chapter 1: Donovan Temple	14
Chapter 2: Overdose	16
Chapter 3: Simon and Jimi	20
Chapter 4: Internet Cafe	24
Chapter 5: CI Grace	28
Chapter 6: Pick Up	36
Chapter 7: The Caretaker	39
Chapter 8: Amy's Story	42
Chapter 9: Commissioner	50
Chapter 10: Jimi's Story	56
Chapter 11: Drowning	64
Chapter 12: Under Cover	66
Chapter 13: The CLT	70
Chapter 14: Territory	72
Chapter 15: Donovan and Jess	74
Chapter 16: Gang Murder	79
Chapter 17: Jimi & Simon	82
Chapter 18: Carpet Factory	88
Chapter 19: Chargrilled	93

Chapter 20: Robert	96
Chapter 21: Robert (2)	99
Chapter 22: Severn Valley	101
Chapter 23: Joshua	104
Chapter 24: Body in the Tree	107
Chapter 25: Manchester	111
Chapter 26: Town Hall	117
Chapter 27: Simon	120
Chapter 28: Raid	123
Chapter 29: Status	127
Chapter 30: Meltdown	130
Chapter 31: Gypsy's	137
Chapter 32: Internet Café (2)	142
Chapter 33: The Catacombs	144
Chapter 34: Hell's Angels	148
Chapter 35: Toby	155
Chapter 36: Jess' Kidnap	157
Chapter 37: Jess' Rescue	164
Chapter 38: Bring in Jimi	169
Chapter 39: Simon's Downfall	184
Chapter 40: Arrested	196
Chapter 41: Deep Cover	204
Chapter 42: The Briefing	210
Chapter 43: Witley & Drakelow	216
Chapter 44: The Bosses	234
Chapter 45: The Docks	243
Chapter 46: Who Wins?	252

Chapter 47: Chief Super	260
Chapter 48: The Syndicate	267
Chapter 49: Epilogue	274

Introduction

This gripping *crime drama* follows Donovan Temple, a dedicated West Mercia police officer stationed in the picturesque and rural Severn Valley of Worcestershire. The story is a masterful blend of sophistication, stylisation, and gritty crime set in the 21st century.

Donovan has a painful past—once a military policeman, he lost his long-term partner to a tragic road accident, which led him to leave the service and return to his childhood home to find solace.

However, Donovan's career at the local police force has not been all smooth sailing. He often feels overlooked for important cases, instead being assigned mundane tasks like petty thefts. But everything changes when his boss—Chief Inspector Victoria Grace—sees potential in Donovan and wants to make him the *poster boy* of the force. While she believes in him wholeheartedly, Donovan struggles with self-doubt and discomfort with her expectations.

Set against the backdrop of the serene Severn Valley, the novel delves into the dangerous world of organised criminal drug gangs who operate in the *County Lines* that have been working under the radar until now.

As their boss demands more from them, Simon and Jimi—two members of an Organised Crime Group (OCG)—must navigate their own moral compass while fulfilling their duties. Meanwhile, readers will be taken on a thrilling journey through various crime scenes and introduced to key characters who are sure to surprise and captivate.

The author of this book is Phil Andrew Young, who is a highly accomplished senior IT consultant from the UK; he retired due to ill health in 2019. A devoted family man with three children and a resident of Worcestershire, Philip self-published his autobiography *2 Much 2 Young* in 2006-7. After a hiatus from his passion for writing, he returns with this gripping crime novel.

Chapter 1: Donovan Temple

A raindrop trickled slowly down the sash window; a gentle pitter-patter providing background noise to Detective Inspector Donovan Temple's contemplations on this summer evening. He sat back in his chair, interlacing his hands behind his head as he watched the raindrop make advancement.

"A DI's job is mostly mundane," he mused aloud, his gaze shifting to the piles of paperwork scattered across his desk. "But it's that 10% that makes it all worthwhile."

The recent influx of lost pets and burglary cases had left him feeling drained, but he refused to let it dampen his spirits.

Just then, a soft nudge at his knee brought his attention back to the present. It was Toby—his loyal chocolate Labrador—reminding him that it was time for their evening walk. Donovan stood up, stretching out his tired muscles before grabbing an umbrella—always prepared for any eventuality.

As they walked through the charming town of Bewdley, Donovan couldn't help but feel a sense of peace wash over him. This place had been his sanctuary after years in the Royal Military Police and the heartbreaking loss of his girlfriend, Grace. Bewdley was familiar and comforting—just what he needed.

Passing by the florists, museum and town hall, they made their way towards the river. They paused at Thomas Telford's bridge, admiring the gentle flow of the River Severn below. Their next stop was the Riverside Café where they were greeted by Joe, the owner.

"Hi, Donovan," Joe said with a warm smile.

"Busy day or has the town been quiet?" Donovan asked.

"Not too shabby for a weekday," Joe replied with a grin. "The usual?"

Joe nodded, bringing over a cappuccino for Donovan and a bowl of water for Toby. As they settled into their routine, Donovan asked about Joe's family.

"Gail is at a council meeting and the kids are as rowdy as ever." Joe chuckled. "Sometimes, I wish I was single again."

"It's not all it's cracked up to be," Donovan bantered back, his thoughts drifting to Jessica, the pub worker he was slowly getting to know.

As Joe cleared tables and chatted with Donovan, the detective couldn't help but feel a sense of longing for the simple joys of family life. But before he could dwell on it too long, his phone rang interrupting his thoughts.

"Hello, Sir, it's Julie, the duty sergeant," a voice on the other end said.

"What can I do for you tonight, Julie?" Donovan responded.

"We've had a reported drug overdose. The boss wants you to investigate it. Shall I get DS Campbell to come in?"

"No need, I'll handle it," Donovan assured her. "I'll be at the station in an hour."

"Well then, no rest for the wicked," he joked to Joe as he ended the call.

"Can I get you a sandwich or something?" Joe offered.

"No thanks, I'll grab something later," Donovan declined as he finished his cappuccino and paid Joe.

As he made his way out of the café, Joe called after him with a playful grin, "See you tomorrow?"

"Not if I see you first," Donovan replied with a chuckle.

Donovan and Toby made their way back through town, preparing for whatever the evening held in store for them.

Chapter 2: Overdose

Donovan treasured his BMW 3 Series M class, a splurge he allowed himself after leaving the military police. He wasn't one for extravagance, but this car was an exception.

He parked in his designated spot at the small-town car park of Bewdley. His dog Toby, hopped onto the backseat as usual and Donovan secured him with a harness. The headquarters were only four miles away, but Donovan couldn't stand the silence. His thoughts could easily turn to darker things. He pressed the car's Google Assist button and requested tracks by Simple Minds, his favourite band. The music filled the car as they made their way.

When they pulled into the HQ car park, Donovan purposely parked away from other vehicles to avoid any accidental dinks to his pride and joy. He and Toby walked up six grey stone steps, through the large double doors, and across the lobby to the duty desk.

"Hi, Julie, what's this drug overdose about?" Donovan inquired.

"It was reported earlier today from Arley by a neighbour. An ambulance, a K-9 unit officer, and a locksmith responded. The paramedics pronounced the casualty dead at the scene," Julie explained.

"Who is there now?" he asked.

"A small CSI team is currently on site. If you hurry in that flashy car of yours, you might catch them," she said and giggled, bending down to pet Toby.

Donovan didn't notice her flirtatious behaviour.

"By the way, your boss wants you to be SIO on this case," she added.

"Okay, I'll head over to Arley now," Donovan said before gathering paperwork from Julie.

He returned to his car, entered the address into his Sat Nav, and resumed playing Simple Minds' music. Arley, a small village in the Wyre Forest district, was only a 30-minute drive away.

As he approached the house, he saw an unmarked CSI van already there and he pulled up behind it. The house was a semi-detached bungalow with the lights on and the front door slightly open.

Donovan entered the house, pulling on his blue latex gloves. He noticed scratch marks on the inside of the front door, most likely made by the owner's dog. The house was in disarray with a strong smell of marijuana lingering in the air. In the living room, a CSI agent was taking photographs of a motionless figure slumped in a worn armchair. The deceased—a man in his 30s with a short mullet hairstyle—had a syringe still hanging from a vein in his right forearm.

A small table to the right of him, next to the chair, held a TV remote, a pack of cigarettes with only six left in it and a car magazine.

"How does everything look? Anything unexpected?" Donovan asked the CSI agent.

"It all seems pretty straightforward. I just need to collect the syringe for testing," the agent replied.

"I would guess that the cause of death is heroin laced with fentanyl. Addicts have difficulty measuring the appropriate dosage for a stronger high when cutting it with fentanyl," Donovan stated.

"What about the time of death? Any signs of rigor mortis?" he asked.

"Yeah, there is some remaining rigour. It looks like death occurred within the last 24 hours," the agent responded. "I can't be more specific without the post-mortem."

Donovan searched through the rest of the house, looking for any out-of-place details.

Starting in the kitchen, he noticed cereal left out on the bar and dirty dishes piled up in the sink emitting a sour stench of spoiled milk. He sifted through a letter tray on the counter and found household bills addressed to Keith Roberts—the deceased, he assumed.

Moving to the front bedroom, Donovan saw an unmade bed and clothes scattered everywhere. The musty odour was unmistakable. It seemed like no one had opened the windows in quite some time. Donovan took note that these were name-brand clothes, not something you would expect a *junkie* to own, as they would have been sold for drug money.

"You can release the body to the coroner once you're done here," Donovan said to the CSI agent, who had followed him into the bedroom and was still taking photos.

"Will do. I'll be finished shortly," the agent responded.

Donovan made his way to the small attached house next door, where Ms Fletcher—a diminutive grey-haired lady—resided. As he approached the front door, he couldn't help but notice the manicured flower beds and perfectly trimmed bushes that framed the entrance.

"Took you long enough," Ms Fletcher remarked in a feisty tone as she opened the door.

Donovan was taken aback by her boldness.

"Sorry. about that, Ma'am," Donovan said with a smile. "You know how it is with cutbacks and all."

Ms Fletcher gestured for him to enter, leading him to a cosy living room filled with an assortment of quaint and old-fashioned furniture. The faint aroma of lavender lingered in the air, adding to the warmth of the space.

Donovan took a seat in a floral-patterned armchair as Ms Fletcher settled into a wingback chair across from him.

"Tell me from the beginning," Donovan prompted, pulling out his notebook and pen.

"What made you think something was wrong?"

"I heard his dog barking constantly from the early hours, waking me up and keeping me awake," she said with frustration evident in her voice.

Donovan noticed the lines of worry etched into her face as he jotted down her words.

"These walls aren't very thick, you see."

"And what time did you hear the barking?" Donovan asked, his pen poised.

"It started around 2 am," she replied, her hands wringing together nervously.

"By lunchtime today, around 1 pm, I'd had enough," she continued with more urgency in her voice. "I decided to knock on his door to see what was going on."

"I didn't get a response from knocking, so I decided to look through his front window." She paused, shuddering at the memory.

"On my tiptoes, I could just about see him lying there. I knocked on the glass, but he didn't respond. So, I called you lot. I saw the paramedics come first, then a locksmith and the dog van. They took his dog away, poor thing. Then, the white van came, the paramedics left, and finally, you arrived."

Donovan carefully noted down every detail she shared, glancing around the room as he did so. The cosy yet cluttered space was a stark contrast to the chaos next door.

As he stood up to leave, Donovan thanked Ms Fletcher for her vigilant observation and praised her for being a part of *neighbourhood watch*, noting the sticker promoting it in her window.

But as he walked back to the police car, a nagging feeling tugged at him. Something about the scene just didn't feel right—too neat and orchestrated. It hinted at something more intriguing lurking beneath the surface, elevating this case from mundane to potentially fascinating—a 10%er.

Chapter 3: Simon and Jimi

"I have a bad feeling about all this, Si," Jimi said, his voice laced with anxiety as he paced the room.

Every step seemed to make the small space feel even more cramped. His bulky frame taking up most of the available floor. The low ceiling pressed down on them, casting sharp shadows that added to the already thick tension in the air.

Simon leaned back into the old, green leather sofa, its once luxurious surface now cracked and patched with age. The worn armrest creaked under his weight as he tried to relax against it.

"What do you expect me to do about it? It's not like I have a say in things," he replied with defeated and resigned tone.

His finger traced the intricate patterns etched into the armrest, trying to focus on something other than the rising unease in the room.

Jimi stopped pacing and turned to Simon; his frustration and desperation evident in his expression.

"I just want to get on with moving all this new product we've been given, so I can finally have some money in my pocket and maybe, just maybe, get out of this game for good," he continued, the tension in his voice palpable.

Simon met Jimi's gaze, his own eyes reflecting a mix of determination and resignation.

"Well, unless we do what the bosses in the OCG[1] want us to do, you can forget about any money in your pocket," he said, his voice dropping to a whisper. "We might just end up on the wrong side of dead if we're not careful."

Jimi's shoulders slumped as he felt the weight of their dire situation pressing down on him. The room felt stifling, the heavy air filled with unspoken fears and looming threats. Simon's words hung in the air like a dark cloud. A stark

---

[1] Organised Crime Group

reminder of the dangerous game they were playing, where one wrong move could cost them everything.

The walls of the room were adorned with faded posters of rap legends, their once vibrant faces now dull and lifeless. They seemed to be watching the conversation with silent curiosity. Outside the window, a neon light flickered on and off, casting an eerie glow that added to the oppressive atmosphere in the room.

Simon looked out at the view of the council estate, its grey concrete buildings seemingly mocking their predicament.

"This latest increase—4 keys of coke, 4 keys of heroin, 20 keys of weed—is a massive amount of product to shift every single week, especially with the small crew we have," Simon said, his frustration evident as he rubbed his temples.

"We need to get these dealers in line and onboard. And we might have to bring in some new blood just to keep up with demand," Simon continued, his voice edged with concern.

He massaged his temples, trying to relieve some of the stress building up inside him.

"Time is not on our side! And all of this while trying to stay under the radar of the feds!" Jimi exclaimed, shaking his head in exasperation.

The room felt even smaller as their predicament weighed heavily on them.

Simon and Jimi had been friends since they were children growing up in Birmingham's notorious council estate known as the *concrete jungle*. It was a place filled with society's misfits and harsh realities that they had managed to navigate together; forming a strong bond that had helped them escape its grip. But at what cost? Their friendship had endured, but the scars from their past still lingered.

Jimi, in his late 20s, had a buzz cut of thick, dark brown hair that framed his angular face. His intense brown eyes seemed to pierce through anyone who met his gaze. His broad, muscular frame was a testament to his dedication to the gym. He exuded an aura of strength and confidence. His brawn often speaks louder than words.

Simon, also in his late 20s, sported a matching buzz cut with his jet-black hair and piercing green eyes. Despite his skinny, wiry frame, he possessed a sharp mind and strategic thinking that made him invaluable to their criminal organisation. His friends jokingly called him *Meerkat* for his alertness and quick reflexes.

But despite their gritty origins on the rough streets of Birmingham Jimi and Simon had developed a taste for the finer things in life. They dressed themselves in designer labels like Sergio Tacchini tracksuits and the latest Nike trainers were their signature look. Thick gold chains adorned their necks, accompanied by expensive watches that glinted in the sunlight.

They emulated the style of contemporary rap artists with their flashy attire and carefully maintained appearances. Regular visits to the Turkish barbers ensured their haircuts were always impeccably sharp. And gadgets were their vice. They always kept up with the latest technology, new mobile phones and PlayStations being their must-have tech.

These luxuries provided a brief respite from their chaotic lives as loyal minions for the OCG. But deep down, they knew it was all just a façade—an attempt to escape their bleak surroundings and make something of themselves. They only had each other, and no girls were allowed—at least, not until they had more power and money.

But as Jimi voiced his worries about a recent increase in their illicit activities, Simon tried to project calmness. He leaned back in his chair and maintained a steady tone as he assured Jimi that they had weathered similar situations before.

Yet, deep down, Simon couldn't shake off his own worries. He knew that with the increase in production came more risks and potential problems to solve. But he needed to hold it together and keep a clear head for Jimi; who didn't handle stress well.

"Yeah, I'm just going to chillax for a while with my PlayStation," Jimi said, trying to brush off his concerns.

He grabbed the controller, hoping to lose himself in the familiar routine of gaming.

Their descent into the world of crime began innocently enough. Enticed by the allure of quick money and a way out of their bleak surroundings, Jimi and Simon started as runners for a local drug gang. The lack of education, job prospects and money pushed them deeper into the life they now led.

Over the past six years, they had climbed the ranks and were now trusted loyalists for the OCG.

Whenever the order was barked by the bosses, "Jump", Simon would always be the first to respond, "How high?"

Then, both of them would jump to action. Non-compliance wasn't an option; they knew the rules and had seen too many people fall by the wayside for breaking them.

Their daily lives were separated, each choosing to rent their own apartments—Simon's in Kidderminster, and Jimi's in Bridgnorth. These locations were strategically chosen, positioned at each end of the Severn Valley railway line for easy access to towns along the route and further out into Staffordshire.

Despite living apart most days, they made sure to meet up regularly to go through their instructions from the bosses; ensuring they were always on the same page.

Theirs was a story of survival, loyalty, and the harsh realities of a life of crime.

Jimi looked up from his gaming, his voice trembling with worry as he asked, "So, what are we going to do now? This latest increase is starting to really concern me."

Simon took a slow breath trying to project an air of calm. He knew Jimi didn't handle stress well, and his own heart was beating wildly with anxiety. But he couldn't let Jimi see that. He needed to stay clear-headed and focused.

"Well, first things first," Simon replied, his tone steady. "I need to go down to the café and get some instructions from the bosses. We've dealt with increases before and managed just fine. No point stressing over something we can't control."

It was a lie, but Simon couldn't show his anxiety. Not when they were involved in such dangerous activities.

As Simon prepared to leave for the café, he couldn't shake off the feelings he had. The uncertainty that hung in the air around them.

Chapter 4: Internet Cafe

Simon parked his car a few streets away from the internet café, making sure to keep his head down and his hoodie up to avoid being caught on any CCTV cameras.

The café was situated in a rundown part of Kidderminster town centre, squeezed between a small sewing shop and a dingy off-licence. Its exterior was dilapidated, with a flickering neon sign that announced: *Internet Here*. Despite the uninviting appearance, Simon made his way inside.

The interior of the café was just as shabby as the outside: the fluorescent lights buzzed and flickered, casting a harsh and cold light over the mismatched furniture and ancient computers. The air was heavy with the stale scent of coffee and lingering traces of burnt toast. A few regulars were scattered throughout, hunched over their screens and lost in their own digital worlds.

The girl behind the counter barely acknowledged Simon's entrance, her attention consumed by her phone. He watched her with a mix of relief and caution. Her indifference could be useful, but he couldn't afford any mistakes.

Approaching the counter, Simon ordered a black coffee with no sugar and received a chipped mug filled with a weak, almost transparent liquid. She slid him a token for the computer without ever looking up from her phone. Simon took the token and mug before navigating his way to the back of the café where rows of outdated computers stood like relics from the Cold War.

He chose the farthest booth, strategically positioning himself against the wall for a clear view of both the entrance and anyone approaching him. As he booted up one of the sluggish machines, its ageing hardware groaned to life.

The linoleum floor tiles were scuffed and stained from years of use, and the air was thick with the scent of frying bacon and old grease. An old jukebox in the corner played a rock ballad, adding to the nostalgic yet melancholic atmosphere.

With the token purchased, Simon inserted it into the computer and began his 30 minutes of use. He quickly typed *Gmail* into the internet browser; his heart hammering in his chest. After a cautious glance around to ensure no one was watching, he clicked on the Gmail icon and entered his username and password.

His inbox appeared on the screen, with only one new message waiting for him. The sender's email address immediately caught his eye: *homerun*. This was the username of his OCG handler; someone, he had never met face to face. The subject line was blank, creating an unsettling sense of anticipation. Simon hesitated before clicking on the message.

The contents were brief:

Eight keys of C, Eight keys of H, 30 keys of W, next shipment next week. Same supply and drop locations.

New line:

Contact bulletin board, ASAP.

Simon mentally made note of the information before deleting the message and logging out of his Gmail account.

He then proceeded to type *https://www.xbullet.com/login* into the browser's address bar. A new encrypted screen opened with a prompt for login credentials.

The OCG had recently switched to this archaic method of communication after almost getting caught when their previous network, *EncroChat*, had been compromised by law enforcement. The French secret service had found a way to hack into its messages and shared this knowledge worldwide, resulting in numerous high-profile criminals and gangs being arrested.

Simon carefully typed out his message.
Was told to contact, ASAP.

He waited for a response.

You need to clean house, not just a slap though, the works, came the reply.

Too many leaks & people on the take, we have names.

Understood, give me the names and we will deal with it, Simon responded.

Worried about the increases in the product, can we hold off until we get things in order? he typed.

No, it is what it is. Just get your shit together. His handler's response was blunt and to the point.

Simon couldn't afford any delays in their operations.

Simon's boss provided him with crucial information that would help them overcome any obstacles, though Simon couldn't yet fathom how. He made a mental note, careful not to leave any trace in writing. This latest intel, coupled with the sudden surge in produce, was a game-changer for their operation.

Simon sat back in his chair, taking a sip of his coffee. The aroma of fresh beans filled his senses as he mulled over the unprecedented growth of their operation. Just a week ago, they had seen a significant increase in produce, and now another one? It was enough to make anyone's head spin. With every sip of coffee, Simon's mind raced with strategies and potential pitfalls.

But upon further reflection, Simon's concern deepened. The sheer volume of the increase was daunting. He wasn't sure, how they would manage it while also enforcing the names he had just been given. It was a delicate balancing act, but there was no turning back now. Everything needed to be executed flawlessly.

With his mind racing, Simon logged off the bulletin board and meticulously cleared his internet browser history to ensure there was no trace of his activity. As he erased each step, the weight of his responsibilities grew heavier on his shoulders. Taking a deep breath, he prepared himself for the next phase of their plan.

Simon grabbed his hoodie from the back of his chair and pulled up the hood before leaving the café to meet Jimi. They had agreed to gather at the beer garden of the Station pub in Kidderminster, just a short walk from the Severn Valley railway station.

As Simon entered the pub's beer garden, he could immediately sense it was a popular spot among locals, who enjoyed the locally brewed ales. The wooden benches were well-worn from countless patrons, and the air was filled with the sweet scent of blooming flowers and the distant chug of passing trains. Simon spotted Jimi already sitting at a table with a pint in hand.

"So, what's the plan, bro?" Jimi asked as Simon took a seat across from him.

"We've got more increases in produce," Simon replied in a hushed voice. "And we need to do some house cleaning. They want the *full monty*, not just a slap on the wrist. A clear message needs to be sent."

"Oh, shit." Jimi paused, processing the news. He took a long sip of his beer, the tension evident in his face. "How many people?"

"More than one. I'll give you names and locations," Simon said, his voice steady despite the weight of the task at hand. "It's a tough call on some of the names, but it has to be done."

"Understood," Jimi replied, nodding slowly.

The increase in produce was undoubtedly good for their business, but managing it while also handling the added responsibility of sending a clear message to their targets was proving to be a logistical nightmare. And to make matters even more challenging, some of the names he had to enforce were familiar; some even close friends. But personal feelings couldn't get in the way of business.

They chose not to discuss things further that day, opting instead to sit back, drink their beers, and enjoy the warm sun on their faces. For a brief moment amidst all the chaos, they were able to pretend everything was okay.

Chapter 5: CI Grace

Donovan's PolDar[2], a sixth sense honed through years of police work, continued to nag at him as he carried out his morning routine. The familiar, comforting smell of freshly brewed coffee wafted through the air as he poured himself a cup and sat down at the kitchen table. As he took a sip, he couldn't shake the feeling that something was amiss; that there was more to the drug overdose scene than met the eye.

As he finished polishing his shoes with precision and care—a habit deeply ingrained from his military days—Donovan found himself dwelling on the details of the case. The casualties identity, the circumstances surrounding the overdose, and any potential leads that could shed light on the situation. Every detail held significance in his meticulous mind, as he visualised each piece of evidence in front of him.

Drawing a deep breath, Donovan knew he couldn't let this rest. His dedication to his job and his unwavering sense of justice compelled him to delve deeper, to uncover the truth, no matter how unsettling it might be.

He was not overly concerned as he trusted in his ability to solve cases, a skill honed over years of being a seasoned detective. He believed that if he stopped thinking about it for too long, the solution would come to him naturally.

Although Donovan did not work out in the gym as much as he should, he still maintained a fit appearance for his 37 years of age. Standing at 6 ft tall with a muscular build, he carried himself with confidence and pride—a reminder of his days serving in the army.

He had already fed and brushed Toby, his loyal chocolate lab who nearly always accompanied him to work. Donovan laced up his brogues with practised ease and checked himself in the mirror one last time before heading out the door.

---

[2] Police Radar

His perfectly tailored suit and neatly combed dark hair gave him an air of professionalism and authority. He grabbed his briefcase containing all of his necessary tools for solving cases and headed out into the bustling streets; his mind already working through the possibilities of the day ahead.

As he walked, the crisp morning air invigorated him. The familiar sounds and smells of the town surrounded him: car horns beeping, delivery vans going about their business, people chatting as they hurried along the pavements, and the faint smell of fresh bread from a nearby bakery.

He loved these quieter moments before the real hustle and bustle of the town took over. It gave him a chance to collect his thoughts and prepare mentally for whatever the day had in store.

His phone buzzed, interrupting his thoughts and bringing him back to reality.

Oh shit, he thought after looking down to see the name of the message sender—Jess.

He had forgotten to call her last night and now he would have to face her wrath.

He typed back:

I know, I'm sorry and will explain, see you later after work, xx, and let out a sigh as he hit send.

Donovan knew he would have to face the music with Jess later. Their relationship had been rocky lately, with Jess often feeling neglected as Donovan's demanding job took up more and more of his time.

He made a mental note to make it up to her somehow. Perhaps, a nice dinner out or a weekend getaway. Anything to smooth things over and prevent another argument. He couldn't let his personal life interfere with his job, but he also couldn't ignore the important people in his life. It was a delicate balance that he strived to maintain.

Donovan took a deep breath, trying to push aside the gnawing concern about the terse message from his partner. His loyal canine companion Toby, wagged his tail happily, blissfully unaware of the tension brewing. Donovan turned up the smooth jazz playing through the car's speakers, finding solace in the soothing melodies that washed over him.

Toby had become a beloved fixture in the office, his friendly demeanour and wagging tail never failing to lift the spirits of the entire team. As Donovan parked the car and made his way inside, he couldn't help but smile at the warm welcome they always received.

Arriving at the station, he greeted his colleagues with a nod. The team were already gathered, discussing the latest developments in their ongoing cases. Donovan listened intently, absorbing every detail and formulating his own theories and strategies. He was known as a strong leader among his peers, always staying one step ahead of the game.

"Alright, everyone," he said, commanding the room's attention. "Let's get to work. I have a good feeling about today."

As he headed toward his boss's office, Donovan mentally prepared himself for the conversation ahead. No doubt there would be questions about the delays in getting results and any lingering issues that needed to be addressed. But with Toby by his side, Donovan felt a sense of reassurance and determination; ready to tackle whatever challenges lay ahead.

Firstly, Donovan made his way over to Amy (DS Campbell), who was sitting at her desk. Amy was a petite powerhouse of a woman; standing at only 5 ft 2 in with brown hair and brown eyes that seemed to miss nothing.

"Morning, Amy," Donovan greeted warmly. "Have you had a chance to look into that overdose case yet?"

Amy looked up from her computer screen, her sharp gaze scrutinising Donovan. "Yes, I've reviewed all the details you sent over," she replied briskly. "I've emailed you with what I have."

Donovan nodded in understanding. "I've already reached out to the family and they're willing to come in. Shall we schedule it?"

"Yes, let's do that, they might know something more about this," Donovan said decisively.

Amy's fingers flew across the keyboard as she began pulling up information on the case.

"I also want to check the toxicology reports and see if there are any connections to previous cases."

Donovan could see the determination in Amy's eyes and felt grateful to have her as his partner. They had been working together for a little over a year now; forming a solid team and almost able to second-guess each other's thoughts. She was his number 2—his right hand—and she was good at it.

"Oh, and the boss wants to see you when you get in," Amy added, not looking up from her screen.

"Yeah, I know. I was on my way there. I'll head there now. Keep an eye on Toby for me?" Donovan said, giving a pat to his faithful dog before heading towards Chief Inspector Victoria Grace's office.

He knocked on the door and heard her voice call out, "Enter."

So, he stepped inside.

Chief Inspector Grace stood with her back to him, gazing out the window at the town's skyline. Donovan couldn't help but notice how striking she looked.

"Morning, Ma'am. You wanted to see me?" Donovan asked, trying to read her expression.

She turned around with a small smile on her lips. "Good morning, Donovan. Yes, I did. How is that overdose case coming along? I wanted to assign it to you since you've seemed a bit down lately. Thought something more challenging might lift your spirits."

"Thanks, for the vote of confidence," he smiled, grateful to have her unwavering support.

The weight of his recent struggles had been lifted by her words and he felt a renewed sense of purpose.

"Yeah, I've been feeling a bit passed over lately, stuck with a caseload that some might consider that of a *slow horse*, shall we say. I've been at this rank for three years now and I feel it's time to move up, if possible. When I first joined the team, I was content with being a DI considering my personal issues, but now I'm ready for more challenging cases to sink my teeth into. You could say my ambition is back."

"Well, if that's how you feel, I'll respect your wishes and see what I can do. Donovan, I have great admiration for you and don't want to lose you. You're a dedicated and hardworking cop with a sharp eye for detail, qualities that are highly valued in our line of work," she said sincerely.

Just then, Donovan's thoughts were abruptly interrupted as his brain sent out an urgent alert. He suddenly realised what had been bothering him about the overdose case: Keith Roberts was murdered! It was like a light bulb had gone off in his head and everything clicked into place.

He knew this was the case because all signs pointed to Keith being right-handed, not left as the crime scene made out. The room where he was found dead was arranged for someone who was right-handed. Belongings were placed on the right side of the table beside his chair, not to the left.

Yet, the syringe used for the fatal dose was found in his right arm, suggesting he was left-handed while administering it himself. Someone had attempted to cover up the murder by making it look like an overdose, but their rookie mistake gave them away.

This new revelation changed everything and without hesitation, Donovan shared his deduction with Chief Inspector Grace. She looked slightly puzzled by his sudden burst of information but remained composed and attentive.

"Well, I expect you to do your best and keep me updated on any developments," she instructed firmly yet supportively. "You'll need a couple of detective constables to assist you. Let's aim to solve this case as quickly as possible."

Donovan nodded with determination, feeling the weight of the case resting on his shoulders. He returned to Amy's desk, a fierce determination in his eyes.

"It just hit me like a bolt of lightning: Keith Roberts was murdered!" he exclaimed in a hushed voice. "The room where he was found was set up to look like an overdose, but they made a mistake. The question now is why? And by who?"

Amy's eyes widened with curiosity and her interest was piqued. "What makes you so sure?" she asked, leaning in closer.

Donovan proceeded to explain his deduction in detail, his mind racing with possibilities. "Everything about the room's setup suggests it was for a right-handed person, yet the syringe was in his right arm…implying he was left-handed when administering the fatal dose. They almost got away with it, but they didn't anticipate someone noticing the small details. We need to find out who was with him that night and why they wanted him dead."

"You're right. We need to dig deeper into Keith Roberts' background and find a motive. People don't go through so much trouble to cover up a murder without a strong reason," Amy agreed determinedly.

Donovan and Amy spent the whole day delving into Keith Roberts' past while setting up their own dedicated workspace, known as the *situation room*. It was equipped with all necessary tools and resources such as computers, desks, phones, an electronic whiteboard, a copier and relevant case materials.

The two newly assigned detective constables, Jane and Mark, were also busy settling into their new roles; a mix of excitement and nervousness evident on their faces.

As mid-afternoon approached, the details of the case began to take shape. Donovan ordered his officers to gather precise information regarding Keith Roberts' movements, meticulously combing through CCTV footage from the surrounding area of his bungalow within the last 24 hours.

As they studied the footage, it became clear that Keith Roberts had a lengthy criminal record: a string of petty thefts, possession of Class A drugs, and even a charge for grievous bodily harm. He was far from being a model citizen. In fact, he had spent one year at Worcestershire Prison's Long Lartin facility; only serving the one year of a two-year sentence before being released just over a year ago.

Their financial checks uncovered nothing in terms of income or savings, which was not surprising given Keith's history. However, it raised questions about how he funded his drug habit and living expenses. The lack of financial resources added an extra layer of complexity to the investigation.

The expedited post-mortem results confirmed Donovan's suspicions; Keith died from a lethal combination of heroin and fentanyl. It was a deadly mix that had taken another life.

As the day drew to a close, no clear motive had emerged. Donovan instructed his team to wrap things up for the night. He and Toby decided to also call it a day, planning to spend the evening with Jess at her workplace—the Little Pack Horse pub.

Donovan and his loyal dog took a brief stroll through Bewdley's Park before entering the cosy pub. The warm atmosphere provided a stark contrast to the intensity of their investigation. As Jess spotted them entering, her face lit up with joy.

Jess was a slender woman standing at 5 ft 5", with her brown hair cut in a chic bob and her sparkling brown eyes radiating warmth. Dressed in a fitted white top and blue jeans, she exuded relaxed confidence at 30 years of age.

"Hi, Jess," Donovan greeted, leaning over the bar to kiss her cheek.

Her scent was a comforting blend of floral perfume and freshness.

"Hey, you," she replied with a grin. "Rough day?"

"You have no idea," Donovan sighed, settling onto a stool. "Do you have any local beer left for a worn-out detective?"

"Always," she said with practised ease, pouring him a pint. "Tell me all about it when you're ready."

Donovan smiled gratefully at her understanding as he took a sip of his beer, letting its smooth bitterness warm him. For now, he was just grateful to be in her company; away from the details of the case, even if only for a little while.

"So, what happened the other night?" Jess asked curiously, playfully narrowing her eyes.

"I got handed a new case late in the evening and time just flew by," Donovan explained, rubbing his temples as if to relieve the memory of his exhaustion. "Before I knew it, it was 4 in the morning. I only had two hours of sleep before I was back at it again. Sorry, for not letting you know."

"I suppose that's to be expected while dating such an important detective," she teased with a smile, her voice filled with affection.

"Grab your drink and sit over there for half an hour. I'll come to sit with you once my shift is over," she suggested, gesturing towards a cosy corner booth bathed in warm light from the pub's dim lamps.

Jess and Donovan spent the early evening catching up on their days. His current case took centre stage in their conversation, although he could only share so much with her. They also exchanged local town news and gossip, sharing small moments of laughter and meaningful glances that spoke volumes about their comfort with one another.

As the night progressed, they bid farewell to the warm, bustling pub and made their way through the quiet, deserted streets towards Donovan's apartment. The cool, crisp air of the evening enveloped them, punctuated by the soft glow of streetlights and the sight of their breaths forming a mist in front of them.

With each step, Jess felt herself growing more and more connected to Donovan. She reached for his hand, intertwining their fingers as they walked in comfortable silence.

As they entered Donovan's cosy apartment, they shed their outer layers and settled into the living room. Jess poured them each a glass of wine while Donovan carefully selected a record from his prized collection. The smooth notes of slow jazz—something Jess had introduced him to—filled the room, creating a serene atmosphere that seemed to cocoon them from the outside world.

Feeling safe and at ease in each other's company, Jess finally spoke up. "Tell me more about your case," she urged gently, her voice barely above a whisper amidst the soothing music.

Donovan let out a heavy sigh before taking a sip of his wine. "It's complicated, Jess. There are so many moving parts, and nothing seems to add up yet. But I promise, once it's all over, I'll tell you everything."

Jess nodded understandingly and placed a reassuring hand on his arm. "I know you will. Just remember to take care of yourself too, okay?"

"I will do," he said with a playful tone as he stroked Toby's head. "After all, I have this boy to look after me."

He nodded gratefully and leaned back into the couch with her by his side. For now, they were content to let the music envelop them and bask in the comfort of each other's presence—a peaceful refuge away from the chaos and stress of their daily lives.

Chapter 6: Pick Up

The sleek, grey Audi Q5 pulled up alongside him, its presence both cautious and imposing.

The passenger door opened with a smooth, almost silent motion, and a man stepped out. His expression was stern and unyielding, his dark eyes leaving no room for resistance.

Without a word, he grabbed the man by his shirt cuff and forcefully pushed him towards the rear of the car, toward the back seat. The man didn't struggle. He knew who he was dealing with and fighting back would be futile.

With a resigned sigh, the man slid into the back seat as the imposing figure joined him. The door shut with a decisive clunk, sealing their fate together in the car's luxurious interior.

Simon sat beside him, giving a curt nod to Jimi who was behind the wheel. Jimi's gaze was cold and calculating as he glanced at them through the rearview mirror. He shifted the car into gear and effortlessly merged into traffic, his movements practised and unhurried.

"It's been a while," Simon remarked casually, but there was an unmistakable edge to his tone.

"Have you been avoiding us?" he continued, narrowing his eyes as he scrutinised the man beside him.

"No, not at all. I've just been busy with other things," the man replied nervously.

His hands fidgeted in his lap, betraying his anxiety.

Jimi—never one to be ignored—interjected from the front seat. "From what I can see, you haven't been busy enough working on our stuff. Your quotas are down, and I'm tempted to teach you a lesson," he said menacingly.

The man's heart raced as he swallowed hard, feeling a lump form in his throat. He knew exactly what kind of *lesson* Jimi had in mind, and it wasn't something he wanted to experience.

"Our OCG is putting pressure on us to increase production, and we don't have room for lazy or careless shoters[3]," Jimi continued, his tone growing more threatening with each word.

"It's tough out there, man. People don't have any doh. Haven't you heard of the *credit crunch*?" the man replied defensively, his desperation evident in his voice, but tinged with a hint of contempt.

He realised his mistake too late.

Suddenly, Simon pulled out a pistol from inside his Harington jacket and pressed it firmly against the man's ribs.

"Don't give me that *credit crunch* bullshit, you fucker. We are not messing around," he screamed loudly into the man's ear, nearly perforating it.

"Just do as you're told, keep your head down and sell!" Simon said calmly now.

"Sort your crew out, bring in more shotters and get a few more cookoo[4] sites up and running, and do it quick," Jimi added to Simon's words.

The car pulled over to the kerb, and Simon opened the door, allowing the man to follow him out of the vehicle. After Simon took his place in the passenger seat, the car pulled away, leaving the shaken caretaker to contemplate what had just happened.

He quickly dialled a number on his phone, his hands trembling as he brought the device to his ear. The weight of their demands pressed heavily upon him as he spoke.

"Hello, it's me," he said nervously. "We've got a problem. The OCG has increased their quota, and I need more shotters and cuckoo locations as soon as possible. Can you help me out?"

As he listened intently to the response on the other end of the line, he furrowed his brow in concern. He jotted down some notes frantically before responding.

"Alright, I'll get on it right away," he said resolutely. "I can't afford to let Simon and Jimi down again. This needs to be handled quickly and discreetly. I'll be in touch."

A weight settled in the caretaker's chest as he ended the call and carefully slid the phone back into his pocket. He could feel the seconds ticking away, each

---

[3] People who sell drugs

[4] Safe houses where drugs are sold from. Usually houses owned by vulnerable people.

one more precious than the last. With a steely glint in his eye, he began his journey; vowing to fulfil every demand placed upon him, no matter the cost.

Every step was deliberate, every breath calculated. The weight of responsibility hung on his shoulders, but he refused to let it slow him down. He was a man on a mission, and nothing would stand in his way.

Chapter 7: The Caretaker

The caretaker was precisely that—a *caretaker* of a local school—he was a key player in the local criminal operation run by Simon and Jimi. While there were other network controllers working for them, the caretaker was special. He excelled at his role and required little management or motivation.

His job as a caretaker at the local high school provided the perfect cover for his illegal activities. Under the guise of maintaining the school and its grounds, he was able to recruit and lead a small gang of dealers; a Fagin-type band with him taking the lead role.

With a discerning eye, he handpicked struggling and vulnerable students who were desperate for money. These young individuals, often from troubled backgrounds, were given drugs to sell under his watchful eye. As their routes and clientele grew, so did his control over them.

But it wasn't just these young dealers that made him valuable to Simon and Jimi. The caretaker also had his own list of larger buyers who purchased significant quantities from him. His dual roles in both the school and the criminal underworld made him an essential asset to the operation.

Standing at 5 ft 11 inch with an average build, the caretaker had blonde hair cut short and a clean-shaven face. His appearance was purposely nondescript, allowing him to blend into any crowd unnoticed.

During school hours, he wore standard overalls provided by the school; effectively camouflaging himself amongst other staff members. But when conducting business for the OCG, he donned casual jeans and t-shirts to further disguise his true identity.

Despite the calm confidence he exuded on the surface, underneath was a man constantly juggling the pressures from above—Simon, Jimi, and the OCG—and the need to maintain his cover and manage his crew of young dealers. Every day was a delicate dance of deception, manipulation, and control.

Since being approached by Simon and Jimi earlier that day, the caretaker had spent hours briefing his crew on the increased demand for drugs. While they grumbled and complained, they all knew the consequences of not complying with their boss' orders—brutal punishment. Reluctantly, they agreed to push more products.

To incentivise their efforts, the caretaker instructed his crew to recruit others to join their ranks. He outlined special deals that would entice buyers into making larger purchases. With meticulous detail, he explained the financial benefits in a way that even the most reluctant dealers couldn't resist. The promise of quick money was a powerful motivator.

He also made a few calls to some of the larger dealers on his payroll, informing them of the increased supply and urging them to make use of it. These conversations were brief but laced with an underlying tension—a shared understanding of the pressure they were all under. The caretaker knew he needed to expand his network of *cuckoos*—individuals who would house the stash—but time was running out.

As the afternoon dragged on, the weight of his responsibilities became almost unbearable. He knew he had to make a trip to the drop-off point soon, as their stock was running low and he needed to deposit the stacks of cash he currently held.

Finally, as evening approached, he made his way to the Stourport canal basin. This picturesque area was located downstream from Bewdley and provided crucial access to the Birmingham canal network—the perfect location for illegal activities like drug trafficking.

As he navigated through the charming Georgian town with its bustling canal basin and nearby funfair, the caretaker couldn't help but feel a twinge of anxiety at the riskiness of his job. But there was no turning back now—he had a job to do for Simon and Jimi and he had to do it well or face dire consequences.

The narrowboat named the *Free Spirit* blended in seamlessly among the other boats in the canal. Its unassuming exterior hid the illicit cargo within, carefully concealed from prying eyes. The peeling paint and rusted metal gave it a worn and weathered patina, adding to its disguise as just another working boat on the water.

He scanned his surroundings, making sure no one out of place was watching before making his way towards the boat. Gaining entry through a padlocked hatch, he stepped into the cramped but functional living space. A small kitchen area occupied one side of the cabin while seating lined the other.

Further towards the back was a bedroom, where a cleverly disguised panel served as a hidden compartment for his merchandise. The hatch opened up, leading into a large crawlspace between the bed's headboard and the boat's bulkhead.

He placed his rucksack on the bed and began unpacking bundles of cash, tightly bound with elastic bands. With practised efficiency, he stashed them away in the crawlspace. This was now someone else's problem.

Next came the drugs, using is holdall to take and store large quantities of heroin, cocaine, and weed. All highly valuable and sought-after substances on the streets. He had worked out exactly how much could fit into the bag and rucksack without raising suspicion. The street value of his current haul alone was an impressive 160 thousand pounds.

Things were about to get riskier for him now with increased volumes came higher risks. He would have to strategically divide and hide his stash; some at his home and some at work in a secret compartment he had created in the janitor's closet at the school.

After securing his supply, he locked up and walked away from the boat with purposeful strides. This was just one drop-off out of many that would happen throughout the week, each one a crucial step in his illegal operations.

As he made his way through the narrow streets of Stourport-on-Severn, his mind was already racing with plans to distribute the product and expand his network of *cuckoos*.

The weight of his actions pressed heavily on his conscience, but he pushed it aside. In this line of work, hesitation and guilt were luxuries he couldn't afford. He had a job to do, and failure was not an option.

Chapter 8: Amy's Story

Donovan had first crossed paths with Amy Cambell, 3 years ago upon his return to the Wyre Forest. From the moment he laid eyes on her, he had been struck by her serious demeanour and no-nonsense attitude.

She exuded professionalism and seemed to have no time for foolishness. But beneath that tough exterior, he sensed a fiery spirit, ready to take on any challenge. He knew that with their combined strengths, they could build a formidable partnership, and maybe even become friends along the way.

―― " ――

Amy Campbell slammed her locker shut, exhaling sharply. Another gruelling shift was done. She rolled her shoulders, feeling the ache of chasing down that shoplifter earlier.

"Heading out, Campbell?" Donovan's voice carried from his desk.

"Yes, Sir. Unless you need me to stay?"

He appeared, shaking his head. "Go home. Get some rest."

Amy nodded, grabbing her bag. As she passed Donovan, he touched her shoulder.

"Good work today," he said quietly.

"Thanks." She managed a tired smile.

Outside, the crisp night air hit her face. Amy breathed deeply, letting the tension slip away. Her phone buzzed. A text from her mum:

"Any luck with that dating app, love?"

Amy sighed. If only it were that simple. Between erratic hours and the constant demands of the job, finding time for romance seemed impossible. Amy pocketed her phone without replying. She'd deal with her mum's well-intentioned meddling later.

It was a nice evening, so Amy decided to walk home, leaving her car at HQ. The walk was quiet, streetlights casting long shadows. Amy's mind drifted to her academy days. The gruelling training, the doubts she'd overcome. Her thoughts drifted, remembering her father's proud face at her graduation.

A proud smile crept onto her face as she thought of her father, a legendary police officer himself who had instilled in her a strong sense of justice and duty. She had followed in his footsteps, determined to make him proud and continue their family tradition of serving and protecting the community.

With each passing day, she had climbed the ranks, determined to prove herself as more than just a woman in a male-dominated field. Now, as a detective sergeant, she stood tall and confident, a shining example of what hard work and determination could achieve.

The weight of her badge on her hip reminded her of the responsibility she held, and she knew that she was ready for any challenge that came her way.

A noise startled her from her daydream. Footsteps, quick and light, from the alley ahead. Amy's hand instinctively moved to her hip, though she was off-duty, had no taser and was unarmed.

A figure burst from the darkness. A woman, wide-eyed and panting.

"Help me!" she gasped, clutching Amy's arm.

Before Amy could respond, two men appeared at the alley's mouth. One brandished a knife.

Amy's training kicked in instantly. She pushed the woman behind her, stance widening.

"Police!" she barked. "Drop the weapon!"

"The men hesitated, exchanging glances," The one with the knife sneered. "Yeah? Where's your badge, love?"

Amy's mind raced. No weapon, no backup. But she couldn't let them hurt her or the woman.

"Last warning," she growled, hoping her voice didn't betray her fear.

The unarmed man lunged forward. Amy pivoted, using his momentum to throw him off balance. He stumbled, crashing into a row of bins.

The knifeman waved the knife wildly. Amy dodged, feeling the blade whistle past her cheek. She grabbed his wrist and twisted hard. The knife clattered to the pavement.

A fist connected with her jaw. Stars exploded in her vision, but she maintained her grip.

Amy pressed the *speed dial* button on the phone's keypad, calling for backup. "HQ, this is Sergeant Campbell badge number 20158. The situation is under control. Two assailants apprehended. Requesting transport and a processing team."

She pocketed her phone, surveying the scene. Flashing lights painted the street in red and blue. The two men, cuffed and sullen, sat in the back of a police van. Amy nodded to herself. Job well done.

20 minutes later, she unlocked her apartment door. Kicked off her boots. Silence—a familiar companion—greeted her. She padded to the kitchen and grabbed a beer from the fridge. The cool bottle felt good against her palm.

Amy settled on the couch and cracked open her laptop. The dating app's cheerful interface blinked to life. She scrolled through profiles, sipping her beer. A doctor with kind eyes. A teacher who loved dogs.

Amy's finger hovered over the *like* button for the teacher's profile. A sharp buzz from her phone made her jump. Donovan's name flashed on the screen.

"Campbell," she answered, voice clipped and professional despite the late hour.

"Amy, it's Donovan. Just got word about the incident. You alright?"

She sank deeper into the couch cushions, suddenly aware of the throbbing in her jaw. "I'm fine. Nothing I couldn't handle."

"Two armed assailants while off-duty? That's not nothing, Amy."

Amy could hear the concern beneath his gruff tone. She closed her eyes, picturing Donovan at his desk, brow furrowed as he pored over the incident report.

"Really, I'm okay," she insisted, though her body ached in protest. "Just a few bruises. Nothing a hot bath won't fix."

Donovan grunted, unconvinced. "Take tomorrow off. That's an order."

Amy opened her mouth to argue, then thought better of it. "Yes, Sir. Thank you."

The line went dead. Amy tossed her phone aside, rubbing her temples. A day off. When was the last time she'd had one of those?

Her gaze drifted back to the dating app. The teacher's profile still glowed on the screen. Amy's finger hovered over the *like* button again. She bit her lip, hesitating.

A sharp knock at the door made her jump. She approached the door cautiously, peering through the peephole.

Her shoulders relaxed. It was Mrs Henley from next door, looking flustered. Amy opened the door.

"Mrs Henley? Is everything alright?"

The older woman wrung her hands. "Oh, Amy dear. I'm so sorry to bother you this late. It's just…I heard a noise in my flat. Like someone was inside. I'm probably being silly, but—"

Amy's cop instincts flared. "Not silly at all. Let me check it out for you."

She grabbed her keys, slipped on her boots and followed Mrs Henley to her apartment. Amy entered first, scanning the dim interior. Nothing seemed out of place.

A soft thud from the bedroom made them both freeze.

Amy's hand twitched, missing her taser. She grabbed an umbrella from the stand instead.

"Stay here," she whispered to Mrs Henley.

Amy crept toward the bedroom; the umbrella raised like a weapon. Her heart pounded, adrenaline surging. She nudged the door open with her foot, muscles coiled to strike.

A blur of motion. Amy swung the umbrella.

And connected with nothing but air.

A sleek tabby cat leapt gracefully from the dresser, landing on the bed with an indignant *Meow*!

Amy lowered the umbrella, tension draining from her body. She let out a surprised laugh.

"It's alright, Mrs Henley!" she called. "Just your cat playing acrobat."

Mrs Henley appeared in the doorway, hand over her heart. When she saw the cat, now licking its paw nonchalantly, she burst into giggles.

"Oh, Mittens! You naughty thing."

Amy smiled, shaking her head at the mischievous feline. "Well, at least, we solved the mystery."

Mrs Henley's laughter subsided into a relieved sigh. "Oh, dear. I feel so silly now. Thank you, for coming to check, Amy. I don't know what I'd do without you next door."

Amy's expression softened. "It's no trouble at all. I'm glad it was just Mittens causing trouble."

Mrs Henley hesitated, glancing at the clock. "I know it's late, but...would you like to stay for a cup of tea? I've got some lovely chamomile that might help us both settle down after all this excitement."

Amy opened her mouth to decline, but something in the older woman's hopeful expression made her pause. She realised how lonely Mrs Henley must get, especially at night.

Amy hesitated, then nodded. "You know what? That sounds lovely."

Mrs Henley beamed, ushering Amy to the cosy kitchen. Soon, the kettle whistled cheerfully. Amy inhaled the soothing scent of chamomile as Mrs Henley poured.

"So, tell me, dear," Mrs Henley said, settling into her chair. "Any young men in your life?"

Amy chuckled, shaking her head. "Not at the moment. Work keeps me pretty busy."

Mrs Henley tsked sympathetically. "It must be so different these days. When I was your age, I was already married with two little ones running about."

Amy's eyebrows rose. "Really?"

"Oh yes," Mrs Henley nodded, eyes twinkling with nostalgia. "I met Harold at a dance hall when I was just 18. He swept me off my feet—quite literally! He was a marvellous dancer."

Amy leaned forward, intrigued. "A dance hall? That sounds so romantic."

Mrs Henley chuckled. "It was, dear. Every Saturday night, all dolled up in our best dresses. The boys would line up on one side, girls on the other. Such excitement in the air!"

She sipped her tea, lost in memory. "Harold asked me to dance, and that was it. We courted for six months, then married. By the time, I was your age, we had little Tommy and Sarah."

Amy's brow furrowed. "It all happened so fast. Weren't you scared?"

Mrs Henley's eyes sparkled. "Scared? Oh my, yes. But also thrilled. Life was different then, you see. We didn't have all these options, all this time, to figure things out. You just...jumped in."

Amy listened, fascinated, as Mrs Henley painted a vivid picture of her youth. The clack of heels on wooden dance floors. The swish of full skirts twirling. The big band music fills the air with brass and rhythm.

"Harold was so handsome in his uniform." Mrs Henley sighed. "He'd just joined the Royal Air Force. When he smiled at me, I felt like I could fly without a plane."

She described their whirlwind courtship. Stolen kisses in the park. Sharing an ice cream sundae at the tea rooms. Love letters were exchanged while Harold was on base.

Mrs Henley's eyes misted over as she continued, "Our wedding day was simple but perfect. I wore my mother's dress, altered to fit. Harold looked so dashing in his uniform. We didn't have much, but we had each other."

Amy listened, entranced, as Mrs Henley described their early married life. The tiny flat above the greengrocers. Learning to cook together, laughing over burnt dinners. The excitement of their first real home, a modest semi-detached with a small garden.

"It wasn't always easy," Mrs Henley admitted. "Money was tight. Harold worked long hours. But we faced everything together."

She smiled, patting Amy's hand. "That's the secret, you know. Finding someone who is your partner in all things. Good times and bad."

Amy nodded, a lump in her throat. She glanced at the clock.

Mrs Henley's eyes twinkled. "Oh, but listen to me prattling on! You must be exhausted, dear."

Amy shook her head, smiling. "Not at all. I've loved hearing about you and Harold."

Mrs Henley beamed, and then her expression grew wistful. "I do miss him terribly. But I'm grateful for every moment we had."

She reached for a photo album on the nearby shelf, flipping it open. "Here we are on our 50th anniversary."

Amy leaned in, studying the image. An older couple, grey-haired but radiant, arms wrapped around each other. Their eyes sparkled with the same joy evident in Mrs Henley's earlier stories.

"You look so happy," Amy murmured.

Mrs Henley nodded. "We were. Right up until the end."

Amy bid Mrs Henley goodnight, her mind swirling with images of dance halls and young love. She padded back to her own apartment, the hallway eerily quiet after the warmth of Mrs Henley's kitchen.

Inside, Amy kicked off her boots and sank onto the couch. Her laptop screen glowed softly, the dating app still open. The teacher's profile smiled back at her.

Amy's fingers hovered over the keyboard. Mrs Henley's words echoed in her mind: "Finding someone who is your partner in all things."

She took a deep breath and clicked *Like*.

Almost instantly, a notification popped up. "It's a match!"

Amy's heart skipped. She hadn't expected such a quick response. A message appeared:

Hi, Amy! I'm Jack. Your profile mentioned you're a police officer—that must be fascinating work.

Amy's fingers flew across the keyboard, her heart racing:

Hi Jack! Yes, it can be pretty intense. What's it like teaching?

Jack's response came quickly:

Never a dull moment! Kids keep me on my toes. But I love it. How about we swap stories over coffee?

Amy hesitated, then typed:

That sounds great. When are you free?

They settled on Saturday afternoon at a cosy café in town. As Amy set her phone down, a giddy feeling bubbled up in her chest. She couldn't remember the last time she'd felt this excited.

She padded to her bedroom, mind whirling with possibilities. What would she wear? Should she bring her badge, just in case? Amy chuckled at herself. This wasn't an undercover op. It was a date.

Amy caught sight of herself in the mirror. A smile played at the corners of her mouth, softening her usually serious expression. She ran a hand through her hair, noticing how the dim light caught the warm highlights. When was the last time she'd really looked at herself, beyond checking for stray hairs or smudged makeup before work?

She leaned closer, studying her reflection. Brown eyes, flecked with gold, sparkled with an excitement she hadn't felt in years. The tiny scar above her left eyebrow—a memento from her first arrest as a rookie—seemed less pronounced tonight. Maybe it was the glow of anticipation warming her cheeks.

Amy's gaze drifted to the framed photo on her nightstand. Her police academy graduation. She stood tall in her crisp uniform, beaming with pride. Her father's arm was draped around her shoulders, his face a mirror of her own joy. She remembered his words that day:

You've got a big heart, Amy. Don't let the job harden it.

Amy touched the photo gently, her father's advice echoing in her mind. She'd worked so hard to prove herself, to be taken seriously. Had she lost something along the way?

Shaking off the melancholy, Amy crawled into bed. The cool sheets felt heavenly against her skin. She stretched, muscles relaxing as she sank into the mattress.

Her mind drifted, replaying the evening's events. The adrenaline rush of the alley confrontation. Mrs Henley's stories of young love. The unexpected excitement of matching with Jack.

Amy closed her eyes, allowing herself to imagine. Coffee with Jack. His warm smile as she described a case. His hand brushed hers as he passed the sugar. Maybe a walk in the park.

Amy's eyelids grew heavy as she nestled deeper into her pillow. The distant hum of traffic faded, replaced by the gentle whir of her bedside fan. Moonlight seeped through the curtains, casting soft shadows across her room.

She drifted into that hazy space between waking and dreaming. Images flickered behind her closed eyes: Mrs Henley twirling in a dance hall, her skirt a blur of colour. Jack's profile photo morphs into a real person, offering her a steaming cup of coffee. Her father's proud smile at her graduation.

The scenes blended, swirling into a kaleidoscope of possibilities. Amy found herself walking through a sunlit park, hand-in-hand with a faceless man. Children's laughter echoed from a nearby playground. A dog bounded past, reminding her of Donovan's loyal Toby.

With a gentle smile on her lips, she allowed herself to drift into a peaceful slumber, knowing that tomorrow would bring new adventures and opportunities. The moon cast a soft glow through the window, illuminating her face and casting shadows across the room. As she drifted off, she could feel all of her worries melt away, replaced by the promise of a brand-new day.

Chapter 9: Commissioner

The news of Karl Hamilton's sudden and tragic death sent shockwaves through the local police force and community. As the respected crime commissioner for the West Mercier Police, his passing was met with a deep sense of disbelief and sorrow.

The initial investigation revealed that the call to the authorities had been made by Hamilton's personal secretary, who—together with his groundskeeper—had discovered his lifeless body with a gunshot wound to the head. The report indicated that the death was instantaneous, raising immediate questions about the circumstances surrounding this shocking incident.

Chief Inspector Grace expressed the department's profound sadness over the loss of their esteemed colleague. "Commissioner Hamilton was a dedicated public servant who worked tirelessly to improve the safety and security of our region," she stated solemnly. "We are committed to conducting a thorough and impartial investigation to determine the exact nature of this tragedy."

The news quickly spread through the community, sparking an outpouring of condolences. Ribbesford House, the historic mansion that Hamilton had overseen, stood silent. Its grandeur was dimmed by the cloud of tragedy that now enveloped it.

As the police delved into the case, the focus shifted to unravelling the mystery surrounding the commissioner's untimely demise. With the groundkeeper as the sole witness, the investigators faced the task of piecing together the events that had led to this shocking loss of life within the hallowed halls of Ribbesford House.

Chief Inspector Grace called Donovan into her office. The room was bathed in the morning light filtering through the blinds, casting striped shadows across her desk.

"Donovan, I want you to be the lead on this, and it goes without saying that we need to keep it as low-key as possible," she said, her tone firm, eyes locked onto his.

"Hamilton liked to be high-profile both in and out of the public eye. He was involved in a lot of key initiatives and policymaking in the force," she continued, her gaze never wavering. "Keep your existing caseload going, but make sure that this one is on the top of your pile."

"No press statements from you; I will deal with all the media attention this will get," she added, emphasising the importance of discretion.

"Certainly, Ma'am. I fully understand and will do my best and get straight on it," Donovan replied, feeling the weight of the responsibility settle onto him.

His mind was already speeding with thoughts about the case.

As he turned to leave her office, his hand on the door handle, he paused. Turning back, he spoke with a hint of uncertainty, "Why me, Ma'am? You have other detective inspectors who have equal amounts of experience to me. Not that I'm not grateful or anything."

Grace's expression softened slightly. "Like I have told you before, I like and trust you," she said, her voice reassuring. "I recently had reason to speak to your old commanding officer based in Hereford.

"He assures me you are a *safe pair of hands*, based on your excellent record when you were dealing with the SAS regiment during your two tours in Afghanistan. Things like this should be relatively easy for you, one would hope," she added, a hint of a smile on her lips.

"I want you to become the poster boy for what modern policing looks like in this region, something, I believe you can live up to," she continued, her tone sober and encouraging.

"You need to increase your profile, hence I'm giving you this. Are you up to it?" she asked, raising an eyebrow, testing his resolve.

"If not, I can always give it to some other career-hungry detective," she added, her voice taking on a challenging edge.

"No, I am up for it! And I just don't want to sound ungrateful for the trust you're putting in me," Donovan replied, his voice steadying with determination.

"So, stop being so insecure and get on with it. I won't be discussing it again," she said curtly, her demeanour shifting back to the no-nonsense leader she was known to be.

Donovan opened the door and left her office, the weight of the assignment pressing on him even more heavily. He needed to make sure he could live up to her and everyone else's expectations. After all, he had been out in the *policing wilderness* for quite some time now and was feeling a little rusty.

Donovan, Amy, and Toby made their way to Ribbesford House in Donovan's car, Roxy Music's 'More Than This' playing softly in the background. The slow ballad matched their sombre moods as they drove the short distance to the scene on that warm summer afternoon. Both were lost in their own thoughts, the gravity of the situation weighing heavily on them.

Upon arrival, the First Attending Officer (FAO) and Scene of Crime Officers (SOCOs) were already at the scene but had paused their work to give Donovan and Amy space to assess what lay before them. The SOCO team had laid down white *eggbox*-style crates, creating a raised common approach path to prevent contamination of the scene.

The entrance door to the study had been forced open, breaking the lock's casement. Inside, directly opposite the entrance, stood an old oak desk with a body slumped forward over its writing area. The man's arms were stretched out in front of him, lifelessly draped over the desk.

The victim was dressed in the attire of a country squire: a houndstooth shirt, a beige hacking jacket, purple corduroy trousers and brown brogue shoes. The ensemble—once a mark of refined taste—now hung lifelessly on his body, adding a tragic irony to the scene.

The wall directly behind the desk, at head height, and the ceiling above it were splattered with a gruesome tapestry of vivid burgundy blood, matted together with dark hair and cream flecks. Mixed flecks of what appeared to be skull and brain fragments.

The scent of death hung thick in the air as Amy stepped closer to the gruesome scene. Her heart pounded in her chest, but she steeled her nerves and forced herself to survey the horrific tableau before her.

The sawn-off shotgun, lay abandoned on the desk, a testament to the violence that had transpired. Amy's gaze was immediately drawn to the victim, his face a shattered and unrecognisable ruin. The entry and exit wounds gaping like dark, accusing mouths.

She fought back the bile that rose in her throat, swallowing hard as she tried to comprehend the level of anguish that must have driven Karl to commit such a desperate act. The handwritten note, its words blotched and smeared with crimson, only added to the sense of tragedy enveloping the room.

The note simply read:

Sorry, Kate, I can't go on, too much pressure. All my Love—Karl.

"Are you okay?" Donovan asked, his voice laced with concern as he placed a steadying hand on Amy's shoulder.

Amy took a deep, steadying breath. "Give me a moment," she said, her voice steady despite the turmoil churning within. "I haven't encountered a scene quite like this before, but…I'll manage."

Steeling her resolve, Amy turned her attention to the task at hand, determined to uncover the truth behind this senseless act and bring some measure of closure to the heartbroken Kate, Karls' wife. It would not be an easy investigation, but Amy knew she had to push forward.

"Have you ever encountered something like this before? You seem surprisingly calm," Amy asked, her voice strained with the weight of the situation.

"I've seen horrific injuries and wounds inflicted by the Taliban during my time in Afghanistan. But nothing quite like this," Donovan replied, his eyes betraying a hint of sadness and pain.

"Unfortunately, I've been exposed to too many unspeakable things. They stick with you, etched into your mind forever. Many of my comrades suffer from PTSD[5] because of it. I consider myself one of the lucky ones, but it never gets easier," he added, trying to push away the disturbing memories that threatened to resurface.

"It seems pretty straightforward as a suicide case goes. What are your thoughts?" Donovan asked, wanting to focus on the task at hand.

"Same here, Boss, all signs point to suicide for me," his partner chimed in.

"Sad to see such a nice bloke go this way," Donovan murmured quietly, shaking his head in disbelief.

They proceeded to interview various members of the staff, gathering information and relocating to the living room. The groundskeeper stood before them in worn clothes, his face weathered from years spent working outdoors.

"Can you describe what happened?" Donovan prompted him.

---

[5] Post Traumatic Stress Disorder

"Well, I arrived for work at 8 am as usual. I was clearing leaves by the big oak tree that can be seen from Mr Hamilton's study window when suddenly I heard a loud cracking noise coming from the house," he recalled.

"It was an unfamiliar sound to me," he added.

"I immediately went over to investigate and found nothing out of place downstairs. That's when I made my way up to the study," he continued.

"Was anyone else around at the time?" Donovan asked.

"No, Sir, not at that time. It was just me," he replied nervously.

"I knocked on the door but got no answer. When I tried to open it, I found it locked. I was worried something might be wrong, so I stepped back and used my shoulder to break the lock. That's when I found Mr Hamilton," he finished with a solemn expression.

As Amy took notes, Donovan thanked the groundskeeper for his help and established that the time of death was around 8:45 am when the gunshot was heard. They then turned their attention to Mr Hamilton's wife, a tall and perfectly rounded woman in her mid-40s.

"I am deeply sorry for your loss," Donovan offered as they sat in the luxurious lounge.

"We just need to understand your husband's state of mind in the days leading up to this," he explained gently.

"He seemed fine from what I could tell. He mentioned having a lot of work to take care of, but nothing he couldn't handle," she replied, trying to hold back tears.

"I had no reason to believe anything was wrong. I can't believe he would do this to us," she sobbed, her composure finally breaking.

Donovan didn't want to push her too hard, but he needed information. "Did you have any indication that things were not going well for him?" he asked carefully.

"Sometimes, he seemed a little down or distant, but that wasn't unusual for him. But nothing that would lead me to believe he would do something like this," she said between sobs.

Donovan nodded sympathetically, understanding the complexity and shock of losing a loved one in such a tragic way.

With a sigh, Donovan leaned back in his chair and signalled the end of the interview. Amy gathered their notes and prepared to leave. They had spent a few hours questioning witnesses; trying to piece together what had happened to Karl Hamilton.

As they walked out of the building and towards their car, Donovan couldn't shake off the feeling that something was still missing from the puzzle. It nagged at him. But for now, all they could do was, head back to headquarters and start on the mountain of paperwork awaiting them.

After arriving back at HQ, Donovan immediately headed to brief his boss, Chief Inspector Grace. She sat behind her desk, her sharp eyes fixed on him as she asked about their findings.

"No, Ma'am, Mr Hamilton just seems to have taken his own life with no interference from others," he reported.

"That's a relief," Chief Inspector Grace responded with a tired smile. "Not a pleasant sight or way to go by any means. From the note he left, it seems depression played a role."

Donovan grimaced at the thought of someone feeling so hopeless that they felt suicide was their only option.

"A terrible shame," he agreed. "But I believe we can write this up as a clear case of suicide."

"Well, I suppose that is good news from a policing standpoint," Chief Inspector Grace said with a nod. "An open and shut case."

"I'll be able to update the press later with that information," she added before dismissing Donovan with a wave of her hand.

As Donovan and Amy worked on writing up the case file—making sure every detail was recorded accurately—they kept an eye out for any new developments in the Keith Roberts murder case. Though one case may have been closed, they knew there were still others waiting to be solved.

Chapter 10: Jimi's Story

Jimi first spotted Simon in the schoolyard. Scrawny kid with hunched shoulders. Easy mark.

"Oi, gimmie your lunch money," Jimi growled.

Simon's eyes flashed. He didn't flinch. "Make me."

Jimi blinked, caught off guard. Then grinned.

They became inseparable after that. Thick as thieves, literally. Started small- nicking sweets from the corner shop. Then graduating to breaking into cars and other petty thefts. The rush was addictive.

One night, as they were prowling for unlocked vehicles, a sleek black Range Rover pulled up.

Tinted windows rolled down. A man in an expensive suit eyed them. "You boys looking for work?"

Jimi and Simon exchanged glances. Could this be their ticket out of the concrete jungle.

"Yeah," Jimi replied, his voice steady despite the pounding in his chest.

The man smiled all teeth. "Get in."

They hesitated. Simon shot Jimi a look; part excitement, part fear. Jimi nodded, almost imperceptibly.

They climbed into the backseat. Leather. Expensive. The car purred to life.

"Names?" The man didn't turn around.

"Jimi. Simon."

"I'm Mr White. You'll be running packages for me. No questions asked. Understood?"

They nodded, caught in the rearview mirror.

The first job was simple. Deliver an envelope. Don't open it. Don't be late.

More followed. Bigger packages. Shadier drop-offs. The money was good. Too good.

One night, curiosity got the better of them. They peeked inside a package. White powder. Kilos of it.

Simon turned pale. "We're out. Now."

Jimi hesitated. The money. The power. It was addictive.

"We can't," he said.

"We have to," Simon hissed.

A car screeched around the corner. Mr White stepped out, flanked by two hulking men.

"Boys," he called, voice icy. "Something wrong with the delivery?"

Jimi's mind raced. Fight or flight.

Simon bolted. Jimi followed, heart pounding.

Gunshots cracked the air. Simon stumbled red blossoming on his shirt.

Jimi grabbed him, dragging him into an alley. Footsteps pounded behind them.

A fence loomed ahead. Jimi heaved Simon over, muscles straining. They tumbled down the other side, landing hard on concrete.

"Run," Simon gasped, clutching his side.

Jimi hesitated. "I'm not leaving you."

"Go!"

Shouts echoed from the alley. Jimi gritted his teeth and made his choice. He hoisted Simon up, half-carrying him as they stumbled forward.

A warehouse appeared. Abandoned. Jimi kicked in a rusted door.

Inside was pitch black. They huddled behind stacks of mouldy crates.

Simon's breathing was laboured. "I'm sorry," he wheezed.

"Shut it," Jimi snapped. "We're getting out of this."

Footsteps outside. Voices.

"Check every building!"

Jimi's mind raced. They were trapped. He scanned the warehouse, desperate for an escape route. A glint of moonlight caught his eye. A broken window, high up on the far wall.

"Can you climb?" he whispered to Simon.

Simon nodded weakly, face pale.

Jimi half-dragged and half-carried his friend across the warehouse floor. Every footstep echoed. Every breath seemed deafening.

They reached the wall. Jimi laced his fingers together, creating a foothold. "Up you go."

Simon struggled, gasping in pain. Blood dripped onto the concrete.

The warehouse door burst open. Flashlight beams cut through the darkness.

"There!" a voice shouted.

Jimi shoved Simon through the window, glass shards slicing his palms. He scrambled up after him, bullets pinging off the metal. They tumbled onto a sloped roof, momentum carrying them down. No time to catch their breath. They hit the ground running.

Sirens wailed in the distance. Getting closer.

"This way," Jimi panted, pulling Simon into a narrow alley.

They weaved through the maze of back streets, putting distance between them and their pursuers. Simon stumbled, legs giving out. Jimi caught him before he hit the pavement.

"Come on, mate. Stay with me."

A door creaked open nearby. An old woman peered out; eyes wide at the sight of them.

"Please," Jimi begged. "Help us."

She hesitated, then nodded, ushering them inside.

The old woman's flat was cramped and musty. Faded wallpaper peeled at the corners. She gestured to a threadbare sofa.

"Sit," she commanded, voice gravelly. "I'll fetch the first aid kit."

Jimi eased Simon down, wincing at his friend's pained groan. Blood soaked through Simon's shirt, sticky and warm.

"We can't stay," Simon wheezed. "They'll find us."

"Shut it," Jimi snapped. "You need help."

The old woman returned; arms laden with supplies. Without a word, she cut away Simon's shirt, revealing the angry red wound beneath.

"Bullet is still in there," she muttered. "I can get it out, but it'll hurt like hell."

Simon nodded weakly. Jimi gripped his hand.

Jimi hesitated before asking, "Are you sure about this?"

"Absolutely," she replied confidently. "I used to be a surgical nurse at the hospital; you'd be surprised by how many gunshot wounds I've seen."

"Do it," Jimi said, mimicking her confidence.

The old woman worked quickly; her gnarled hands steady. Simon bit down on a rolled-up towel, muffling his screams. Jimi held him down, muscles straining.

Minutes stretched into an hour. Finally, a small metal ping—the bullet dropped into a dish.

"Done," the woman said, wiping her brow. "He needs rest now."

Jimi nodded, exhausted. "Thank you. I'm Jimi. This is Simon."

"Mary," she replied. "You boys in trouble?"

Jimi hesitated. "Yeah. Bad people after us."

Mary's eyes narrowed. "OCG?"

Jimi's head snapped up. "How'd you—"

"I've seen it before," she said, voice hard. "My Tommy got mixed up with them years back. Never saw him again."

Silence fell. Simon's ragged breathing filled the room. Jimi's mind raced.

"We need to move," he said. "They'll be combing the area."

Mary shook her head. "Not tonight. He is too weak."

She was right. Simon's face was ashen, eyes glassy with pain.

"I know a place," Mary continued. "Safehouse. We'll go at dawn."

"How do you know about safe houses?" Jimi inquired, trying to pass the time as they waited.

"I have my ways," Mary replied with a sly grin. "Living in this concrete jungle has taught me to always be on my guard. I have connections, people who owe me favours, like you now." Her smile was gentle yet knowing, hinting at a backstory of loss and survival.

Jimi nodded, tension coiling in his gut. "What if they come here?"

Mary's lips thinned. She shuffled to a cabinet and pulled out a sawn-off shotgun.

"Let them try."

Dawn came too slowly. Jimi paced, peering out windows, jumping at every sound. Simon drifted in and out of consciousness.

Finally, Mary nodded. "Time to go."

They helped Simon to his feet. He swayed, gritting his teeth against the pain. Jimi slung Simon's arm over his shoulder, taking most of his weight.

Mary led them through a back door, into a narrow alley. The streets were deserted, bathed in the grey light of early morning. They moved slowly, every step agony for Simon.

"Just a bit further," Mary whispered.

A car engine rumbled in the distance. Jimi's heart raced. He scanned for cover, finding none.

The car rounded the corner. Black Range Rover. Tinted windows.

"Run!" Jimi hissed.

They stumbled forward. Simon gasped in pain. The car accelerated.

Mary veered left, towards a derelict building. She fumbled with a key, hands shaking.

The Range Rover screeched to a halt.

The lock clicked open. They tumbled inside, slamming the door shut. Footsteps pounded outside.

"Downstairs," Mary struggled, leading them to a hidden trapdoor.

They descended into darkness. The cellar reeked of mould and decay. Mary fumbled with a flashlight, illuminating a narrow tunnel.

"Old drug smuggling route, forgotten by most," she explained. "Leads out of the city."

A muffled shout from above. Fists pounding on the door.

"Go," Mary urged.

Jimi hesitated. "Come with us."

Mary shook her head, a sad smile on her wrinkled face. "This is my fight too. For Tommy."

The door splintered upstairs. Mary shoved them towards the tunnel.

Jimi and Simon stumbled through the dank tunnel, hearts pounding. The sounds of pursuit faded behind them. After what felt like hours, they emerged into a sunlit forest clearing.

"We made it," Simon wheezed, collapsing against a tree.

Jimi scanned their surroundings, muscles tense. "For now."

A twig snapped. They froze.

Mr White stepped into view; hands raised. "Easy, boys. I'm alone."

Jimi shifted, shielding Simon. "What do you want?"

"To talk." Mr White's voice was calm. "You've impressed me. Not many could've escaped like that."

He reached into his jacket. Jimi tensed, expecting a gun. Instead, Mr White pulled out a thick envelope.

"Your payment. Plus extra, for the trouble."

Jimi hesitated, eyeing the envelope. Mr White smiled, a wolf in an expensive suit.

"There's more where that came from," he said smoothly. "Much more."

He gestured around the clearing. Sunlight dappled the forest floor, birdsong filling the air.

"Beautiful, isn't it? Peaceful. This could be your life, boys. No more concrete jungle. No more scraping by."

Mr White's words painted a seductive picture. Jimi felt Simon shift beside him, leaning forward slightly.

"I know you're scared," Mr White continued. "But you've got talent. Skill. Loyalty. That's rare in our world. Valuable."

He pulled out a small tablet and tapped the screen. An image appeared—a picture of the countryside, a Georgian town with quaint streets and manicured lawns on neat houses. An escape from the lifeless concrete.

"This could be yours," Mr White said, gesturing to the tablet. "A house in the country. Clean air. Good schools for your kids someday. No more looking over your shoulder."

The image shifted, showing a gleaming sports car parked in a circular driveway. "And this. Top of the line. Bulletproof, of course."

Another swipe revealed stacks of cash and piles of gold bars. "Financial security. For life."

Jimi's breath caught. He glanced at Simon and saw the longing in his friend's eyes.

Mr White continued, his voice hypnotic, "Think about it. No more council flats with paper-thin walls. No more dodging bill collectors. No more watching your mum work three jobs just to keep the lights on."

He zoomed in on the country house. "This one has got a pool. Home theatre."

Mr White zoomed in further, revealing luxurious details. A sprawling kitchen with marble countertops and state-of-the-art appliances. A master bedroom larger than their entire council flat, with a walk-in closet and an en-suite bathroom boasting a jacuzzi tub.

"The garage fits six cars," Mr White said smoothly. "Pick your favourites. Lamborghini, Ferrari, Aston Martin—they're all yours."

He swiped again, showing a private jet. "For your holidays. How about a villa in the Maldives? Or skiing in the Swiss Alps?"

Jimi's mind reeled. He'd never left Birmingham, let alone the country. He was only 18, and he found it all intoxicating.

Mr White continued in his seductive purr voice, "You'll have access to the best clubs, the finest restaurants. VIP treatment everywhere you go. No more queuing outside in the rain, hoping to get in. You'll waltz right past the velvet ropes."

He swiped again, revealing a montage of glamorous scenes. Beautiful people in designer clothes, laughing and clinking champagne glasses on a yacht. A private island with pristine white sand beaches. A penthouse suite overlooking a glittering city skyline.

"This is the life you deserve," Mr White said. "The life you've always dreamed of."

Simon leaned in closer, captivated by the images. Jimi couldn't blame him; they were mesmerising.

Mr White tapped the screen once more. A document appeared. "All you have to do is sign. One signature."

The document glowed on the screen, a digital key to unlock a world of luxury. Mr White's words painted vivid pictures in Jimi's mind.

The signature was a blood oath, a binding contract that granted access to a world of depravity and destruction. Little did they know that it would consume them completely; taking everything they held dear and leaving behind only a trail of shattered dreams and broken lives.

"Imagine, waking up every morning in Egyptian cotton sheets, softer than anything you've ever felt. You'll step onto heated marble floors, padding to a bathroom with a rainfall shower and a view of rolling hills. No more cold flats with dodgy plumbing."

He swiped again, revealing a home office with floor-to-ceiling bookshelves and a mahogany desk. "You'll have your own private library. First editions, rare books. Knowledge at your fingertips."

Another swipe showed a state-of-the-art gym. "Personal trainers, nutritionists, massage therapists—all on call. You'll be in the best shape of your life."

The images flashed by faster now, a dizzying kaleidoscope of luxury. A private cinema with plush leather recliners. A wine cellar stocked with rare vintages. A rooftop garden with a glass-bottom infinity pool overlooking the countryside.

"Your own personal chef," Mr White continued. "Michelin-starred. He'll prepare whatever your heart desires, day or night. Caviar for breakfast? Wagyu beef for a midnight snack? It's all yours."

He zoomed in on the master closet. "Designer clothes. Tailored suits. Shoes handcrafted in Italy. You'll never wear the same outfit twice if you don't want to."

The two boys were swallowed whole, their minds consumed by the seductive images and enticing words that washed away the grime of their impoverished streets. Jimi was desperate for this dream. It was a lifeline to something better. With trembling hands, the boys signed on the dotted line—they were in; committed to this irresistible escape from reality.

They had recruited him, and Jimi never looked back.

Chapter 11: Drowning

The doorbell rang and she mindlessly swung the door open, not bothering to check who it was. Before she could react, a large hand snaked around her throat, squeezing tightly and slamming her back against the hallway mirror.

The glass shattered into a million tiny shards, embedding themselves in her skin as she struggled against her attacker. But it was no use. She was no match for Jimi, one of the notorious enforcers from the OCG. He said nothing as he tied her hands behind her back with zip ties and gagged her with a piece of rag.

She was helplessly dragged out of her own home and shoved into the trunk of Jimi's car. She could feel every bump in the road as they drove towards an unknown destination. Fear gripped her as she wondered what horrors awaited her.

After what felt like an eternity, the car finally stopped, and she heard the sound of a gate opening. The car started. Moving forward to its destination.

Jimi forced her out of the car and into the darkness, illuminated only by his powerful headtorch.

He remained silent as he pushed her in her back, down a dirt path and through a hole in a fence. Her heart raced as she realised that they were heading towards a body of water.

"Please," she begged, "don't hurt me."

But Jimi remained stoic, silent, showing no mercy as he led her onto a workmen's platform and then onto the edge of the sluice gates.

With one swift motion, he removed the zip ties from her wrists and pushed her over the edge into waist-high, murky water. She thrashed and screamed, but Jimi only held onto her tighter by her hair.

And then she saw it—the look in his eyes that sent chills down her spine. He had been given orders to dispose of her, and he would do so without hesitation.

"Please, please, I beg you—"

He shoved her head down with brutal force, ignoring her desperate attempts to fight back. As they thrashed about in the water, he relentlessly pushed her deeper and deeper until she was completely submerged. Her panicked struggles slowly gave way to an eerie stillness, her body lifeless and heavy in his grasp.

Overwhelmed by a sudden surge of guilt and regret, he released her limp form and watched as it floated away from the shore. He had committed murder without hesitation, following orders that left a bitter taste in his mouth. The thought of facing consequences for his actions was suffocating.

Determined to erase any trace of the horrific deed, he changed into fresh clothes and drove off. As for *disposing of the evidence*; he set the car ablaze in a clearing in the forest with a warped sense of satisfaction.

But even as he walked away from the scene, his mind raced with the haunting image of her lifeless body floating downstream. It would only be a matter of time before someone discovered the truth. Yet he kept walking, leaving behind nothing but destruction and death in his wake.

Chapter 12: Under Cover

For days, they had been tirelessly working on the Keith Roberts case, piecing together bits of evidence and leads. They knew that opportunity and means were established, but the elusive motive evaded them.

The team had spent countless hours sifting through footage from neighbours' doorbell cameras and nearby CCTV cameras. Grainy images captured a few visitors throughout the day, their faces hidden from view. A grey Audi SUV appeared on one of the CCTV tapes, with two passengers inside. One got out to spend time in the house, while the other stayed behind in the car, only returning later to pick up their companion. Again, no faces were discernible, but they were people of interest.

By this point, they were convinced that Keith was involved in some sort of illegal activity—perhaps, a small-time drug dealer with too many visitors to be considered mere friends. But who could he have gotten mixed up with? That was still a mystery.

They had managed to retrieve a partial licence plate from the CCTV footage, but it came back as *unknown* in the DVLA database—most likely a fake plate. Tracking the vehicle through multiple cameras, they eventually lost sight of it. It appears the car had either stopped to switch plates or had been abandoned somewhere.

All of this information was laid out in the situation room for everyone to see. The whiteboard now held photos of Keith and his house, along with various pieces of evidence. Donovan had even moved his things into the room so he could work more efficiently alongside Amy, Jane and Mark, the two DCs.

Just then, the duty sergeant walked in.

"Boss, here's another one for you—a suspected suicide by drowning in Trimpley by the river." He handed Donovan a thin case file.

"Three deaths in three days…aren't we popular," Donovan quipped. "Thanks."

"Amy and I will head out to the scene and check it out. Keep us updated if anything else comes up while we're out," he instructed the DCs, who nodded in response.

They didn't rush. The body wasn't going anywhere, and it was a beautiful summer's day. They took Donovan's car and drove 5.5 miles to the reservoir, the sound of Fleetwood Mac filling the air.

As they drove, Amy turned to Donovan.

"How's things with Jess these days?" she asked.

Donovan didn't mind the personal question. He and Amy had been friends and colleagues for years now.

"You know how it is. The job can put a strain on any relationship. But Jess is understanding…most of the time," he said and chuckled. "Sometimes, I think she prefers Toby's company over mine."

"What about your love life?" He asked her.

"Non-existent," she laughed. "Dating is tough these days. I've tried using dating apps, but all I seem to attract are crazies who belong in our custody cells."

"So, swiping left and right isn't working out for you?" he joked.

"The decent ones run for the hills when they find out I'm a cop. Lucky, if I even get a third date!" she exclaimed.

"I've never tried online dating myself, and I doubt I'd have much luck anyway. I'm more old-fashioned—luckily, I met Jess locally, otherwise, I'd probably be single forever." Donovan admitted.

"Well, at least you have Toby for company," Amy teased.

"He might want some feline companionship himself one day…who knows," Donovan smirked.

"Maybe I should invent a dating app for dogs? But I bet some crazy has already done it." He laughed out loud.

The friendly chatter came to an end as they reached the entrance gates of the reservoir. The once gleaming gates were now rusted, with a faded sign warning, *Keep Out*, and another below it declaring, *Members only*. An intercom sat next to the signs, its metallic exterior glistening in the sunlight.

Amy stepped out of the car and pressed the buzzer, her voice muffled as she spoke to someone on the other end. After a few moments, she returned to the car, and they drove through as the gate slowly raised.

The reservoir was a sprawling expanse of water, with two distinct pools—one for boating and recreation, and the smaller one reserved for angling. It was nestled next to the River Severn and cut through by the Severn Valley railway. The picturesque setting made it a popular destination for locals who enjoyed outdoor activities or simply wanted to take in its beauty.

Passing by the shimmering pools, they continued down a dirt track until they reached their destination. The forensics van was already there, its presence a stark contrast against the tranquil surroundings. Donovan parked behind it, and they all got out of the car.

He let Toby off his leash so he could roam freely for a bit, his wagging tail betraying his excitement. Ignoring the police officers who had cordoned off the area, Toby bounded through the lush grass surrounding them.

Donovan eventually handed Toby's leash to a young police officer and he and Amy ducked under the cordon tape. They walked along the riverbank until they reached the water's edge where a body lay face upwards.

The woman was dressed in a light summer blouse and white jeans, but her once vibrant features were now pale and lifeless. Her arms displayed cuts and scrapes from what he assumed was being pushed over sharp rocks before coming to rest by the edge of the river. Amy leaned in closer to examine her.

"What do you see, Amy?" Donovan asked, always valuing her insights.

"She appears to be in her early 30s, well-groomed with manicured nails and neatly done eyebrows," she reported. "Based on her condition, I'd say she has been in the water for a few days."

Putting on a pair of latex gloves, Amy began to search through the woman's clothing.

"I can't find any form of identification on her," she said as she completed her initial analysis.

"Nothing else seems out of the ordinary, Boss. Looks like a clear case of suicide," she concluded.

Just as they were about to leave the body, Donovan noticed something. "Can someone hand me a magnifying glass?" he requested from one of the forensics team members, who promptly obliged.

Bending down to get a closer look, he pointed out a faint mark under the woman's chin.

"It seems to be some sort of pressure mark, possibly from a struggle," he noted. "Do you see it too?"

"Yes, Boss. It's barely visible but I can make it out," Amy confirmed his findings.

"Let's get an autopsy done ASAP. While everything points to suicide, we need to be sure," Donovan decided.

With that, they made their way back to the car, first retrieving Toby who was happily playing with some nearby branches. They retraced their steps and headed back to headquarters, eager to begin unravelling the mystery behind this tragic death.

Chapter 13: The CLT

The morning after the suicide drowning, Donovan received the autopsy results. The headline declared the cause of death to be *freshwater asphyxiation*. The pressure marks that Donovan had observed under her chin confirmed that she had been strangled, but it was not the direct cause of death.

This revelation added a new layer of complexity to the case, as it now appeared to be a staged suicide.

Using IDENT1—the UK's main fingerprint database—they were able to identify the woman. However, her name and other information were heavily redacted, indicating that she was either an undercover officer or a spook. This raised suspicions and made for a more challenging investigation.

Two suspicious deaths in two days: an overdosed body and a staged suicide. Were they connected? Was there a serial killer at work? These questions remained unanswered as Donovan's boss summoned him to her office later that day.

He noticed two men sitting with her when he approached. She introduced them as DCI Steven Murdock and DI Wayne Nash from the County Lines Taskforce (CLT) based out of Birmingham HQ. They explained to him that *County Lines* are the transportation of illegal drugs across police and local authority boundaries.

They were investigating the recent drowning victim Elaine Rodgers who had been working undercover for over two years within an Organised Crime Group. According to their last contact with her, she had uncovered something significant and was planning on meeting with OCG leaders in person before being killed. The CLT wanted to collaborate with Donovan's team and share their knowledge base and redacted information on Elaine's reports.

Donovan agreed to this arrangement and expressed his condolences for their loss. After exchanging business cards, they parted ways with promises of future cooperation.

However, Donovan's chief inspector reminded him to keep her informed of any developments and not to let anything catch them by surprise. "With this *cooperation*, progress may be slowed down as everything would have to be run by the CLT first," Donovan said, but he was determined to work closely with them and get to the bottom of this suspicious death.

She leaned back in her leather chair, the creak of its mechanism adding a sense of seriousness to their conversation.

"Yes, it will," she said firmly. "But if the tables were turned, we would insist on the same protocols being in place. She was one of ours after all."

He left her office and returned to the situation room, where his team eagerly awaited his instructions. The bright lights overhead seemed to buzz with anticipation as he briefed them on their new task force assignment. He could see the excitement in their expressions at the thought of something out of the ordinary.

However, Donovan knew he needed to keep them grounded and focused. He reminded them that their main priority was solving the Keith Roberts murder case, and not to lose sight of that goal. He was determined to keep their motivation high and his foot on the peddle.

Later that day, they were granted access to the exclusive CLT knowledge base. As Donovan pored over the extensive research and notes on *County Lines*, he couldn't help but feel a sense of admiration for Elaine Rodgers' impressive career. Despite its risks, she had dedicated herself to dismantling this criminal network. And now, she had become a victim of it.

Donovan added her name and details to the *murder board*, determined to bring her killer to justice. He made a mental note to himself, promising to do everything in his power to seek justice for Elaine's untimely and brutal death.

Chapter 14: Territory

The moonless night was eerily quiet as he sprinted down the deserted street, his heart pounding in his chest. The only sound was the rapid thudding of his footsteps against the pavement and the occasional bark of a distant dog.

He could feel the adrenaline coursing through him, urging him to run faster and escape from his pursuer. The figure chasing him was shrouded in all black, their face obscured by a balaclava. In their hand, they held a gun that glinted in the moonlight. He knew he had to act fast if he wanted any chance of survival.

Just moments ago, he had been discussing drug deals with his friend in a car parked inconspicuously three streets away. But now, he found himself being hunted down like prey on this dark and desolate street. He had no time to make phone calls for help or find a hiding place. All he could do was run.

As he calculated his next move, he spotted a nondescript house to his right and made a split-second decision to seek refuge inside. He leapt up the porch steps and frantically rang the doorbell, hoping someone would answer. The middle-aged woman who lived there opened the door warily, only to be shoved aside by him as he barged into her home.

He slammed the door shut behind him, trying to keep his assailant out. But it was futile.

With one powerful kick, the door burst open and Simon, the notorious enforcer for his rival gang, stepped inside with gun in hand.

Simon brandished a deadly semi-automatic pistol, and bullets flew through the air as Simon pursued him through the house, firing indiscriminately, one bullet catching the lady owner in her arm, and causing chaos everywhere they went. They crashed through rooms and furniture until they ended up in the dining room where Simon delivered three fatal shots to his target's chest.

Simon quickly checked his body and satisfied that his job was done, he quickly exited through the back door and jumped into a waiting car before speeding away into the night.

Later, catching up with Jimi, Simon reported on his success. But he couldn't help but feel uneasy about the innocent woman that he may have accidentally shot during the chase. He worried about getting caught by the police and the consequences of their illegal actions catching up to them.

As they drove off to get some much-needed drinks, Simon's hands shook from the adrenaline rush and the weight of their violent lifestyle weighing heavily on him.

―― " ――

The duty sergeant's phone rang at 10:30 pm, interrupting the silence of the police station. Her heart sank as she heard the news of another death. A shooting had occurred in Bridgenorth, leaving one person dead and another injured. The gravity of the situation was evident in her voice as she relayed the details to Donovan, who was immediately called in by his boss to attend to the scene.

Chapter 15: Donovan and Jess

The evening sun cast a warm glow through the apartment windows as Donovan and Jess settled onto the couch, Toby curled up contentedly at their feet. Donovan sighed, running a hand through his hair.

"I'm sorry, we haven't had much time together lately," he said. "These murder cases have been relentless."

Jess gave him a sympathetic smile. "I understand. The pub has been crazy busy with all the summer tourists too."

They fell into a comfortable silence, the gentle sound of the river drifting in from outside. Donovan found his thoughts wandering to his ex-partner, as they often did on quiet evenings like this. He felt a familiar pang of grief, but it was softer now, less sharp than it used to be.

Jess seemed to sense his mood shift. She reached out and took his hand, giving it a gentle squeeze.

Donovan squeezed back, grateful for her understanding. He turned to look at Jess, really look at her, taking in her kind eyes and the freckles sprinkled across her nose. A wave of affection washed over him.

"You know," he said softly, "I'm really glad you're here."

Jess' smile widened. "Me too."

Toby chose that moment to let out a contented sigh, stretching his paws out in his sleep. They both chuckled, the tender moment lightening.

"So, tell me about these cases," Jess prompted, tucking her legs under her on the couch. "Anything I should be worried about in our sleepy little town?"

Donovan shook his head. "Nothing for the general public to be concerned about. It's just…frustrating. Two seemingly unrelated murders in a week. No clear connections, no obvious motive in one of them. It's like trying to put together a puzzle with half the pieces missing."

Jess nodded thoughtfully. "That does sound frustrating. Any leads at all?"

Donovan ran a hand over his face. "A few, but nothing solid yet. We're re-interviewing witnesses, and combing through security footage. It's just…time-consuming."

"And time is something you don't have much of lately," Jess said softly.

"Yeah," Donovan agreed, his voice tinged with regret. He looked at Jess, the sunlight caught her hair, turning it to spun gold. "I'm sorry about that. You deserve better."

Jess leaned in, resting her head on his shoulder. "Hey, none of that. I knew what I was getting into when I started dating a detective." She paused, her voice taking on a playful tone. "Besides, absence makes the heart grow fonder, right?"

Donovan chuckled, wrapping an arm around her. "Is that so?"

"Mhmm," Jess hummed. "Though I wouldn't object to a little less absence."

"Noted," Donovan said, pressing a kiss to the top of her head. "Maybe we could plan a weekend away soon. Head up to the Lake District, do some hiking?"

Jess lifted her head, her eyes sparkling. "That sounds perfect. Though knowing our luck, a body would turn up in the woods the moment we arrived."

"Don't jinx it," Donovan groaned, but he was smiling.

They lapsed into comfortable silence again, content in each other's company. Donovan found himself thinking about his ex-partner again, but this time, the memories didn't bring the usual sharp pang of grief. Instead, he felt a bittersweet warmth, a fondness for the time they'd shared. He realised, with a start, that he was finally ready to let go of the past and fully embrace his present—and future—with Jess.

As if sensing his thoughts, Jess stirred beside him. "Penny for your thoughts?" she asked softly.

Donovan took a deep breath. "I was just thinking…about my ex-girlfriend."

Jess tensed slightly, but her voice remained gentle. "Oh?"

"Yeah," Donovan continued, tightening his arm around her reassuringly. "But it's different now. I…I think I'm finally ready to move forward. Properly, I mean."

Jess sat up, her eyes searching his face. "Are you sure?"

Donovan nodded slowly, meeting Jess' gaze. "I am. She will always be a part of me, but…I'm ready to build a future with you, Jess. If that's what you want too."

Jess' eyes welled up with tears, but she was smiling. "Of course, it is, you big idiot," she said, her voice thick with emotion.

She leaned in and kissed him softly.

Donovan felt lighter than he had in years. He hadn't realised how much he'd been holding back, afraid to fully commit to Jess out of some misplaced sense of loyalty to her memory. But now, sitting here in the warm glow of the setting sun, with Toby snoring gently at his feet, he knew he was exactly where he was meant to be.

"So," Jess said, her eyes twinkling, "tell me more about this weekend getaway you mentioned. I could use a break from pulling pints for sunburnt tourists."

Donovan grinned, pulling her closer. "Well, I was thinking we could rent a little cottage up near Windermere. There's this place I know, tucked away in the hills. It's got a view of the lake that'll take your breath away, especially at sunset when the water turns to liquid gold."

Jess sighed contentedly, nestling into his side. "That sounds perfect. We could go for hikes during the day, maybe rent a little boat?"

"Absolutely," Donovan agreed. "There's a great trail that winds up through the fells. It's a bit of a climb, but the view from the top…you can see for miles. Rolling green hills, dotted with sheep, the lake stretching out below like a mirror. We could pack a picnic, make a day of it."

Jess' eyes lit up. "Oh, and we could stop at that little cheese shop in town! Remember the one, we found last time? With the cave-aged cheddar that was so sharp it made your eyes water?"

Donovan laughed. "How could I forget? I think I can still taste it."

As they continued to plan their getaway, the room filled with the warm glow of possibility. The setting sun painted the walls in hues of gold and amber, casting long shadows that danced across the floor. Toby stirred at their feet, rolling over with a contented grunt, his tail thumping gently against the hardwood floor.

Donovan found himself getting caught up in Jess' enthusiasm, his mind conjuring images of misty mornings.

The sun had nearly set, casting long shadows across the room. Donovan and Jess were still nestled on the couch, lost in conversation about their upcoming trip. The air was filled with the gentle hum of anticipation and the soft whisper of possibility.

"Oh, and we absolutely must try that little bistro in Ambleside," Jess was saying, her eyes sparkling with excitement. "I've heard they do the most amazing sticky toffee pudding."

Donovan chuckled, pulling her closer. "I thought this was supposed to be a hiking trip, not a culinary tour of the Lake District."

"Why can't it be both?" Jess retorted with a grin.

As the sun sank below the horizon, its final rays flooded into the room, casting everything in a golden glow. The distant sound of the river could be heard through the open sash windows, the gentle rush of water over rocks. Donovan felt a sense of peace and happiness envelop him as he cuddled closer to Jess, cherishing the warmth of her presence and their shared excitement for what was to come.

Just as Jess was describing a quaint tea shop, she'd read about, with its homemade scones and clotted cream, the tranquil atmosphere was shattered by the shrill ring of Donovan's phone. The sound cut through the peaceful evening like a knife, causing Toby to startle awake with a confused whine.

Donovan's face fell as he reached for the device, already knowing what this call meant.

He answered with a terse, "Detective Donovan here."

His face tightened as he listened to the voice on the other end of the line. The warm glow of the evening seemed to fade, replaced by a cold, harsh reality. Jess watched his expression change, her own smile fading as she realised their perfect moment was slipping away.

"I understand. Yes, I'll be there as soon as possible," Donovan said, his voice clipped and professional.

He ended the call and turned to Jess; his eyes filled with regret. "I'm so sorry, Jess. There's been another murder."

Jess nodded, trying to hide her disappointment. "It's okay. I understand. Duty calls, right?"

Donovan jumps to his feet, his hand raking through his hair in frustration. "This time it's a brutal gang killing. And they didn't just take out their target— an innocent woman is lying injured as well." His gut twists with determination. "I have to go. I'm sorry."

Jess watched as Donovan hurried to gather his things, his movements practised and efficient. She could see the tension in him, the way his frame tightened as he mentally prepared for what lay ahead. As he shrugged on his coat, he turned to her, his eyes softening for a moment.

"I'll make this up to you, I promise," he said, leaning in to kiss her cheek.

"Just be careful," Jess replied, squeezing his hand.

With a final apologetic glance, Donovan was gone, the door clicking shut behind him. The apartment suddenly felt emptier, the golden glow of the evening fading into a cooler blue twilight. Jess sighed, looking down at Toby, who was staring at the door with his head tilted.

"Well, boy," she said, reaching down to scratch behind his ears, "looks like it's just you and me tonight. How about we go for a walk?"

At the word *walk*, Toby's ears perked up and his tail began to wag furiously. Jess couldn't help but smile at his enthusiasm. She grabbed his leash from the hook by the door, and Toby immediately started prancing in excited circles.

As they stepped out of the apartment building, the cool evening air enveloped them. The sky was a canvas of deep purples and blues, with the first stars just beginning to twinkle into view. The street lamps had flickered to life, casting pools of warm light on the cobblestone streets of Bewdley.

With a swift gesture, Jess beckon'd for Toby to follow as they headed out to enjoy the last bit of warmth before nightfall. Jess' thoughts drifted to days walking with Donovan and Toby in the lakes.

Chapter 16: Gang Murder

Donovan manoeuvres his way through the narrow, winding streets of Bridgnorth; a charming town nestled in the historic county of Shropshire. As he drove, he couldn't help but admire the quaintness of the town, with its picturesque buildings and cobblestone streets.

As he reached Rosehill Drive, Donovan took note of how peaceful and serene the town felt in the stillness of night. The once-polluted River Severn now shimmered under the light of the moon, offering a tranquil escape for fishermen and nature lovers alike.

However, the calmness was soon disrupted by the distant blue flashing lights of police cars, signalling that something had gone awry in this otherwise idyllic town. Donovan quickly parked his car and approached the cordoned-off house, where two officers stood guard outside.

A small crowd of curious neighbours had gathered nearby, eager for any information about the commotion and just being generally nosy.

His partner Amy was already there, talking to one of the officers. Both Donovan and Amy dressed in their crime scene suits as they entered the taped-off house. Inside, they found a team of forensic experts diligently documenting every detail—from bullet holes to blood splatter.

The strong halogen lamps lit up each room as they made their way through the house, finding a faint smell of gunpowder mixed with stale tobacco. In the lounge, Donovan's attention was drawn to a 3D imaging tripod surrounded by numbered bullet holes made by an automatic pistol. He couldn't help but wonder how the victim had managed to evade being fatally shot for so long before ultimately succumbing to multiple gunshot wounds.

As they moved into the dining room, Donovan's eyes fell upon the lifeless body lying face-up on the floor. The victim's open eyes seemed to bore into him, silently pleading for answers. Three gunshot wounds marred his chest—a stark contrast against his pristine Adidas sports top and unzipped hoodie. Blood pooled around the body, seeping into the carpet below.

"Tell me what you're seeing, Amy," Donovan instructed in a sombre tone.

"It's a male, late 20s," she replied, her voice reflecting the gravity of the situation.

"Looks like he was dressed decently and unarmed from what I can see."

Donovan searched the victim's pockets and found a wallet with a driver's licence identifying him as Patrick O'Brian from Liverpool. He also discovered a small bag of marijuana, hinting at possible ties to illegal activities.

"It seems this could be a botched gang hit," Donovan speculated, his mind racing with possibilities. "Not as clean as someone wanted."

"Did you speak to the homeowner?" he asked Amy, already planning their next steps.

"I talked to one of the officers who interviewed her before she was taken to the hospital," she replied, referring to the preliminary statement taken at the scene.

According to the homeowner, she didn't know the victim or his attacker. However, they would need to confirm this with a more formal statement later.

"Is she okay?" Donovan asked.

"She got shot in her arm, a straight-through wound, she will be fine," Amy responded, reviewing her notes.

"Thank goodness for small mercies," Donovan replied.

This was unlike anything they had encountered in Shropshire before; automatic weapons used on innocent civilians? It was every law enforcement officer's worst nightmare and a field day for the media.

"The CSI team will be here for hours. Let's start running Patrick O'Brian's name through our database and see if we can identify any next of kin or gather more information about him," Donovan instructed Amy.

"Also, make sure to collect any CCTV footage or doorbell camera recordings from nearby residents. Someone must have seen something," he added.

"Got it, Boss. Why don't you head home and get some rest? It's been a long night," Amy suggested, noticing how exhausted Donovan looked.

Taking her advice, Donovan thanked her and headed home, eager to finally get some much-needed rest. Little did he know, these cases would turn out to be the most challenging and shocking of his career in the Wyre Forest so far.

———— " ————

He drove home in the quiet solitude of his car, allowing his thoughts to drift through his mind like wispy clouds on a breezy day. The weight of the past few days hung heavy on him as he thought about the cases he now led. Each one seemed like a new puzzle, and he couldn't help acknowledging they were all connected in some way.

The sheer number of deaths in such a short amount of time had sparked much suspicion within him.

"All you need is just one piece of the puzzle to fit into place," he mused, "one crucial detail to unravel the rest."

But where would that missing piece come from? It seemed elusive, just out of reach, taunting him with its elusiveness and teasing him with its importance.

As he continued down the winding road, his mind raced with possibilities and theories; determined to crack open the mystery and bring justice to those criminals who deserved everything the police could throw at them.

Chapter 17: Jimi & Simon

Jimi's footsteps were an abrupt rhythm against the wooden floorboards, back and forth like a caged animal. The room was a box of black and greys, too small for the giants of anxiety that wrestled within him. Each time, he turned on his heel, Simon came into view, an island of calm amidst Jimi's tempest.

"Simon," Jimi started his voice a tightrope of tension. "It's Fenix, mate. He is on the list." His gaze flicked to the carpet, then back up to meet Simon's unreadable expression.

A beat passed. Simon didn't move, just watched Jimi with eyes too steady for comfort. "And?" His words sliced the air, precise, waiting.

"Christ, Simon!" Jimi threw his hands up, exasperation giving way to a desperate edge. "He is a friend. From way back."

"Jimi," Simon's tone held a hint of steel, though his posture remained unchanged, "you know how it works."

"Friends, Simon." Jimi's breath hitched, betraying him. "People we fucking came up with!"

Silence hung heavy between them. Simon didn't respond immediately, letting Jimi's words echo in the confines of the room. There was no escaping the reality of the situation, no door left unguarded by duty and dark promise.

Simon leaned forward, the leather of the sofa creaking as he perched himself on the edge of it. "Jimi," he said, voice low and deliberate, "orders are orders. You know what happens if we don't follow through."

"Consequences?" Jimi spat out the word as if it burned his tongue. His fists balled at his sides. "What about right and wrong, Simon?"

"Morality?" Simon's chuckle was a dry leaf skittering across a pavement. "That's a luxury we forfeited long ago."

"Did we?" Jimi shot back, pacing quickening. The walls seemed to press closer with each step, the space shrinking around him. "Or did we just stop giving a damn?"

"Careful." The warning in Simon's voice was clear as shattered glass.

"Careful?" Jimi's laugh was sharp, without humour. "We're way past careful, mate."

Jimi's shadow clashed with the flickering lamplight, a dance of doubt across the walls. Simon watched him, an un-moving silhouette against the dim glow.

"Listen," Simon's voice cut through the tension. "We've done things. Things that can't be undone." His eyes held Jimi's, unblinking. "There's no stepping off this train."

"Can't?" The word lodged in Jimi's throat, a bitter pill. He stopped pacing. The room stilled, save for the clock ticking, relentless, marking time they didn't have.

"Can't," Simon affirmed. "You know the stakes."

"Stakes—" Jimi echoed, his gaze drifting.

A photograph on the wall caught his eye. Laughter once shared, is now a relic framed in innocence. He remembered the shutter click, the flash. Simpler times. His heart clenched.

"Look at us," he murmured, voice barely a whisper. The image stared back, haunting. "How did we get here, Si?"

Simon remained silent, allowing the past to seep into the present, a ghost between them. Jimi's hands fell to his sides, the fight seeping out of him like air from a punctured tyre.

"Choices," Simon finally said. "Or lack thereof."

"Right," Jimi nodded.

A hollow agreement, filled with echoes of a life they once knew.

Simon leaned back, the leather groaning under his weight. "It's about loyalty, Jimi," he said, his voice steady as a heartbeat. "To the OCG. To each other."

"Power? Protection?" Jimi spat the words out like they tasted foul. He turned away from the photograph, his hands finding his hips, fingers digging in as if to anchor himself.

"Exactly." Simon's gaze didn't waver. "They've got our backs."

"Until when?" Jimi's eyes darted around the room, searching for something, anything, that made sense anymore. "Until we're no longer useful?"

"Jimi." Simon's voice hardened. "We need them."

"Need?" Fire flared in Jimi's chest. "Or trapped?"

"Same thing now, isn't it?" Simon's lips twisted into a semblance of a smile, but his eyes stayed cold.

Jimi's head shook before he could stop it, denying everything Simon stood for.

"What's the price, Si?" His voice broke through the tension between them, raw and ragged. "Our souls?"

"Too late for that kind of talk." Simon's dismissal was a slap to the face.

"Is it?" Jimi's voice rose, defiance building like a storm. "Fenix is a friend, Si. A brother!"

"Orders are orders." Simon's shrug was a betrayal, a chasm opening wide.

"Right." Jimi's breaths came fast, too fast. "Orders." His mind raced, a maze with no exit.

"Think about it, Jimi." Simon's voice sliced through the chaos. "We can't afford doubt."

"Can't we?" The question hung heavy in the air, a thread about to snap.

"Think about it," Simon repeated, his tone final, like the closing of a coffin lid.

Simon surged from the leather, his presence suddenly towering over Jimi's shorter but muscular frame. A firm hand clasped Jimi's shoulder, a silent command for solidarity.

"Focus on the endgame," he said, his voice low and steady. "Remember what we're in this for—the rewards are within reach."

Jimi flinched, the touch igniting a spark of rebellion. He shrugged off Simon's grip, stepping back, repulsed, his pulse hammering in his ears.

"Rewards?" He spat the word out like it tasted foul. "We're not scavengers, Si. We used to stand for something."

"Used to," Simon echoed, a subtle edge slicing through the two words.

"Right." Jimi's eyes were wide, haunted. "I can't—this list—" He choked on his thoughts, each name a smothering weight. "They're not just hits, they're people. Fenix—" His voice trailed, the name dissolving into silence.

"Collateral damage," Simon interrupted, his face a mask of resolve. "Necessary sacrifices."

"Is that what we are now?" Jimi's question was a bullet, fired point-blank. "Executioners?"

"Survivors," Simon corrected, his tone unyielding.

"Survival at this cost?" Jimi's hands balled into fists, his knuckles bone white. "Where does it end, Si?"

Simon's jaw clenched, his answer lodged somewhere deep, unspoken. Silence enveloped them, heavy as a shroud.

The air crackled with tension, the silence between them a chasm. Simon's eyes narrowed, his patience fraying like a worn rope.

"Hesitation is a luxury we can't afford," he said, each word edged in steel. "You know what's at stake."

Jimi recoiled as if struck, the ghosts of their past actions flickering across his face.

"We've already paid in blood," he muttered, but it was the shadow of defiance, fleeting.

"Turn back?" Simon's laugh was dark, devoid of humour. "There's no road home for people like us, people lower down the food chain."

"People like us?" Jimi's laugh was a bark; raw and harsh. "Is that what you call this? We're monsters, parading in human skin."

"Speak for yourself," Simon countered, standing firm, immovable as stone. "I do what must be done."

"Must be done?" The words erupted from Jimi, bitter as bile. "For what? For who?" His voice cracked, betraying the storm within.

"Survival isn't pretty," Simon replied, his voice flat, a mirror to his eyes.

"Pretty?" Jimi's hands shook his laughter—now a howl. "There's nothing pretty about betrayal. You're heartless!"

"Better heartless than dead," Simon shot back, his own resolve hardening like ice.

Jimi's breath hitched, his fury spent, leaving only the raw edges of his soul exposed.

"Dead," he whispered. "Maybe we already are."

Silence clawed at the room, thick and oppressive. Simon's words, a lingering poison in the air, ate into the space between them. He watched, his expression unreadable, as the fire drained from Jimi's eyes, leaving behind the cold ash of defeat.

"Dead," Jimi whispered again, the word a ghost on his lips.

A muscle twitched in Simon's jaw, but he said nothing more, offering no comfort, no rebuke—only the stark reality of their existence hanging heavy in the quiet.

Jimi's gaze dropped, his defiance crumbling like a cliff-side worn by relentless waves. The silence bore down, an invisible weight upon his shoulders.

In his periphery, the photograph on the wall taunted him—a scornful reminder of a past untainted by blood.

A shudder ran through Jimi's frame. In that stillness, a choice took root, dark and decisive.

"Enough." The word was barely audible, yet it cut through the stillness like a blade.

Simon's eyes followed as Jimi surged to his feet. Resolve stamped on his features, Jimi strode across the room, each step a declaration. The air seemed to shift, reacting to the sudden burst of movement.

"Where do you think you're going?" Simon's voice sliced into Jimi's back, sharp, demanding.

"Out," Jimi's reply came terse, final.

"Jimi—" Simon began, but the words dissolved into the growing distance as Jimi reached the door.

The handle turned with a click, a small sound that marked a vast decision. Without looking back, Jimi pulled open the door, stepping over the threshold. His heart hammered a frantic drumbeat against the cage of his ribs.

The door slammed shut with a resonance that felt like a full stop to one chapter and the forced start of another, all too uncertain. Simon remained seated, the echo of the door's closure slowly fading into the dense quiet left in Jimi's wake.

The night air clawed at Jimi's flushed cheeks as he burst from the confines of his flat. Lights from Bridgenorth's sleepy streets cast long shadows that seemed to reach for him. He staggered forward, the Saharan wind drying the tears in his eyes and whipping away the suffocating heat of anger and fear.

He walked. Past the flickering streetlamps. Past the shuttered windows. Each step a desperate beat in the rhythm of his escape. The quaint town was a dark maze, but in its twisted paths, he searched for the thread of reason; for the solace of solitude to quiet the storm within.

Time lost meaning. Streets turned to blurs. And then, clarity washed over him with the starkness of the night sky. What now? The question gnawed at him. Loyalty or conscience? A gypsy friend's life hanging in the balance.

His breath steadied. Resolve hardened. He couldn't run forever. Jimi turned back, the decision anchoring each step towards the flat.

The door creaked open with a soft whisper compared to the slam that had marked his exit. Simon looked up, the ghost of a smirk playing on his lips.

"Find what you were looking for?" His voice was a smooth stone skimming across the surface of tension.

"Let's just get this over with," Jimi muttered, sinking into the leather of the couch opposite Simon.

"OCG is planning to expand," Simon began, the words spilling out like pieces on a chessboard. "Northwest counties. More power, more reach."

Jimi's mind spun, latching onto the words. Northwest. Power. Reach. Could it be…an out?

Simon continued, oblivious to the illogical gears turning in Jimi's head, "We follow through, we're set. You understand?"

"Understood." The lie tasted like ash, but it was necessary.

For Fenix. For himself. Jimi nodded, the plan embedding itself in the folds of his mind. Maybe arrested by the police. Maybe that could be his chance, his way out. Maybe a deal was to be done?

"Good," Simon said, leaning back with satisfaction. "We stick to the plan. We do as we're told."

For now, Jimi agreed silently—for now.

Chapter 18: Carpet Factory

As the night grew darker, the four of them huddled together in Fenix's cramped and musty caravan. The stench of old fabric and sweat filled the air as they drank and played poker—their chosen form of entertainment.

Jimi, a master at the game, skilfully manipulated the cards with deceptive ease thanks to tips he had learned from a sinister acquaintance in his days in the concrete jungle. He knew how to put on a good show, purposely winning some rounds while losing others to maintain appearances. As the drinks flowed freely, Jimi took on the role of dealer using his cunning card skills to guarantee that only he and Fenix were left in the game.

The caravan was situated in a traveller's campsite just outside Stourport-on-Severn, a notorious hub for criminal activity. The OCG had deep roots within this community, with its leaders turning a blind eye to their illegal operations if they received their cut of the profits. Fenix and his closest comrades were part of this ruthless fraternity. They were known for their ability to traffic illicit goods quickly and discreetly. They were an invaluable asset to the OCG in this area.

Over time, Jimi had ingratiated himself into their inner circle and become a crucial liaison between them and the OCG's higher-ups. However, he never forgot where his true loyalties lay—firmly with his bosses in the OCG.

Fenix, a short man with fiery red hair and ragged clothing, was far from being a skilled poker player. But tonight, he seemed to be having all the luck thanks to Jimi's expert card dealing. The other two players—Michael and Shamus—were Gypsies from the same campsite who had already declared themselves out of the game after suffering heavy losses against Fenix. But it was all part of Jimi's plan.

As they continued playing and drinking well into the night, Fenix grew increasingly intoxicated but remained alert. Jimi, on the other hand, carefully regulated his alcohol intake, knowing he needed a clear mind for what was to come.

"Let's call it a night, Fenix," Jimi suggested, his tone suggesting no argument.

"Just because you know I can beat you, you want to quit. Typical," Fenix sneered.

"Okay then, one final hand and we both go *all-in*. Let's see who has the bigger balls," Jimi countered with a wicked smile.

As a dealer, Jimi dealt the last hand and after several rounds of intense card flipping, they both went *all-in*. The final card revealed that Fenix had won with a straight flush.

"Told you, mate, you can't beat me!" Fenix gloated as he scooped up his winnings from the table; amounting to about a hundred pounds according to Jimi's estimation.

"Yeah, but I'll have you next time," Jimi replied nonchalantly.

"I've got Simon coming to pick me up. I can't drive in this state," Jimi announced, signalling an end to the evening's revelries.

Fenix knew Simon but wasn't as close to him as he was with Jimi. As they waited outside for Simon's arrival, they chatted casually about girls and football, until the sound of a car pulling up interrupted them. Fenix stood up first and opened the caravan door for Jimi to leave.

But instead of walking out like any ordinary night, Jimi swiftly turned around and seized Fenix by the arm. With startling strength and speed, he whirled Fenix around and pinned him down onto one of the caravan seats while covering his mouth with his hand. Simon rushed in to help but Jimi already had everything under control.

It was clear that Fenix was no match for his superior physical prowess.

Fenix's eyes widened in shock and confusion as Simon and Jimi forcefully bound his hands behind his back with tight zip cable ties, the rough material digging into his skin. The sting of the tape against his mouth was a harsh reminder of his current situation. His mind was clouded, both from the effects of alcohol and the sudden turn of events.

Simon opened the back door of the sleek grey Audi, urging Fenix inside with a rough shove. He landed on the plush leather seats next to Jimi, who was holding a concealed Walther P99 pistol. Fenix struggled to speak through the tape, his muffled protests falling on deaf ears.

The car pulled away smoothly, its powerful engine barely making a sound. Jimi kept the gun pressed into Fenix's side, ready to use it at any moment.

As they drove, Fenix's mind raced with fear and confusion. He had no idea what was happening or where they were taking him. His thoughts were interrupted as Jimi removed the tape from his mouth with a sharp rip.

"What the fuck is going on? What do you want?" Fenix demanded, panic lacing his voice.

"We know someone has been skimming money off the top of our operations, and all signs point to you," Jimi said calmly.

Fenix shook his head vigorously. "I swear, I don't know anything about missing money."

"We'll see about that," Jimi replied coldly.

He quickly replaced the tape over Fenix's mouth, not wanting to engage in conversation at this point. They would reach their destination soon—an old, abandoned, small, carpet factory on the outskirts of Kidderminster.

Simon stayed with the car as Jimi led Fenix at gunpoint through overgrown bushes and along a path until they reached the factory. The building was dilapidated, its roof half open to the elements and the other half covered in crumbling asbestos sheeting. It had been left to rot for decades and now served as a haven for what Jimi had in store.

Jimi flicked a hand torch to show the way and he led Fenix inside, the sound of their footsteps echoing through the empty space. He turned on a generator, one he had put in place earlier that day, allowing him to illuminate the factory with bright halogen *builders* lights.

The once bustling factory floor was now littered with tall, upright, abandoned carpet looms; some still holding threads and patterns from their last use. In the centre of the vast space, Jimi had placed a rusty metal chair for Fenix to sit on. He forced him down onto it and tightened his restraints even further. He bound Fenix to the chair with a heavy chain and padlock, pinning his arms and torso firmly in the chair.

With a quick, fluid motion, Jimi removed the tape that had been covering Fenix's mouth, causing him to recoil in fear. His eyes darted around the dimly lit room, trying to find an escape route.

"This is mental!" he exclaimed, his voice trembling with panic.

Jimi towered over Fenix; his thick arms crossed over his chest.

"Look, mate, you've been caught red-handed. But the bosses think you're not smart enough to have pulled this off alone." He paused and leaned down closer to Fenix. "So, who helped you?"

Fenix shook his head, sweat beading on his forehead. "I don't have a clue what you're talking about."

Without warning, Jimi slapped him hard across the face, leaving a trail of blood from his split lip.

"Don't give me any of that shit! You need to fess up and give me names," Jimi growled.

Despite the beating and relentless questioning from Jimi, Fenix remained defiant. But as the morning sun started to filter in through the factory skylights Jimi could see cracks forming in Fenix's resolve. He was sure that Fenix had been skimming money. Simon had told him so and, therefore, it must be true.

Fenix's face was swollen and bruised, blood dripping from his two split eyelids and a broken nose. He could barely see through his swollen eyelids or speak through his split lip. But he held on, clinging to the hope of negotiating his way out of this mess.

"I told you; I didn't do anything wrong, and I don't know anyone else who did either," Fenix managed to say between spitting out blood.

"You're full of shit, Fenix," Jimi spat back.

"You're just a lousy liar. I trusted you as a mate and now you've gone and fucked it all up, and all for just a few quid."

"Give me some names and I might go easier on you," Jimi said, his aggression rising.

"I don't know any names," Fenix responded weakly, his voice now tired and shallow from the beatings.

Jimi knew he had to increase the pressure to get what he wanted. He went to the back of the room where a can of petrol sat and brought it over to Fenix. Slowly, he unscrewed the cap and waved the can in front of Fenix's face, letting him smell the fumes.

Fenix's eyes widened in fear as he realised Jimi's intentions. He struggled against his restraints, but they held firm.

"What are you doing? No, no!" he pleaded as Jimi poured the contents of the can over his head, drenching him in petrol.

"You gonna tell me or am I going to light you up?" Jimi threatened.

At this point, Fenix knew it was futile to hold out any longer. He could see the fire flickering in Jimi's eyes and knew he meant business.

"Okay, okay…I'll tell you who I've heard might be involved. It's Liam."

Jimi nodded, a smug smirk spreading across his face.

"See, that wasn't so hard, was it? This could have been over hours ago if you'd just cooperated. And we both know you've been dipping into the pot, so let's not bother talking about that anymore. Any other names you want to give up?"

Fenix shook his head weakly. "No, I don't know anyone else." His voice was barely a whisper now as he resigned himself to his fate.

Jimi's heart ached as he looked into Fenix's eyes and saw the fear and confusion reflected there. He knew that his old friend had no idea of the danger he was in; no knowledge of the sinister plot that had been set in motion.

With a heavy heart, Jimi reached into his pocket and pulled out a book of matches. He struck one against the rough edge and watched as the flame flickered to life, the rest of the matches ignited. He then tossed the book into Fenix's lap.

In an instant, the petrol-drenched clothing burst into flames, creating a massive fireball that shot up five feet above Fenix's head. The intense heat and brightness of the flames were almost blinding; their outer edges were tinted with yellow and blue at their core.

As Fenix's screams tore through the air, Jimi calmly stepped back, careful to avoid the growing inferno. He couldn't bear to watch his former friend suffer this fate, but he also couldn't bring himself to intervene. The guilt weighed heavily on him as he walked away from the blazing spectacle behind him.

Fenix's screams gradually faded as he lost consciousness, succumbing to the overwhelming pain and realisation of what Jimi had done. Flames continued to spread rapidly across his body until they eventually consumed him completely.

Jimi didn't dare look back or dwell on the gruesome scene that he had just orchestrated. Killing a friend was not something to be proud of, but it was a necessary sacrifice for his own survival.

Chapter 19: Chargrilled

The phone rang out, piercing the quiet of the situation room and pulling Donovan and his team out of their work. The voice on the other end informed them of a suspected murder in a disused carpet factory. Without hesitation, they set off for the scene.

Amy read the case file out loud as they drove, noting that it appeared to be gang-related based on the initial modus operandi. She continued to skim through the sparse contents of the file:

Burned to death and no witnesses were the only headlines.

She said out loud. It was clear this would be a challenging case.

They arrived at the factory, located in a remote area with only a PC and forensics team present. As they approached, the road turned from tarmac to dirt, leading across a field to the entrance of the factory. The familiar smell of smoke and gasoline lingered in the air.

"Donovan, my man!" The lead forensics investigator greeted him with a smirk. "You just can't stay away from these intense cases, can you?"

"Yeah, lucky me," Donovan replied sarcastically. "What do we have here?"

"It's quite gruesome, I must warn you." The forensics lead grimaced before continuing. "A male Caucasian completely charred, burnt to death covered in petrol."

Donovan's stomach churned at the thought.

"Any fingerprints or evidence for identification?"

"Unfortunately, not. We're thinking dental records will be our only option." The lead investigator gestured towards some footprints nearby. "We're taking moulds of these prints though."

"Thanks," Donovan said as he made a mental note to expedite the identification process.

"Let's get this body over to the coroner ASAP after we finish here."

He turned to Amy and motioned for her to follow him inside leaving Toby tied up outside. Adjusting their eyes to the dim lighting first, then shifting to bright lights that illuminated the scene. Donovan and Amy approached the victim.

Even with the warning, Donovan wasn't prepared for what he saw. The body was nothing more than a human-shaped pile of melted flesh and bone, something out of a hammer horror movie he thought, but worse. Any features or distinguishing marks were burned beyond recognition. Donovan was cautious not to disturb anything, afraid it might crumble to ash at his touch.

"Anything catch your eye, Amy?" Donovan asked, trying not to show his own discomfort.

"Not really, Boss," she replied, her voice strained from trying not to gag. "Just the overwhelming 'burnt to a crisp' vibe."

Donovan nodded in agreement. "The accelerant used appears to be petrol. We'll have to rely on forensics for any identification."

As they continued their examination, Donovan noticed something near the victim's neck: bent metal that looked like a necklace of some kind. He called over the forensics team to bag it up and send it to the lab for cleaning and analysis.

"The duty sergeant mentioned a possible gang connection," Donovan said as they finished up.

"Given the brutality of this murder, I'd say it's safe to rule out suicide," Donovan said wryly.

"A bit obvious that, Boss." Amy let herself laugh a little.

Amy gathered herself and shuddered at the thought. "Whoever did this is clearly dangerous. And based on the footprints, there may have been more than one person involved."

"Maybe, or just kids playing, leaving footprints," Donovan responded.

"Brutal is the right word to use though." Donovan sighed as they made their way back to the car, collecting Toby along the way.

They drove off, leaving behind a scene of horror and mystery that would surely test their skills as investigators.

"It's like we're chasing shadows," Donovan grumbled, exhaustion evident in his voice.

"I have a sinking feeling that this is just the beginning," Amy added with a grim expression.

Nodding solemnly, Donovan felt a sense of defeat wash over him.

"Let's regroup back at HQ and go back to the basics. We need a breakthrough," he suggested.

Donovan scrolled through his phone until he found the perfect song to match the chaos and confusion surrounding them: 'Mad World' by Tears for Fears. The haunting melody echoed through the car, mirroring the madness of their current situation.

With heavy hearts, Donovan and Amy stood in front of the whiteboard covered in photos, notes, and electronic strings connecting them all. From petty theft to brutal murders, their investigation had taken a dark turn in just one week; leaving them no closer to solving any of the crimes.

Chapter 20: Robert

As the sun began to set, Simon made his way to his friend's house, his mind heavy with the task he had been commanded to do by his bosses. He couldn't shake the feeling that things were spiralling out of control. He knew that he had no choice but to follow their orders or face their wrath.

Rob's house was a quaint 1970s townhouse nestled on a quiet side road in the idyllic village of Hampton Loade. Simon arrived at the front door and knocked, steeling himself for the conversation that lay ahead.

A few moments later, Rob opened the door. His long blonde hair was tied back with bands, and he wore a black t-shirt adorned with *motorhead* in bold letters across the chest, tour dates were listed down the back of it. He was one of Simon's *shotters*, and his home was being used for *cuckooing*.

"Hi, Si, it's good to see you, man," Rob said nervously, surprised by Simon's unexpected visit.

"Hey, Rob, how've you been?" Simon responded, offering a plastic carrier bag filled with beer cans and a bottle of rum as a peace offering.

"I'm great, thanks. Come on in," Rob replied, welcoming Simon into his home.

Simon stepped inside and waited in the hallway while Rob led him into the cluttered lounge.

"Take a seat, mate." Rob gestured towards an old leather chair with cracks lining its surface.

Simon sat down and leaned forward, placing his carrier bag on the cluttered coffee table.

He pulled out two beers and handed one to Rob. The sound of their cans opening filled the room as they pulled on the ring pulls, they both took sips.

"How's business?" Simon asked.

"It's steady, could be better. People just don't have the cash these days," Rob replied, beginning to relax now that he realised this wasn't a serious meeting.

As they continued to chat, Simon shared their plans to expand their drug operation and increase sales. Rob nodded along, not fully understanding everything due to his high-functioning autism. But Simon knew how to accommodate him and make him feel comfortable.

Suddenly, the doorbell rang. Rob excused himself and answered it, speaking briefly with a petite girl who had come for drugs. He returned to the lounge and slid open a drawer in the dresser against the wall. Inside were small bags of heroin, cocaine and cannabis. He handed them over to the girl and she handed him a wad of cash before leaving.

Rob came back inside and placed the money into the same drawer. Despite the seemingly normal conversation between friends, Simon couldn't shake off the underlying tension and danger that lurked beneath the surface.

As Simon observed the small-time drug deal unfold before him. He couldn't help but feel a sense of nostalgia wash over him. It had been a while since he had been this close to an actual drug deal.

The two men carried on with their casual conversation, masking the underlying tension in the air. They spoke of football, music and girls, trying to distract themselves from the reality of their illegal transaction. As they finished off the remaining cans of beer, the evening slowly crept by.

Simon knew what he had to do next, but he couldn't bring himself to do it just yet. He asked for a couple of glasses and opened the bottle of rum. He poured out a measure for himself and another for his friend, dropping a small pill into his glass and waiting for it to dissolve, then exchanging a casual *cheers* before taking a sip. But Simon noticed that Rob was drinking too quickly, his speech beginning to slur as the effects of ketamine set in.

Without hesitation, Simon continued to refill Rob's glass, watching as his friend became more disoriented and eventually passed out on the sofa.

With a heavy heart and tears filling his eyes, Simon stood up and grabbed a cushion from the couch. He placed it over Rob's face, pushing down hard and holding it there. He checked for signs of life—no breath or pulse could be felt. Rob was dead.

Feeling sick with guilt, Simon took out a syringe from his pocket; one preloaded with a deadly combination of heroin and fentanyl. He wanted to make sure it looked like an accidental overdose, not murder. Donning latex gloves, he injected Rob's lifeless body with the lethal concoction before setting about cleaning up the scene.

Wiping down any surfaces he may have touched, including the rum bottle, Simon cleaned up meticulously. He even washed his glass before placing it back in the kitchen cupboard where it belonged. Satisfied with his efforts, he collected his empty beer cans and left the house.

As he walked down the street, Simon made sure no one was around to witness his departure. His hood pulled up, he carried a bag containing his empty cans and fled to the car he had parked a mile away. The cool night air offered little comfort as he drove away, knowing what he had done and desperately trying to justify it in his mind.

He only hoped that his plan to make it look like an overdose would work. He was unaware of the fatal mistake he had made in administering drugs to a dead body; drugs that could not flow through the veins of a dead man who had no heartbeat to pump it around. As he drove on, the weight of his actions weighed heavy on his soul.

Meanwhile, back at the house, the lifeless body of Rob lay on the couch. He became a tragic victim of Simon's desperate attempt to cover up their drug use gone wrong. And with every passing moment, the truth grew closer to being revealed in an autopsy report.

As he drove away in his car, Simon couldn't shake the thought of Rob's lifeless body lying alone in the house. His heart pounded with guilt and fear as he reached for the burner phone and dialled 911 for the ambulance service. He quickly reported the overdose and gave them the address, making sure to put the phone down before anyone could trace it back to him.

The burden of his actions settled heavily on his shoulders as he sped away into the night, leaving behind a scene of chaos and despair.

Chapter 21: Robert (2)

Donovan sat in the cosy corner booth of the Little Pack Horse pub, enjoying his dinner with Jess. The dim lighting and chatter of patrons created a warm atmosphere, and he was grateful for the company after a long day at work.

As they chatted and laughed, Donovan's phone suddenly rang. He excused himself and answered, hearing the urgent voice of HQ on the other end. A drug overdose case had just come in, and they needed his expertise.

Quickly scribbling down the details in his pocket notebook, Donovan called Amy to pick him up. Even though he had only had one pint of beer and wasn't over the legal drink-drive limit, he didn't like to risk driving after even a small amount of alcohol.

"I have to go, duty calls," he said to Jess apologetically.

She nodded understandingly. "It's a shame, I was enjoying the company."

"Can you drop Toby off at my place?" Donovan asked Jess as they walked out of the pub. "You could always hang around for a nightcap."

Jess smiled and agreed. A short time later, Amy pulled up outside in her car. Donovan gave her the address in Hampton Loade, and she punched it into her satnav before they drove off.

As they made their way through the quiet streets, Donovan couldn't resist trying to tease Amy.

"So, is this your mess in the car? Bit of a tip," he joked.

Amy rolled her eyes but couldn't help smiling. "You know how it is, a busy lady with no time to clean!"

"I can't believe all these sweet and chocolate wrappers," Donovan continued teasing. "What's your name, Cadbury?"

Amy tutted playfully and shook her head as they arrived at the scene of the overdose. The paramedics had already confirmed the death and had left, leaving only first response teams on site.

After changing into CSI suits, Donovan and Amy approached the house where the overdose had occurred. They walked down the pathway and into the lounge, where they found the body of a young man with a needle still in his arm. Initial signs pointed towards a drug overdose.

Donovan carefully inspected the body, starting at the head and working his way down. Nothing immediately stood out to him. He then turned his attention to the rest of the room, with Amy following closely behind. The living space seemed like that of a typical young bachelor, with few personal items on display. Donovan opened a large dresser and found various drug paraphernalia, indicating personal use.

"It all seems a bit too perfect," Donovan remarked, furrowing his eyebrows. "A bit too easy. Just like the other overdose/murder."

Amy nodded in agreement. "I get what you mean. It just doesn't feel right."

They continued searching through the rest of the house, finding a name on household bills—Robert Lightfoot. They made a note to run his name when they returned to HQ.

After about an hour at the scene, Donovan and Amy left, leaving a police officer to take statements from nearby neighbours. There was no need for them to duplicate efforts.

Donovan instructed Amy to drop him off at his apartment before heading home herself to get some rest. There was nothing more they could do tonight, but they knew they would have a skeleton shift at HQ who would reach out to Robert Lightfoot's next of kin and report back any findings in the morning.

Chapter 22: Severn Valley

The sun was setting as they sat in the cosy corner of Kidderminster's King and Castle pub, sipping on pints of frothy beer. The warm atmosphere of the old-style pub—located adjacent to the Severn Valley railway—was bustling with people—not just steam enthusiasts, but also those seeking a taste of the pub's legendary beer and lively ambience.

As they waited for their train to Bridgnorth, the two men talked and laughed, enjoying each other's company. This was a routine trip for them, one they had done over 50 times before. They knew how to blend in and keep a low profile.

When the announcement came for their train, they finished their beers and gathered their coats before making their way out onto the open platform. A magnificent steam locomotive awaited them, ready to take them on their journey.

They boarded the 19:00 hrs train, which would make stops at Bewdley, Arley, Highley, Hampton Loade and finally Bridgnorth. Though not the most affordable or convenient mode of transportation, it allowed them to move around the county unnoticed amongst tourists and rail enthusiasts.

Observing the other passengers selecting their carriages and getting on, the two men hung back before choosing a compartment at the rear of the train. It was large enough for the two of them to share, offering privacy and comfort during their 1 hour and 15-minute journey to Bridgnorth.

As they settled into their seats opposite each other, the guard and ticket master blew a whistle signalling for departure. The carriage jolted forward as the engine took up slack between the cars, slowly pulling away from the station.

The compartment was adorned with dark blue upholstered bench seats facing each other. The ceiling and panelled walls were made of richly stained oak wood with brass luggage rails running along either side of the cabin. On one side of the compartment was a door, opening to the outside, with a pull-down window and brass handle. The other side had a wooden and glass sliding partition door with privacy blinds attached to each window.

The door slid open, revealing the train's guard. "Tickets please," he requested.

Simon handed over six crisp £10 notes and four pounds in exact change for their return tickets to Bridgnorth. The guard punched the tickets with a small hand punch before returning them to Simon.

"Thank you, lads. Just a reminder, the last train back is at 21:00 hrs tonight. Enjoy your journey," the guard said before moving on.

Simon stood up and pulled down the blinds facing the corridor, ensuring their privacy.

"Don't want everyone knowing our business," he joked.

His partner—a small-time foot soldier in their organisation—sat across from him having black hair, cropped short and being an average build. This journey was not out of the ordinary for them as Simon often handled these meetings.

"So, what exactly are we doing here tonight?" his partner asked curiously.

"We just need to pick up some coin and deliver it to the narrow boat. It's too much for one person to carry without being seen," Simon explained with a sly grin.

The train chugged along the tracks, stopping first at Bewdley station and then continuing to Arley. As the countryside passed by in a blur, Simon's mind raced with thoughts of what was about to happen. He knew his next stop, Highley station, would be a crucial moment.

As the train slowed to a stop at Highley, Simon heard someone trying to board their carriage. He quickly informed them that the seats were reserved, successfully deterring them from joining him and his partner. But as they moved to another compartment further up the train,

Simon's hand reached behind his back and with a swift, practised movement he retrieved his Glock semi-automatic pistol. His partner, Liam, was caught off guard by the sudden motion and let out a gasp of shock.

"Stay calm and sit down," Simon ordered with ice in his voice, pointedly aiming the gun at Liam. "You'll be okay if you just do as I say."

Liam pleaded for mercy, insisting he had done nothing wrong. But Simon knew better. Fenix had given him up when tortured by Jimi, and the ruthless OCG wanted their pound of flesh for skimming money off the top. And now, Simon had been tasked with teaching him a brutal lesson.

"It's out of my hands," Simon said coldly. "But I have no choice but to follow orders."

He gestured towards the platform exit door, his grip on the gun never faltering as he instructed Liam to stand with his back to him and hands raised above his head. As Liam reluctantly complied, Simon stood behind him with the calculated distance between them, ready to strike at any sign of resistance.

"Now open the door," Simon commanded, his voice laced with deadly intent.

Trembling with fear, Liam continued to plead for his life as he opened the door. But it was too late. Simon had planned every detail. He was timing his execution perfectly so that it coincided with the train's fastest point while surrounded by dense foliage to conceal any signs of a struggle.

With one precise, swift kick and a single shot to the nape of Liam's neck, he fell out of the moving train without making a sound. Liam was dead.

"Job done," Simon said softly to himself.

Simon closed the door and wiped away any traces of blood with his handkerchief, his expression betraying no emotion as he sat down in his empty seat. He tried to suppress the guilt and remorse that threatened to consume him for taking the life of someone he once considered a friend.

As the train pulled into Bridgnorth station, Simon quickly disembarked and blended into the crowd, making sure to keep his face hidden from any platform cameras. He took a taxi back to his flat, relieved that he had completed his task without being caught.

No money was collected that night. It was all just a ruse to lure Liam onto the train and carry out the OCG's orders. But deep down, Simon couldn't help but feel haunted by what he had done. After all, Liam had children for God's sake.

It was a tough decision, but in this world of organised crime, it was always a matter of *them or us*. The heaviness of his actions threatened to crush him as he lay awake in bed, unable to escape the haunting memories of this fateful night.

Chapter 23: Joshua

Simon and Jimi stood outside in the crisp night air; their faces set in determination as they prepared to carry out their orders. They both knew the risks of this mission, but they had no choice. It was their job to keep things quiet and to make sure no one found out about their involvement. They had decided upon making it look like a suicide it being the best option.

Joshua—or Josh as they knew him—had been working with them for three years now. He was a trusted member of their crew, specialising in dealing drugs on a larger scale than most shotters. But recently, they had received word from the top that he had been dipping into the profits for his own enjoyment.

Despite feeling uneasy about the situation, Simon and Jimi drove up to Josh's apartment complex at 8 pm. The building was an old converted coaching house, with Josh's apartment located above a *middle mews*. As they approached cautiously—keeping an eye out for any possible CCTV cameras—Jimi used his knowledge of the local area to guide them through safely.

Jimi buzzed Josh's apartment and waited for a response.

"Who is it?" came a male voice over the intercom.

"It's Jimi and Simon," Jimi answered confidently.

They were both eager to get inside and complete their mission quickly, without drawing any unwanted attention.

After receiving confirmation from Josh and being let inside, they climbed the stairs to his front door. Jimi knocked, and after a brief moment of hesitation, Josh opened it slightly to peer through the gap. He seemed ready to slam it shut, if necessary, always cautious and suspicious of unexpected visitors. But when he saw that it was indeed Simon and Jimi standing there, he relaxed and let them in.

The interior of Josh's apartment was like a luxurious man cave—all dark leather furniture and sleek chrome accents. A large TV playing the evening news bulletin dominated one wall, while a PlayStation and a Bang and Olufsen HiFi system took up another corner of the room. The plush grey carpet was soft underfoot, highlighting the expensive taste that Josh clearly had.

They all settled down on the large sofa and chair. Simon and Jimi sat together while Josh took a seat on the nearby chair.

"What brings you guys here?" Josh asked, trying to hide his agitation.

"Just wanted to check in…see how everything is going for you," Jimi replied casually.

"Things are good, no complaints from me," Josh said, his tone still tense.

"You mind if I use your bathroom?" Jimi suddenly asked, standing up from the sofa.

"No, go ahead. It's just through that door on the left," Josh said, gesturing towards the back of his apartment.

Jimi made his way around the back of Josh's chair to reach the bathroom door, giving Simon a subtle nod as he passed by. They both knew what their next move was. They needed to confront Josh about the missing money.

As he passed Josh, Jimi pounced on him, his large body moving with a stealth-like grace as he took Josh in a headlock. Jimi's right arm was wrapped tightly around Josh's neck, cutting off his air supply and causing him to gasp for breath.

Josh's vision began to blur, and darkness crept at the edges of his consciousness. Desperately, he reached behind his back where he had hidden a pistol earlier while making tea for his guests. He had a gut feeling that something was not right and needed protection.

With shaking hands, Josh pulled out the gun, fully exposing it and pointing it at Simon who was still seated on the sofa. Jimi's hold on him loosened slightly, allowing Josh to take in gulps of air.

"Back the fuck off!" Josh shouted, spitting out the order.

Simon raised his hands in surrender while Jimi released his hold completely.

"Okay, okay, let's all take it easy," Simon said calmly.

"I don't believe you have the guts to use that thing," he continued.

"You've really messed up this time. You stole from the boss men, and they want revenge," Simon said with a hint of fear in his voice.

"What do you suggest we do about that?" Simon asked earnestly.

"We can't just pretend like nothing happened."

"You thought you could come here and beat me up? Well, I'm not going to take it," Josh said, still pointing the gun at them both.

"I have been a loyal servant for years now, no complaints."

"We never intended to beat you," Simon said with a sly smile.

He nodded at Jimi who pulled out a large knife from inside his jacket pocket. With expert precision, he bent over Josh's shoulder from behind and plunged the blade straight into his chest. The sharp edge sliced through muscle and tissue effortlessly, piercing Josh's left lung and entering his heart.

The knife went in deep until its hilt was pressed against Josh's chest. Surprisingly, there was little blood spilling out despite the fatal wound, the knife muting any flow. Jimi and Simon were thankful for this, knowing that it would make their escape easier.

Josh collapsed into the chair, his lifeless body slumping forward. He had died instantly from the knife wound. Jimi quickly took Josh's gun from him and checked its magazine, finding no bullets inside and nothing in the chamber. Josh had been bluffing, though they didn't know it at the time.

"We need to wipe down the knife's handle and search the flat for any evidence linking to us or to drugs or the OCG," Simon said to Jimi.

"Give me the gun, I'll dispose of it later," he replied as he cleaned off any fingerprints from the weapon.

They spent the next hour tearing through the apartment, searching for anything that could incriminate them. They found half a kilo of cocaine and heroin hidden away in various places, along with rolls of cash in a bedside drawer which they took with them.

Hastily, they emptied drawers onto the floor and tore apart furniture looking for any hidden compartments where Josh may have stashed something incriminating. Their hearts pounded with adrenaline as they frantically tried to cover their tracks.

Could this look like a botched robbery? That's what they hoped for. With nothing else left to do, they left the apartment and disappeared into the darkness of night without looking back, trying not to think about what they had just done. For them, killing had become almost routine now, an easy way out of their problems.

Chapter 24: Body in the Tree

His canine companion darted off into the dense forest, an action that was not out of the ordinary. However, this time she returned with a muddy and tattered brown Lofa shoe clamped tightly in her jaws.

_____ " _____

The weight of hopelessness settled heavily on Donovan as he sat at his cluttered desk, surrounded by cases that seemed to be going nowhere. He rubbed his tired eyes and let out a deep sigh before gathering his team around the whiteboards for another strategy session.

"Team, we're at a standstill here," he began, frustration evident in his voice. "We need to apply Occam's Razor to these cases and simplify things."

One of the PCs raised their hand. "What's Occam's Razor?" they asked.

"It's a philosophical tool used for *shaving off* unlikely explanations," Donovan explained. "In other words, we need to eliminate any complex theories and focus on more straightforward possibilities."

He turned to the whiteboard, pens ready in hand. "Let's start with the number of killers involved. Due to the differing modus operandi of each murder, it's safe to assume there is more than one killer at play here."

"But could it be three killers?" another team member chimed in.

Donovan shook his head. "My gut feeling, or PolDar as I like to call it, tells me that's highly unlikely. But we can't rule it out completely just yet."

He gestured towards the whiteboard filled with clues and evidence photos. "This won't magically reveal the killer(s) to us, but it will help us gain some clarity from this chaotic mess of answers we currently have."

"We've been at this for a week now with little progress," he continued with a heavy sigh. "Our boss is getting impatient, and so are we. Let's focus on what we do have. We'll start by expanding our search for any connections to the cars involved, utilising the CLT's database to see if there are any leads there."

The team nodded in agreement and quickly set to work, reorganising the evidence boards and typing away on their computers with renewed determination.

Just as they were getting into a rhythm, the duty sergeant burst in. "Boss, we've just received a report of a suspected murder near Hampton Loade," he announced breathlessly.

Donovan thanked him and took the case file, already mentally preparing himself for another long day. He and Amy hopped into the car and made their way to the scene. Choosing a playlist containing *Moby* to accompany them, they arrived on the scene but had to park a quarter of a mile away and continue on foot. Toby eagerly led the way.

Upon arrival, they found the usual scene: forensic teams and a lone police constable buzzing around, gathering evidence. The pathway leading to where the body was found was shrouded in dense trees and bushes, making it difficult to see anything before reaching the area.

Donovan handed Toby over to the PC and suited up in his own forensic gear before making his way through a small gap in the bushes with Amy close behind.

"Beautiful day to be out here," one of the forensic officers remarked with a hint of sarcasm.

Amy couldn't help but chuckle. "Couldn't agree more."

"It's been quite a busy week for us," another officer chimed in.

"You're telling me," Amy replied with a sigh. "Any breakthroughs on your end?"

The officer shook his head. "Nope, not our job. You're the detectives, we just collect and analyse evidence."

Despite the grim situation, they all shared a small laugh before getting back to work.

Donovan's eyes immediately fell upon the lifeless body, hanging six feet in the air and caught in a tangle of branches. The young Caucasian male was suspended like a grotesque puppet, his limbs twisted at unnatural angles. Donovan could see signs of head trauma from where he stood, even before forensics confirmed it with their expert opinion.

"It appears to be a gunshot wound, entry point at the back of his skull and exit point through his mouth," one of the team members stated.

Donovan nodded, already coming to the same conclusion.

"Are there any other visible injuries?" he asked.

"Some bruising, but that's most likely from the fall after death," Forensics replied.

"Based on the state of the body and surrounding area, I'd say this happened a few days ago," they added.

"Taking into account the positioning of the body, it's safe to assume that he was shot and then pushed off a train. It's the only logical explanation," Donovan declared.

"Agreed," both Amy and forensics chimed in.

"Can we get him down, please?" Donovan requested.

After taking all necessary photographs, forensics carefully lowered the body from its precarious perch in the bush. As Donovan inspected the victim more closely, he noticed something missing—a shoe.

"Where's his other shoe?" he asked.

"Over here, Sir. A member of the public's dog found it nearby," responded one of the officers on the scene.

Thanking them for their help, Donovan bent down to examine the body further. The evidence was clear: a medium calibre gunshot wound with severe damage to the lower jaw and face.

"It seems that whoever had killed this man did not expect him to be found so quickly," Donovan said.

"What makes you think that?" Amy inquired.

"The location. This spot is dense with bushes and trees, making it the most secluded area along the train line. I have a feeling that the killer chose it carefully and planned the murder beforehand," Donovan explained.

"It's possible that the killer got lucky with such a remote location, but finding the body so soon is not their ideal scenario. It could've been months, even years before this discovery, leading to more decomposition and fewer clues for forensics to work with," he added.

While Amy searched through the victim's pockets, Donovan surveyed the scene once more before they headed back to headquarters.

"Let's hope we catch a break on this one. Shooting on the Severn Valley railway is not a common occurrence," he remarked.

"There must be witnesses," Amy pointed out.

"We can only hope. I like to call these unusual cases *10 percenters*," Donovan said with a smirk, still trying to lighten the mood amidst the grim situation.

As they drove back to HQ, both detectives were lost in thought about the strange case unfolding before them. At the station, they added the railway shooting to their whiteboard of active cases and awaited any updates from forensics.

"Boss, I may have something," a young DC approached Donovan.

"I did some digging like you suggested and found references to a Grey Audi Q5 spotted near areas of interest. No identifiable licence plate numbers, but there was a name linked to the car—Simon," she reported.

"Excellent work! Keep searching for more information on this Simon character," Donovan instructed as he added his name to their board with a question mark beside it.

They would anxiously await the results from forensics and the post-mortem in the morning. Donovan—tired and restless—had to leave and attend the local council meeting in Bewdley. Gail—wife of the café owner Joe—had specifically requested that he provide an update on the high-profile suicide of Karl Hamilton and the recent string of violent deaths in the area. Donovan's boss saw this as an opportunity for good PR, so she agreed for him to go.

The night air was getting cooler as Donovan made his way through the quiet streets to the town hall. He couldn't shake off the feeling of unease as he contemplated what he would say at the meeting.

Chapter 25: Manchester

The Audi Q5 glided through the murky streets, a sleek predator. Jimi's fingers tapped the steering wheel, a staccato rhythm matching his impatience. Simon leaned forward, eyes flicking left and right, piercing the shadows that clung to alleyways and doorways.

"Left here," Simon murmured, his voice barely above a whisper.

Jimi swung the car around the corner, the engine purr a quiet threat. Streetlights cast an orange haze, but their quarry was not one to hide in the light. They needed the dark, where grudges grew like mould.

"Slow down," Simon instructed, his gaze locked on a figure ambling ahead.

Jimi eased off the accelerator, the Q5 creeping up behind the unsuspecting man. Their target, a silhouette against the dim glow of a flickering streetlamp, ambled with the false security of his own territory.

"Gotcha," Jimi breathed out.

They pulled alongside the man. Simon rolled down his window, feigning a confused driver. "Oi, mate, you know how to get to Market Street from here?"

The man stopped, turning towards them, his face etched with lines of life on the streets. He peered into the car, the trap set.

"Market Street, yeah?" he began, stepping closer.

That's when Jimi struck. A swift motion, a gleam of metal. The gun was in his hand, the barrel steady despite his pounding heart.

"Get in the car," Jimi's voice didn't rise, it didn't need to.

The threat was clear in the cold steel pressed against the man's chest. Fear bloomed in the rival's eyes, a silent scream where bravado died.

"Jimi!" the man started, a plea forming on his lips.

Jimi's reputation preceded him.

"Shut it," Jimi cut him off, his finger caressing the trigger like a lover's touch. "You're coming with us."

Simon's shadow stretched out on the pavement as he unfolded himself from the passenger seat; a dark ghost against the car's sleek form. He reached for the rear door with a mocking bow.

"After you."

The bound man hesitated, his eyes darting between Jimi's unwavering gun and the open door of the Q5.

Words tumbled over his tongue in a frantic jumble, "This ain't right. I swear—"

"Save it," Jimi snapped, pointing at him with his pistol.

With a shuffling gait, the man complied, wincing as he manoeuvred his tied hands to slide into the backseat. The door slammed shut, a definitive note of captivity.

The engine hummed as they resumed their hunt through the city's veins. The streets were less illuminated here and shadows were clinging to corners like old secrets. Simon flicked a glance at Jimi—a silent signal—before turning his attention to the rearview mirror, where fear twisted the man's features.

"Look," the man said, his voice trembling, "whatever you think I've done, we can sort this—"

"Sort?" Simon's laugh was dry, devoid of any real mirth. "You're way past sorting, mate."

Jimi kept his eyes on the road, the gun now resting casually in his lap. Each building they passed seemed to absorb the sound of the man's shallow breaths—the tension was palpable—thick enough to choke on.

"Please, listen," the man pressed, straining against the binds at his wrists. "I didn't mean to cross—"

"Didn't mean?" Simon cut in, his tone sharp as the knife he kept in his boot. "You didn't stumble into our turf by accident."

Streetlights flickered overhead, casting brief illuminations on the trio like a spotlight on the theatre of the damned. The car moved like a predator, unhurried, sure of its prey.

"Please—" It was barely a whisper now, a last-ditch plea thrown into the void between life and death.

"Quiet," Jimi ordered, the word slicing through the desperation.

Silence settled heavily. The only sound is the car's tyres whispering across the asphalt, a serenade to the inevitable.

The Audi Q5 rolled to a halt, its headlights cutting swathes through the darkness of the car breaker's yard. Dust swirled in the stark glow of the floodlights as Jimi killed the engine. For a moment, all was silent save for the ticking of cooling metal.

"Out," Jimi grunted, his fingers digging into the man's arm with vice-like intent.

Simon mirrored him on the other side; their movements were practised and efficient. The man's feet stumbled on the loose gravel, his pleas spilling out in ragged gasps.

"Please, I have a family," he choked, eyes wide and darting from one captor to the other.

"Shut it," Jimi snapped back, his grip unyielding as they hauled him toward an ominous pile of crushed cars.

The shadows loomed large, the shapes of twisted metal like the contorted limbs of giants.

"Wait, wait—" The man's words came out in a breathless staccato, but Simon's cold chuckle cut through the desperation.

"Jimi, you hear something?" Simon asked, feigning curiosity.

"Wind's talking again." Jimi replied, his voice devoid of emotion.

"Mercy, please, have—"

"Mercy?" Simon said his tone acid. "That's rich."

The man's struggles grew frenetic, his body writhing in their grasp, but it was no use. The combined strength of his captors was unassailable, their resolve as unforgiving as the steel that surrounded them.

"Jimi, look at him. He thinks he is getting out of this." Simon's smile was a blade, sharp and gleaming in the harsh light.

"Pathetic," Jimi muttered, his face a mask of stone.

They stopped, the man now dwarfed by a mountain of discarded vehicles. His whimpers bounced off the cold metal, a symphony of fear playing to an audience of indifference.

"Please—" It was a whisper lost in the vastness of the yard, the word hanging in the air, heavy with the scent of oil and rust.

"Done begging?" Simon asked, almost bored.

"Never started," Jimi responded, his eyes never leaving the man.

There was a finality in his stance; an end written in the lines of his face and the set of his shoulders.

"Let's finish this," Simon said, his voice a low rumble, a prelude to silence.

Jimi's hand was steady. The man before him—a mix of defiance and terror etched into his face—seemed to shrink with the cold touch of metal against his skin. A shiver ran down the captive's spine, a silent scream in a body too paralysed by fear to move.

"Any last words?" Jimi's voice was almost a whisper, edged with darkness.

The man's eyes darted wildly, searching for an ounce of mercy in a sea of malice.

"I—"

The sound tore through the stillness of the night, a single, brutal punctuation. The man's body crumpled into a lifeless heap against the backdrop of twisted metal and shadow. Jimi had shot the man, point-blank, against his right temple. The exit wound exploded outward with vivid red blood.

Silence returned, swallowing the echo of the shot as if the yard itself was complicit in the deed.

"Clean," Simon remarked, his tone clinical.

He turned away, footsteps deliberate on gravel. In his outstretched hand—an envelope thick with notes passed to the breaker's yard owner—a hushed covenant sealed under the floodlights' unforgiving glare.

"Make sure it's done right," Simon said, the threat woven into his casual demeanour.

"Always is," came the gruff reply, a voice used to such transactions, untouched by the weight of what it enabled.

They watched as the car, now a steel coffin, ascended, gripped by the crane's iron jaws. The machinery groaned, a guttural chorus to the final act. With a jolt, the car surrendered to the crusher—its structure protesting until it was silenced—compressed into silence.

"Like he never existed," Jimi mused, eyes not leaving the crushed remains.

"Exactly." Simon's lips curled into a semblance of a smile, devoid of humour.

The yard owner counted his money again, nodding his satisfaction, oblivious or indifferent to the stain it left on his hands.

"Let's go," Jimi said.

The two men turned their backs on the scene, their shadows long in the light of the departing day.

The Audi Q5 cut through the night, its engine a low growl against the silence. Streetlights streaked past, casting intermittent shadows across Jimi's face as he drove. A smirk is tugging at his lips.

"Did you see his face, right before—" Simon's voice trailed off into a chuckle, the sound hollow and cold.

"Picture perfect," Jimi replied, his laughter mingling with Simon's—a twisted duet.

The rearview mirror flashed a view of empty streets, but their echoes of cruelty filled the car.

"Like rats, they scurry when we come knocking." Simon flicked on the radio, only to switch it off again.

The music couldn't compete with the adrenaline that pulsed through him.

"Think he had time to regret crossing us?" Jimi asked, his voice playful yet edged with steel.

"Regret? Doubt it. Fear, though—" Simon let the word hang, savouring the memory of power over life and death.

Jimi nodded, satisfaction rolling off him in waves. The car sped on, unmarked by the violence left in its wake.

"Too easy," Simon mused aloud, his gaze fixed on the passing blur of the city. "It's all just too easy."

"Means we're good at what we do." Jimi's laugh was a dark thing, scratching at the confines of the car.

"Or maybe everyone else is just bad at staying alive," Simon countered, the corner of his mouth twitching upwards.

A comfortable silence settled between them; the kind shared by those who need not speak to communicate. It was the silence of complicity, of shared darkness.

As the Audi drove onto the bypass, the town's glow dimmed behind them. Ahead lay only darkness, a fitting path for two souls so devoid of light.

"Easy," Jimi repeated, the word less a boast now, more a whisper of unease.

He gripped the steering wheel tighter, chasing the thrill that once was, but now seemed an echo of itself.

Simon didn't respond as he was lost in thought. The realisation was there, sharp and unwelcome. Murder had become their currency, traded without thought, spent without remorse.

"These streets won't forget us," Simon finally said, breaking the quiet.

"Nor we…them," Jimi agreed, his smile fading as the Audi devoured miles of road.

The streets emptied around them, the town falling away as they drove towards the outskirts. Their laughter faded into the night, a chilling duet that danced with the shadows.

Chapter 26: Town Hall

The monthly local council meeting was always a highly anticipated event in the small community. People flocked to it, eager to hear updates on planning applications and local events. But this particular meeting had been called as an exception due to the recent surge of incidents in the area.

The meeting took place in a grand room above Bewdley town's museum, housed in a magnificent Tudor-style building that exuded history and charm. The room was filled to the brim with concerned citizens, local councillors and even the MP.

"The word must have gotten around," Gail remarked as she took her seat next to Donovan.

"Well, it's big news for such a small community," Donovan replied, taking a seat at the front of the room between Gail and the chairperson, who happened to be the lady mayoress.

The buzz of conversation filled the air, but as soon as the mayoress banged her gavel and called for order, silence fell over the room.

"Thank you all, for coming to this exceptional evening's meeting," she began.

"We have a special update from the police on the recent incidents. DI Donovan Temple—who is leading the investigations—will provide an update and answer any questions we may have." She gestured towards Donovan to stand up and speak.

"Greetings everyone," he started, his voice tentative but friendly. "It's good to see some familiar faces here tonight."

"As you all know, we've experienced several concerning incidents over the past week. A lot more than usual, which is why I'm here." He paused briefly before continuing, "We've had two suspected overdose deaths, one drowning believed, one fatal fire, and two fatal shootings, one of which was just reported today."

Donovan quickly ran through each incident before delivering some unsettling news. "I can confirm that we are treating all suspected overdoses as murders."

He went on to explain that they had yet to make any arrests in connection with the other deaths, but they were following multiple leads.

"Thank you, for your update, DI Temple. Are there any questions?" The mayoress addressed the room.

A middle-aged woman from the public gallery raised her hand and spoke up, "Why do you think there's been an increase in violent crimes? This area is usually so peaceful, it's all very scary. Should we be afraid?"

Donovan took a deep breath before answering. "To answer your question in parts, we believe that the rise in violent crimes can be attributed to organised criminal activity in the area. We're not sure why this has happened, but we are working on uncovering the reasons."

He added, trying to reassure the worried residents, "You should not fear. This is not normal, and the criminal gangs do not typically involve members of the public in their business."

But not everyone was convinced.

"What about the late-night noise from people leaving pubs? It's becoming unbearable," another resident chimed in.

Donovan shifted uncomfortably in his seat before responding. "That's not something I have jurisdiction over, but I can assure you that, as a local resident myself, I am invested in finding a solution." He hoped the mayoress would move on to the next topic and spare him from further questioning.

Thankfully, she wrapped up the formalities and ended the meeting. As Donovan exited the room, he met up with Jess who had come to listen to him speak.

"How do you think it went?" he asked her.

"Overall, it went well. But clearly, people are scared, and who can blame them?" she replied with a sigh.

"It's frustrating. I was hoping for more leads by now. But I have a feeling…something will break soon," Donovan said determinedly.

They walked out into the night together, searching for answers in the darkness surrounding their once-peaceful community.

As the evening wore on, Donovan and Jess found themselves curled up on the couch, her head resting on his chest as they watched a movie. He had let her choose the program, wanting to make her happy. With each passing minute, the warmth of his body and the steady rise and fall of his chest lulled her into a state of tranquillity.

The soft glow from the TV illuminated their faces, casting shadows against the walls and filling the room with a cosy ambience. Donovan's eyes grew heavy as exhaustion finally caught up with him, and he dozed off, his arm instinctively wrapping around Jess as they both drifted off into a peaceful slumber.

Chapter 27: Simon

As Donovan and Amy entered the office, they were met with a flurry of activity. Fingerprints from the railway killing had come back with a hit from the database. The dead person was Liam Grainger from Kidderminster. Jane, the DC, had already printed off his lengthy rap sheet and placed it on top of a stack of papers ready for Donovan's perusal.

Glancing at the sheet, Donovan remarked to Amy, "As I would have expected, a laundry list of crimes but nothing too serious."

"It says here he was married. Let's go inform his wife about his demise and conduct an interview before she has time to process everything," he said decisively.

They made their way to Liam's home in a neighbourhood known for its troublesome history with the police. The area was lined with 1970s semi-detached houses that seemed to blend together into one monotonous block of pebble dash. As they approached the house, they could hear the sounds of children laughing and playing inside.

Donovan knocked on the door and could hear shuffling and murmurs from within before it finally swung open. Standing before them was Mrs Grainger; a woman in her late 20s with bleached blonde hair. Her eyebrows still bore traces of her natural brown colour, and her roots were growing out. She wore a white t-shirt, black jeans, and Nike running shoes.

"Who are you?" she asked sharply.

"Are you Mrs Grainger?" Donovan inquired.

"Why? Who is asking?" she replied suspiciously.

"We are the police. May we come in?" Donovan presented his warrant card as proof.

"What's he been up to now?" she sighed, waving them inside.

The hallway was littered with clothes and toys strewn about haphazardly. Half-empty glasses sat on every available surface; evidence of a chaotic household. In the heart of it all sat a massive 70-inch TV, dominating the living room. Donovan and Amy stood in silence as Mrs Grainger perched herself on the edge of a chair.

"Unfortunately, we are the bearers of bad news. We found Mr Grainger's dead body late yesterday near Hampton Loade," Donovan said solemnly.

Mrs Grainger sat in stunned silence at this news, her face drained of all colour.

"His death is being treated as a murder. He was shot," Donovan continued.

"Do you have any idea why someone would want to kill him?" he probed gently.

She wiped away a stray tear and tried to compose herself. Donovan offered her his handkerchief, but she declined.

"No, I don't know of anyone who would want to harm him. He was a good husband and father to our kids. But everyone knew he liked to have a bit of fun, always up to something. Nothing major though, at least not that I know of," she replied with a hint of sadness in her voice.

"What were his movements yesterday?" Donovan pressed further.

"We spent the morning together and went down to the local playground with the kids. Later in the day, he said he was meeting a friend for a few beers," she answered.

"A friend? Do you remember their name?" Donovan asked.

"Yes, it was Simon. I don't know his last name though," she said thoughtfully. "He used to go drinking at the King and Castle quite often."

Donovan and Amy exchanged glances at the mention of that name again—Simon.

"Why do you think Liam was on a train yesterday evening?" Donovan shifted gears with his questioning.

"I have no idea. He never mentioned going anywhere. I just assumed he crashed at Simon's place for the night…something, he did when he drank too much, so he wouldn't wake up me or the kids," she explained.

After informing Mrs Grainger of the need for her to officially identify her husband's body in the coming days, Donovan and Amy handed her their contact cards in case she needed anything else. As they made their way back to their car, they could see Mrs Grainger sitting on the couch with her youngest child in her lap—a sombre reminder of the human toll that crime takes.

Donovan sent Amy to interview the staff at the King and Castle and the train guardsman who had been working on the night of Liam's death, determined to get to the bottom of this case.

Back at the bustling police headquarters, Donovan and his team were hard at work trying to piece together the case. The computers whizzed. DC Mark finally had a breakthrough and discovered a surname for their suspect—Franklin.

Donovan wasted no time in pulling up this name on the database, revealing a lengthy criminal record dating back to Franklin's youth. From petty theft to more sinister crimes, it was clear that he was not a pleasant individual.

As they delved deeper into his file, they found an address in Kidderminster associated with him.

"Excellent!" exclaimed Donovan, feeling a surge of excitement at finally getting some solid evidence.

But before taking any action, he knew he had to brief his superiors and reach out to DI Wayne at the CLT to decide on the best course of action.

Amy returned from her errand bearing CCTV footage from the King and Castle pub. The bar staff confirmed that Franklin and another man, Liam, were regulars there on the night of the crime.

Unfortunately, when they spoke to the elderly guardsman on duty that evening, he could not recall seeing the two suspects. He sheepishly apologised, citing his old age as a factor in his forgetfulness.

However, reviewing the CCTV footage revealed undeniable proof of Franklin and Liam's presence at the pub that night. They even managed to put names to faces as they watched the two men drinking together. But much to their frustration, the footage did not capture them leaving the bar.

Donovan quickly sought approval from his boss and DI Wayne for their planned raid on Franklin's house early the next morning. With everything in place, they went home to rest. Then, in the morning they anxiously waited for dawn to break in hopes of finally getting their man.

Chapter 28: Raid

The team stood on high alert, their fingers tightly gripping the cold metal of their loaded firearms. Simon's reputation for violence preceded him, and they were prepared for the worst.

As they approached the small suburban residence, Donovan took charge, signalling for quiet. No sirens or flashing lights would be needed for this operation. They had one goal: to apprehend Simon without drawing any unwanted attention.

Donovan led the way, with Amy and three firearms-trained PCs behind him. One of them held a door battering ram, ready to take down any obstacles in their way. They moved silently up the pathway towards the white UPVC door that blocked their entry. This was a house of multiple occupancy, and one of the flats belonged to Simon. With housing plans in hand, they knew exactly where to go.

Their hearts raced with adrenaline as they waited for Donovan's signal.

"Breach, Breach. Armed police!" he finally yelled.

The PC with the ram swung it back and forth, hitting both hinges of the door with precision. The loud bangs echoed through the quiet neighbourhood as the door came crashing down, giving them access to Simon's flat.

"Armed police!" Donovan shouted repeatedly, making sure everyone inside was aware of their presence.

They rushed in, guns drawn, and made their way up the stairs towards Simon's room. Once again, the PC used the battering ram to break down the entrance door. Donovan followed closely behind, ready for anything.

Simon was caught off guard by all the noise and commotion. He jumped out of bed and swung a punch at Donovan, who quickly ducked and retaliated with an elbow to Simon's rib cage. The blow winded Simon, causing him to gasp for air.

Donovan swiftly took control, using his skills from his days in military police training to subdue Simon. He twisted his wrist into an ikkyo move from the

Aikido martial art, causing Simon to fall to the ground in pain. Amy quickly handcuffed him as Donovan pinned him down with one knee in his back and a firm grip on his arm.

"You're under arrest for suspicion of murder," Donovan declared.

Simon was caught off guard again, now fully awake and processing what was happening.

"Stay down," Donovan warned, as he pushed harder on Simon's back.

Amy read him his rights, cautioning him that anything he said could be used against him in court. With Simon in custody, Donovan allowed him to put on some clothes before they took him away in a makeshift shirt made from his duvet, they did not want to unshackle him to put on a shirt.

"Any weapons we should know about?" Donovan asked sternly.

Simon played dumb, refusing to give any information away. But Donovan had a search warrant for this address and wasn't leaving without answers. The PCs began combing through every inch of Simon's flat, searching under the bed, rifling through drawers and even checking above them a small attic space in the hallway above.

As Simon sat there—still in shock from the sudden turn of events—he couldn't help but think how foolish it would be for him to keep any incriminating evidence at his own home.

With heavy disappointment weighing on his shoulders, Simon stood in the barren living room of his flat. He watched as the detectives finished their search, packing away any potential evidence. They then escorted him to headquarters, where he was promptly thrown into a bleak cell.

The room was completely stripped, save for a window that offered a sliver of light, a toilet in the corner, and a thin blue plastic-coated mattress that seemed barely used. The door had a small portal for guards to observe from and a slot for food to be passed through.

After being processed and photographed, Simon was left alone to contemplate his situation for what felt like hours before being brought into an interrogation room. Donovan—with Amy by his side—sat across from Simon at a large black desk.

"This interview is being recorded. Please, state your name," Donovan began.

"I am DI Donovan Temple," he announced.

"I am DS Amy Campbell," Amy followed.

"Simon Franklin," Simon stated, trying to maintain composure.

"Just so you are aware, this room is under video surveillance and my fellow officers may watch this interview," Donovan warned.

"Let's begin," he prompted.

"Why have you brought me here?" Simon asked, already feeling defensive.

"We have reason to believe that you are connected to the murder of a man three days ago," Donovan responded bluntly.

"That's not true! I had nothing to do with it," Simon protested, shaking his head vehemently.

"Where were you on the evening of 25 June?" Donovan pressed.

"I was out drinking with a friend and then went home," Simon explained.

"With whom and where did you go?" Donovan probed further.

"We started at the Station Inn and then went to the King and Castle. You can ask the staff there; they know me well. I was with my friend Liam Grainger," Simon revealed.

"What happened after that?" Donovan inquired.

"I went home, like I said. I was alone," Simon maintained, growing increasingly agitated. "And Liam went home, I think."

"Any witnesses to corroborate your story?" Donovan questioned.

"No, I was by myself," Simon insisted, his façade of calm cracking under the pressure.

"Well, we have reason to believe that you boarded a Severn Valley train with Liam and then killed him," Donovan stated bluntly, not mincing words.

"That's absurd! Liam was my friend. Why would I want to kill him?" Simon exclaimed in shock and disbelief.

"I didn't even know he was dead until now!" he added, attempting to feign grief for his supposed friend.

"I think I should speak to my lawyer now," Simon demanded, reaching his breaking point.

"I'm not going to answer any more of your bullshit questions," he declared firmly.

With that, Simon provided the name and number of his solicitor to Donovan. The name was all too familiar to the detective—this solicitor represented some of the most notorious and wealthy criminals in the area. Donovan couldn't help but wonder: how Simon could afford such a high-priced solicitor or have him on speed dial.

The interview soon concluded, with Simon refusing to answer any further questions, proclaiming *no comment* repeatedly. A few more agonising hours passed before Simon's solicitor finally arrived and spoke with him.

After a brief conversation with Donovan, the solicitor confidently insisted that they release his client due to lack of evidence. It infuriated Donovan that he did not have enough to keep Simon locked up at this time.

Simon was eventually released on bail later that day. He couldn't believe how quickly they had found Liam's body. He thought he had chosen a remote enough location to hide it completely. But he wasn't surprised that he was picked up for questioning as he hadn't been very discreet when hiding from sight earlier in the evening with Liam.

He walked away from the police station with a sneer on his face, mocking those who had arrested him.

Chapter 29: Status

Chief Inspector Grace sat at her desk, staring at the stack of files and evidence surrounding the cases her team had been working on. Her frustration was palpable as she knew they were all working tirelessly to solve the string of murders and overdoses that had plagued their area. She took a deep breath and called for her team to gather around the whiteboards in the situation room.

"I know we are all tired and just as frustrated as I am with our lack of progress," she began. "But I need a full briefing so I can provide an update to the chief superintendent."

Donovan—acting as a lead detective—stood beside her and began to recount the timeline of events from the first overdose-turned-murder up until the most recent arrest. He spoke of victims and evidence, trying to make sense of it all.

"Keith Roberts was the first victim," Donovan explained, his eyes scanning over his notes. "We believe he was a drug dealer based on forensics and local camera footage. But we have no leads on a motive or suspect, making this case run cold."

He then moved on to discuss the killing of undercover policewoman Elaine Rodgers, revealing that her death was connected to her work exposing a criminal gang; the OCG behind. However, they were still unable to determine what information she was about to expose before her untimely demise.

"The post-mortem provided us with a DNA sample under her fingernails, but we have yet to identify who it belongs to," Donovan continued.

Chief Inspector Grace interrupted, asking about the County Lines Taskforce's involvement in the case.

"They haven't made any significant progress either," Donovan admitted. "But we are keeping each other updated."

Donovan then delved into details about another murder that seemed gang-related, with evidence pointing towards a rival gang claiming turf, and with the assailant leaving behind a few footprints as clues.

"The most gruesome scene was at the carpet factory," Donovan continued, his voice sombre. "But forensics haven't found much evidence other than a medallion that was around the victim's neck. We are still waiting on forensics to analyse it."

Grace interrupted again, expressing her frustration with the slow progress of forensics, "Make sure the lab knows that these cases are a high priority, no excuses," she said with a touch of anger in her voice.

Donovan quickly moved on to the second overdose-turned-murder, explaining that the victim had been asphyxiated and then staged to look like an overdose. He noted the similarities between this case and the first, suggesting a clever killer trying to cover their tracks.

"And finally, we have Simon Franklin as a suspect for the Severn Valley railway killing," Donovan said, tapping a picture of the smug-looking man on the whiteboard.

"But he lawyered up quickly and isn't talking. We need a witness who can place him and the victim on the train together."

Chief Inspector Grace nodded, taking in all of the information before dismissing her team to continue their work.

She knew they were doing everything they could, but she couldn't shake off her own dissatisfaction with their lack of progress. She was determined to find answers and bring justice to the loved ones of those who had lost their lives.

The chief inspector's voice was stern as she spoke with Donovan, "I do think that we can say with confidence that all of these crimes are drug-related and are most likely the same crime group who are cleaning house." She looked around the room, measuring up the mood.

"We do, however, need to catch some breaks," she continued, "these will only come from dogged determination from the team, something I know we all want." Her words hung in the air, heavy with the weight of the situation at hand.

"Thank you, for the update, Donovan," she said, looking at her colleague. "I agree with you about this all feeling like an OCG's work, and that we need more evidence to corroborate this theory."

"How are you doing for manpower?" she asked, concern evident in her tone.

"Due to the sheer increase in cases, I have authorisation for spending on overtime, but no increase in headcount, at this point," she said.

"We seem to be managing, Ma'am. We are all a bit tired but are soldiering on," he added with determination.

"Keep on going over each case, keep digging, and keep me informed please," Chief Inspector Grace instructed.

She knew it was important to stay updated and involved in every aspect of the investigation.

After the briefing, Chief Inspector Grace remained frustrated. She had been through countless cases before and knew that sometimes it was just a waiting game. But she also trusted in her team and in the process—a big break would come, it always did. Until then, they would continue to tirelessly work towards solving these murders and bringing justice to those affected by them.

Chapter 30: Meltdown

Donovan's footsteps echoed through the apartment as he paced back and forth, the floorboards creaking under his weight. His mind raced, thoughts swirling like a tempest. The linked cases consumed him, an unsolvable puzzle taunting his every waking moment.

Clenching his fists, he felt the burden of responsibility bearing down on him. Lives hung in the balance, and he was the one tasked with bringing justice. But doubt crept in; insidious whispers that he wasn't good enough, that he'd fail.

The door clicked open, and Jess entered. Her presence brings a momentary reprieve from his inner turmoil. Concern etched lines around her eyes as she took in Donovan's haggard appearance.

"Donovan, what's wrong?" Her voice was soft, laced with worry.

She crossed the room, closing the distance between them. Reaching out, she placed a gentle hand on his arm, the warmth of her touch seeping through his shirt.

Donovan stopped pacing abruptly. He met her gaze, seeing the depth of her concern reflected back at him. The words stuck in his throat as the admission of his fears was too heavy to voice.

He shook his head. "It's these damn cases, Jess. I can't...I don't know if I can solve them."

The doubt in his voice was visible, a stark contrast to the confident detective he usually portrayed. His shoulders slumped, the weight of his worries dragging him down.

Jess' grip on his arm tightened a silent reassurance. "Talk to me, Donovan. Let me help you carry this burden."

Donovan took a shuddering breath, the words tumbling out in a rush, "I'm convinced these cases are connected, Jess. The victims, the MO, it's too similar to be a coincidence." He ran a hand through his hair, frustration evident in the gesture. "But I'm missing something, a piece of the puzzle that ties it all together."

He began pacing again, his footsteps echoing in the quiet apartment. "If I can't figure this out, I'm sure more people will die. Their blood will be on my hands." His voice cracked the guilt and fear consuming him.

Jess listened attentively. Her eyes were filled with empathy. She understood the weight of responsibility Donovan carried in the lives that depended on his skills as a detective. But she also knew the man beneath the badge, the one who had solved countless complex cases before.

She stepped in front of him, halting his pacing. "Donovan, look at me." Her tone was gentle but firm. "You are one of the best detectives out there. Your instincts, your ability to see patterns others miss…it's what sets you apart."

Donovan met her gaze, a flicker of hope in his eyes.

Jess continued, "Remember the Blackwell case? Everyone thought it was a dead end, but you refused to give up. You followed your instincts and uncovered the truth."

She placed both hands on his shoulders, her touch grounding him. "You have the skills and the determination to crack these cases too. Don't let doubt consume you."

Donovan's breaths slowed, Jess' words penetrating the fog of his mind. She was right. He had solved tough cases before, relying on his instincts and tenacity. He couldn't let fear paralyse him now.

"I don't know what I'd do without you, Jess." His voice was rough with emotion. "You always know how to pull me back from the edge."

Jess smiled softly. "That's what partners are for. We've got each other's backs, no matter what."

Donovan nodded, a newfound determination settling in his chest. He couldn't let the perpetrators win, and couldn't let more innocent lives be lost. He had to trust in his abilities and push forward.

With Jess by his side, he felt a glimmer of hope. Together, they would unravel the twisted threads of these cases and bring justice to the victims. No matter how dark the path ahead, they would face it head-on.

Jess' brow furrowed, her eyes studying Donovan's face.

"You need a break," she said softly. "Just for a little while."

Donovan shook his head, ready to protest, but Jess held up a hand. "Hear me out. Let's take Toby for a walk. Some fresh air and a change of scenery might help clear your mind."

He glanced at the case files scattered across his desk, the weight of responsibility tugging at him. But the earnest look in Jess' eyes made him pause. Maybe she was right. Maybe a momentary escape was exactly what he needed.

"Alright," he conceded, pushing back from the desk. "A quick walk with Toby. But then it's back to work."

Jess' face brightened, a smile tugging at the corners of her mouth. "Deal."

Donovan grabbed Toby's leash from the hook by the door, the familiar jingle of tags bringing a sense of comfort. The loyal Labrador bounded over, tail wagging eagerly.

As they stepped outside, the air filled Donovan's lungs, invigorating his senses. Toby trotted ahead, his nose to the ground, exploring the scents of the neighbourhood.

The rhythmic sound of their footsteps against the pavement settled into a soothing cadence. Donovan's mind began to wander; the suffocating weight of the cases temporarily lifted from his shoulders.

Jess walked beside him, her presence a steady anchor in the tumultuous sea of his thoughts. She didn't push for conversation, understanding his need for quiet reflection.

As they rounded the corner, a group of children playing in a nearby park caught Donovan's attention. Their laughter and carefree spirits were a stark contrast to the darkness he faced daily. It was a reminder of why he did this job, and why he fought so hard for justice.

With each step, Donovan felt his resolve strengthen. He couldn't let the perpetrators win, couldn't let more lives be shattered. He had to trust in his abilities and keep pushing forward, no matter how daunting the task.

Jess was right. This brief respite was exactly what he needed to recharge and refocus. With a renewed sense of determination, Donovan knew he was ready to dive back into the investigation; to unravel the twisted threads that connected these heinous crimes.

As they turned back towards home, Donovan's mind was already racing with fresh ideas and angles to explore. The break had given him clarity, and he was eager to put it to use.

Donovan's hand gripped Toby's leash tightly as they navigated the bustling streets of Bewdley. The faithful lab trotted happily beside him, his tail wagging with each new scent that caught his attention. Donovan envied Toby's ability to find joy in the simplest things; wishing he could shed the weight of the cases as easily as his furry companion.

Jess pointed to a quaint little bookshop tucked between a coffee house and a vintage clothing store.

"Let's check it out," she suggested, her eyes sparkling with curiosity.

Donovan nodded, grateful for the distraction. As they stepped inside, the musty smell of old books enveloped them; a comforting scent that reminded him of long afternoons spent in his grandfather's study.

They wandered through the narrow aisles, their fingers trailing along the spines of well-worn novels and dusty tomes. Jess pulled out a book, flipping through its pages with a smile.

"I used to love this series as a kid," she reminisced, her voice soft with nostalgia.

Donovan glanced over her shoulder, recognising the colourful illustrations. "The Adventures of Timmy and his Dog," he read aloud, a faint smile tugging at the corners of his mouth. "I remember reading those to my little sister."

For a moment, they were lost in shared memories, the weight of the present temporarily forgotten. It was a reminder of simpler times, of innocence not yet tainted by the cruelty of the world.

As they continued to browse, Donovan's mind began to wander. He found himself drawn to the mystery section, his eyes scanning the titles for anything that might spark a new perspective on the cases.

Jess noticed his focus and gently touched his arm.

"Hey, remember why we're here," she reminded him, her voice gentle but firm. "This is supposed to be a break from all that."

Donovan sighed, his shoulders slumping slightly. "I know, I just can't help it. These cases…they're always there, lurking in the back of my mind."

"I get it," Jess said, her eyes filled with understanding. "But you need to give yourself permission to step away, even if it's just for a little while. You'll come back to it with fresh eyes and a clearer head."

Donovan knew she was right. He forced himself to turn away from the mystery section, focusing instead on the warmth of Jess' hand on his arm and the solid presence of Toby at his side.

They continued to meander through the shop, letting the peaceful atmosphere wash over them. For a brief moment, the world outside ceased to exist, and Donovan allowed himself to simply be present; to breathe in the musty air and lose himself in the pages of a book.

As they finally emerged back onto the street, Donovan felt a sense of calm settle over him. The cases were still there, waiting for him, but he felt more equipped to face them now. With Jess by his side and Toby leading the way, he knew he could tackle whatever challenges lay ahead.

A deafening bang shattered the tranquillity, sending Toby into a frenzy of barks. Donovan's heart raced, his body instinctively dropping into a crouch as his hand reached for a weapon that wasn't there.

"It's just a car backfiring," Jess said, her voice distant, drowned out by the rush of blood in his ears.

But Donovan was no longer on the streets of Bewdley. The acrid smell of gunpowder filled his nostrils, and the scorching desert sun beat down on his back. Shouts and gunfire echoed around him, a chaotic symphony of violence and desperation.

He moved swiftly, his boots kicking up clouds of dust as he darted between crumbling buildings. His partner, Mackenzie, was close behind, her breathing heavy and laboured. They had to reach the target, had to complete the mission before it was too late.

A bullet whizzed past Donovan's ear, the searing heat of its passage a stark reminder of the danger they faced. He pressed on, his focus narrowing to a single point, a singular purpose. There was no room for fear, no time for hesitation.

They rounded a corner, and there it was, the source of all this chaos and destruction. Donovan's grip tightened on his rifle, his finger hovering over the trigger. One shot, one chance to end this madness.

But then, a flicker of movement caught his eye. A child—no more than six years old—emerged from the shadows; her wide, terrified eyes locking with his. At that moment, the world seemed to stand still, the weight of his decision bearing down on him like a physical force.

Donovan blinked, the memory dissipating like smoke in the wind. The streets of Bewdley came back into focus, the gentle hum of everyday life replacing the cacophony of war. He drew a shaky breath, his heart pounding in his chest.

Jess' concerned gaze met his, her hand still resting on his arm. "Donovan, are you alright?"

He nodded, swallowing hard. "I'm fine. Just…just a memory."

"Your military days?" Jess asked softly, understanding etched in her features.

"Yeah." Donovan raised his hands to his face, washing away distant memories, his thoughts racing. "It's those experiences, Jess. They've made me who I am today. The things I've seen, the decisions I've had to make…they've given me the strength to keep going, to keep fighting for what's right."

Jess smiled, her eyes shining with pride. "You're a remarkable man, Donovan. Your past has shaped you, but it doesn't define you. You've taken those experiences and used them to become an even better detective, a better person."

Donovan felt a surge of gratitude, a warmth spreading through him. "I couldn't do it without you, Jess. Your support, your belief in me…it means everything."

"I'll always be here for you," Jess promised, her voice firm and unwavering.

Donovan nodded as his determination reignited. The doubts that had plagued him seemed to melt away, replaced by a newfound sense of purpose. He couldn't let the weight of his responsibilities crush him, couldn't let the fear of failure consume him.

"You're right," he said, his voice steady and strong. "We'll find the truth, no matter how deep we have to dig."

Jess grinned, her hand slipping into his as they continued their walk. Toby trotted ahead, his tail wagging happily. The sun broke through the clouds, casting a warm glow over the streets of Bewdley.

Donovan felt a renewed sense of hope, a flicker of light in the darkness. With Jess by his side and his military experience guiding him, he knew he had the strength and resilience to face whatever challenges lay ahead. The cases would be solved, the perpetrators brought to justice. He wouldn't rest until the truth was revealed, no matter the cost.

The door clicked shut behind them as they stepped into the familiar atmosphere of his home. Donovan strode to his desk, his steps measured and deliberate. He settled into his chair, the well-worn leather creaking beneath his weight.

Jess watched him from the doorway, her eyes soft with understanding. She knew the fire that burned within him, the unrelenting desire for justice that drove him forward. It was one of the many reasons she loved him.

Donovan reached for the case files, his fingers tracing the edges of the manila folders. The weight of the pages felt heavy in his hands. He flipped open the first file, his eyes scanning the evidence and clues that had become so familiar.

But this time, something felt different. The pieces of the puzzle seemed to shift and rearrange themselves, forming new patterns and connections. Donovan leaned forward; his brow furrowed in concentration.

"There's something here," he murmured, his voice barely audible. "Something, I missed before."

Jess moved closer as her curiosity piqued. "What is it?"

"It might be nothing or something," he responded with vagueness.

He grabbed a pen, scribbling furiously on a scrap of paper. Names, dates, and locations swirled together, forming a web of potential leads. Jess watched in silent fascination, marvelling at the way his mind worked.

Jess leaned in, her own mind whirring with possibilities. "You think you found a lead?"

Donovan nodded, a grim smile tugging at the corners of his mouth. "It's more than that. It could be a breakthrough."

He stood abruptly, the chair scraping against the hardwood floor as he said, "We need to run these leads, talk to these witnesses again. There's something we're missing, something that will tie it all together."

Jess grinned, her own excitement building. "You'll crack this case wide open."

Donovan gathered the files, his shoulders squared with renewed determination. The road ahead wouldn't be easy, but he was now ready for the challenge. With Jess by his side and the truth within reach, he knew they would prevail.

The game was afoot, and Donovan was more than ready to play.

Donovan strode out of the apartment, he breathed deeply, feeling the weight of the case files in his hands, the tangible evidence they were about to unravel.

He climbed into his sleek black car and revved the engine, eager to make it to the police station. The rush of adrenaline from his time spent with Jess and Toby still coursed through his veins, energising him for the journey ahead. As he drove, a small smile tugged at the corners of his lips, and a warmth spread through his chest, making everything feel right at that moment.

Chapter 31: Gypsy's

Donovan's mind was swirling with the weight of his current caseload. He desperately needed a break from the constant grind of chasing leads, wanting to solve these crimes. Perhaps, just a small breakthrough, a glimmer of hope to keep him going.

"Boss, we have had a result. It's about that burnt and bent metal found on the carpet factory victim's body," one of the constables called out, snapping Donovan back to attention.

He leaned in as the constable continued, "Forensics managed to clean it up, and they have emailed over an image of it. I have sent it to you."

Donovan sat at his cluttered desk and quickly opened the email, revealing a front and back picture of what appeared to be a pendant. The front image resembled Saint Christopher's face, but different somehow. And on the back, there was written: Saint Sara.

Curiosity piqued; Donovan immediately turned to his computer for answers. He typed in the words *Saint Sara*, and the search results confirmed to him that she was the patron saint of Romani Gypsies.

Finally, a lead. However, small and tentative it may be. Excitement fluttered in Donovan's stomach as he shared the finding with his team.

"We know of a local gypsy community who have had links in the past with organised crime. I think we should pay them a visit," he said to Amy.

"They can be quite guarded when it comes to talking to the police," she warned.

"I'm aware. We need to tread carefully and not give too much away during our conversations," Donovan replied.

They hopped into Donovan's car and headed towards the gypsy encampment. As they drove, Donovan played songs by Joy Division, setting an eerie tone for their investigation.

Upon arrival, they were met with a hidden entrance obscured by trees and bushes. The town planning committee had given in to pressure from local residents who didn't want a traveller's site near their homes, *out of sight, out of mind*, or so the saying goes.

Passing between two grand pillars topped with sculpted horse heads, they entered the site and were greeted by about 20 caravans. The first few were stationary vans, while the rest were mobile travellers.

Donovan pulled up outside the first static caravan and was immediately welcomed by the tranquil surroundings—save for a few dogs wandering freely. Two young men were working on a broken quad bike near one of the vans, they had its engine strewn out in front of them. As Donovan and Amy approached, they set aside their tools and came over to greet them.

"Nice ride, mate," one of the young men said, admiring Donovan's car.

"Thank you. It's my pride and joy," Donovan replied, trying to keep things light.

"What brings you here?" the man asked.

"We're looking to speak with whoever runs this site," Donovan stated.

"And what for?" the man inquired.

"Well, that's something we would discuss with them in private," Donovan replied firmly.

The man eyed Donovan suspiciously but ultimately relented.

"You'll need to speak with Nathan then. He runs this place, and his van is the first one there," he said, pointing towards a nearby static caravan.

Donovan thanked him for the information before making his way towards Nathan's van. He was determined to get some answers from the site manager himself.

Donovan ascended the two wooden steps and rapped his knuckles against the door, Amy close behind him. The door creaked open to reveal a gentleman with a full head of silver hair and a matching beard. His attire was far from what one would expect from a stereotype of a gypsy.

He wore a crisp, blue Ralph Lauren shirt tucked into black chino trousers, paired with black Dr Martens boots. His eyes were piercing blue, giving him an air of intelligence and confidence.

"Can I help you?" he greeted them with a warm smile.

"Hello, we're from the police. I'm DI Temple and this is DS Campbell," Donovan introduced themselves.

"Well, come on in then. It's always nice to have some company," the man replied, opening the door wider for them to enter.

Inside, the caravan was immaculate, almost opulent. The seating area was covered in plastic to protect it from stains and every surface gleamed with polish.

"Would you like some coffee or tea?" the man offered.

"We won't be staying long, just here for a routine visit to assist us with an ongoing investigation," Donovan declined politely.

"How can I help?" Nathan asked.

"Are you aware of anyone going missing from this or any other nearby site?" Donovan inquired.

"People go missing all the time around here, especially young men going looking for work or chasing after girls," the man shrugged.

"We're specifically interested in someone who wears these items," Donovan said, pulling out photos of the pendant and laying them on the table in front of Nathan.

Nathan picked up the images and studied them closely.

"I might know who this is…or I might not. Depends on what you want him for," Nathan replied coyly.

"He hasn't done anything wrong. We found this pendant on a dead person, a few days ago, and we're trying to identify him and figure out why he was killed," Donovan explained.

Nathan's face drained of colour, and it took him a few moments to compose himself.

"I've seen this pendant before, on a guy named Fenix. He has a van on the site," Nathan finally spoke up.

"When did you last see him?" Donovan asked.

"A few days ago. He had some friends over for a card game, something he does every now and then," Nathan recalled.

"Do you know who he was playing with?" Amy pressed for more information.

"The usual bunch of reprobates…some from the site and a few outsiders," Nathan replied.

"Any names?" Amy urged.

"I can't be sure. I don't pay that much attention. But there was Michael and Shamus from the site and a regular friend of his named Jimi. Nice guy, comes by every once in a while," Nathan said, rubbing his head as if trying to remember.

"Are Michael and Shamus around now?" Amy asked.

"Yeah, you were just speaking to them outside," Nathan confirmed, standing up and opening the door to call out to the two men.

The men approached the door, and Nathan warned them not to make a mess or touch anything under threat of his wife's anger.

"These people need to speak with you," Nathan instructed them as they entered the caravan.

"Nathan says you were playing cards with Fenix a few nights ago. Is that right?" Amy asked the two men.

"Could have been us," one of them replied nonchalantly, the same man who held a tyre iron earlier.

"Who might you be?" Amy inquired; her sharp gaze fixed on the man standing before them.

"My name is Shamus," he replied confidently, his dark eyes meeting hers without hesitation.

"Well Shamus, this is not a time to be smart with us. We believe your friend Fenix was killed around the time of that card game," Donovan stated sternly, crossing his arms over his chest.

"I would rather not do this down at the station, but it remains an option," Amy responded, her expression unreadable.

"We were just playing poker, having a good time and drinking," Michael added, nervously shifting his weight from one foot to the other.

"What time did you finish?" Amy probed, her detective instincts kicking in.

"It was about 1:00 am. It was a good night apart from Fenix wiping us out of our money," Michael admitted with a sheepish grin.

"We left him playing with the other guy, Jimi," Shamus chimed in, glancing around anxiously.

"Was that the last you saw of Fenix?" Amy pressed on.

"Yeah, we went off to bed. It was getting late," Michael confirmed.

"Okay, I think we have finished for now. Thank you, for your time," Donovan said to the two men with a nod.

"Any chance we can take a look at Fenix's van while we are here?" Donovan asked, turning to Nathan who had remained quiet until now.

"I'm not sure about that," Nathan hesitated, rubbing his hand over his well-kept beard.

"I could get a court order, but why waste time with that?" Donovan countered calmly.

"Yeah okay, I have a spare key. All the vans leave one with me, just in case," Nathan finally relented with a sigh.

They left Nathan's van and walked up to where Fenix lived. His van was small in comparison to many of the others, a testament to his bachelor lifestyle.

Nathan opened the door, and they entered the tiny space. The van was surprisingly tidy except for a large quantity of empty beer bottles littering the table.

There wasn't much to search, everything appearing as expected with no signs of drugs or large amounts of cash. No clues were found to shed light on what had happened that fatal night.

Donovan thanked Nathan and told him they would be sending over a forensics team regardless, cautioning him not to touch anything in the meantime.

As they drove away, Donovan couldn't help but feel satisfied with how the interview had gone.

"I think that went well, considering?" he remarked to Amy.

"Yes, I agree. I believe the two lads when they tell us they didn't witness anything suspicious," Amy replied with a nod.

"Well, we have another name to check on now—this Jimi character. I have a feeling he is very much a person of interest and may be linked to Simon," Donovan stated thoughtfully.

"We need to see if the CLT have any information on him," Amy agreed, her mind already processing the next steps.

Donovan couldn't wait to get back to HQ and delve into this new evidence. It felt like things were finally starting to fall into place, and he could feel it in his bones.

Chapter 32: Internet Café (2)

The weight of the situation weighed heavily on Simon's mind as he anxiously sought out a quiet place to communicate with his bosses.

The police were closing in, and their recent actions had surely caused some commotion. Despite his and Jimi's efforts to keep things discreet, they couldn't evade all scrutiny. Simon was particularly disappointed that the railway shooting had been discovered so quickly. He thought he had chosen the perfect spot to eliminate Liam.

And while the rival gang shooting was always going to be messy, it was necessary to send a clear message. Luckily, the police had not mentioned this incident during his interview, so there was a chance he could get away with it.

He instructed Jimi to lay low for now and reached out to his boss for guidance. Fear gripped him as he waited for a response, knowing that his own life could be at stake.

Eventually, he found himself alone in an internet café with only one other person, a girl working behind the counter. He had made sure to check for any potential followers before entering the café, carefully navigating through shops and streets.

After ordering a lukewarm coffee and internet tokens, he settled into a PC, selecting one furthest from the counter, With a token inserted, the computer sprung to life and Simon typed in the URL: *https://www.xbullet.com/login*.

Once connected, he began typing out a report of his encounter with the police:

Police pulled me in, they knew things and wanted to pin them on me. I covered my tracks though.

Almost immediately, a response came from his boss.

Yes, we know. Concentrate on moving product, for now, we will sort out the feds.

Relieved that his bosses were aware of his situation and taking action, Simon continued with his instructions:

Instruct key dealers to get produce from a new location we have set up. The narrowboat might be under surveillance.

His boss responded promptly:

The new location is the catacombs under Witley Court. Look it up on Google.

Taking a moment to do as instructed, Simon searched for *Witley Court* and was met with multiple results. One in particular caught his eye:

Witley Court was once one of the great country houses of England. An impressive early 17th-century mansion. Fire devastated it in 1937.

Though there was no mention of catacombs, Simon knew they were hidden beneath the surface, making it the perfect location for their operations.

His boss further added:

Meet with the Hell's Angels, get them to Kidnap DI Donovan's girlfriend as some security…get him to back off.
We have a new Hub, our main outpost, Drakelow Tunnels, Wolverley. Ge the Angels to run security for it. Let us know how you get on.

His boss ended the session.

As he logged out of the bulletin board and prepared to leave, Simon couldn't shake off the feeling of being watched. He quickly called Jimi on his burner phone and arranged to meet up. He was keeping a watchful eye over his shoulder as he left the café.

Chapter 33: The Catacombs

The quaint village of Great Witley—nestled in the northwest region of Worcestershire—was home to the once grand and illustrious Witley Court. However, its beauty was marred by a tragic fire in 1937 that left it nothing but ruins.

Since Simon's arrest, they had abandoned their flashy Audi Q5 and opted for a more inconspicuous 10-year-old Vauxhall Astra. As they pulled up outside the dilapidated stately home at lunchtime, Jimi, the caretaker, and Simon couldn't help but feel a sense of foreboding.

Despite its current state of disrepair, the house still exuded an air of grandeur as its towering ruins loomed over them. The remnants of ornate walls, battlements, and arched windows hinted at its former splendour.

"Isn't this a bit bold for a drug operation?" the caretaker voiced his concern as they approached the decaying structure.

"What do you mean?" Jimi asked.

"People come here to see the ruins and whatnot. There could be prying eyes everywhere," the caretaker replied.

"That's exactly why it's perfect. It's right under everyone's noses but out of sight. I think it's quite clever," Simon chimed in.

"To each, their own," shrugged the caretaker, clearly not sharing Simon's enthusiasm.

"I thought using a narrowboat as a drop location was risky enough, but this takes it to a whole new level," the caretaker remarked.

"And our recent changes and increase in product volume are on a whole new level too," Simon added with a sly grin.

"How are we doing with distribution this week? Are we meeting quotas?" Simon redirected the conversation back to business, always focused and determined.

"I have all hands on deck. We recruited more dealers and got some cuckoos up and running," the caretaker reported.

"I haven't seen or heard from those other dealers who were encroaching on our territory since their guy got killed," the caretaker observed, wondering if Simon had a hand in it.

"Things are looking good. People are coming back to us for gear, and we're getting it to them. But losing the narrowboat was a blow," the caretaker admitted, still feeling the sting of their previous setback.

"Well, at least I won't have to break your kneecaps then," Jimi joked, but the caretaker didn't find it amusing.

"Losing the narrowboat was necessary. It was only a matter of time before the feds caught onto our game and took you and the other dealers down," Simon stated matter-of-factly.

As they stepped out of the car and cautiously made their way towards the main house, they were unsure of where to go or how to find the elusive *catacombs*.

Turning a corner, they found themselves face to face with a young man leaning against a wire fence that cordoned off the ruins, a warning sign posted nearby indicating: *construction work in progress*.

The man approached them casually. "Do you happen to have a light?" he asked in a local accent with hints of Welsh.

Simon handed him his lighter, and he lit up his cigarette.

"It's a beautiful day for a visit. You guys are just here sightseeing?" he inquired.

"We're actually here for some business as well," Simon responded cryptically.

The man gave Simon an appraising look before speaking again, "Are you Trapping[6]."

"Could be," Simon responded.

The man grinned, acknowledging that Simon was aware of the slang being used was well-informed and had been sent by the right person.

"Good to meet ya, the bosses said you would be coming. Follow me."

---

[6] The act of selling drugs

They followed him, their footsteps echoing through the abandoned building. The towering brick stately home loomed over them, casting shadows that seemed to stretch and twist in the light.

He led them around the back of the building and through a gap in the fence, their guide navigating with ease as if he had done this many times before. As they approached a set of steps, another young man emerged from the shadows blocking their path.

"It's okay, they are with me," the first man said confidently.

The second man nodded and then blended back into his hiding place.

The four of them descended stone stairs, stopping briefly to allow their newfound colleague to open a rusty steel door that blocked their way. The door creaked open, revealing a dark tunnel that stretched out before them. They continued their journey, the sound of dripping water and distant shuffling filling the air.

"What is this place?" Simon asked, his eyes scanning the walls for any signs of life.

"This leads down into a maze of tunnels that spread out under the fountain and out into the grounds. They go on for miles," the man responded.

"Don't people try to come down here?" Simon asked cautiously.

"Sometimes, but we tell them we are security, and they just accept it and walk away," the man replied nonchalantly.

"It never ceases to amaze me how gullible people are," Jimi chimed in with a laugh.

"A bit like you, Jimi," Simon joked, earning a scowl from his friend.

As they walked deeper into the tunnel, their way was lit by a string of electric lights hung on hooks along the wall. It was clear that someone had taken great care to keep these tunnels hidden yet functional.

The tunnel widened into a spacious room, comparable in size to a medium-sized swimming pool. It was filled with various types of equipment and people diligently working away. Four work benches were stationed throughout the room. Each was occupied by someone deeply engrossed in their individual tasks.

According to the man, the first bench was used for cutting cocaine, the second for heroin, and the third for prepping pills. On the fourth bench, there was a money-counting machine where they would neatly bundle their profits.

They proceeded to the rear of the room, where they stepped into another area. This space was significantly larger than the previous one and contained storage units for both finished products and raw materials. On one side, there were shelves attached to the wall, holding large quantities of a white powder—kilo blocks of cocaine.

On the other side, there were sacks filled with an off-white powder—uncut heroin. In between were bags meticulously filled with cannabis, ready for sale. And finally, at the back, there were bundles upon bundles of bank notes wrapped in plastic film, standing at least two metres tall.

"That's more money than I have ever seen!" the caretaker exclaimed, his eyes widening in disbelief.

"Don't get any bright ideas, men have died for less," Simon warned sternly.

"This is doing drugs on an industrial scale!" Jimi exclaimed, his voice filled with equal parts awe and horror.

"Gather up what you need for this week's supply on the way out," Simon instructed.

"From now on, you will get your supply from here and drop off the cash," he continued.

"I will need to bring a few more key dealers here over the next few days to introduce them," he said, turning to talk to the man beside him.

"That's not a problem," the man replied calmly.

"I will let my boss know you have been here and what your plans are," he added before leading them out of the room, through the tunnels and back to their car.

As they drove away, the caretaker was lost in thought about how he had gotten involved in this dangerous world. He knew that he may have to return here in less than a week if sales were good. It was a risky operation, but it also showed just how determined and powerful their bosses were.

Chapter 34: Hell's Angels

Simon pulled up to the Barbarians clubhouse. This would be his first encounter with this notorious biker gang. He pulled himself together and approached the clubhouse located on this otherwise quiet council estate in Kidderminster. He knocked at the door and a figure opened it beckoning him in.

Inside, cigarette smoke hung thick in the air. Gruff voices and clanking beer bottles fell silent as Simon entered. A dozen pairs of eyes locked onto him.

"Boys," Simon nodded, making his way to an empty chair at the table.

The chapter president, a hulking man with a greying beard, leaned forward. "Right, let's get down to business. We've got two items on the agenda tonight."

Simon's gaze swept the room, noting the tense anticipation.

"First up, the Donovan situation," the president continued. "We've got intel on his girl, Jess. Works at the Little Pack Horse pub in Bewdley. Seems she is his weak spot."

"We need him to back off the OCG," he continued.

A wiry man with tattoos snaking up his neck leaned in. "I've been watching her. Pretty little thing. Brown hair, always smiling. Leaves work around midnight...most nights."

"Good," the president nodded. "We grab her, Donovan will come running."

Simon's stomach churned, but he kept his face impassive. "What's the plan?"

The president unrolled a crude Bewdley town map on the table. "Two of us on bikes. We'll wait here," he jabbed a meaty finger at an alley. "When she walks by, we snatch her. Quick and quiet."

"What about cameras?" someone asked.

Simon says, "It can't be a snatch after work, I know she is off for a few days, a snitch of mine told me. It must be from her house, outside where she parks. I can provide a van for you to use."

The bikers exchanged glances, a mix of suspicion and intrigue flickering across their faces. The president's eyes narrowed, scrutinising Simon.

"You seem to know a lot about this girl, mate," he growled. "Care to share how?"

Simon shrugged, maintaining his cool demeanour. "I've done my homework. It's what I'm here for, isn't it?"

A burly man with a shaved head slammed his fist on the table. "I don't like it. Smells fishy. We stick to the original plan."

"Hold on," the wiry man interjected, leaning forward. "Simon has got a point. A van is less conspicuous than bikes. We could park it right outside her place, no one would bat an eye."

The room erupted into a heated debate. Voices rose, and chairs scraped.

The president raised a hand, silencing the room. "Alright, alright. Let's hear Simon out. What's your angle on this?"

Simon leaned back, feigning nonchalance. "Look, I've been tailing her for weeks. She has got a routine. Every Tuesday and Thursday, she goes for a run at 6 am. Starts at her flat, loops around the park, and ends back home. That's our window."

The tattooed man nodded slowly. "Less people around at that hour. Could work."

"But what about the dog?" a voice piped up from the back.

"She has a dog," the wiry biker interjected.

Simon's brow furrowed. "What dog?"

The president smirked. "Ah, maybe you don't know everything after all. Donovan has got a big chocolate lab. Follows the girl sometimes when she runs."

Simon's mind raced, adapting quickly. "The dog, right? I've seen it. But that's why the van is perfect. We wait until later when she is alone."

He leaned in, voice low and persuasive, "Look, I've got it all worked out. We park the van near her flat around 3 pm. She usually gets home from errands then. No dog, no witnesses. We grab her fast, drive her straight to Snuff Mill."

The president's eyes gleamed with interest. "Snuff Mill, eh? Good thinking. Remote, abandoned. Perfect spot to make the call."

Simon nodded, warming to his improvised plan. "Exactly. We get her there, nice and isolated. Then, we ring Donovan. Tell him to back off the OCG or his girl gets it."

The room hummed with approval.

The tattooed man grinned, revealing a row of gold teeth. "I like it. Clean, simple. No mess."

The president leaned back, stroking his beard thoughtfully. His eyes darted around the room, gauging the reactions of his men. Slowly, he shook his head.

"It's too risky," he said, his voice gravelly. "We're dealing with an ex-military cop here. This Donovan bloke is not some pushover. He is SAS trained, for Christ's sake. Two tours in Afghanistan. What if he tracks us down before we can make the call?"

Simon leaned forward with his eyes intense. "That's precisely why we need to act now. Every day we wait, Donovan gets closer to dismantling our operation. This is our chance to turn the tables."

The president's brow furrowed. "I don't know," he repeated, but his resolve was wavering.

Simon pressed his advantage. "Look, I've got a mate who owes me a favour. He has got a nondescript white van, perfect for the job. Clean plates, and tinted windows. We use that, two of your best men, and we're in and out before anyone notices."

The room fell silent, tension thick in the air. Simon could almost hear the gears turning in their heads. He held his breath, waiting.

Finally, the president nodded slowly. "Alright, Simon. We'll do it your way. But if this goes south, it's on your head. Got it?"

Simon nodded, relief flooding through him. "Understood, you're the boss."

The president's gaze swept the room, landing on two burly men. "Spike, Parker—you're on this. Don't fuck it up."

They nodded, faces grim.

"Now, onto the second item," the president continued, his voice dropping. "The Drakelow Tunnels at Wolverley."

A ripple of tension passed through the room. Simon leaned in; ears pricked.

"Our friends in the OCG have set up shop there, their new hub," the president explained. "A new distribution hub for product and cash. They need muscle to keep it secure."

He unrolled a detailed map of the Wolverley area, pointing to a series of markings. "Three main entrances here, here and here. Natural chokepoints, easy to defend. But there's a network of smaller tunnels—potential weak spots."

The wiry man with the scarred face leaned over the map, tracing the network of tunnels with a calloused finger. "These smaller passages, they're a problem. Too many ways in."

Simon studied the intricate web of lines. "What about collapsing some of these tunnels? Create a more defensible perimeter."

The president nodded approvingly. "Good thinking. We've got some demolition experience in the club. Jack, that's your area, right?"

A stocky man with close-cropped hair grunted in affirmation, "Yeah, I can rig some controlled blasts. Seal off the weaker points."

"We'll need more than that," the tattooed man chimed in. "Even with a tighter perimeter, we're spread thin."

The president tapped the map, his finger landing on a series of red X's. "We've got five strategic points here. Each needs a two-man team, rotating shifts. High-powered rifles, night vision, the works."

Simon leaned in, studying the terrain. "What about motion sensors? We could set up a perimeter, give us an early warning system."

The tattooed man nodded approvingly. "I like that. We've got a guy who can rig those up, an ex-military electronics specialist."

"Good," the president grunted. "Now, inside the caves themselves, we need to think smart. The acoustics in there are tricky—sound carries, echoes. Makes it hard to pinpoint where threats are coming from."

The wiry man with the scarred face continued, "We set up a series of speakers throughout the cave system. Connect them to a central control panel. If we get intruders, we can pump in disorienting sounds: gunfire, footsteps, voices. Throw them off balance."

Simon nodded, impressed. "Psychological warfare. I like it."

The president leaned back, a gleam in his eye. "Now we're talking. What else?"

A barrel-chested man with a shaved head spoke up. "We could rig up some strobe lights too. Disorient them visually as well as aurally."

"Good, good," the president nodded. "But what about our own people? How do we make sure they don't get caught in the crossfire?"

Simon tapped his temple. "Night vision goggles with built-in comms. Our guys can coordinate in the dark, even with the strobes going."

The president nodded, a wicked grin spreading across his face. "Now we're cooking. What else?"

Jacko, the demolitions expert, leaned in. "We could rig some of the smaller tunnels with trip wires. Not explosives—too risky. But smoke bombs, flash bangs. Disorient anyone trying to sneak in."

"Good thinking," the president agreed. "What about the main cavern? That's where the product and money will be stored."

The wiry man with the scarred face pulled out a small notebook, sketching rapidly. "We build a series of false walls. Hide the real stash behind them. Anyone who manages to get in will waste time searching empty caves."

Simon studied the sketch, his mind racing. "We could take it a step further. Create a labyrinth."

The president's eyebrows raised. "Go on."

"We use those false walls but make them movable. Hydraulic systems, are controlled from a central point. We can literally change the layout of the caves on the fly."

A low whistle echoed through the room.

The tattooed man leaned forward, eyes gleaming. "That's some James Bond shit right there."

"It gets better," Simon continued, warming to his idea. "We install pressure plates throughout the floor. As intruders move, we track their progress, shifting walls to funnel them where we want."

Jack nodded approvingly. "We could add some nasty surprises too. Trap doors leading to spiked pits, for example."

The president's grin widened and his eyes gleamed with malicious delight. "Boys, I think we've got ourselves a plan."

He stood, pacing around the table, his massive frame casting long shadows in the dim light.

"Let's recap. We've got the perimeter secured with motion sensors and snipers. The tunnels are rigged with traps and false leads. And the main cavern—" he paused, chuckling darkly, "well, that's going to be our very own house of horrors."

Simon leaned back, watching the excitement build in the room. The bikers were practically salivating at the prospect of their impenetrable fortress.

"Now, let's talk logistics," the president continued. "Jack, you'll oversee the demolitions and trap setups. Spike, you're in charge of the electronics: sensors, comms and the works." The president turned to the wiry man with a scarred face. "Rodgers, you're on security rotations. I want a tight schedule, no gaps."

Rodgers nodded, already scribbling in his notebook.

"Now, for supplies," the president continued. "We'll need to move carefully. Can't have a sudden influx of construction materials raising eyebrows."

The tattooed man spoke up, "I've got a mate who runs a demolition company. We can siphon off materials from his jobs, bit by bit."

"Good," the president nodded. "What about the tech?"

Spike leaned forward, his eyes glinting. "I've got connections in the dark web. We can source the high-end tech without raising flags. Untraceable crypto payments, dead drops for delivery. It'll take time, but we'll get what we need."

The president nodded; satisfaction etched on his weathered face. "Good. Now, timeline. I want this fortress operational in three weeks. No excuses."

A chorus of affirmations echoed through the room. Simon watched, mind racing, as the bikers began divvying up tasks. He'd gathered more intel in one night than weeks of surveillance. The OCG would be pleased.

"Alright, that's enough for tonight," the president growled, glancing at his watch. "Meeting adjourned. Simon, stick around a minute."

Simon's pulse quickened as the room emptied, leaving him alone with the president. The hulking man leaned in close, his breath reeking of stale beer and cigarettes.

"You've got a good head on your shoulders, Simon," he growled. "But remember, we're watching you. One wrong move—"

He left the threat hanging. Simon nodded, keeping his face impassive. "Understood, Boss. I'm here to help."

The president grunted, seemingly satisfied. "Alright, get out of here. We'll be in touch about the girl."

Simon stood, carefully stretching his cramped muscles. He'd been sitting rigidly for hours, every nerve on high alert. As he made his way to the door, he could feel the president's eyes boring into his back.

Outside, the cool night air hit him like a slap. Simon took a deep breath. He strode to his car, mind racing. He needed to contact his real employers—the OCG—immediately. These plans were too valuable to sit on, the kidnapping and the tunnels.

He slipped into the driver's seat, hands shaking slightly as the last remnants of adrenaline coursed through him. The bikers' plan was ambitious, borderline insane. But if they pulled it off.

Simon started the engine, peeling away from the kerb. He drove aimlessly, circling the quiet streets of Kidderminster, paranoia gnawing at him. After 20 minutes, satisfied he wasn't being tailed, he pulled into an empty car park and sat, thinking through what had just transpired and reviewing text messages on his phone.

Chapter 35: Toby

Toby's usual playful and boisterous demeanour had been absent all day. Normally, he relished following Donovan around the office, surrounded by all the delightful *playthings* that Donovan called his colleagues. Toby loved being the centre of attention, enjoying the fuss and pats lavished upon him.

His favourite moments were when they went out in the car, with Donovan taking him for a short walk before attending crime scenes. Sometimes, he even let Toby off his leash to explore on his own; knowing he could trust his furry friend not to run off. As he lay in the backseat of the car dozing while Donovan did his work. Toby knew that Donovan was his best friend.

But today, Toby felt ill.

"Don't you think Toby seems a bit under the weather?" Donovan asked Amy.

"Yes, Boss, he didn't even beg for my lunch like he usually does," she replied.

"I'm going to take him to the vet. I can't stand to see my best friend suffer. Can you cover for me?" Donovan requested.

"Of course, Sir," Amy agreed.

Donovan rushed Toby to the veterinarian's office. Thankfully, it was nothing serious—just a little stomach bug he must have picked up somewhere, but it was taking its toll, taking him off his legs. With some prescribed medicine and rest for the next 24 hours or so, Toby would be back to his energetic self in no time.

The vet also advised against any outings with Donovan for a few days to allow for proper recovery. Considering this news, Donovan met with Jess and explained the situation. He asked her to look after Toby during the day until he was fully recovered. Luckily, Jess was owed some time off work and enjoyed having Toby around.

Donovan knew she would spoil him with love and attention, but it would be hard not having his faithful crime-fighting companion by his side for the next few days.

Donovan dropped Toby off at Jess' and returned to work. His team were eager to hear the news about Toby and were relieved to hear it was nothing serious.

Chapter 36: Jess' Kidnap

Jess had spent the morning meticulously cleaning her cosy flat, making sure every surface was dust-free, and every item was in its designated place. She also took care of her beloved canine companion, Toby, who was still feeling under the weather.

Located at the far end of Bewdley, Jess' flat sat on the ground floor of Baldwin House; a historic building named after its former resident and Prime Minister Stanley Baldwin. The exterior boasted elegant Georgian architecture, while the interior had been tastefully refurbished with a mix of modern and traditional elements.

As she finished up her chores, Jess couldn't help but marvel at how perfectly her flat suited her lifestyle. It is a convenient location, just 200 yards from her workplace at the Little Pack Horse pub was an added bonus.

But as the clock struck 1:00 pm, she realised it was time to venture out for some much-needed grocery shopping. Putting Toby's lead on, she exited through the rear entrance of her flat and made her way to her car parked in the designated bay.

Lost in thought about shopping lists and meal plans for the week ahead, Jess barely registered her surroundings. Toby walked beside her, his nose eagerly sniffing at every new scent that crossed their path. The afternoon sun shone down on them, casting warm rays across the car park and creating long shadows on the pavement.

Juggling her phone and handbag, Jess fumbled for her car keys as she approached her vehicle. Her mind was preoccupied with upcoming meetings, appointments, and a dinner date that almost slipped her mind.

But as she reached for the door handle, a sudden movement caught her eye. A figure emerged from behind a parked van, startling her heart into skipping a beat. Instinctively clutching Toby's leash tighter, Jess took a step back as the figure moved closer. With each step, their features became clearer until she could finally see who it was.

The two men had been lying in wait for several hours, concealed behind a semi-derelict garage adjacent to Jess' flat and the parking bays. But Jess had not noticed them emerging from their hiding place, nor did she pay much attention to them as they approached her.

One stood tall at 6 ft, while the other was shorter at 5 ft 7". They both wore casual t-shirts, jeans, and biker boots, looking ordinary by all accounts. Jess' gaze flickered up from her car keys as she felt the taller man invade her personal space; his chin almost touching the top of her head. She could detect a strong smell of stale beer and cigarettes on the assailant's breath.

"What the hell!" Jess exclaimed, trying to back away but stopped short by the man's grip on her wrist.

Strangely, she could smell his aftershave, Tom Ford she thought, remembering it was one she had bought for Donovan on his birthday.

The man's grip only tightened around her wrist, causing her to wince in pain. Toby watched helplessly, his barks growing more frantic as he sensed the danger his friend was in. Meanwhile, the shorter man spoke in a calm voice, though there was an underlying threat that sent shivers down Jess' spine.

"We don't want to hurt you, but you need to cooperate," he said, his grip never loosening.

"Just do as we say, and this will all be over soon."

Panicked thoughts raced through Jess' mind as she searched for a way to escape. But the men had her completely surrounded, and any sudden movements could provoke them. Even Toby's loyal presence seemed powerless against these two strangers.

Reluctantly, Jess nodded her understanding, her body going limp as she resigned herself to their demands. She let go of Toby's leash. The taller man quickly bound her hands with cable ties, rendering her unable to break free. Toby whined and circled helplessly nearby; torn between wanting to protect his friend and feeling helpless in his current condition.

As the shorter man gestured to the taller one, Jess' heart sank as she realised this wasn't a random encounter. These men had been planning this for some time.

"Let's get her in the van," he said. "We need to move quickly before anyone else shows up."

The men opened the sliding door and pushed Jess onto the backseat.

The van pulled out of the visitor's bay and onto the main road. Jess was sitting helplessly in the backseat with her bound wrists. Fear and panic began to consume her as the reality of her situation set in.

Her voice trembled slightly as she spoke, fear gripping at her chest. "Where are you taking me?" she asked, trying to keep her composure.

"Somewhere safe, for now," the man in the passenger seat replied, his tone sounding more like a warning than reassurance.

Jess' mind raced as they drove through the town's streets and country lanes, her heart pounding in her chest. She knew Donovan was a police officer, but these men didn't seem to be intimidated by that. They had a clear agenda, and she was just a pawn in their game.

The car weaved in and out of traffic with expert precision, causing Jess' adrenaline to spike even higher. She desperately searched for a way to escape or contact help, but her hands were bound, and she had no means of communication.

As they continued their journey, Jess couldn't help but wonder what fate awaited her at the end of it. Were these men using her as leverage against Donovan or did they have something more sinister planned? The uncertainty only added to her growing sense of dread.

Toby had been left behind; he had wanted to do more to help Jess. Guilt and disappointment washed over him for not being able to intervene effectively in the chaotic situation. He sat for a while by Jess' car in the hope she would come back, then left to make his way to Donovan.

As he walked down the streets towards their apartment, Toby kept a sharp eye out for any sign of his master. He knew his friend would be worried when he found out what had happened, and Toby relied on Donovan's wisdom and experience to guide them through this ordeal.

Toby made his way back home. His illness weighed heavily on him, slowing down his pace and dulling his senses. But he pushed through, determined to find Donovan and figure out their next steps.

Finally, reaching their apartment building, Toby sat anxiously outside their door, waiting for Donovan's return.

―――― " ――――

The van came to a sudden stop and the men got out, their heavy footsteps crunching on the overgrown vegetation. Jess looked up at the dilapidated structure before them, dread coursing through her as she realised what this place was.

The men led her inside, pushing open the creaky door. The interior was dark and musty, the air thick with the smell of decay. Cobwebs hung from the corners and the floorboards groaned under their weight.

As they neared deeper into the building, Jess couldn't help but think of the dark history of this *Snuff Mill*. What horrors might have taken place within these crumbling walls? She knew escape would be nearly impossible in this forgotten and forsaken place.

---- " ----

Donovan closed the door of their apartment behind them, a sense of unease settling over him. It wasn't like Jess to not answer his calls, no matter how busy she was.

He set his keys on the kitchen counter and turned to Toby, who sat patiently by his side.

"Let's figure out what's going on," Donovan said with forced calmness.

His mind was racing with worry for Jess, and he knew, that whatever it was, they needed to act fast.

He rummaged through the cupboard, searching for a treat to offer Toby. Finally, he found a bag of dog biscuits and held one out to his eager friend.

As Toby crunched away, Donovan opened his phone and pulled up Jess' contact information. His fingers hovered over the keys as he hesitated, unsure if he should try calling her work number. But he needed answers, and this seemed like the best option.

The phone rang several times before it was finally picked up by a cheerful voice, "Hello, Little Pack Horse, how can I help you?"

Donovan cleared his throat nervously. "Hi, this is Donovan, Jess' partner. I'm trying to reach her, but she is not answering her phone. Did she come in at all today?"

There was a brief pause before the voice responded, "Oh, hi, Donovan. I'm afraid Jess isn't working today."

"Okay, that's fine," Donovan replied with forced calmness. "I knew she had some time off booked with you, I just wondered." He quickly ended the call and set his phone down on the table.

Donovan felt a knot of worry form in his stomach. This wasn't like Jess to not answer her phone or miss work without telling him first. Something definitely didn't feel right.

"I'm starting to get really worried—" he murmured to Toby, who looked up at him with concerned brown eyes.

——— " ———

Donovan's phone rang, jolting him out of his thoughts. He saw that it was Jess' number and answered eagerly.

"Hello? Where are you?" he said, hoping to hear her voice on the other end.

"Sorry, she can't come to the phone right now," a man's voice announced, instantly, sending alarm bells ringing in Donovan's mind.

"Do as I say, and no one will get hurt," the man continued, his tone calm and threatening.

"You need to back off the murder cases you have been working on for the past few weeks. The OCG doesn't like you snooping around," he said, his words sending a chill down Donovan's spine.

"Leave well alone for a few weeks until the OCG has covered things up," he added, his voice dripping with menace.

Donovan understood the gravity of the situation, but he also knew he couldn't just sit back and let these criminals control him.

"I understand," he replied tentatively, trying to buy himself some time to come up with a plan.

"But if you lay a finger on Jess, I will come after you with everything at my disposal," Donovan warned, feeling his protective instincts kick in for the woman he loved.

"Let me speak to Jess, just to make sure she is okay," he insisted, hoping to gain some reassurance from hearing her voice.

Jess eventually came on the line, her voice trembling with fear. "Hi…it's me. I'm okay…scared, but okay," she said quietly before the man took back the phone.

"We will call every day, so you know she is alright, as long as you do what we say," the man stated before ending the call abruptly.

Donovan sat back in his chair, his mind reeling with thoughts and emotions. He knew he shouldn't back off from pursuing justice for those who had been murdered, but he also didn't want Jess to suffer for his actions. It was a difficult decision, one that weighed heavily on his heart.

Donovan's night was a restless blur. Every creak of the apartment, every distant siren jolted him awake. His mind raced with scenarios, each worse than the last. Toby whined softly, sensing his distress. The digital clock's red numbers ticked by agonisingly slow: 2:17, 3:42, 4:55.

Dawn's pale fingers crept through the blinds, finding Donovan slumped at the kitchen table. His eyes were bloodshot, stubble darkening his features. Coffee cups littered the surface, cold dregs testament to his vigil.

He showered mechanically but the steaming was water doing little to clear his head. Donovan's reflection stared back, hollow-eyed and grim. He straightened his tie, an armour of normalcy.

The drive to HQ was surreal. Morning commuters were going about their business, joggers were jogging, and parents were taking their children to school, all very normal.

Donovan pulled into the station parking lot, his mind still churning. He nodded mechanically to colleagues as he made his way to his desk. The familiar buzz of phones and clacking keyboards felt oddly muffled as if he were underwater.

He booted up his computer, fingers flying across the keys as he accessed the phone tracking software. A few tense moments passed as the system searched. Then—a hit.

Jess' phone pinged near Snuff Mill, an abandoned industrial site on the outskirts of town. Donovan's breath caught in his throat. The mill's dark history of accidents and rumours of criminal activity made his stomach churn.

He pulled up satellite imagery, studying the crumbling brick buildings and overgrown grounds. Dense woods surrounded the complex, perfect for concealment. Donovan's eyes narrowed as he spotted a dirt-access road, barely visible through the trees.

Donovan's fingers hovered over the keyboard, hesitating. He knew he should report this, and follow protocol. But the thought of bureaucracy slowing things down while Jess was in danger—made his chest tighten. He needed someone he could trust implicitly.

"Amy," he called softly, motioning her over.

Amy approached, her brow furrowing at Donovan's tense expression.

"What's wrong?" she asked, leaning in close.

Donovan's voice was barely above a whisper. "Jess has been kidnapped. OCG involvement. They're using her to blackmail me into backing off our murder cases."

Amy's eyes widened, but she kept her composure. "Christ," she breathed. "What do you need?"

Donovan leaned in closer, his voice low and urgent. "Amy, I need your help Jess was taken yesterday afternoon. Men ambushed her in the parking lot of her flat. They've got her at the old Snuff Mill."

Amy's eyes widened in shock. "My God, Donovan. How do you know?"

He quickly filled her in on the phone call, the threats, and his tracking of Jess' phone. "The OCG is behind this. They want me to back off our recent murder investigations."

Donovan's fingers drummed nervously on his desk. "I can't go through official channels. If word gets out, they might—" He could not finish the thought.

Amy nodded grimly. "I understand. What's your plan?"

"I need to scout the area first," Donovan said, pulling up satellite imagery on his screen.

"Let's formulate a plan. See if we can deal with this ourselves or, at least, with a small team we can trust not to talk," Donovan said, keen to get things moving.

Donovan and Amy huddled over his desk; voices low as they pored over the satellite images. The abandoned Snuff Mill sprawled across the screen, a maze of dilapidated buildings and overgrown paths.

"There," Donovan pointed, tracing a faint line through the dense foliage. "That old access road could be our best bet for a quiet approach."

Amy nodded; her brow furrowed in concentration. "What about thermal imaging? We could use drones to get a heat signature layout of the buildings and people in it."

Donovan's eyes lit up. "Brilliant. I've got a contact in the tech division who owes me a favour. He can keep it off the books."

They spent the next few hours meticulously planning, their voices barely above whispers. Donovan sketched a rough layout of the mill complex on a scrap of paper, marking potential entry points.

They needed to move fast. The OCG was regrouping, and he could not allow this to happen.

Chapter 37: Jess' Rescue

Donovan's heart raced as he crouched behind a crumbling stone wall, peering at the dilapidated Snuff Mill. The old building loomed before them, its broken windows like dark, hollow eyes. He could feel Toby trembling with anticipation beside him, the Labrador's muscles taut and ready to spring into action.

"Amy," Donovan whispered to his partner, "take the firearms team around back. I'll create a distraction at the front."

Amy nodded, her face grim with determination. As she silently directed the team to their positions, Donovan turned to Toby.

"Ready, boy?" he murmured, scratching behind the dog's ears.

Toby's tail wagged once in response.

With a deep breath, Donovan stood and approached the mill's entrance with Toby at his heels. He could hear muffled voices coming from inside. His hand instinctively moved to his holster, fingers brushing the cool metal of his service weapon.

As he neared the door, a floorboard creaked beneath his foot. The voices inside fell silent. Donovan froze, his breath caught in his throat. Suddenly, a shout erupted from within.

"Someone is here!" It was Spike's voice, panicked and angry.

Donovan's training kicked in. In one fluid motion, he kicked open the door and rolled inside, drawing his gun as he moved. Toby bounded in after him, a low growl rumbling in his chest.

The scene before them was chaos. Jess was tied to a chair, her eyes wide with fear and hope as she saw Donovan. Spike stood beside her, his gun wavering between Donovan and Jess. Parker was scrambling for his own weapon, caught off guard by the sudden intrusion.

In that split-second of confusion, Donovan acted. He fired a warning shot into the ceiling, the sound deafening in the enclosed space.

"Police! Drop your weapons!" he shouted, his voice commanding and steady despite the adrenaline coursing through him.

Spike hesitated; his gun still trained on Jess. Donovan's eyes narrowed, his mind racing through possible scenarios. He couldn't risk a direct shot with Jess so close.

That's when Toby made his move. With a fierce bark, the Labrador lunged at Spike, clamping his powerful jaws around the man's gun arm. Spike cried out in pain and surprise, his weapon clattering to the floor.

Seizing the opportunity, Donovan sprinted forward, closing the distance to Parker in three long strides. Parker raised his gun, but Donovan was faster. With a swift Aikido move, he redirected Parker's arm, twisting it behind his back and forcing him to drop the weapon. In one fluid motion, Donovan swept Parker's legs out from under him, pinning him to the ground.

"Stay down!" Donovan growled, securing Parker's hands behind his back with zip ties.

Meanwhile, Toby had Spike cornered—the man cowering against the wall as the dog stood guard, teeth bared. Donovan quickly moved to subdue Spike, disarming him and binding his hands as well.

With both assailants neutralised, Donovan rushed to Jess.

"Are you alright?" he asked, his voice softening as he worked to untie her bonds.

Jess nodded, tears of relief streaming down her face. "I knew you'd find me," she whispered, her voice shaky but filled with gratitude.

As Donovan helped Jess to her feet, Amy and the firearms team burst through the back entrance, weapons raised. They quickly assessed the situation, lowering their guns when they saw the suspects were already subdued.

"Nice work, Donovan," Amy said, a hint of admiration in her voice. "And you too, Toby," she added, giving the Labrador an approving nod.

Toby wagged his tail, clearly pleased with himself. He trotted over to Jess, nuzzling her hand as if to reassure her that everything was okay now.

Donovan wrapped his arm around Jess, holding her close as the reality of the situation began to sink in.

"It's over," he murmured, pressing a kiss to her forehead. "You're safe now."

As the firearms team began to secure the scene and process the suspects, Donovan led Jess outside into the cool night air. She was shaking slightly, the adrenaline wearing off and the shock setting in. Donovan draped his jacket over her shoulders and guided her to sit on a low stone wall.

"Deep breaths," he said softly, rubbing circles on her back. "You're doing great."

Toby sat at Jess' feet, his head resting on her knee as if he understood she needed comfort. She absently stroked his fur, drawing strength from the dog's steady presence.

Amy approached them, notepad in hand. "I hate to do this now, but we need to get your statement while it's fresh," she said apologetically.

Jess nodded, her voice steadier as she recounted the events of her capture and captivity. Donovan listened intently as she described how Parker and Spike had ambushed her outside her house, forcing her into a van at gunpoint. Donovan felt a mixture of rage and relief wash over him: rage at what she had endured, and profound relief that she was now safe.

As Jess finished giving her statement, the wail of approaching ambulance sirens filled the air.

Donovan squeezed her hand reassuringly. "Let's get you checked out, just to be safe," he said gently.

Jess started to protest but then nodded, the exhaustion finally catching up with her.

As the paramedics approached, Donovan turned to Amy. "I'm going to ride with her to the hospital. Can you handle things here?"

Amy nodded, her expression understanding. "Of course. I'll wrap things up here and meet you at the hospital later for a full debrief."

Donovan helped Jess onto a stretcher, Toby trailing behind them loyally. As the paramedics loaded her into the ambulance, Donovan turned to his canine partner.

"Good boy, Toby," he said, kneeling down to ruffle the lab's fur. "You really came through for us tonight."

Toby's tail wagged happily, and he licked Donovan's hand.

"Stay with Amy, okay? I'll see you soon," Donovan instructed.

Toby sat obediently, watching as Donovan climbed into the ambulance beside Jess.

As they drove away from Snuff Mill, the flashing lights of police cars still illuminating the old building, Donovan held Jess' hand tightly. She looked pale and shaken, but a small smile played on her lips as she gazed up at him.

"I can't believe you found me," she whispered. "How did you do it?"

Donovan squeezed her hand gently. "We triangulated the phone call from Parker and Spike. But honestly, I would have turned over every stone in the county to find you."

Jess' eyes welled with tears. "I was so scared, but I kept thinking about you. I knew you wouldn't give up."

As the ambulance wound its way through the quiet streets, Donovan felt a mix of emotions washing over him: relief, lingering fear, and a deep, overwhelming love for the woman beside him. He made a silent vow to himself that he would never let anything like this happen to Jess again.

At the hospital, doctors examined Jess thoroughly, treating her for minor cuts and bruises. Donovan never left her side, holding her hand through each test and procedure. As dawn broke, casting a pale light through the hospital room window, Jess was finally cleared to go home.

Amy arrived just as they were preparing to leave, Toby trotting happily at her heels. The Labrador rushed to Jess, tail wagging furiously as he showered her with affectionate licks.

"Easy, boy," Donovan chuckled, gently pulling Toby back. "She is still a bit sore."

Amy handed Donovan a file. "Preliminary report," she explained. "Spike and Parker are in custody. They were hired by the OCG, they belong to a biker gang who have close ties with criminal activity. They hired them to kidnap Jess and keep you from going after them."

Donovan's eyes narrowed as he flipped through the report. "The OCG," he muttered, his voice low and dangerous. "The report confirms that they were behind this."

Jess looked between them, confusion and worry etched on her face. "The OCG? What does that mean?"

Donovan sighed, running a hand through his hair. "The Organised Crime Group. The force has been tracking them for months. They're involved in everything from drug trafficking to money laundering."

"And now kidnapping," Amy added grimly. "They're escalating, Donovan. This is personal now."

Jess shuddered, and Donovan wrapped an arm around her protectively.

"We'll get them," he promised, his voice filled with determination. "But right now, I need to get Jess home and safe."

Amy nodded. "Of course. Take care of her. I'll keep digging and let you know if anything new comes up."

As they left the hospital, Donovan felt a renewed sense of purpose. The OCG had crossed a line, and he was determined to bring them down. But for now, his priority was Jess.

They arrived at Donovan's flat, Toby bounding ahead to check each room before settling at Jess' feet. Donovan helped Jess to the couch, wrapping her in a soft blanket.

"You should rest," he said softly, brushing a strand of hair from her face.

Jess caught his hand, her eyes meeting his. "Stay with me?" she asked, her voice barely a whisper.

Donovan nodded, settling beside her. As Jess drifted off to sleep, her head resting on his shoulder, Donovan's mind raced. The OCG had made this personal, and he knew they wouldn't stop here. He needed to end this.

Toby whined softly, sensing his master's unease. Donovan reached down to scratch behind the dog's ears, finding comfort in the familiar gesture.

"We'll get them, boy," he murmured. "We'll make sure they can't hurt anyone else."

As the morning light filtered through the curtains, Donovan's phone buzzed quietly. It was a text from Amy:

New lead on the murders, Meet at the station.

Donovan looked down at Jess, still peacefully asleep. He hated the thought of leaving her, even for a moment, but he knew this lead could be crucial. Carefully, he eased himself off the couch, making sure not to wake Jess. He scribbled a quick note explaining where he'd gone and left it on the coffee table.

"Toby, stay," he whispered firmly to the lab. "Guard Jess."

Toby's ears perked up at the command, and he settled into a protective stance next to the couch. Satisfied, Donovan grabbed his coat and keys, taking one last look at Jess before quietly slipping out the door.

The station was a hive of activity when Donovan arrived. Amy was waiting for him, a stack of files in her arms and dark circles under her eyes suggesting she hadn't slept.

Donovan was ready to work through another long day, determined to see things through to the end.

Chapter 38: Bring in Jimi

Donovan spotted Jimi exiting McDonald's, Big Mac in hand. He nodded to Amy.
"Go."
They moved fast. Jimi saw them coming. His eyes went wide. The burger hit the pavement.
He bolted.
Donovan's team fanned out, cutting off escape routes. Jimi darted between parked cars, desperate. Donovan pursued, gaining ground with each stride.
Jimi glanced back. Mistake. He stumbled.
Donovan lunged, tackling him to the asphalt. They skidded, Jimi thrashing.
"Stop resisting," Donovan commanded, voice low and steady.
Jimi went limp. Defeated.
Donovan cuffed him efficiently, then helped him up. "Let's talk, Jimi. Nice and easy."
Amy pulled up in the unmarked car, engine purring, she got out to help. Donovan guided Jimi into the backseat, Amy sliding in beside him.
"You, okay?" Donovan asked, previously eyeing Jimi's scraped palms.
Jimi nodded, sullen. "Didn't do nothin'."
"We'll see about that," Amy said, her tone professional but not unkind.
Donovan took the wheel, Amy in the back with Jimi. The town blurred past as they headed to the station. Silence hung heavy.
At a red light, Donovan's phone buzzed. Text from an unknown number:
Watch your back, Detective.
His body tensed up. He deleted it and said nothing.
The station loomed ahead. Donovan parked, his mind racing. He bet that the OCG sent that text. Connected to Jimi? Bigger fish?
"Let's go," he said,
The station's glass doors hissed open. Fluorescent lights buzzed overhead, casting harsh shadows. Jimi shuffled between them, his head down.

Officer Chen looked up from the front desk, eyebrows raised. "Busy day, Detective?"

Donovan nodded, guiding Jimi past. Their footsteps echoed in the tiled hallway.

At the holding cells, Donovan unlocked the first empty one. The door's hinges creaked.

"In you go, Jimi. Sit tight."

Jimi slumped onto the bench, avoiding eye contact. The cell door clanged shut.

Donovan turned to Amy. "Coffee?"

"God, yes."

They headed to the break room. The ancient coffee maker sputtered and steamed. Donovan grabbed two chipped mugs from the cupboard.

Amy leaned against the counter; arms crossed. "So, what's our play here?"

Donovan poured the coffee, its bitter aroma filling the cramped space. "Let's give him time to stew. An hour, maybe two."

"Good cop, bad cop?" Amy asked, accepting her mug with a nod.

"Too cliché." Donovan sipped, grimacing at the burnt taste. "We'll start friendly, build rapport. Then hit him with the evidence."

Donovan puts his mug down on the table, his voice dropping to a dangerous whisper. "The DNA evidence from under the fingernails of that undercover cop. It puts him right at the scene, hands-on killing." His eyes narrowed as he leaned in closer, his tone almost menacing. "Someone is going down for this."

"Damn." Amy whistled low. "That's solid."

"It's a good solid start." Donovan rubbed his temples. Donovan nodded; his eyes distant. "But Jimi is small fry. We need to leverage this, get him to flip on the bigger players."

Amy sipped her coffee, considering. "The OCG has got its tentacles deep. Jimi might be too scared to talk."

"That's where you come in," Donovan said, a hint of a smile playing at his lips. "You've got a way with people, Campbell. If anyone can get him to open up—it's you."

She raised an eyebrow. "Flattery will get you everywhere, Temple."

The ancient wall clock ticked away, its hands jerking forward in fits and starts. Donovan glanced at it, then drained the last of his coffee.

"Time's up. Let's move him."

They made their way back to the holding cells, footsteps echoing in the empty corridor. Jimi sat hunched on the bench, picking at a loose thread on his sleeve.

"Up and at 'em, Jimi," Donovan called, unlocking the cell. "Let's have a chat."

Jimi's eyes darted between them, wary. He stood slowly, shoulders slumped.

Amy stepped forward, voice gentle. "This way. Watch your step."

They led him down the hall, past the hum of ancient air conditioning. The interview room door loomed ahead, its paint peeling at the edges.

Donovan paused, hand on the doorknob. He turned to Amy, voice low. "Remember, we're building trust. No pressure, not yet. Let him think we're on his side."

Amy nodded; her brown eyes sharp. "Got it. I'll play the sympathetic ear."

They took their seats, the two detectives at one side of the table and Jimi at the other.

"For the purposes of the tape, I am DI Temple," Donovan said, voice professional.

"I am DS Campbell," Amy said. Toying with the pen in her hand.

"Jimi say your name," Donovan asked.

"I am James Monroe," Jimi replied.

Donovan leaned back in his chair, eyeing the man across the table. Jimi sat there, face impassive, his muscular arms crossed over his chest. The stark lights cast harsh shadows across his features.

"So, Jimi," Donovan began, his voice deceptively casual. "Want to tell me where you were last Tuesday night?"

Jimi shrugged. "Home. Watching telly."

"Anyone who can verify that?"

"Nah. Live alone, don't I?"

Donovan nodded, then slid a photograph across the table. It showed a woman's face, pale and bloated.

"Recognise her?"

Jimi barely glanced at the photo. "Should I?"

"Well, considering we found your DNA under her fingernails, I'd say yeah, you should."

Jimi's neck tightened, but he kept his cool. "I saw a lot of girls that night. Maybe I met her at a club, but I can't recall."

Donovan leaned forward; his eyes boring into Jimi's. "This wasn't just some random hookup, and you know it. This woman was an undercover officer, and her body was found in the Trimpley Reservoir. Care to explain how your DNA ended up under the fingernails of a drowned cop?"

A flicker of unease crossed Jimi's face, quickly replaced by a sneer. "Sounds like you lot fucked up, sending a bird to do a man's job. Maybe she got in over her head."

Donovan's fist slammed onto the table, causing Jimi to flinch. "Don't play games with me. We know you're an enforcer for the *County Lines* OCG."

Jimi's eyes narrowed, a dangerous glint appearing in them. "You don't know shit."

Donovan stood up, circling the table slowly. "Oh, but we do. We've been watching your little organisation for months. We know about the drug shipments, the protection rackets, the whole operation. And now, you've gone and killed one of ours."

Jimi remained silent, his gaze following Donovan as he moved around the room.

"Here's what I think happened," Donovan continued, his voice low and menacing. "I think she got too close. Maybe she overheard something she shouldn't have or saw something incriminating. And you, being the loyal attack dog—that you are—were sent to take care of the problem."

He leaned in close, his breath hot on Jimi's ear. "But she fought back, didn't she?"

Jimi's fist tightened, a muscle twitching in his cheek. His eyes darted to the two-way mirror, then back to Donovan.

"You're talking out your arse," he growled, but there was a hint of uncertainty in his voice.

Amy took over the questioning and pressed on, sensing weakness. "She scratched you when you tried to grab her, didn't she? Left evidence under her nails. Rookie mistake for an enforcer like you."

Jimi's composure cracked. "You don't know what you're dealing with," he hissed. "I'm small fry. You come after me, the bosses will make your life hell."

"Is that a threat?" Amy asked, raising an eyebrow.

"It's a fucking promise," Jimi snarled. "You think drowning one cop is bad? Cross the wrong people, and you'll be fishing bodies out of that reservoir for weeks."

"Well, they tried to scare me off by kidnapping my girl, but they failed. They come after me or mine and they will fail again," Donovan interjected.

Donovan's eyes hardened. He grabbed Jimi by the collar, yanking him forward. "Listen here, you piece of shit. You just admitted to drowning an officer. You're going down for this, and you're taking your whole organisation with you."

Jimi's bravado faltered. "I didn't say that. You can't prove anything."

"Oh, but we can," Donovan said, releasing him with a shove.

Donovan is suddenly shifted. He pulled his chair closer, leaning in with a conspiratorial air.

"Look, Jimi, I'll level with you. We've got you bang to rights on this one. But I'm not interested in small fry like you. I want the big fish."

Jimi's eyes narrowed suspiciously. "What are you getting at?"

"I'm talking about a deal," Donovan said, his voice low. "You give us names, dates, locations—everything you know about the OCG's operations, and we can make this murder charge…disappear."

Jimi scoffed. "You expect me to rat? I'd be a dead man walking."

"We can protect you," Amy pressed. "Reduced sentence or even a new identity maybe, relocation—the works. It's a hell of a lot better than spending the rest of your life in prison."

Jimi shifted uncomfortably in his chair. Conflict was evident on his face. He glanced at the two-way mirror again, as if trying to see who might be watching from the other side.

"How do I know you'll keep your word?" he asked, his voice barely above a whisper.

Donovan leaned back, a hint of triumph in his eyes. "Because this isn't just about you anymore, Jimi. This is about taking down an entire criminal empire. Your cooperation could save lives, and prevent more bodies from ending up in that reservoir."

Jimi's shoulders slumped, the fight seeming to drain out of him. "They'll kill me if they find out," he muttered.

"Not if we get to them first," Amy countered, her soft voice a welcome break from Donovan's questioning. "But we need your help to do that."

There was a long moment of silence as Jimi appeared to weigh his options.

Finally, Jimi let out a heavy sigh. "Alright," he said, his voice rough. "I'll talk. But I want everything in writing. Full immunity, witness protection…the works."

"We will do what we can, dependent on the information you provide," Amy responded.

Donovan nodded, trying to contain his excitement. "Of course. We'll draw up the paperwork right away."

As he stood to leave the room, Jimi's voice stopped him, "One more thing, Detective."

Donovan turned back. "Yes?"

Jimi's eyes were cold, his face set in grim lines. "When you go after them, be careful. These aren't your average thugs. They've got people everywhere: cops, judges, politicians. You start digging, you might not like what you find."

"We understand," Donovan replied, trying to mask his unease at Jimi's warning. He opened the door and signalled to the officer waiting outside. "Bring in the paperwork and get a stenographer. We're going to be here a while."

As they waited, Jimi's demeanour changed. The tough exterior crumbled, replaced by a nervousness that manifested in fidgeting hands and darting eyes. When the stenographer arrived and set up her equipment, Jimi took a deep breath.

"Alright," he said, his voice barely above a whisper. "I'll start from the beginning. The OCG…it's bigger than you can imagine. The leaders call themselves *The Syndicate*, and they've got their fingers in everything: drugs, weapons, human trafficking, you name it."

Donovan leaned forward, hanging on every word. "Go on."

"They use Simon as their middleman. Simon is my best mate, and an enforcer, but an enforcer with brains. Simon confides in me, tells me everything."

Jimi hesitated, then continued, "Simon…he is the key to a lot of this. He is not just another enforcer like me. He is the one who connects the bosses to the street-level operations."

Donovan's eyebrows shot up. "Simon? Simon who?" He was hanging in the knowledge he knew what Jimi was about to say.

"Simon Franklin," Jimi said, his voice low. "We came up together, been mates since we were kids. But he has always been smarter…more ambitious. He is the one who got me into this life."

After Jimi's confirmation, Donovan's belief that Simon was a middleman was solidified.

Donovan scribbled furiously in his notebook. "And what exactly does Simon do for the Syndicate?"

Jimi leaned back, a haunted look in his eyes. "Everything. He arranges the drug shipments, coordinates the protection, even handles some of the more.. delicate matters personally."

Jimi swallowed hard. "Like drowning undercover cops, yeah. Simon…he is the one who ordered the hit on your officer. Said she was getting too close, asking too many questions."

Donovan's grip tightened on his pen. "And you carried out the order?"

Jimi nodded; shame evident on his face. "I didn't know she was a cop; I swear. Simon just said she was a problem that needed solving. I didn't ask questions…that's not how things work with the Syndicate."

"Tell me about the night it happened," Donovan pressed.

Jimi closed his eyes as if trying to block out the memory. "I went to her house that night. It was late, maybe 11 pm. I knew her routine; she'd be alone, probably getting ready for bed. I rang her doorbell."

He paused, taking a shaky breath. "She answered the door. I…I grabbed her from behind and covered her mouth so she couldn't scream. She fought hard, that's when she must've scratched me. But I overpowered her, tied her up, gagged her."

Donovan's face remained impassive, but his knuckles were white as he gripped his pen.

"I put her in the boot of my car and drove to Trimpley," Jimi continued, his voice hollow. "It was so quiet out there, just the sound of the water. I…I dragged her to the water's edge," Jimi continued, his voice shaking. "She was struggling, trying to scream through the gag. I…I pushed her in. Held her under until the bubbles stopped."

Jimi's face was ashen, his eyes unfocused as if reliving the moment. "I can still see her eyes: wide with panic, staring up at me through the water. I didn't know she was a cop, I swear. But it doesn't matter, does it? I still killed her."

Donovan leaned back, disgust and anger warring on his face. "No, it doesn't matter. A life is a life."

"What happened after?" he pressed.

Jimi shrugged listlessly. "I burnt out the car I was in, covering my tracks. Then, I went home. Showered. Threw away my clothes just in case. Reported back to Simon that the job was done."

Donovan nodded, his mind racing. He glanced at Amy, who gave him a subtle nod. Time to dig deeper.

"Jimi," Donovan said, his voice low and steady, "I need you to think carefully. Was this the only time Simon asked you to…handle a problem?"

Jimi's eyes darted around the room, his Adam's apple bobbing as he swallowed hard. "I…I don't know if I should—"

"Remember our deal," Amy interjected softly. "Full cooperation for protection. We need to know everything."

Jimi's shoulders slumped. He ran a hand through his hair, leaving it standing on end.

"No," he whispered. "It wasn't the only time."

Donovan leaned forward, his chair creaking. "Tell me about the others."

Jimi's voice trembled as he spoke. "There were…others. Two staged overdoses, made to look like accidents. Simon handled those personally. He has got a way to make things look natural."

Donovan's voice was cold and hard as he spoke. "He made a mistake and now we have confirmation that it was murder. We suspected Simon, but you just confirmed our suspicions."

Donovan wanted Simon, but he was aware that one villain's testimony against another would not be sufficient on its own.

Donovan nodded, encouraging him to continue.

"Then there was the gang shooting," Jimi said, his eyes unfocused. "Rival outfit from Liverpool trying to muscle in on our territory. Simon orchestrated the whole thing. Shame about the poor lady who got shot though." He paused, swallowing hard. "But that's not the worst of it."

Donovan leaned closer. "Go on."

Jimi's voice dropped to a hoarse whisper. "Fenix…he thought he was untouchable. Skimming profits, selling products on the side. The OCG found out, they told me and Simon to make an example of him."

"The carpet factory fire. That was you?"

Jimi's nod was accompanied by haunted eyes. "I played poker with him and got him drunk," he confesses. "I brought him to the abandoned carpet factory where I tortured him until he gave me more names. Finally, I poured petrol over him and set him on fire." Jimi's voice is solemn as he recounts his actions.

He paused, swallowing hard. "I…I worked him over for hours. Fenix held out longer than I expected. Tough bastard."

Donovan's stomach churned at Jimi's confession. The room fell silent, save for the soft whir of the recording equipment. Amy shifted in her seat, her eyes meeting Donovan's. A wordless exchange passed between them.

"Jimi," Amy began, her voice gentle but probing, "what about the Severn Valley railway incident? The shooting on the heritage steam train last week?"

Jimi's head snapped up; eyes wide. "How did you—"

"We have our sources," Donovan interjected smoothly. "But we need confirmation. Was Simon involved?"

Jimi's gaze darted between them, weighing his options. Finally, he slumped back in his chair, defeated. "Yeah," he muttered. "It was Simon."

Amy leaned forward; pen poised over her notebook. "Tell us everything."

Jimi took a deep breath, his eyes distant. "It was Simon's idea. We'd gotten the name from Fenix before…before he died. Liam Grainger, a small-time dealer working out of Kidderminster. He'd been skimming off the top for months, thinking we wouldn't notice."

Donovan nodded, encouraging him to continue.

"Simon…he has always had a flair for the dramatic. Said a simple hit was too boring. He wanted to send a clear message." Jimi's voice dropped to a whisper. "So, he came up with this plan. The Severn Valley railway, you know? That heritage steam line that runs through the countryside."

Amy scribbled furiously in her notebook as Jimi spoke.

"Simon arranged it all. Bought tickets for the last train of the day, and made sure Liam would be on it. I think he even may have bribed the conductor to keep one of the carriages empty." Jimi's voice was barely above a whisper now, his eyes unfocused as if seeing it all play out again.

"Simon…he is meticulous, you know? Planned it all out like some twisted work of art. A vintage steam engine, chugging through the countryside at twilight. Almost romantic, if you didn't know what was coming."

Jimi's voice grew hollow as he continued, "Simon took Liam for a drink first. Some quaint pub in Kidderminster, all exposed beams and brass fittings. Bought him pint after pint, acting the mate. Liam never suspected a thing."

Donovan leaned in, captivated by the grim tale.

"They boarded the last train just as the sun was setting. Simon had timed it perfectly. The sky was on fire, all oranges and purples. Liam was three sheets to the wind by then, stumbling onto the platform."

Jimi's eyes were distant, reliving the scene. "The train itself was a thing of beauty. Steam billowing from the engine, obscuring the platform in a ghostly fog. They found their carriage empty, just as Simon had arranged."

Jimi's voice grew hushed, almost reverent as he recounted what Simon had told him. "The train lurched into motion, wheels screeching against the tracks. Simon led Liam to the rear of the carriage." He paused, swallowing hard. "You could see the steam from the locomotive, billowing past the windows and you could smell the embers from the engine."

Donovan and Amy sat motionless, hanging on every word.

Jimi's voice grew even quieter, barely audible over the hum of the lights. "Simon waited for the perfect moment. The train rounded a sharp bend, wheels screeching against the rails. In that instant, he drew the gun."

Donovan leaned forward, hanging on every word.

"It was over in a heartbeat. One moment, Liam was swaying drunkenly, admiring the twilight landscape. The next—" Jimi's voice cracked. "Simon put the barrel to the base of his skull and pulled the trigger."

Amy's pen froze mid-sentence, her knuckles white around the grip.

"The gunshot was swallowed by the train's roar. Liam crumpled like a marionette with cut strings. But Simon wasn't done."

Jimi's voice trembled as he continued. "Simon…he didn't stop there. He had Liam open the door, and after shooting him, he kicked him out. Liam's lifeless body fell from the train. The train was still rounding the bend, wheels screaming against the rails."

Donovan leaned in, his face a mask of grim fascination.

Jimi's eyes were unfocused, reliving the scene through Simon's recounting. "Liam's body tumbled out into the darkness, vanishing in an instant. One second there, the next…gone."

Jimi's voice grew hushed, and he continued, "Simon told me how the body disappeared into the night; like it had never existed. The train kept chugging along, oblivious to the horror it left behind. Steam billowed past the windows, obscuring the countryside in a ghostly fog."

He paused, swallowing hard. "But that wasn't the end of it. Simon…he is a meticulous bastard, you know? He waited until the train reached the next station.

Bridgnorth, I think. As passengers disembarked, he slipped out, mingling with the crowd."

Jimi's eyes were distant, lost in the retelling. "Simon described how the station looked like something out of another time. Gas lamps flicker on the platform, casting long shadows. The air was thick with steam and the scent of coal. Volunteers in period costume, oblivious to what had just gone down."

Donovan's mind reeled with the grim details of Simon's methodical brutality. He took a deep breath, refocusing on the larger picture.

Donovan couldn't believe how intricate Jimi's storytelling was, especially since he assumed he was just a brute enforcer.

"Jimi," he said, leaning forward, "we need to know more about the OCG's current operations. What are they up to now?"

Jimi's eyes darted nervously around the room. He licked his lips, hesitating. "You don't understand," he whispered. "These people…they're everywhere. If they find out I've talked—"

"We can protect you," Amy interjected softly. "But only if you give us everything."

Jimi closed his eyes, shoulders slumping in defeat. When he spoke again, his voice was barely audible. "Witley Court," he said. "The old ruins. There's more there than meets the eye."

Donovan leaned closer his eyes narrowed. "Witley Court? The old ruins? What's going on there?"

Jimi shifted uncomfortably, his gaze darting between Donovan and Amy. "It's…it's not what you think. The ruins above ground, they're just for show. It's what's underneath that matters."

"Go on," Amy prompted gently.

Jimi took a deep breath. "There are catacombs beneath Witley Court. Most people don't know about them. The OCG…they've turned it into a manufacturing and storage facility. A fortress, really."

Donovan leaned forward, his voice low and urgent. "What kind of storage?"

"Drugs," Jimi whispered. "More than you can imagine. Cocaine, heroin, synthetic stuff I've never even heard of. And cash. Stacks and stacks of it." Jimi leaned in, his voice dropping to a whisper. "When you approach the ruins, it looks like any other tourist spot. Crumbling walls, overgrown gardens. But there's always someone watching. They've got cameras hidden in the trees, motion sensors in the grass maybe."

He paused, glancing nervously at the door before continuing, "There's a man who greets visitors. Looks like a builder maybe. But he is OCG…through and through. If he doesn't recognise you, he'll spin some tale about the ruins being closed for restoration."

Jimi's eyes grew distant as if seeing it all play out. "But if you're one of them, if you know the right words, *County Lines* slang…everything changes. He'll lead you to a hidden door, tucked away behind a fallen column. It looks like solid steel, but it slides open at his touch."

Jimi's voice dropped even lower, his eyes darting around the room. "Once you're through that door, it's like stepping into another world. The air gets cooler, damper. The walls are rough stone, slick with moisture. Ancient-looking lights line the walls, but they're electric."

He paused, swallowing hard. "The catacombs…they go on for miles. Twisting, turning passages that could swallow a man whole. It's a maze down there, designed to confuse anyone who doesn't belong. But I got showed the way once with Simon and the caretaker."

Donovan's ears perked up at the mention of the name *caretaker*, but he chose not to address it at that moment.

Donovan leaned in, captivated. "And what's down there, Jimi?"

"About 300 yards in, there's another door. Massive steel, like something out of a bank vault. I think it's got a keypad."

Jimi's eyes grew distant, his voice hushed with awe. "Behind that door…it's like entering another world. The passage opens up into a cavernous chamber, easily the size of a medium-sized swimming pool. The ceiling soars overhead. Ancient stone pillars, thick as tree trunks, support the weight above."

He paused, swallowing hard. "The air down there…it's thick with the scent of chemicals and money. You can taste it on your tongue."

Donovan leaned in, hanging on every word.

"Four massive workbenches dominate the space," Jimi continued. "Each one a hive of activity. The first bench, that's where they cut the cocaine. White powder everywhere, like some twisted winter wonderland. Men in hazmat suits, working with surgical precision."

Jimi's eyes grew unfocused as he continued, his voice barely above a whisper. "The second bench…that's where they press the heroin. The air is thick with a sickly-sweet smell, like overripe fruit. They've got these industrial presses, stamping out little bricks wrapped in wax paper. Each one marked with the Syndicate's symbol—a coiled snake."

He paused, licking his lips nervously. "The third bench is for the synthetics. That's where things get weird. It's like something out of a sci-fi film. Bubbling beakers, centrifuges whirring. They're cooking up stuff I've never even heard of. Drugs that can make you forget your own name or see through time."

Donovan and Amy exchanged a glance, their faces grim.

"The fourth bench…that's where the money lives. It's like nothing you've ever seen. Stacks of bills, higher than a man. The air crackles with static from the counting machine. They're running non-stop, day and night."

He leaned in, eyes wide. "This isn't your corner store money counter. It's an industrial-grade machine, the size of a small car. The noise is deafening; a constant whirr and click as they process millions in cash. When near to it the smell of money is so thick you can almost taste it."

Jimi paused, swallowing hard. "But that's not even the half of it. There's another room, just as big as the first. You access it through a hidden door in the back, disguised as part of the stone wall."

It swung open Jimi's eyes grew distant, his voice dropping to a reverent whisper. "The second chamber…it's a sight that would make your head spin. As soon as that hidden door swings open, you're hit with a wave of cold air. They've got industrial-grade air conditioning running full blast down there."

He leaned in, his words tumbling out faster now. "The room is easily as big as the first, maybe bigger. But where the first chamber was all about production, this one's pure storage. Imagine row after row of steel shelving units, stretching as far as the eye can see. Each shelf is loaded with product, ready for distribution."

Donovan and Amy exchanged glances; their faces grim as Jimi continued.

Jimi's voice was unwavered. "On one side, it's all neatly packaged drugs. Bricks of cocaine wrapped in plastic and each one stamped with the Syndicate's snake symbol. Also, some heroin bricks are stacked like Lego blocks. Pills in every colour of the rainbow, packed in vacuum-sealed bags. Bags of weed broken down into sellable sizes."

He paused, taking a shaky breath. "But the other side…that's where the real treasure is. Money. More cash than you've ever seen in your life."

Donovan leaned forward; his eyes intense. "How much?"

Jimi shook his head, a humourless laugh escaping his lips. "More than I could count if I had a hundred years. There's this…this mountain of cash. It's like something out of a cartoon, you know? A perfect cube, maybe two metres on each side and 10 feet tall."

Jimi's eyes were wide, almost feverish as he continued, "That cube of cash…it's not just thrown together. It's a work of art. Stacks of bills, all neatly arranged. 50s, 20s: each denomination has its own layer. From a distance, it looks like some twisted rainbow made of money."

He leaned in, lowering his voice. "But that's not even the craziest part. See, the Syndicate doesn't trust banks. Too much risk of getting caught. So, from what Simon tells me, they've turned that chamber into their own private vault."

Donovan and Amy exchanged glances as Jimi went on.

"Along the back wall, there's a row of safety deposit boxes. Not your standard bank boxes, mind you. These are military-grade. Reinforced steel, biometric locks. I heard Simon say they could survive a nuclear blast.

"Those safety deposit boxes…they're not just for show. Simon told me once, when he was drunk, about what's inside. It's not just cash and drugs. We're talking about secrets that could bring down well-known people."

He leaned in closer, his words tumbling out in a rush. "There are files in there, detailing every dirty deal the Syndicate's ever made. Names of corrupt people, judges on the take, cops who've looked the other way. Dates, times and amounts paid. It's all there, meticulously documented."

Donovan and Amy sat motionless, hanging on every word.

"What about the caretaker?" Donovan prompted.

Jimi's eyes widened at the mention of the caretaker. He glanced nervously at the door before leaning in closer.

"The caretaker," he whispered, "that's not a name you throw around lightly. He is…he is something else entirely."

Donovan leaned forward, his voice low and urgent. "Tell us about him, Jimi."

Jimi took a shaky breath. "The caretaker…he is not what you'd expect. Just a normal-looking bloke, nothing gangster about him. Looks like he should be teaching not running a drug empire."

"But appearances can be deceiving," Amy prompted.

Jimi nodded. "Oh, yeah. The caretaker…he has got a day job, see? Works at a secondary school in Kidderminster. An actual caretaker."

"He has an essential part of the *sales* department." Jimi lets out a laugh.

"That's all I have to share," Jimi stated, ending the interview abruptly.

"Are you certain, Jimi?" Amy pressed.

"Yes, there's nothing else to say. I've said enough already." Jimi responded with a hint of sadness in his voice.

"You did well cooperating. It was the smart choice," Amy reassured him.

Donovan gestured for a police constable to come in through the 2-way mirror.

"Please, escort Jimi back to his cell," Donovan instructed.

"Jimi, we will discuss what happens next soon," Donovan added before leaving with the officer.

As Jimi left, the door closed behind him.

"If Jimi is correct, gaining access to Witley Court could bring down not only the OCG but also several other shady individuals," Donovan explained.

"Yes, it would inflict significant damage." Amy concurred.

"Let's keep this information confidential for now. We can't be sure who we can trust, or even if Jimi is telling the truth. I need time to strategise," Donovan advised.

After turning off the interview recorder, they gathered the case file and their notes before exiting the room. Each lost in their own thoughts, wondering about the next steps and the importance of being careful. Only time would reveal the outcome.

Chapter 39: Simon's Downfall

Donovan paced the station, frustration etched on his face. He clenched his fists, knuckles white. Simon was out there, free. The thought made his skin crawl.

"Amy," he called, voice low and urgent.

She appeared in the doorway, alert. "Sir?"

"I need you on Simon. Now." Donovan's eyes blazed with intensity. "He is slippery, but he'll slip up. We just need to be there when he does."

Amy nodded, already reaching for her jacket. "What's the plan?"

"Shadow him. Every move, every stop. I want to know where he goes, who he talks to." Donovan leaned in close, his voice barely above a whisper. "He is cocky as hell. Thinks he is untouchable I bet. That's when they make mistakes."

Amy's eyes narrowed; determination etched on her face. "I'm on it."

Donovan grabbed her arm, his grip firm but not unkind. "Be careful. This guy is dangerous. Don't engage unless absolutely necessary."

"Bring Mark along for backup and make sure to have your service weapon on hand. This guy could be armed," he advised.

She nodded, a hint of a smile playing on her lips. "I'll be a ghost, Sir."

As Amy left, Donovan turned to the evidence board. Photos, timelines, scraps of information. Not enough. Never enough. He ran his fingers through his hair, exhaling slowly.

The station around him hummed with activity, but Donovan barely noticed. His mind was on the chase, piecing together fragments of the case. Simon's smug face during the interview when his brief arrived. The families of the victims, their grief palpable. The weight of it all pressed down on him.

His phone buzzed: Amy.

"He is on the move," her voice crackled.

"Stay on him," Donovan ordered, his voice taut with tension. "But keep your distance. We can't risk spooking him now."

Amy's reply came in a hushed whisper. "Got it. He is heading east on foot. Looks like he is in a hurry."

Thoughts raced in Donovan's head. East. What was there? He pulled up a mental map of the area.

"There's an internet cafe a few streets that way. Could be his destination."

"Copy that," Amy confirmed.

Donovan could hear her measured breathing as she moved. He pictured her, small but determined, weaving through the streets.

"He has gone inside," Amy reported moments later. "Internet cafe, just like you said."

Donovan's fingers drummed against his desk.

"Good. Wait outside. Let me know if he makes any moves. I bet he is checking in with his bosses, getting the low down on any next steps."

Minutes ticked by, each one an eternity. Donovan's phone buzzed again.

"He is on the move," Amy whispered. "Heading north now."

"Stay with him," Donovan ordered, his voice tight. "But be careful. He might be getting paranoid."

Amy's footsteps quickened, her breath coming in short bursts. "He is looking over his shoulder a lot. I think he suspects something."

Donovan's heart raced. "Don't lose him. But don't let him see you either."

The town pulsed around them. Traffic hummed. Pedestrians bustled. Amy wove through it all, her eyes never leaving Simon's back.

"He has turned east again," she reported. "We're approaching the railway station."

Donovan's mind whirred. "The lockers. I bet he is heading for the lockers."

Amy's breath caught. "The lockers? What's he storing there?"

"Evidence," Donovan growled. "Stay on him, but don't let him spot you. I'm on my way."

Simon slipped into the bustling railway station, his eyes darting. Amy followed, her small frame allowing her to weave through a crowd of teenagers who were on their way to school. A cacophony of announcements over the Tannoy and shuffling feet filled the air.

She watched as Simon approached a bank of lockers, his movements jerky and nervous. He fumbled with a key, hands shaking. The locker door creaked open.

Amy's heart raced. She edged closer, pretending to study a timetable. From the corner of her eye, she saw Simon pull out a duffel bag.

Suddenly, he froze. His head snapped up, eyes scanning the crowd. Amy ducked behind a pillar, pulse-pounding.

Amy held her breath, pressed against the cold concrete pillar. Her heart hammered in her chest. She risked a glance around the edge.

Simon was on the move again, duffel bag clutched tightly to his side. He weaved through the crowd, head low, shoulders hunched. Amy waited for a beat, then followed.

Her phone vibrated. Donovan.

"What's happening?" His voice was tense, urgent.

Amy kept her voice low, blending with the station's ambient noise. "He has got a bag from the locker. Heading towards the exit now."

"Stay on him," Donovan ordered. "I'm five minutes out."

Simon walked through the station doors, and out into the bustling street. The morning rush was in full swing. Cars honked, cyclists weaved, pedestrians jostled. Amy slipped into the flow, keeping Simon in her sights.

Amy's voice crackled through the phone. "I think he has spotted me, Donovan. I can't follow any closer without blowing my cover."

"Don't lose him. I'm almost there."

Simon darted across the street, narrowly avoiding a taxi. The driver leaned on his horn and shouted abuse out of the window, but Simon didn't flinch. He clutched the duffel bag tighter, knuckles white.

Amy weaved through the crowd, keeping Simon in her peripheral vision. Her heart raced, adrenaline coursing through her veins. She ducked behind a newspaper stand as Simon glanced back again.

"He is paranoid," she whispered into her phone. "But he hasn't ditched the bag."

"Good," Donovan replied. "That bag is our key. Whatever is inside could nail him, real physical evidence is what we need."

Simon ducked into an alleyway, his footsteps echoing off the grimy brick walls. Amy hesitated, then followed. The alley was a maze of large bins and fire escapes, the air thick with the stench of rotting garbage.

Suddenly, a screech of tyres. Donovan's unmarked car skidded to a stop at the alley's entrance. Simon whirled, eyes wild, trapped between Amy and Donovan.

"Freeze!" Donovan's voice boomed. "It's over, Simon."

Simon's eyes darted, searching for an escape. He lunged for a rusty overhead fire escape, the duffel bag swinging wildly. Amy was faster. She tackled him, both crashing to the grimy pavement. The bag flew open, spilling its contents.

The contents of Simon's bag were scattered across the alley. Guns clattered on the pavement, their metal glinting in the dim light. A black balaclava tumbled out, rolling to a stop at Donovan's feet. Training shoes, their soles caked with mud, spilt from the torn duffel.

Donovan's eyes narrowed as he surveyed the scene. He crouched, carefully picking up the balaclava with a gloved hand. A faint, acrid smell hit his nostrils. Gunshot residue.

"We've got him," he muttered, a grim smile playing on his lips.

Amy kept Simon pinned, her small frame belying her strength. Simon struggled, his face contorted with rage and fear.

"You've got nothing!" he spat, but his voice quavered.

Donovan approached; his steps measured. "We've got everything, Simon. Game over."

Amy received a nod from him, and she grabbed Simon by the arm to help him stand. The suspect's confidence disappeared, replaced by a pale complexion. Donovan recited his rights in a calm and deliberate manner.

They marched Simon to the waiting police car, a small crowd of onlookers gathering at the alley's entrance. Whispers and pointed fingers followed them. Amy kept a firm grip on Simon's arm, her eyes scanning for any sign of trouble.

The drive to the station was tense and silent. Simon stared out the window, his reflection haunted and gaunt in the glass. Donovan's hands were tight around the steering wheel, his mind already racing through the interrogation to come.

At the station, a flurry of activity greeted them. Officers bustled about, their faces a mix of curiosity and grim satisfaction. The air hummed with tension and the smell of stale coffee.

Donovan marched Simon past rows of desks cluttered with case files and half-empty mugs. Phones rang incessantly, their shrill tones punctuating the low murmur of voices. Amy followed close behind, her eyes never leaving Simon's hunched form.

They reached the interrogation room, a stark space with cinderblock walls painted an institutional beige. A single table dominated the centre, flanked by three metal chairs. The overhead lights buzzed.

"Sit," Donovan ordered, his voice low and controlled.

Simon slumped into the chair; his earlier bravado completely evaporated. His eyes darted around the room, taking in the stark walls, the two-way mirror, the camera in the corner. Sweat beaded on his forehead.

Donovan sat across from him, his posture relaxed but alert. Amy stood in the corner, arms crossed, her gaze unwavering.

They announced themselves to the interview tape and moved on.

"Let's start from the beginning, shall we?" Donovan's voice was calm, almost conversational.

He laid out the evidence bags one by one. The guns. The balaclava. The shoes.

Simon's eyes followed each item, his breathing growing more rapid with each reveal. The lights hummed, casting a sickly pallor over his face.

"Those aren't mine," Simon croaked, his voice barely above a whisper.

Donovan leaned forward, his eyes boring into Simon. "We both know that's a lie. I bet your prints are all over them. The mud on those shoes? It probably matches samples from both crime scenes. We will soon find out; they will be processed overnight."

Simon's shoulders slumped. The fight drained out of him visibly, like air from a punctured tyre.

"I want a lawyer," he mumbled, eyes fixed on the table.

Donovan exchanged a glance with Amy. She nodded almost imperceptibly and left the room, her footsteps echoing in the hallway.

The silence stretched, thick and oppressive. Simon fidgeted, his fingers drumming an erratic rhythm on the metal table. Sweat darkened the collar of his shirt.

Minutes ticked by, each one feeling like an eternity. The lights buzzed incessantly, torching the two men.

Donovan leaned back, eyes never leaving Simon. The interrogation room felt smaller by the minute, its beige walls closing in. The air grew thick with tension.

The door creaked open. A man in an impeccable suit strode in, leather briefcase in hand. Simon's lawyer. His polished shoes clicked on the linoleum floor.

"I'm afraid this interview is over," the lawyer announced, voice smooth as silk. "My client has nothing more to say."

Donovan was angry. "Your client was caught red-handed with evidence linking him to two murders."

The lawyer smiled, all teeth and no warmth. "Alleged murders, Detective. And I'm sure there's a perfectly reasonable explanation for those items."

Simon perked up, hope flickering in his eyes. But Donovan saw the cracks in his façade.

Simon's lawyer cleared his throat, his polished demeanour a stark contrast to Simon's dishevelled appearance. "My client is willing to cooperate, but we'll need assurances."

Donovan's eyes narrowed. "Assurances? He is looking at two counts of first-degree murder!"

The solicitor leaned forward, his voice low and measured. "Three, actually. And information on a larger operation."

The room fell silent. Even the buzz of the lights seemed to dim. Donovan's mind raced, piecing together the implications.

"Three?" he finally managed, his voice barely above a whisper.

Simon nodded; his earlier bravado completely gone. He looked small, defeated.

"There's…there's more to this than you know."

"You would be surprised at what we know, your old friend Jimi told us a lot of things, including your involvement in these murders," Donovan countered.

The lawyer produced a thick manila folder from his briefcase. "My client has information on a new strategic location, a trafficking ring. Names, dates…everything."

Donovan's eyes narrowed as he studied the folder. His fingers itched to open it, to dive into the wealth of information it surely contained. But years of experience had taught him caution.

"Let's hear it," he said, voice low and controlled.

Simon licked his lips nervously, glancing at his lawyer for reassurance. The solicitor nodded almost imperceptibly.

"It's big," Simon began, his voice barely above a whisper. "Possibly international. They move people, drugs…weapons. I was just a small part of it."

Donovan leaned forward, his chair creaking under the shift in weight. "Names," he demanded.

Simon disclosed, "I've earned the bosses' trust, and they are giving me more responsibilities. They're satisfied with my performance and want me to have a bigger role in local operations. In fact, today they shared some information with me that I can pass on to you."

Simon hesitated, then spoke. Names tumbled out, each one sending a jolt through Donovan. People in the spotlight. Businesspeople. Even a few law enforcement officials. The scope was staggering.

The lawyer pushed the folder across the table.

Donovan's fingers hovered over the folder, his mind racing. The promise of breaking open a massive criminal enterprise tantalised him. But the cost. He glanced at Simon, the man's eyes feverish with desperation.

"Before we go any further," Donovan said, voice low and measured, "I need more specifics. Not just names, but dates, locations, concrete evidence."

Simon nodded eagerly, words spilling out in a frantic torrent. "There's a shipment coming in next week. Guns and people, packed in shipping containers. They're using the old cannery wharf in Felixstowe as a front. I can give you the exact time, the dock number, everything."

"Also, I have information, about a place called Drakelow Tunnels," Simon said, his voice steady.

Donovan's eyes widened. He knew of Drakelow Tunnels. A sprawling complex, perfect for a covert operation. His mind raced with the tactical implications.

"It's being prepared—as we speak—as the OCG's new hub, somewhere safe to run operations out of."

"When's it going live?" he demanded.

"Already live," Simon replied, his voice steadier now. "They brought in the first major shipment last Friday. Cocaine, mostly. And cash. Lots of it."

Donovan's question hung in the air; the tension palpable as they discussed their plan.

"Who is guarding it?" he finally asked.

Simon's response was quick and confident. "Hell's Angels," he said. "A team of 20 of their best. They rotate shifts, so there's always someone on guard."

The words sent a shiver down Donovan's spine, knowing that these were not men to be taken lightly. Their reputation preceded them: fierce, ruthless, and loyal to their own. Shrouded in mystery and danger, the Hell's Angels were not to be underestimated.

The lawyer interjected smoothly, "Of course, this information comes at a price. My client expects certain…considerations."

Donovan thought for a while. The weight of the decision pressed down on him.

Donovan sat bolt upright. The promise of a bigger bust dangled before him, tempting. But as he looked at Simon, really looked at him, something didn't sit right.

He opened the folder, scanning its contents. Dates, names, locations. It all seemed too neat, too convenient. His eyes narrowed.

"This is impressive," Donovan said, voice carefully neutral. "But it's not enough."

Simon's face fell, panic flickering in his eyes. "What do you mean? It's everything!"

Donovan stood, pacing the small room. The lighting cast harsh shadows across his face. "It's a story, Simon. A good one, but just a story."

He pulled out crime scene photos, laying them on the table one by one. The victims' faces stared up at them, accusing.

"This is real," Donovan growled.

Donovan pulled out a small, worn notebook from his pocket. He flipped it open, revealing pages of cramped handwriting.

"Remember Jimi?" Donovan asked, his voice low and dangerous. "Your old partner in crime?"

Simon's face drained of colour. "I don't know what you're talking about," he stammered.

Donovan slammed his hand on the table. "Like I said, Jimi talked, Simon. He left this with us."

He began to read from the notebook. Dates, times, locations. Detailed accounts of murders. Simon's name came up again and again, each mention more damning than the last.

Simon's lawyer shifted uncomfortably. "Detective, I must object—"

Donovan cut him off with a sharp gesture. "No. Your client's little song and dance ends now."

He turned back to Simon, eyes blazing. "We've got you, Simon. Dead to rights. Jimi's evidence puts you at every scene. The mud on those shoes? It will match samples that forensics took. And that balaclava? It's got gunshot residue all over it, used when you killed your gangland rival."

Simon slumped in his chair, the fight draining out of him. His lawyer's polished façade cracked, revealing a flicker of genuine concern.

Donovan continued, his voice low and relentless, "The guns in that bag? Ballistics will match them to the murders, the gang killing and the execution of Liam Grainger. And I bet when we process your prints, we'll find a match to the partials we lifted from Robert Lightfoot's house."

He leaned in close, his words barely above a whisper. "You're going down for this, Simon. No deal. No clever escape. Just cold, hard justice."

Donovan's brows furrowed in a scowl as he spoke, "Thanks. for the information by the way. However, we have decided to pass this time."

Simon's façade crumbled, his false confidence fading away. He couldn't hold back the flood of emotions any longer and collapsed into tears, hiding his face in his hands. His body trembled with conflicting feelings, unsure of how to process this overwhelming moment.

Donovan straightened, his voice regaining its professional edge. "Simon Franklin, I am charging you with four counts of first-degree murder. You do not have to say anything, but it may harm your defence if you do not mention when questioned something which you later rely on in court. Anything you do say may be given in evidence."

The words echoed in the small room, each one another nail in Simon's coffin. His lawyer sat stunned; briefcase forgotten at his feet.

Donovan nodded to the two-way mirror. The door opened, and two uniformed officers entered. The officers pulled Simon to his feet, the click of handcuffs echoing in the silent room. He stumbled, legs weak, as they led him out. The lights of the hallway seemed to sear his eyes after the dim interrogation room.

They marched him past bustling desks, ringing phones, and the low hum of conversation. Officers paused in their work, eyes following Simon's shuffling progress. The weight of their stares pressed down on him, suffocating.

The processing room was a stark contrast: clinical and impersonal. Simon's fingerprints were taken, each press of ink a damning piece of evidence. The flash of the camera for his mug shot was blinding, capturing his haunted expression for posterity.

As they led him to the cells, Simon's world narrowed to the sound of their footsteps echoing off concrete walls.

Donovan watched as Simon disappeared down the corridor, his shoulders slumped in defeat. He let out a long breath, the tension of the past weeks finally beginning to ebb away.

Amy appeared at his side; her face flushed with the thrill of success. "We did it," she said, her voice barely above a whisper.

Donovan nodded, a small smile tugging at the corners of his mouth. "We did."

They made their way back to the incident room, the buzz of activity washing over them. Officers bustled about, phones rang, and the ever-present hum of computers filled the air. But there was an undercurrent of excitement, a palpable sense of victory.

Donovan strode through the station, purpose in every step. The din of ringing phones and shuffling papers faded as he approached Chief Inspector Grace's office. He paused at the door, straightening his tie and taking a deep breath.

"Come in," CI Grace's voice called from inside, muffled but authoritative.

Donovan entered, the plush carpet muting his footsteps. CI Grace sat behind an imposing mahogany desk, framed by towering bookshelves filled with leather-bound law texts. Sunlight streamed through Venetian blinds, casting zebra-like shadows across the room.

"Ma'am," Donovan began, his voice steady despite the adrenaline still coursing through him. "We've got him. Simon Franklin is in custody and has been charged."

Donovan closed the door behind him, taking a seat across from CI Grace. He leaned forward, his voice low and intense.

"I had a hunch and had him tailed. We caught Simon red-handed. Amy tailed him to the train station where he retrieved a duffel bag from a locker. Inside, we found the murder weapons: two pistols whose ballistics match the crime scenes. There was also a balaclava with gunshot residue and a pair of muddy shoes."

Grace's eyebrows rose. "Impressive work, Donovan. But I sense there's more."

Donovan nodded. "Simon tried to bargain. Claimed he had information on a larger trafficking operation. Names, dates, the works. But it didn't add up."

"There may be something in some of it, we will follow it up."

He paused, pulling out Jimi's notebook. "Remember Jimi, Simon's old partner? He pointed us in the direction of this when we interviewed him."

Donovan spread out the contents of Jimi's notebook on Grace's desk. "This is the key, Ma'am. Jimi documented everything before we moved him to a safe house. Dates, times, locations—all corroborating our evidence and putting Simon at every crime scene."

Grace leaned forward, eyes scanning the pages. "My God," she breathed.

"There's more," Donovan continued. "The mud on Simon's shoes? It's bound to be a perfect match to samples from both murder sites. And his fingerprints? They will be all over the guns."

He pulled out a series of photographs. "These are from traffic cameras near Robert Lightfoot's house. See that figure in the shadows? The build and his gate match Simon perfectly. And look at the timestamp—just 10 minutes after our estimated time of death."

CI Grace nodded, her face grim.

CI Grace leaned back in her chair, absorbing the weight of the evidence. "Outstanding work, Donovan. This is airtight."

Donovan nodded, his expression a mix of satisfaction and weariness. "There's more, Ma'am. We executed another search warrant on Simon's flat while he was in custody. On the premise, he may have moved things there after the last search. It came back a goldmine."

"I had a chance to look over it after his interview and before coming in here."

He pulled out his phone, swiping through a series of photos. "Hidden in a false bottom of his wardrobe, we found a laptop. IT is still cracking it, but what they've found so far is damning. Detailed plans of his murders, seems he liked to make notes and plan."

Grace's eyes widened. "My God."

"In his kitchen," Donovan continued, "we found a drawer full of burner phones. We will be checking numbers as we speak." Donovan paused, letting the weight of the evidence sink in. He pulled out a plastic evidence bag containing a worn leather-bound book. He continued, his voice low and intense, "Simon documented everything. His thought processes, his motivations. It's like a window into a psychopath's mind."

CI Grace leaned forward; her eyes fixed on the journal. Donovan flipped it open, his voice barely above a whisper as he read:

"The rush of power when I pulled the trigger…it was intoxicating. Watching the life drain from his eyes, knowing I held his fate in my hands. It's addictive."

He looked up, meeting her horrified gaze.

Donovan closed the journal, his fingers lingering on its worn cover. "It goes on like that for pages, Ma'am. Detailed accounts of each murder, his thoughts, and his plans for future victims. It's…chilling. The diary of a maniac."

Grace sat back, her face ashen. "My God, Donovan. This is beyond what we imagined."

"There's even more," Donovan said, his voice tight. He pulled out a small USB drive. "This was hidden in a false bottom of Simon's bedside table. Our tech team cracked it open this morning after the arrest."

He inserted the drive into Grace's computer, pulling up a series of files. "It's a goldmine of information. Not just on Simon's crimes, but on a network of criminals he was connected to. Names, dates, locations of drug deals in the *County Lines* operation."

CI Grace leaned forward, her eyes widening as she scanned the information.

Her eyes darted across the screen, absorbing the magnitude of the information. "This…this is unprecedented, Donovan. It's not just Simon we're looking at here. This could bring down an entire network."

Donovan nodded, his face grim. "It's bigger than we ever imagined, Ma'am. The connections go deep. Politicians, business leaders, even a few names in law enforcement."

He stood, pacing the length of Grace's office. Sunlight streamed through the blinds, casting alternating bars of light and shadow across his face.

"We need to move carefully…and fast. If word gets out before we're ready, people will scatter. Evidence will disappear."

She nodded, her fingers steepled under her chin. "Agreed. We'll need to coordinate with other departments, the CLT, and maybe even bring in MI5. This goes beyond our jurisdiction."

"I can handle all the responsibilities in this area, Ma'am. However, I will need you to work with the chain of command, avoiding anyone named, and other task forces to coordinate everything."

"I agree, we can regroup in the morning and discuss our next steps."

Donovan stood up from his chair in her office and headed out for the evening, his mind still buzzing with all that had happened during the day.

Chapter 40: Arrested

The high school loomed its brick façade a silent sentinel against the dusk-dulled sky. Donovan's hand shot out, the entrance yielding to his forceful shove. The doors slammed behind them, their report bounding down the vacant corridors. He exchanged a terse nod with Amy, and they moved.

"Office," he said, a whisper more than enough in the hollow expanse of the institution after hours.

"Got it." Her voice, cool and even, betrayed none of the adrenaline that Donovan felt coursing through his veins.

Their strides were measured, swift—a tandem rhythm punctuating the stillness. Tile floors offered no forgiveness for the urgency of their steps. Donovan's eyes scanned ahead, his senses razor-honed. He knew the layout; he'd memorised it, every possible exit mapped in his mind.

They rounded a corner, and there it was—the caretaker's office. But it wasn't just any caretaker waiting inside. This one had secrets, dirty ones, tucked away among the mops and buckets.

"Police!" Donovan shouted, announcing their presence.

It was protocol, but he might as well have set off a siren for the effect it had on the man inside.

The caretaker's head snapped up, his face a canvas of panic. For a moment, their eyes locked—Donovan's eyes hard and unyielding, the caretaker's eyes wide with fear. A second stretched, taut as a wire.

Then, he moved a sudden blur against the backdrop of cleaning supplies. His hand dove into the cart, emerging with a bag—bulky, its contents unmistakable even through the thick plastic.

"Stop!" Amy's command was sharp, a blade thrown into the space between them.

But the caretaker was already fleeing, the door flung open in his wake. His desperation was visible, a live thing that filled the corridor as he stumbled out.

"Go!" Donovan didn't need to say more.

They were after him, their pursuit as relentless as the pulse beating in Donovan's ears. The chase was on, the prey running, but Donovan was close. Always close.

Donovan's breath came in quick bursts, his vision narrowing to the fleeing figure ahead. Amy's presence was a shadow at his side.

"Left!" he shouted, muscles coiling as they veered sharply.

Their soles screeched against the sheen of the corridor, a discordant symphony to their pursuit.

"Watch out!" Amy's warning cut through the din as the caretaker hurled a stack of textbooks behind him.

They hit the floor with a thunderous clap, pages fluttering like wounded birds. Donovan leapt, barely clearing the debris. Amy followed suit, nimble and unscathed.

"Persistent," she grunted, more a statement of respect than annoyance.

"Comes with the badge," Donovan replied, eyes never leaving the caretaker's retreating form.

The hallway seemed to stretch, an endless tunnel lined with metal lockers, each one a silent witness to the chase. The caretaker's desperation painted his movements erratic and dangerous. He snatched a chair from a nearby classroom, tossing it into their path without looking back.

"Damn!" Donovan's exclamation was sharp as he swerved, feeling the air shift where the chair had been moments before.

Amy mimicked the manoeuvre, her agility a testament to hours spent in training.

"Split up." Her voice was taut, ready for his call.

"Keep on him!" Donovan decided, unwilling to risk losing sight of their quarry.

They plunged deeper into the labyrinth of the school. The caretaker was always a step ahead, his trail marked by chaos: papers scattered across the floor, a trash can overturned, its contents strewn like an afterthought.

"Corner him," Donovan panted, strategy overtaking raw pursuit.

"Got it," Amy's reply was clipped, her mind already mapping out the caretaker's possible escape routes.

"Can't let him get away," Donovan muttered under his breath, though he knew Amy thought the same.

This was more than a chase; it was the tightening of a noose, the closing of a net. And they were at its centre, drawing inexorably closer to the man who controlled the local gang of minors.

"End of the line!" Amy called out, her voice echoing off the walls as they neared the final stretch.

The caretaker glanced over his shoulder, his eyes wild. A silent plea for freedom was etched into his features before he disappeared around another bend.

"Almost there," Donovan pushed, every sinew straining, every instinct honed on the capture.

"Stay sharp," Amy breathed, her warning needless but not unwelcome.

This was the hunt, and they were the hunters. Nothing would stop them now.

Donovan's breath came in rapid bursts, his heart hammering against his ribs as he surged forward. The distant clamour of the caretaker's flight was a siren call, propelling him through the school. Adrenaline coursed through them, each stride eating up the space between hunter and hunted.

"Left!" Amy's voice sliced through the tension, sharp and certain.

She was right on his heels, her presence a steady thrum in his peripheral awareness.

He veered left. Ahead, the echo of footsteps grew louder, more frantic. The caretaker was close, too close to slip away.

"Keep the pace," Donovan grunted, his words clipped.

They were gaining ground, he could feel it in the slight hitch of their target's rhythm.

Amy's reply was a grunt, her focus laser sharp.

The chase funnelled them towards the double doors at the end of the hallway. Pushed open by desperate hands moments before, they swung back with a slow creak that seemed at odds with the urgency of pursuit.

Through the threshold, the scent of chlorine assaulted Donovan's senses. His eyes registered the gleaming tiles of the swimming pool area just as a splash reverberated against the high ceiling.

In a decisive motion, the caretaker plunged into the water without hesitation. The surface seemed to swallow him whole as he disappeared beneath the shimmering liquid, his bag of illicit goods still clutched tightly in his hand. He fought against the confines of the water, his clothes now drenched and weighing him down.

Desperation filled his movements as he struggled to reach the safety of the other side. Every muscle in his body strained against the resistance of the water, determined to keep him submerged. But he refused to let go of his precious cargo, even as it threatened to pull him under.

Donovan let out a bark as he skidded to a sudden halt near the edge. Amy followed suit and stopped beside him, her restraints at the ready, her gaze locked on the struggling figure in front of them.

"Can't believe this," she muttered.

Donovan didn't waste any time, quickly removing his jacket and giving orders. His eyes were fixed on the pool, where the caretaker was floundering. Time was of the essence.

"Be careful," Amy called after him, but Donovan was already moving, his body coiled for the dive that would bring the chase to an inevitable close.

Without hesitation, Donovan's body pierced the water's surface with a clean dive. The chill of the pool clamped around him like a vice, seizing his breath. He kicked hard, propelling himself upwards. Breaking through, he gasped, eyes snapping to the caretaker's flailing form.

"Stop!" His voice was a thunderous command lost amidst the chaos of splashing water.

The caretaker ignored the call, thrashing wildly, trying to distance himself. Donovan surged forward, muscles coiled with purpose. Each stroke cut through the water with precision, a silent promise of impending capture.

Distance closed, Donovan reached out, fingers grazing the man's sleeve. The caretaker jolted and tried to jerk away, but Donovan was relentless. He latched onto the fabric, pulling himself closer.

"Got you," he hissed.

Their bodies collided in a tumultuous dance of desperation. The caretaker swung an elbow; Donovan deflected it smoothly with his Aikido training surfacing like instinct. Grappling ensued, limbs entangled in a struggle for dominance.

"Enough!" Donovan's tone was steel as he twisted the man's arm behind his back, leveraging his own weight.

A moment's advantage and he was on top, pressing the caretaker's torso against the pool edge.

"Give up," he growled, each word punctuated by the heave of their chests.

"Can't...breathe—" the man gasped, water lapping at his lips.

"Then, stop fighting." Donovan's grip was ironclad but controlled, eyes drilling into the caretaker.

Panic flickered across the man's face before his body went limp, surrender etched in every line. Donovan kept him afloat, ensuring his head remained above water. The fight seeped out of the scene, leaving only the echo of their ragged breathing.

"Secure?" Amy called from the edge, ready to move in.

"Secure," Donovan confirmed, dragging the defeated caretaker towards her outstretched hands.

Heaving the caretaker's sodden weight up onto the poolside, Donovan's lungs screamed for air. Water cascaded from his drenched clothing, pooling around his feet. The man's struggle had ceased, but his chest heaved in heavy erratic breaths. Amy was at Donovan's side in an instant, her handcuffs glinting under the harsh overhead lights.

"Turn around," she declared, voice echoing off the tiled walls.

The caretaker complied, a defeated slump to his shoulders. Metal clicked shut around his wrists, a sound that signalled the end of the chase and the beginning of justice.

"Walk," Donovan ordered, his tone allowing no room for resistance.

They moved through the corridors, the janitor's wet shoes leaving smeared prints on the shiny floor—an unwitting path back to the scene of his crimes.

The interrogation room was stark. The only sounds were the hum of the fluorescent light and the shuffle of papers as Donovan prepared to dive into the caretaker's world of deceit. Across the table, the man sat, cuffs chaining him to reality.

"Name?" Donovan started, his voice even and cold.

"Michael...Michael Davis," came the reluctant reply.

"Michael, you know why you're here." Donovan leaned forward, eyes never leaving the caretaker's face. "Let's not waste time."

Davis's gaze shifted, but Donovan was unrelenting.

"Who are you working for?" His words were sharp, each one etched with the promise of uncovering the truth.

"I...I can't—" Davis stammered, fear creeping into his eyes.

"Can't or won't?" Donovan's question sliced through the tension.

"Look, I'm just a small piece—" the caretaker began, but Donovan cut him off.

"Small pieces make up the bigger picture, Davis. Start talking, or every second of your silence adds another brick to the cell wall you'll be staring at for years."

Amy watched, her expression unreadable, but her presence a silent force by Donovan's side.

"Okay! Okay," Davis caved, sweat beading on his forehead. "I'll talk, just…you have to protect me."

"Your cooperation is your protection," Donovan assured, his words a lifeline thrown into turbulent waters.

"Start from the beginning," he commanded, settling back into his chair.

He knew the road ahead would be long, but every confession they pried from this man brought them one step closer to dismantling the network that had poisoned their streets.

The names tumbled from Davis's lips, a cascade of guilt and desperation. Donovan scribbled each one, his hand steady despite the churn in his gut. Amy's pencil tapped a relentless rhythm on her notepad, a metronome to the caretaker's downfall.

"Jason…Lily…Marcus," Davis gasped, voice breaking on the syllables.

"Kids," Donovan muttered, more to himself than anyone else.

Amy caught his eye, her expression tight.

"We have choices to think about, Donovan. What's the play?" Her words were crisp, cutting through the hum of the fluorescent lights above.

He paused, the weight of their futures pressing down on him. These were children, their lives branching out before them. A hard-line could snap those branches, and leave them withered before they had a chance to grow.

"Caution," he decided, the word tasting like a bitter compromise on his tongue. "We bring them in, talk straight. Scare them right."

"Right." Amy nodded, understanding the tumult beneath his stoic façade.

"Think that'll save them?" she asked, her voice low enough that only Donovan could hear.

"Hope is all we have," he replied, locking away the doubt that clawed at his resolve.

He turned to Davis, who slumped in his chair, the fight drained out of him.

"Your part is done," Donovan told him, standing up. The sound of his chair scraping back was a full stop to the interrogation. "Let's see if we can write a different ending for these kids."

Chains clinked as the caretaker's wrists were bound, a metallic symphony to his downfall. He shuffled forward, each step a surrender to the consequences of his actions. Donovan watched, eyes narrowed, reading the slump of the man's shoulders, the defeat etched into his downcast face. 10 years—time is enough for regret to fester and redemption to feel like a distant dream.

"Justice," Amy murmured, her voice steady despite the adrenaline that still hummed in their veins.

"Or just the start," Donovan replied, his tone flat but his mind ablaze with what lay ahead.

They stepped out of the interview room, the door closing with a decisive click behind them. Donovan felt the chapter close on the caretaker, even as his own story raced on, pages turning faster than he could read them. The organised crime group lurking behind the scenes was a hydra; cut one head off, two more would sprout.

"Next steps?" Amy asked, aware of the gears turning behind Donovan's stony façade.

"Follow the trail," he said, the words sharp, cutting through the fog of victory. "The caretaker talked. Now, we make those names count."

"Lead the way, Sir." Her eyes matched his intensity, ready for whatever was next.

"Already on it." He was moving before the sentence finished, his stride purposeful, his resolve steeling him for the work ahead.

The caretaker was just a pawn, a single thread pulled from a larger web. The true fight was still to come, and Donovan would be at the forefront, dismantling the darkness piece by painstaking piece.

Donovan strode into the station's open office, the buzz of activity a stark contrast to the sterile silence of the interview room. Amy was a shadow at his side—her gaze sweeping the room—absorbing every detail as if it held a clue they couldn't afford to miss.

"Do you have anything to report," Donovan snapped to the team clustered around a mess of files and laptops.

"Still piecing it together," one PC replied, fingers flying over keys. "But we're onto something."

"Good." The word sliced through the tension like a knife.

Donovan leaned over a desk, eyes darting across a digital map peppered with pins and strings of data. Each point is a lead, a node in an intricate criminal network.

"Here." Amy pointed to a cluster of markers on the screen. "These are the schools. Connections run deep."

"Too deep," Donovan muttered.

It wasn't just about drugs. It was about futures derailed, and innocence lost.

"Surveillance?" he questioned, voice sharp as glass.

"Up and running," another PC confirmed.

"Patterns?"

"Emerging."

"Time is not a luxury we have," Donovan said, terse.

Every second squandered was another kid at risk, another deal made.

"Understood." The team's response was a chorus, unified.

Amy leaned in close, her words for Donovan alone. "We've got this. They can't hide forever."

"Then let's bring the shadows into light," Donovan replied, his focus razor-edged.

The team nodded, their expressions mirroring Donovan's unyielding determination. They were a unit, battle-hardened and ready for the war that waged beyond the station's walls.

"The next 24 hours are critical," Donovan announced, locking eyes with each member of his team. "I want updates on the hour. No stone unturned."

"Got it, Boss," they echoed.

"Let's move!" Donovan commanded.

Chairs scraped against the floor, the sound of a battle cry. Screens glowed brighter, fingers typed faster, and Donovan and Amy stood at the helm like two sentinels guarding the line between order and chaos.

With determination etched into their faces, they exit the station and set forth on their mission; to apprehend the dealers and put an end to their poisonous drug peddling. They move toward the schools' gates.

At last, they spot a group of youths, huddled together looking through a set of soccer playing cards, and exchanging small packages. With swift action, they close in on the suspects and make the arrests. It's a small victory in the war against drugs, but it's one step closer to a safer community for all.

Chapter 41: Deep Cover

CI Grace's heels clicked a staccato rhythm against the polished floorboards as she entered the clandestine space in Bromsgrove. Each step reverberated, filling the sterile expanse with an undercurrent of urgency. Fluorescent lights buzzed overhead, slicing through the dimness and casting angular shadows that flickered like spectres on the walls.

At the centre of it all, a large table bore the weight of coffee jugs, cups and four senior officers; their silhouettes etched sharply against the brilliance. Two men and two women; they were bastions of law in a world teetering on the brink of chaos. Their faces—maps of anticipation laced with threads of concern—lifted as Grace made her entrance.

She gave a curt nod to each, a silent acknowledgement of the stakes at play. Her gaze lingered a second longer on the woman to her right, whose eyes reflected a history of hard-won battles and the scars to prove it. Another officer—a man with steel in his jaw—met Grace's eyes with a stoic resolve that spoke of countless nights staring down danger.

The gravity of the meeting pulled at the air, thickening it with unspoken oaths and unwavering commitment. This was not merely a gathering; it was a conclave where decisions would ripple through the underbelly of crime and justice alike.

Grace took her seat, the head of the table becoming her command centre.

"Status on the *County Lines*?" one of the men demanded, his tone slicing through any residual silence.

The large file before CI Grace thumped down, its contents pregnant with evidence and strategy.

The officers shifted, a silent symphony of starched uniforms and anxious energy.

One cleared his throat, leaning forward. "We've hit snags," he said crisply. "Surveillance compromised at two locations. Couriers are spooked, going to ground."

"Talk," CI Grace pressed, her fingers drumming a staccato rhythm on the tabletop.

"Insiders have clammed up, possible leak." A woman's voice, taut as a wire. "And there's more problems on the street. Rivals are getting twitchy, violence escalating."

"Numbers?" Grace didn't miss a beat.

"Three stabbings last week. Two ODs," another officer added, his words clipped.

"Collateral damage is mounting," Grace acknowledged, her eyes hard as flint.

The room held its breath, the ticking clock now a metronome to their pulse.

"Secrecity," CI Grace stated flatly, her gaze cutting through the room. "Jimi's list has names that can't afford to see daylight." Every head around the table was motionless, eyes locked on her. "A single leak," she continued, leaning forward so that the shadows from the overhead light fell across her face, "could unravel us all."

She paused, letting the words hang in the air, heavy with implication. The officers understood; that the grim reality of their work required the silence of tombs. Grace reached into her file and drew out two photographs, placing them on the table like cards in a high-stakes game.

"Operation Witley and Operation Drakelow," she declared, her voice slicing through the tension. She tapped the first photograph, an image of sprawling gardens and the haunting shell of a grand house—Witley Court. "We'll cut off one of the main arteries here."

Then, her finger moved to the second photograph, depicting the yawning mouth of Drakelow Tunnels. "And here, we go for the heart, the OCG's main hub."

"DI Temple," Grace announced, her tone brokered no argument. "He has Drakelow." Her eyes flicked to the officer, who sat straighter, the weight of the task settling on his shoulders.

"DS Campbell," she continued, turning to another, who nodded sharply at the mention of her name, "Witley is hers."

Grace studied the pictures for a moment, her expression unreadable. These were her chosen, her most capable, and this was their proving ground. With the objectives laid bare, the plan unfolded—a tapestry of interwoven fates and precision tactics.

"Expect resistance. Expect the unexpected," she warned; her every word etched with the clarity of experience. "These locations are our battlegrounds. Control them, and we turn the tide."

The sting operations were more than mere raids; they were a statement—a show of force against a tide of crime that had flooded their streets. Grace knew the risks, and so did her team. But as she watched the resolve harden in the faces around her, she also knew there was no turning back.

"Entrances?" A furrowed brow from the senior officer on Grace's left punctuated the air of tension. "Witley has got too many variables."

"Controlled entry points." Grace's reply cut through the uncertainty. "DS Campbell, her team locks them down. No in or out without her say-so."

"Drakelow's tunnels—what about signal issues?" another officer chimed in, his voice etched with concern.

"Tech is ahead of it," she said, tapping the file before her. "We're installing repeaters throughout. Communication stays clear."

A nod, then silence, broken only by the rustling of papers as the officers digested the strategy; their eyes flickering over the blueprints and maps like hawks over a battlefield.

"Armaments?" The question came sharp, quick.

"Non-lethal, where possible," CI Grace stated, her gaze unyielding. "We're there to apprehend, not escalate."

"Backup?"

"Two units on standby. Immediate deployment if things go sideways." Her words were clipped, and decisive.

"Press?"

"Blackout, until we're done." She paused, letting the finality of her word settle. "No leaks. Full stop."

"Transport for the suspects?"

"Secured. Unmarked and out of sight." CI Grace's hands remained still, her poise unshaken even as her mind raced through every contingency.

"Intelligence support?"

"24/7 surveillance. We've got eyes everywhere, even in the sky, a drone," she affirmed, her confidence unwavering; a reflection of the countless hours poured into planning each meticulous detail.

"Rules of engagement?" This time, the question held a note of gravity that matched the weight of responsibility resting upon them all.

"Minimum force, maximum efficiency. But protect our teams at all costs." Her directive was clear; there was no room for misinterpretation.

"Collateral?"

"Evacuation protocols are in place. Civilians are not part of the equation." CI Grace met each inquisitive gaze head-on, her resolve steeling her against the rising tide of what-ifs.

"Understood." The collective voice of her officers melded into a single affirmation of trust and readiness.

"Questions?" Grace's gaze lingered on each face.

One by one, they shook their heads, their expressions etched with resolve.

"Good." Grace's nod was curt, final.

She shuffled in her chair, feeling the heat of the operation pressing down on her. As the silence stretched, it became a pact, an unspoken vow that bonded them to the cause, to each other.

"Then we're set." Grace stood, her movements deliberate. "Remember, success is in the details. We need to stay sharp and our lines of command secure, the five people in this room are the only ones who now have all the details."

CI Grace's chair scraped back, a sharp report that shattered the silence. "I trust you," she declared; her voice ironclad with certainty. Her eyes locked with each officer in turn, a silent exchange of vows. "Every one of you."

"Agreed," they echoed, a chorus of reinforced steel.

"Remember," Grace leaned in, her shadow stretching across the table like an omen, "secrecy is our ally. Not a word beyond these walls."

"Understood," came the collective response, a low murmur of assent.

"Votes of confidence?" she pressed.

"Unanimous," confirmed a stern-faced officer, his nod as solid as the conviction in his voice.

"Ready," affirmed the third, determination etched into every line of his being.

"Prepared," concluded the last, her eyes alight with the fire of readiness.

"Then, it's time." Grace stood, the movement crisp, purposeful.

The officers mirrored her, rising as one entity, a phalanx braced for battle.

"Operations commence after my team briefing," she stated, the finality in her tone leaving no room for doubt or debate.

Their nods were sharp, decisive.

The senior officers filed out, steps measured, and face masks of resolve and readiness. The door closed with a soft click, sealing the pact made within those four walls.

The door thudded shut behind her as she left, its echo a solitary note amidst the silence of the corridor. Her pulse thrummed in her ears. Each beat was a countdown to the operations that would soon unfold under the cover of darkness.

She strode on, the dossier clasped under her arm, its contents as volatile as nitro-glycerine. With every step, her mind spun, a relentless carousel of strategies and scenarios. Operation Witley. Operation Drakelow. Names etched into her consciousness, their success or failure hers to own.

Trust. The word hung in her chest like a talisman. She had imparted it unto them, those senior officers with their squared shoulders and steady nods. But trust was a gamble, a leap of faith when every instinct screamed caution. Had she been right to lay such weight upon their shoulders? They were good police officers, seasoned, yet doubt was a bitter pill, always lurking in the shadows.

"Temple. Campbell." Their faces flashed in her mind's eye, sharp and focused.

The best she had. Yet even the mightiest sword could not cleave through treachery if it came from within. She knew too well the cost of misplaced confidence; history was littered with its casualties.

A sigh escaped her, a ghost of vulnerability. It was a luxury she couldn't afford—not now. Not with so much at stake. A thread of steel wove itself through her resolve, hardening her. They were chosen, handpicked for this moment. They would rise to the occasion; they had to.

"Focus," she whispered to herself, the word slicing through the whirlwind of thoughts.

The mission was clear. Secure the drugs, the money, the strong boxes. Minimise harm. Protect the innocent. They were more than operatives executing commands; they were guardians at the gates, defenders of order.

Her fingers brushed the cool metal of the door handle at the end of the corridor, ready to step out into the night. The air outside would taste of coming rain and the electric charge of impending action. There was no turning back now. No room for hesitation.

"Zero hour," she repeated, the two words a silent vow.

DI Donovan, DS Campbell, arbiter of fates in an unseen war. Her footsteps ceased their rhythmic march, pausing at the threshold of what would come.

Ahead lay a chessboard town, where tonight, the pawns and knights would move at her command.

The door swung open, and a rush of cool air greeted her. CI Grace emerged into twilight's embrace, the day's end casting long shadows across the precinct steps. Her lungs filled with the scent of rain and petrol, the tang of a town bracing for the storm.

Fatigue suddenly washed over her, making her realise the weight and stress of these cases on her well-being.

She stood still, just one heartbeat, letting the weight settle—a mantle heavy with risk, threaded with duty. She tasted the resolve on her tongue, sharp as iron. There was no room for doubt, not when lives hung in balance, teetering on the edge of her decisions.

"Campbell. Donovan." she exhaled their names, like a prayer to steady her pulse.

They were her aces in a high-stakes game, pieces she'd manoeuvred into position with a precision that brooked no chance.

A car honked impatiently nearby, slicing through her reverie. Focus snapped back; time was slipping away, trickling into the darkening streets where danger multiplied with the shadows.

"Ready," she whispered to the dying light.

The word was a promise, forged in the crucible of her will to bend chaos into order. She could feel the operations unfolding ahead, each move critical, every second counting down to confrontation.

Grace stepped off the kerb, her stride resolute, shoes clicking a staccato rhythm against the pavement. Each step was a declaration, a silent command to the night: yield your secrets, give up your ghosts. She was a tempest brewing on the horizon of the Wyre Forests underbelly, ready to unleash justice in swift, unrelenting waves.

One last glance at the station's entrance when she arrived back, its windows reflecting the first flickers of streetlights, and then, Grace Donovan pushed forward into the gathering dusk, her mind a whirring engine of strategy and anticipation. The chapter closed, but the story—her story—marched onward, relentless as the coming storm.

Chapter 42: The Briefing

Donovan, Amy and Chief Inspector Grace huddle together in CI Grace's office. They discuss what they know so far and how they will take down the organised crime groups operating locations at Witley Court and Drakelow Tunnels.

Amy and her team will take down Witley Court and Donovan and another team take down Drakelow Tunnels. They need to keep things quiet, only telling their teams the plans at the last minute. Once done, they will use any information such as names to serve arrest warrants on people named, using other police forces and maybe MI5.

Donovan leaned in, his voice low. "We hit both locations simultaneously. No room for error."

Amy nodded, her eyes sharp. "My team can handle Witley Court. We'll need tactical gear, maybe some night vision."

"Agreed," Chief Inspector Grace said. "Donovan, you'll lead the Drakelow op. Choose your team carefully, firearms-trained, of course."

Donovan's mind raced, mapping out the underground tunnels. "We'll need breaching charges. And a communications expert to help keep the two teams aligned."

Grace tapped her desk. "Absolute secrecy until go-time. If word leaks, this whole operation falls apart."

"What about after?" Amy asked. "Once we have names…locations?"

"We coordinate with other forces," Grace said. "Cast a wide net. MI5 if necessary."

Donovan felt the familiar pre-mission tension coiling in his gut. "We'll need to move fast once we breach. These aren't amateurs we're dealing with."

Amy's lips tightened. "Agreed. My team will focus on securing evidence and any digital devices. We can't let them destroy anything."

"Good thinking." Grace nodded. "Donovan, your priority is apprehending the key players. We need them alive."

Donovan's mind flashed to the tunnels' layout. "There could be hidden exits. We'll need a perimeter team."

Grace leaned back, her chair creaking. "I'll coordinate with local units. They can set up roadblocks, but quietly."

Donovan rubbed his chin, the stubble rough against his calloused hand. "We'll need specialised equipment for Drakelow. Those tunnels are a maze."

Amy leaned forward, her compact frame tense. "What about thermal imaging? Could help identify hidden rooms or escape routes."

"Good call," Donovan nodded. "I'll requisition some from the tactical unit. We'll also need portable signal boosters. Can't risk losing comms down there."

Grace's phone buzzed. She glanced at it, frowning. "Just got word. Simon has been moved to maximum security. He is not talking but, at least, he is contained."

Donovan tightened. One less variable to worry about, but Simon's silence meant they were flying blind.

"Any progress on cracking his encrypted files?"

"Cyber team is working on it," Grace replied.

Amy pulled out her tablet, fingers flying across the screen. "I've been mapping potential escape routes from Witley Court. There's an old tunnel system, supposedly sealed off decades ago. We can't rule out they've reopened it."

Donovan leaned in, studying the blueprint. "Good catch. We'll need ground-penetrating radar to check for any hidden passages. I know a guy in the engineering corps who can lend us some equipment off the books."

Grace nodded approvingly. "Do it. What about transportation? We can't risk using marked vehicles."

"I've got a contact at a private security firm," Donovan offered. "They've got a fleet of unmarked vans we can use. Bulletproof, with secure comms built-in."

"Wow, do you know every person in town, Donovan?" Grace asked with a smile, relieving the tension.

"Well, it's kind of my job. Ex-MP and all that," Donovan replied playfully, causing both of them to laugh.

Amy's brow furrowed. "What about air support? A drone could give us real-time intel once we breach."

Donovan snapped his fingers. "Brilliant, Amy. I've got a contact in the RAF who owes me a favour. We could borrow a Watchkeeper drone, top-of-the-line surveillance tech. I used them before out in Afghanistan with the SAS."

Grace raised an eyebrow. "That's military-grade equipment, Donovan. Are you sure we can get clearance?"

"Leave that to me," Donovan assured her. "It'll give us thermal imaging, night vision, and secure data links. Perfect for coordinating both teams."

Amy pulled up a 3D render of Witley Court on her tablet. "Look here," she pointed to a section of the sprawling estate. "Looks like some old servant quarters left after the fire, could be a weak point. We could use shaped charges to create a distraction while the main team enters through the front."

Donovan nodded, impressed. "Good thinking. For Drakelow, we'll need to approach it from multiple angles. The main entrance is too obvious."

He pulled up a detailed map of the tunnel system on the large screen. "There are three secondary entrances we can use. Team Alpha will breach here," he pointed to a ventilation shaft on the eastern side. "Team Bravo will come in through this maintenance access point to the north. I'll lead Team Charlie through this drainage tunnel to the south."

Amy studied the map intently. "Those tunnels are a maze. How will you navigate once inside?"

Donovan grinned. "I've got that covered. Remember, I have Toby? I'll bring him with Team Charlie. His nose will guide us through the dark better than any map."

Grace nodded approvingly. "Excellent thinking, Donovan. But how will you protect Toby?"

Donovan's eyes gleamed. "Already on it. I've got a custom-made K9 tactical vest for him. Kevlar-lined, with a camera mount and a GPS tracker. I wanted to protect him while out on the job with me, but I went a bit OTT with it, another favour. He'll be safer than any of us."

Amy leaned in, intrigued. "What about comms? We can't risk any radio chatter leaking."

"I've got that covered too," Donovan replied. He pulled out a small, sleek device from his pocket. "New tech from a friend at GCHQ. Quantum encryption. Unbreakable, even if they intercept the signal."

Grace whistled, impressed. "You really do know everyone, don't you?"

Donovan shrugged, a hint of a smile on his face. "It's not about knowing everyone. It's about building trust and maintaining relationships. You never know when they'll come in handy."

Grace nodded, then turned to a large touchscreen on the wall. "Let's go over the timeline. We need precision down to the second."

The screen lit up with a detailed schedule. Donovan studied it, his mind racing through scenarios.

"H-hour minus three," he began. "Teams assemble at separate staging areas. Final equipment checks, comms test, and mission briefing."

Amy chimed in. "H-hour minus two, we move out. Separate routes, avoiding detection. Radio silence except for emergency channels."

"H-hour minus 30 minutes," Donovan continued. "Teams in position. Drone goes airborne for final recon."

CI Grace pointed to the map, her finger tracing the routes. "H-hour minus 15 minutes, snipers and perimeter teams in position. Donovan, your explosives expert preps the breaching charges."

Donovan nodded, his mind racing through the intricate details. "Right. We'll use thermobaric charges on the main entrance. Less structural damage, but the overpressure will stun anyone inside. For the side entrances, shaped charges to minimise collateral."

Amy leaned in, her brow furrowed. "What about electronic countermeasures? They might have surveillance systems we don't know about."

"Good point, EMP generators. We'll trigger them 30 seconds before the breach. Should fry any cameras or alarms they've got set up. I can get hold of a couple."

Grace's eyes widened. "Impressive. When can we execute?"

Donovan glanced at his watch, calculating. "We need at least 72 hours to gather all the specialised equipment and brief the teams. I'd say…Thursday night, 02:00 hours. That gives us a cover of darkness and minimal civilian presence."

Amy nodded, her fingers flying over her tablet. "I'll start prepping my team."

Grace pulled up a weather report. "Thursday looks good. Clear skies, new moon. Perfect conditions for the op."

Donovan felt the familiar surge of adrenaline, the pre-mission buzz electrifying his nerves. But this was different. Bigger. More complex than anything they'd tackled before.

"We need more manpower," he said, his voice low and urgent. "This operation is too massive for just our teams."

Grace nodded, her expression grim. "I've been thinking the same. We'll need to bring in officers from Birmingham and Wolverhampton."

Amy's eyes widened. "That's risky. How do we keep it quiet?"

Donovan leaned back, his mind racing. "We use a cover story. A major training exercise. Multi-force collaboration on a fictional scenario."

Grace snapped her fingers. "Brilliant. We can even leak some false details to the press. Make it seem like a routine drill."

"I know just the reporter," Amy added.

Donovan nodded, his mind already racing through the final details. "Alright, let's lock it in. Thursday at 02:00."

He pulled up a satellite image of both locations on the big screen. "We'll need to account for every variable. Amy, what's the status of your team's night vision capabilities?"

Amy tapped her tablet, pulling up an inventory list. "We've got the latest gen-4 goggles. Thermal imaging overlays, heads-up display for team positions. They're good, but we could use a few more."

"I've got a contact at the SAS who can lend us some of their prototypes," Donovan offered. "They're testing some new tech augmented reality overlays, AI-assisted target identification. Might give us an edge."

Grace leaned in, impressed. "That sounds like something out of a sci-fi film, Donovan. Are you sure we can get access to that kind of tech?"

Donovan's eyes gleamed. "Absolutely. My old CO owes me a favour. These goggles are game changers. They can identify heat signatures through walls, highlight potential weapons, even suggest tactical entry points based on structural analysis."

Amy whistled low. "That could give us a massive advantage, especially in the maze-like layout of Drakelow."

"Exactly," Donovan nodded. "And for Witley Court, the AR overlay can highlight potential hiding spots or secret passages based on the building's architecture."

Grace tapped her chin thoughtfully. "What about communications inside the structures? Those thick walls could interfere with our signals."

Donovan's eyes lit up. "I've got just the thing. Remember that quantum encryption tech I mentioned? It comes with a mesh network capability. We can deploy micro-repeaters throughout the buildings as we advance. They're about the size of a coin, stick to any surface, and create a self-healing network. Even if some get destroyed, the others automatically reconfigure to maintain coverage."

Amy leaned forward, intrigued. "That sounds incredible. How do we control them?"

"They're semi-autonomous," Donovan explained, "The control unit uses swarm AI to optimise their placement. As we move, they'll deploy themselves to maintain optimal signal strength. They even have built-in motion sensors to alert us to any movement in cleared areas."

Grace shook her head in amazement. "You never cease to surprise me, Donovan. Anything else up your sleeve?"

"No, Ma'am," Donovan's voice was firm and resolute, "I think that's all we can do in terms of technology. We'll need medics at both locations, but my part is finished."

His fingers tapped against the desk as he spoke, his mind already jumping to the next step. "We have a solid plan, now it's just a matter of executing it. 72 hours from this moment. Let's do this," Donovan declared with determination, "let's finally take out these bastards for good."

Amy and CI Grace nodded in agreement, their expressions mirroring Donovan's fierce determination. This was their chance to end the reign of criminality once and for all, and they were ready to give it their all.

Chapter 43: Witley & Drakelow

00:15. The tension crackled in the air as Donovan surveyed his team. Kevlar vests snug, weapons checked and double-checked. He knelt, adjusting Toby's protective gear.

"Final briefing," Donovan's voice cut through the hum of preparation. "We hit Drakelow at 02:00 sharp. Three entry points. Remember your assigned routes."

Amy confirmed over her radio, her eyes fierce. "My squad is prepped for Whitley. We'll sync our watches at 01:55."

Donovan unrolled a detailed map of Drakelow's labyrinthine tunnels. "Pay attention. These old shafts are treacherous. Team Alpha, your ventilation shaft entry is tight. Watch for unstable sections."

A young officer raised his hand. "Sir, what if comms fail underground?"

"Signal boosters," Donovan replied, tapping his vest. "But if all else fails, fall back to your entry point. No heroics."

The minutes ticked by each second ratcheting up the tension. At 01:30, Donovan's team moved out, vehicles cutting through the night. Toby sat alert beside him; ears pricked.

01:55. Watches synced.

Donovan's voice crackled over the radio, "Go dark. Radio silence until breach."

02:00. "Execute."

Team Charlie slipped into the drainage tunnel with Toby leading the way. Water sloshed around their ankles. Donovan's night vision painted the world in eerie green.

Ahead, a metal grate. Shaped charge in place.

"Fire in the hole," Donovan whispered.

The explosion was muffled, but the grate blew inward. Toby surged forward, nose to the ground. Donovan followed, MP5 at the ready.

The tunnel opened into a vast chamber. Stacks of crates lined the walls. The stench of chemicals hung thick in the air.

A shout. Gunfire erupted. Muzzle flashes lit up the darkness.

"Contact!" Donovan barked into his radio.

He dove behind a crate, bullets whizzing overhead.

Toby growled; hackles raised. Donovan peered around the cover. Three Hell's Angels, automatic weapons blazing.

He popped up and squeezed off two rounds. One biker went down.

More gunfire from the left. Team Alpha had breached. The bikers were caught in a crossfire.

"Vault!" Donovan shouted. "Secure the vault!"

Donovan sprinted forward, Toby at his heels. Gunfire erupted from a side passage. He dove, rolling behind a stack of pallets. Bullets splintered wood inches from his head.

"Team Bravo, status!" he barked into his radio.

Static crackled. Then:

"Heavy resistance at the north entrance. We're pinned down!"

Donovan gritted his teeth. "Hold position. We're coming to you."

He signalled to two officers. "Cover me."

Donovan burst from cover, Toby leading the charge. The lab rushed past in a blur of green night vision. Chemical fumes burned his nostrils.

A biker loomed, swinging a crowbar. Donovan dropped and swept the man's legs. As he fell, Donovan's elbow found his temple. The biker went limp.

They rounded a corner, bullets ricocheting off the concrete. Donovan spotted Team Bravo pinned down behind overturned tables. He signalled his men to provide covering fire.

"Flashbang out!" Donovan yelled, lobbing the grenade.

It detonated with a blinding flash.

Toby surged forward, latching onto a stunned biker's arm. Donovan followed, dropping two more with precise shots.

"Push to the vault!" he ordered.

The team advanced, securing room after room. Drug paraphernalia littered tables. Money counters whirred, forgotten.

A massive steel door loomed ahead. The vault.

"Breaching charge," Donovan commanded.

The explosion rocked the tunnel. As the smoke cleared, Donovan's night vision revealed mountains of cash and drug parcels stacked to the ceiling.

"Clear!"

Donovan surveyed the vault, his mind racing. Cash stacks reached nearly to the ceiling; shrink-wrapped bricks of narcotics filled industrial shelving units. The sheer scale was staggering.

"Secure and catalogue everything," he ordered his team. "By the book. I want every gram accounted for."

As his officers got to work, Donovan tapped his radio, "Campbell, report. What's your status at Whitley?"

Static crackled. Then Amy's voice, breathless but steady:

"Donovan, you won't believe this. We've breached both main chambers. It's a goddamn labyrinth down here."

Gunfire echoed in the background.

Donovan tensed. "Casualties?"

"Negative," Amy replied. "But heavy resistance. These guys aren't going down easy."

Donovan paced; frustration etched on his face. "Hold your position and regroup, I can't send backup at the moment."

"Understood," Amy's voice crackled. "We've got this. Campbell out."

Toby's low growl drew Donovan's attention. The dog's ears were pricked, nose twitching.

"What is it, boy?"

Toby padded towards a far corner of the vault, sniffing intently at the wall. Donovan followed, running his hand along the rough concrete.

There. A faint seam.

"Over here!" he called to his team. "There's something behind this wall."

They worked quickly, using small charges to blow the hidden door. As the dust settled, Donovan's night vision revealed a small, secret chamber.

A figure emerged from the shadows; hands raised.

Donovan's blood ran cold. The face staring back at him was one he knew all too well, but he must be a ghost.

"Commissioner Hamilton?" Donovan's voice was barely a whisper.

The man they'd all believed dead stood before them, very much alive. His eyes darted nervously between Donovan and the armed officers.

"Lower your weapons," Donovan ordered, not taking his eyes off Hamilton. "Sir, we…we thought you were dead. Your suicide—"

Hamilton's laugh was bitter. "Faked. Had to disappear. Things got…complicated."

Toby growled, sensing the tension. Donovan's mind raced. If Hamilton was here, in a secret room connected to a drug vault—

"You're involved in all this," Donovan stated flatly.

Hamilton's shoulders sagged. "It wasn't supposed to go this far. I just needed to pay off some debts. Then, it spiralled out of control."

"You're under arrest, Sir."

As he moved to cuff Hamilton, a deafening explosion rocked the tunnel. The ground shook violently.

"What the hell?" Donovan steadied himself against the wall.

His radio crackled to life:

"Sir! The main tunnel is collapsing! We need to evacuate now!"

Donovan grabbed Hamilton's arm. "Move! Everyone out!"

They raced through the crumbling passageways, dodging falling debris. Toby led the way, navigating through the chaos.

Another explosion. Part of the ceiling caved in ahead of them.

"This way!" Donovan shouted, veering down a side tunnel.

Water was rising fast, flooding in from somewhere. They splashed through ankle-deep, then knee-deep water. It surged, now waist-deep and rising fast. Donovan pushed forward, dragging Hamilton along, Toby swimming beside them. The tunnel groaned ominously, dust and small rocks raining down.

"There!" an officer shouted, pointing to a maintenance ladder barely visible in the murky water.

Donovan shoved Hamilton towards it. "Climb! Now!"

As the others scrambled up the rungs, Donovan swept the area with his night vision, ensuring no one was left behind. Toby paddled anxiously at his side, whining.

"Go on, boy," Donovan urged, giving Toby a boost onto the ladder.

A deafening crack split the air. Donovan looked up to see a massive slab of concrete falling directly towards him. He dove, narrowly avoiding being crushed.

But as he surfaced, gasping for air, a sharp crack echoed through the tunnel. White-hot pain exploded in Donovan's left arm. He'd been shot.

"Sniper!" he shouted, voice raw.

The water churned around him as he struggled to stay afloat. Blood seeped from the wound, turning the murky flood a sickening crimson. Donovan gritted his teeth, fighting to keep his head above water.

Toby yelped, leaping from the ladder back into the surging current. The loyal dog paddled furiously towards his injured master, whining with concern.

"No, Toby! Get back!" Donovan ordered, but the Labrador ignored him.

Another shot rang out, the bullet whizzing past Donovan's ear. He couldn't see the shooter in the chaos of the collapsing tunnel. Debris rained down, churning the rising water into a frothy maelstrom.

Toby paddled closer, his chocolate fur slick and dark in the murky flood. Donovan reached out with his good arm, fingers grazing the dog's Kevlar vest.

The deafening sound of a third gunshot pierced through the air, ripping Donovan's heart in two as he watched in slow motion. With eyes wide and filled with horror, he saw the bullet strike Toby directly in the chest, lifting the beloved dog half out of the water before plummeting back down.

A gut-wrenching cry escaped from Donovan's lips, echoing off the crumbling walls that seemed to mock his despair. But Toby didn't yelp, didn't sink into the depths of the murky water. Instead, the fiercely loyal Labrador shook his head in confusion, refusing to give up as he continued to swim towards his master against all odds.

Donovan's heart raced as he realised Toby's Kevlar vest had saved him. Relief flooded through him, giving him a surge of adrenaline. He grabbed Toby's vest, using it to stay afloat.

"Good boy," he whispered, his voice hoarse.

Another shot rang out. Donovan ducked, pulling Toby close. He scanned the darkness, searching for the shooter.

There. A faint glint of metal in the shadows.

Donovan drew his sidearm, steadying himself against Toby. He took a deep breath, ignoring the searing pain in his arm. Time seemed to slow.

Two rapid shots. The sniper's rifle clattered to the ground.

"Clear!" Donovan shouted.

"Boss!" A voice called from above. "Rope is coming down!"

A thick cord splashed into the water beside them. Donovan gripped it with his good arm, wrapping it around Toby's vest.

"Pull him up first!" he shouted.

Toby whined, reluctant to leave his master. But strong hands hauled the dog to safety.

The rope came down again. Donovan's arm screamed in protest as he was lifted from the churning water. He gritted his teeth, fighting to stay conscious.

Fresh air hit his face as he emerged from the tunnel. His team pulled him onto solid ground. Toby was there instantly, licking his face.

"Sir, we need to move," an officer urged. "The whole complex is unstable."

Donovan struggled to his feet, leaning heavily on a nearby wall. "Hamilton?"

"Secured, Sir. Along with all the evidence we could salvage."

Donovan staggered forward, his team supporting him as they rushed to evacuate the collapsing tunnels. The ground shook beneath their feet, a deep rumbling echoing through the caverns. They emerged into the cool night air, sirens wailing in the distance.

As medics swarmed around him, Donovan's radio crackled to life. Amy's voice cut through the chaos, breathless but triumphant:

"Donovan, do you copy? We've secured Whitley Court. You won't believe what we found."

He winced as a paramedic tended to his wounded arm. "Go ahead, Campbell. What's your status?"

"We've got the strongboxes," Amy reported, her voice tinged with excitement. "Six of them, heavy as hell. We had to fight our way through a small army to get them, but it was worth it."

Donovan's face fell as he surveyed the collapsed entrance to Drakelow Tunnels. Clouds of dust still billowed from the rubble, obscuring the flashing lights of emergency vehicles. The ground rumbled ominously.

"How much did we lose?" he asked, his voice hoarse.

Officer Jensen shook his head grimly. "Most of it, Sir. When that last section caved in, it took nearly everything with it. The vault is buried under tons of rock now."

Donovan closed his eyes, picturing the mountains of cash and drugs now entombed in the earth. All of the planning, countless man-hours, all that evidence—gone.

But as he looked at Karl Hamilton, handcuffed and flanked by two officers, a glimmer of hope sparked in Donovan's chest.

"We didn't lose everything," he said, his voice gaining Donovan pressed the radio to his ear, wincing as the movement jostled his injured arm. "Campbell, listen carefully. We've got a situation here you need to know about."

He paused, glancing at Hamilton's defeated form. The former commissioner's eyes were downcast, his shoulders slumped.

"We found Karl Hamilton. Alive."

The radio crackled with static. Then, Amy's voice, incredulous:

"What? Hamilton? But…how?"

Donovan recounted the discovery in the hidden chamber, his words tumbling out in a rush. He described Hamilton's faked suicide, the secret room connected to the drug vault, and the implications of his involvement.

"Jesus," Amy breathed. "The commissioner? In on all this?"

"It gets worse," Donovan continued. "The tunnel is collapsed. We lost most of the evidence. But we've got Hamilton. And those strongboxes you recovered might be our saving grace."

Donovan's mind raced, piecing together the bigger picture. "Campbell, I need you to secure those boxes. Use every precaution. If Hamilton was involved, there's no telling how deep this goes or who else might be implicated."

"Understood," Amy replied, her voice steely with determination. "I'll have them under 24-hour guard until we can crack them open."

Donovan ended the call, his gaze sweeping over the chaotic scene. Paramedics bustled around, tending to injured officers. The rumble of heavy machinery grew louder as rescue teams prepared to clear the tunnel entrance.

He knelt beside Toby, running his hand through the dog's damp fur. "You saved my life in there, boy," he murmured.

A commotion near the perimeter caught his attention. Donovan squinted through the swirling dust and flashing lights. A sleek black SUV had pulled up, its tinted windows gleaming ominously in the night.

The rear door swung open. A tall figure emerged his crisp suit a stark contrast to the muddy, battered officers around him.

Donovan's stomach dropped. He recognised that silhouette.

"Chief Superintendent," he muttered under his breath.

The man strode decisively towards them, his face a mask of barely contained fury. As he drew closer, his eyes locked onto Hamilton's hunched form.

"What in God's name is going on here, Donovan?" he demanded, his voice cutting through the chaos.

Donovan straightened, ignoring the throb in his arm. "Sir, we've uncovered a major conspiracy. Commissioner Hamilton—"

"I can see that," Chief Superintendent snapped, cutting Donovan off. His eyes narrowed as he took in Hamilton's dishevelled appearance. "Explain. Now."

Donovan squared his shoulders, meeting his superior's gaze unflinchingly. "Sir, we raided Drakelow Tunnels as planned. We found a massive drug operation, along with—"

He gestured towards Hamilton. "Commissioner. In a hidden chamber connected to the vault."

Chief's face paled visibly. "Impossible," he whispered.

Hamilton looked up, his eyes hollow. "It's true, Richard. I'm sorry."

Donovan's instincts prickled at the familiar use of the chief's first name. He filed that information away for later.

"The tunnels collapsed during extraction," Donovan continued. "We lost most of the physical evidence, but we—"

Chief Superintendent's face—contorted with rage, his finger jabbing accusingly at Donovan. "You've jeopardised everything! Years of work trying to break this OCG—gone!"

Before Donovan could respond, the screech of tyres cut through the night. A sleek, midnight-blue Audi A4 skidded to a halt at the perimeter, kicking up a cloud of dust. The driver's door flew open.

Chief Inspector Victoria Grace emerged, her blonde hair gleaming under the emergency lights. She strode purposefully towards the group.

"Stand down, Richard," she called out, her voice sharp as a whip crack.

Chief Superintendent spun to face her. "Victoria? What are you doing here?"

"Saving my best officers from your misplaced wrath," she replied coolly, coming to stand beside CI Grace stood tall, her eyes sweeping over the chaotic scene.

She placed a steadying hand on Donovan's shoulder, her gaze never leaving the chief superintendent's face.

"Richard," she began, her voice low and controlled, "what you're witnessing here is the culmination of a deep-cover operation."

Chief Superintendent's brow furrowed. "What are you talking about? I wasn't informed of any—"

"Precisely," CI Grace cut him off. "You weren't informed because we couldn't risk it. The corruption runs deeper than you can imagine."

She gestured towards Hamilton, who seemed to shrink under her gaze. "Karl here isn't just a dirty citizen. He is a lynchpin in a network that stretches across multiple agencies, private sectors, even into the halls of the parliament."

CI Grace's words hung in the air, heavy with implications. She took a step forward, her presence commanding attention despite the chaos surrounding them.

"For the past few weeks," she continued, her voice dropping to a near whisper, "we've been running a shadow operation. Its tentacles reach into every corner of this conspiracy."

Chief Superintendent's face paled. "Impossible. I would have known"

"Would you?" Her eyes flashed. "That's precisely why you were kept in the dark. We couldn't be certain who was compromised."

She reached into her coat, producing a small, encrypted tablet. With a few deft swipes, she pulled up a complex web of connections. Names, dates, bank transactions—all illuminated in a dizzying array of data.

"This," she said, holding up the screen, "is what we've uncovered so far from one of their enforcers who is now in protection."

"We expect to have more evidence from stronghold boxes recovered tonight from our other operation, led by DS Campbell, at Witley Court."

Chief Superintendent staggered back, his face ashen. "My God," he whispered, eyes fixed on the tablet's screen.

CI Grace nodded grimly. "Exactly. The scope of this is unprecedented."

Donovan's mind raced, processing this new information. He glanced at Hamilton, seeing the former commissioner in a new light.

"So, Hamilton's suicide—"

"A carefully orchestrated ploy," CI Grace confirmed. "We needed him to appear compromised to draw out the bigger players."

"Sorry, Donovan. I could not let you in on it."

She turned to Hamilton, her expression softening slightly. "You can stand down now, Karl. You've done your part."

Hamilton's shoulders sagged with visible relief. "Thank God," he muttered. "I wasn't sure how much longer I could keep this up, poor Kate, this will be a shock to her."

Donovan inquired, "So who was the deceased individual found at Karl's residence?"

CI Grace replied, "It was a cadaver, likely an unknown vagrant with a similar body type as Karl."

Chief Superintendent's eyes darted between CI Grace, Hamilton and Donovan. "I don't understand. Why wasn't I informed? I could have helped coordinate—"

"Because we didn't know who to trust," CI Grace cut in sharply. "This conspiracy goes deep, Richard. Very deep."

Donovan stepped forward, wincing as he jostled his injured arm. "Sir, with all due respect, keeping you in the dark was necessary. We couldn't risk tipping off the wrong people."

Chief Superintendent's face flushed red. "Are you implying that I—"

"We're not implying anything," CI Grace interjected smoothly. "We're stating facts. This operation was need-to-know, and you didn't need-to-know Until now."

She turned to Donovan. "Your team's work tonight was crucial. Despite the setbacks, we've made significant progress. The strongboxes from Whitley Court could be the key to unravelling this entire network."

Donovan nodded, his mind forever racing. "Campbell's team is securing them now. We'll need a safe location to analyse the contents."

"Already arranged," CI Grace replied. "A secure facility is standing by. We move everything there within the hour."

Chief Superintendent seemed to deflate, the anger draining from his face. "I...I had no idea," he muttered.

CI Grace's expression softened slightly. "None of us did, at first. That's how insidious this thing is."

She turned back to Donovan. "We need to move quickly. Every minute we delay, gives them a chance to cover their tracks."

Donovan straightened, ignoring the throbbing pain in his arm. "Understood. I'll coordinate with Campbell to get those strongboxes transported immediately."

He tapped his radio, "Campbell, do you copy?"

"Go ahead, Donovan," Amy's voice crackled through.

"We need those strongboxes moved, ASAP. Secure transport is en route to your location. Trust no one outside your immediate team."

"Copy that," Amy replied, her voice tense. "We're locked down tight here. No one is getting near these boxes without going through us first."

CI Grace nodded approvingly. "Good. Now, we need to secure Hamilton and get him to a safe house. His testimony will be crucial."

Chief Superintendent cleared his throat. "I...I can handle that," he offered, his voice subdued.

CI Grace fixed him with a steely gaze. "No, Richard. You won't be handling anything related to this operation moving forward."

"Whose orders?" he demanded, his voice seething with anger.

"A special oversight committee has given approval for these operations," she answered.

Chief Superintendent's face flushed. "Now, see here, Victoria—"

"This isn't up for debate," she cut him off sharply. "Until we can verify everyone's involvement, you're to be considered a potential security risk. For now, you're on administrative leave, effective immediately."

Donovan watched as chief superintendent's shoulders slumped in defeat. The man who had moments ago been bristling with authority now looked small and lost.

"I understand," he muttered, not meeting anyone's eyes.

CI Grace turned to two nearby officers. "Escort the chief superintendent home. He is not to access any police systems or communicate with anyone involved in this investigation. Clear?"

The officers nodded, moving to flank the dejected man.

As they led the chief superintendent away, she turned back to Donovan. "We need to move fast. The collapse of Drakelow Tunnels will alert our targets. They'll be scrambling to cover their tracks."

Donovan nodded grimly. "Agreed. What's our next move?"

Her eyes gleamed with determination. "We follow the money. Those strongboxes from Whitley Court are our best lead. I want you to personally oversee their transport and analysis."

"What about Hamilton?" Donovan asked, glancing at the former commissioner.

"I'll handle his debriefing personally," CI Grace replied. "His information could be the key to unravelling this whole conspiracy."

Donovan's radio crackled to life.

Amy's voice came through, tense and urgent:

"Donovan, we've got a situation here. Multiple vehicles approaching Whitley Court fast. Looks like a small army."

Donovan's blood ran cold. "Hold your position, Campbell. Reinforcements are on the way."

He turned to CI Grace, who was already barking orders into her phone. "I need to get to Whitley Court, now."

She nodded, tossing him a set of keys. "Take my Audi. Go."

Donovan sprinted to the sleek vehicle, Toby hot on his heels, the pain in his arm forgotten after injections of painkiller.

As they peeled out, tyres squealing, he heard Amy's voice again over the radio:

"They're here! Heavy firepower. We're outnumbered."

The Audi's engine roared as Donovan pushed it to its limits. Trees whipped by in a dark blur.

"Hold on, Amy," he muttered through gritted teeth.

Toby whined from the backseat, sensing the tension. Donovan's head filled, calculating distances and angles of approach. Whitley Court loomed ahead, a gothic silhouette against the night sky.

Gunfire erupted, muzzle flashes lighting up the darkness. Donovan killed the headlights, relying on muscle memory to navigate the winding approach.

"Amy, status!" he barked into the radio.

Static crackled, then Amy's voice, breathless:

"Pinned down in the east wing, above ground. They're trying to flank us!"

Donovan spotted the attackers' vehicles; sleek black SUVs, professional grade. This was no ordinary gang. He counted at least six vehicles, meaning they were severely outnumbered.

He slammed on the brakes, skidding to a stop behind a stone wall.

"Toby, stay," he commanded as he leapt out, assault rifle at the ready.

Gunfire intensified from the east wing. Donovan crouched low, using the wall as cover as he assessed the situation. Two SUVs blocked the main entrance. Armed men in tactical gear poured out, moving with military precision.

His radio crackled:

"Donovan! We can't hold them much longer. The strongboxes—" Amy's transmission cut off abruptly.

He had to act fast.

Staying low, he sprinted towards the east wing, using the shadows for cover. The attackers were focused on the main entrance, giving him a slim chance to flank them.

Donovan's breath came in short bursts as he ran. He reached the side of the building, pressing his back against the cool stone.

Gunfire erupted above him, gunfire bouncing off the once ornate walls. Donovan could hear Amy shouting orders to her team.

He peered around the corner. Two men in black tactical gear were setting up a breaching charge on a side wall. Donovan raised his rifle, took a deep breath, and squeezed the trigger twice.

Both men dropped. The breaching charge clattered to the ground, unused.

Donovan sprinted forward, scooping up the charge. He slapped it onto a wall and detonated it, blasting his way ahead.

Smoke billowed as he charged through, rifle at the ready. Two more attackers spun towards him, caught off guard. Donovan dropped them with precise shots before they could raise their weapons.

"Amy!" he shouted over the din of gunfire. "Where are you?"

"East side!" her voice called back. "In the old corridor!"

Donovan ran, adrenaline helping to mask the pain in his arm. As he reached the burnt-out east wing, a hail of bullets forced him to dive for cover behind an overturned column.

He could see Amy and her team at the end of the hall, pinned down behind makeshift barricades made of rubble. Between them stood four heavily armed assailants, focused on Amy's position Donovan's thoughts raced, assessing the situation in a heartbeat. The four assailants had their backs to him, focused entirely on Amy's position. He had the element of surprise, but he was outnumbered and outgunned.

Time seemed to slow as Donovan formulated his plan. He reached into his tactical vest, fingers closing around a flashbang grenade. With practised precision, he pulled the pin and lobbed it down the corridor.

"Eyes!" he shouted, hoping Amy's team would understand.

The grenade detonated with a blinding flash and deafening bang. The assailants staggered, disoriented. Donovan seized his moment.

He vaulted over the fallen column, rifle raised. Two quick bursts dropped the first two attackers before they could regain their bearings. The third managed to swing his weapon around, but Donovan's instincts took over; his body moving with precision honed by years of military training.

As the third attacker swung his weapon around, Donovan dropped into a crouch, the bullet whistling harmlessly overhead. In one smooth motion, he swept the assailant's legs out from under him.

The man crashed to the ground, his rifle clattering across the debris-strewn floor. Donovan pounced, driving his elbow into the attacker's solar plexus. The man gasped; the air driven from his lungs.

The fourth assailant, recovering from the flashbang, raised his weapon. But Amy, seizing the opportunity Donovan had created, jumped over her makeshift barricade. She tackled the gunman with a leap, her smaller frame belying her strength as she drove him into the wall.

Donovan spun, his rifle finding its mark as Amy grappled with the last assailant. A single shot rang out and the man slumped to the ground.

"Nice timing," Amy panted, brushing dust from her tactical vest.

"Likewise," Donovan replied, scanning the corridor for any remaining threats. "Status on the strongboxes?"

Amy gestured towards the corner of the building they were defending. "Secured over there. We rigged them with explosives as a last resort."

Donovan nodded grimly. "Let's move them before more company arrives."

They worked swiftly. Amy's team formed a protective perimeter as Donovan and two officers manhandled the heavy strongboxes out of the makeshift safe area. Each box was a small fortune in weight, their contents a mystery that could unravel a vast conspiracy.

As they loaded the last strongbox into the armoured transport vehicle, Donovan's radio crackled to life.

CI Grace's voice cut through the static:

"Donovan, we've secured a route to the safe facility. You'll have air support for the journey."

The rumble of helicopter rotors filled the air, growing louder as a black and white police chopper appeared on the horizon. Donovan nodded to Amy, who climbed into the passenger seat of the transport. He took the wheel, Toby settling in the back, alert and ready.

The convoy set out, cutting through the night like a well-oiled machine. The armoured transport led, flanked by two police cars. Above, the helicopter kept a watchful eye on the road ahead, their powerful searchlights scanning for any potential threats.

Donovan's knuckles were clenched around the steering wheel as they wound down narrow lanes and through small streets.

The convoy moved through narrow country lanes, headlights cutting through the inky darkness. Donovan's eyes darted constantly, scanning for threats. The weight of the strongboxes in the back of the transport seemed to press down on him, a physical reminder of the stakes.

As they approached the outskirts of Stourport-on-Severn, the landscape began to change. Fields gave way to industrial buildings, looming silent and watchful in the night. The Foley Park Industrial Estate materialised like a fortress; its high fences topped with razor wire glinting in the moonlight.

The facility itself was unremarkable at first glance—a nondescript warehouse among many. But as they drew closer, Donovan noted the subtle signs of heavy security. Cameras swivelled silently, tracking their approach. Armed guards patrolled the perimeter, their movements precise and vigilant.

At the gate, a heavily armoured checkpoint loomed. Donovan slowed the transport to a crawl, his nerves on edge as armed guards approached. One of them, a stone-faced woman with piercing green eyes, scrutinised their credentials with painstaking thoroughness.

"Clearance code?" she demanded, her voice sharp as a razor.

Donovan recited the complex alphanumeric sequence CI Grace had texted him. For a heart-stopping moment, silence reigned. Then, with a nod, the guard stepped back.

"Proceed to Bay 3."

The massive gate groaned open, revealing in-depth security measures beyond. Retinal scanners, biometric locks, and what looked like a small army of guards awaited them. Donovan guided the transport through, hyper-aware of every bump and turn.

Inside the cavernous warehouse, the true nature of the facility revealed itself. What appeared unremarkable from the outside was a marvel of technology within. Donovan guided the transport to Bay 3, a reinforced concrete platform illuminated by harsh, clinical lighting.

As they came to a stop, a team of technicians in white lab coats swarmed the vehicle. They moved with practised efficiency, attaching sensors and scanners to the strongboxes before carefully unloading them onto waiting for trolleys.

Donovan and Amy watched as each box was whisked away through a series of doors, disappearing into the bowels of the facility. The process was meticulous, each box was treated as if it contained volatile explosives rather than documents and evidence

"Impressive setup," Amy murmured, her eyes wide as she took in the surroundings.

Donovan nodded, noting the layers of security surrounding them. "Let's hope it's enough to keep this evidence safe."

As the last strongbox disappeared into the facility's inner sanctum, CI Grace approached, her face lined with exhaustion but her eyes sharp.

"Excellent work, both of you," she said. "The contents of those boxes could blow this whole case wide open. Our team will work through the night to analyse everything."

She paused, taking in their battered appearances. "You two look dead on your feet. Go home, and get some rest. We'll reconvene for a full debrief at 13:00 hours."

Donovan felt the adrenaline that had been sustaining him begin to ebb away, replaced by bone-deep weariness.

He nodded gratefully. "Yes, Ma'am."

As they exited the facility, the first hints of dawn were beginning to paint the sky in soft hues of pink and gold. Donovan felt the weight of the night's events settle heavily on his shoulders. CI Grace offered to take Donovan and Amy home; Donovan was the first drop. He climbed into the Audi, Toby jumping into the back seat with a weary huff between him and Amy.

The drive home was a blur of empty roads and sleepy towns just beginning to stir. Donovan's mind raced, replaying the night's events, but his body ached for rest. As they pulled up near his modest apartment in Bewdley, the sun was peeking over the horizon, bathing everything in a warm, golden light.

Donovan fumbled with his keys, his injured arm protesting the movement. Inside, the familiar scents of home: old books, leather, and the lingering aroma of last night's dinner—a curry from the local takeaway.

He stumbled into his apartment, the weight of exhaustion settling heavily on his shoulders. He fumbled for his phone, wincing as the movement jostled his injured arm. His fingers danced across the screen, tapping out a quick message to Jess:

Safe home. Long night. Will call later. Love you, XX.

He hit send, then knelt beside Toby, who was looking up at him with worried brown eyes. Donovan ran his hand through the dog's soft fur, scratching behind his ears.

"You were amazing tonight, boy," he murmured, his voice rough with fatigue. "Saved my life back there in the tunnels. Best partner a man could ask for."

Donovan inspected the hole in Toby's bulletproof vest. "Money well spent," he mused, trying to imagine the severity of the situation if Toby hadn't been wearing it.

Toby's tail thumped against the floor, his whole body wiggling with joy at the praise. Donovan smiled, feeling some of the tension from the night's events start to Donovan stood, his muscles protesting every movement. He shuffled towards the bathroom, Toby padding loyally behind him. The shower beckoned, promising to wash away the grime and tension of the night.

He turned the water on, adjusting the temperature until steam began to fill the small space. As he peeled off his tactical gear, wincing at the sight of dried blood on his arm, Donovan caught a glimpse of himself in the mirror. Dark circles shadowed his eyes, and a day's worth of stubble peppered his jawline.

He wrapped plastic film around his injured arm in an effort to protect it from getting wet, then stepping under the hot spray, Donovan let out a long, weary sigh. The water cascaded over his battered body, soothing aches he hadn't even realised were there. He watched as rivulets of dirt and blood swirled down the drain, carrying away the physical remnants of the night's chaos.

As he lathered and rinsed, Donovan's mind drifted, replaying the night's events in a hazy, dreamlike sequence. The thunderous collapse of Drakelow Tunnels, the fierce gunfight at Whitley Court, the revelation of Hamilton's true role—it all swirled together in a kaleidoscope of adrenaline-fuelled memories.

Stepping out of the shower, Donovan dried off gingerly, careful of his injured arm. He slipped into a pair of soft flannel pyjama bottoms and an old, faded t-shirt that smelled of home and comfort. The familiar scents and textures helped ground him, pulling him back from the edge of exhaustion-induced delirium.

Toby waited patiently by the bedroom door, his tail wagging slowly as Donovan emerged from the bathroom.

Donovan shuffled towards his bedroom, Toby padding softly beside him. The room was bathed in a warm, golden glow as sunlight filtered through the half-drawn curtains. His queen-sized bed, with its rumpled navy-blue quilt and plush pillows, looked like an oasis of comfort.

He sank onto the edge of the mattress, feeling the familiar give of memory foam beneath him. Toby hopped up, circling three times before settling at the foot of the bed, his chocolate fur a stark contrast against the dark bedding.

Donovan reached for his phone on the nightstand, squinting at the screen. A message from Jess blinked back at him:

Glad you're safe. Sleep well, hero. Call me when you wake up. Love you too.

A small smile tugged at his lips as he set the phone down and ease Donovan eased himself back onto the pillows, his body sinking gratefully into the soft embrace of the mattress. He pulled the navy quilt up to his chest, its familiar weight a comforting presence. Toby shifted, inching closer until his warm body pressed against Donovan's side.

The room was quiet, save for Toby's soft, rhythmic breathing. The faint scent of lavender from the sachet Jess had placed in his drawer mingled with the earthy aroma of Toby's fur.

Donovan's eyes grew heavy as the night's events replayed in his mind, fading like a distant dream. The deafening crash of the tunnels felt far away now. He closed his eyes and let himself drift into sleep, hoping for peaceful dreams.

Chapter 44: The Bosses

Simon blinked as the harsh sunlight assaulted his eyes. The bustling streets of Birmingham stretched before him, a cacophony of noise and motion. His heart raced, a sickening cocktail of fear and anticipation churning in his gut.

His phone vibrated. With trembling fingers, he pulled it from his pocket and stared at the screen. Unknown number:

Meet at the Vaults. 9 pm. Come alone.

The message seared into his brain. The OCG bosses. Summoning him already, mere hours after his release. No chance to breathe, to think.

He clenched his jaw, shoving the phone back into his pocket. Sweat beaded on his forehead despite the cool air. Passersby jostled him as they hurried about their lives, blissfully unaware of the darkness awaiting him.

Simon sucked in a breath and started walking, letting the flow of the crowd propel him forward. The meeting place was across town. He had hours to kill, and too many thoughts crowding his mind.

A lifetime in prison. A lifetime to plan, to stew in his anger and resentment. And for what? To jump right back in, indebted to the very men who left him to rot?

He had no choice. The alternative was a swift death in a back alley. The OCG didn't tolerate loose ends. Simon was many things, but he wasn't ready to die. Not yet.

His feet carried him through the city centre, past shops and cafes, mothers with prams and businessmen barking into cell phones. The world kept spinning, oblivious to the cancer metastasising in its underbelly.

He sat for a while with a coffee, looking out of a large plate glass window, watching the world pass him by. Taking multiple refills to pass the time.

As the sun began its descent, Simon found himself across from the Vaults. Decrepit and dark, the old bar loomed like a black hole, ready to swallow him whole. He hesitated only a moment before squaring his shoulders and crossing the street.

The bosses were waiting, and he had debts to pay.

Simon slipped into the shadowy alleyways, his footsteps echoing against the damp cobblestones, leading him deeper into the heart of the city's underbelly. His senses were on high alert, every flicker of movement catching his eye, every distant sound making his muscles tense.

He moved swiftly, his head down, hands shoved deep into the pockets of his worn leather jacket. The weight of the past pressed down on him, memories of his time behind bars threatening to suffocate him. But he pushed them aside, focusing on the task at hand.

The alleyway narrowed, the buildings looming higher, blotting out the fading daylight. Shadows danced along the walls, their shapes distorted and menacing. Simon's heart raced, adrenaline pumping through his veins. He knew the dangers that lurked in these forgotten corners of the city. The desperate souls who would do anything to survive.

A sudden clatter behind him made Simon whirl around, his fists clenched, ready for a fight. But there was nothing there, just a stray cat darting into the darkness. He let out a shaky breath, cursing himself for his jumpiness.

Finally, he reached his destination. The entrance to the underground bar was hidden beneath a nondescript building, its façade crumbling and unremarkable. Simon paused, his hand resting on the rusted metal door. He could feel the thrumming of music reverberating through the ground, the muffled sounds of laughter and clinking glasses.

He steeled himself, pushing away the fear that threatened to consume him. This was it. No turning back now. With a deep breath, Simon yanked open the door and descended into the dimly lit depths, ready to face whatever awaited him.

The bar was a world unto itself, a seedy haven for the city's criminal underworld. The air was thick with the stench of cigarette smoke and stale beer, the walls adorned with peeling posters and flickering neon signs. Simon scanned the room, his eyes adjusting to the low light. Patrons hunched over their drinks, their faces obscured by shadows, their conversations hushed and furtive.

He made his way to the bar, his shoulders hunched, his gaze fixed straight ahead. The bartender, a grizzled man with a scar running down his cheek, barely glanced up as Simon approached.

"I'm here to see the bosses," Simon said, his voice low and steady.

The bartender jerked his head towards a door at the back of the room, hidden behind a tattered curtain. Simon nodded, tossing a crumpled five-pound note onto the bar for the bartender's trouble. He weaved his way through the crowd, ignoring the curious glances and whispered speculations.

As he reached the curtain, Simon paused, his hand hovering over the fabric. Behind that door lay his fate, the path he had chosen. There was no going back, no second chances. He drew in a deep breath, steeling himself for whatever lay ahead.

With a final glance over his shoulder, Simon pushed aside the curtain and stepped into the unknown, ready to face the top dogs of the criminal underworld.

Simon stepped into the dimly lit backroom, and the air is thick with the acrid smell of cigar smoke. A single overhead light cast an eerie glow, illuminating a secluded booth in the far corner. There, the OCG bosses lounged, their eyes glinting with a dangerous mix of power and menace.

Shadows danced across their faces, obscuring their features, but Simon could feel the weight of their gaze upon him. His palms grew slick with sweat, his heart pounding against his ribs like a caged animal desperate for escape.

He approached the booth, each step feeling like a mile. The bosses watched him, their expressions unreadable, their postures relaxed yet coiled with latent aggression.

"Simon," the one in the middle spoke, his voice low and gravelly. "Take a seat."

It was not a request, but a command. Simon obeyed, sliding into the booth, the cracked leather creaking beneath him. He clasped his hands together, willing them to stop trembling.

The boss to the left, a woman with a razor-sharp bob and eyes like chips of ice, leaned forward. "We've heard things about you, Simon. Good things."

Simon swallowed hard, his mouth dry. "I'm here to prove myself."

The boss on the right, a man with a jagged scar bisecting his eyebrow, chuckled. "Prove yourself, huh? We'll see about that."

The middle boss, clearly the leader, studied Simon intently. "You're fresh out of prison. You've got a lot to learn, a lot to prove."

"But you did good, you did your bit of time and didn't grass, and we like that about you," he continued.

"Thanks, for getting me out so quickly," Simon responded.

"Just one of the benefits of having a crooked judge in your pocket," the leader said, a smile crossing his face.

Simon met his gaze, a flicker of defiance sparking within him. "I'm a quick study."

The woman smirked. "We'll put that to the test."

The leader leaned back, his fingers steepled. "We've got big plans, Simon. Plans that require loyalty, discretion, and a certain…ruthlessness."

Simon's mind raced, the implications of those words sinking in. He knew he was stepping into a world of shadows. A world where the lines between right and wrong blurred into nothingness.

But he had no choice. This was his path now, his only chance at survival. He nodded, his jaw set with determination.

"I'm in," he said, his voice steady. "Whatever it takes."

The bosses exchanged glances, a silent communication passing between them. The leaders' lips curled into a smile, but it held no warmth.

"Welcome to the family, Simon," he said, his words laced with a chilling finality. "Let's get down to business."

The leader leaned forward, his elbows resting on the table. "We're expanding our operations, Simon. Bigger risks, bigger rewards."

Simon listened intently, his heart pounding in his chest.

The woman chimed in, her eyes glinting. "We're branching out, diversifying our portfolio."

Simon's mind raced, trying to keep up with the implications.

The scarred man grinned, a predatory edge to his smile. "People smuggling, Simon. That's where the real money is."

Simon felt a chill run down his spine. He knew the depths of human depravity, but this…this was a whole new level.

"Felixstowe docks," the leader explained, his fingers tracing invisible lines on the table. "Our gateway to the world. We've got contacts, routes, everything in place."

Simon's thoughts whirled, the magnitude of their plans sinking in. He was no stranger to crime, but the scale of their ambitions was staggering.

"It's a well-oiled machine," the woman said, her voice tinged with pride. "We've got it all figured out. The logistics…the bribes…the manpower."

Simon's palms were slick with sweat. He knew he was in deep; too deep to back out now.

The leader fixed Simon with a piercing stare. "And that's where you come in, Simon. You're our eyes and ears on the ground. Our enforcer, our problem solver."

Simon met his gaze, a flicker of determination burning within him. He knew he was walking a tightrope, balancing between survival and damnation.

But he had no choice. This was his life now, his destiny.

"I'm ready," he said, his voice steady. "Just point me in the right direction."

The bosses exchanged nods, a silent agreement sealing Simon's fate.

"Welcome to the business, Simon," the leader said, his words carrying the weight of a death sentence. "Let's get to work."

The bosses leaned forward, their eyes boring into Simon's soul. "We need fresh ideas, Simon. Ways to expand our empire, tighten our grip on things."

Simon's mind raced the adrenaline pumping. He knew his next words could make or break him.

"The docks are just the beginning," he said, his voice measured. "We need to think bigger. Diversify."

The leader raised an eyebrow. "Go on."

Simon licked his lips, his thoughts crystallising. "We've got the drugs, the smuggling. But what about protection rackets? Extortion? Every business in town should be paying us money, it's old school but it will work."

The bosses exchanged glances, a flicker of intrigue in their eyes.

"And how would we make that happen?" the woman asked, her tone challenging.

Simon leaned back, a slow smile spreading across his face. "We start small. Take over the local gangs, and absorb their territory. Then, we move on to the legitimate businesses. Restaurants, nightclubs, construction firms. We make them an offer they can't refuse."

The leader nodded, a glimmer of respect in his eyes. "You've got vision, Simon. I like that."

Simon's heart pounded, a mix of fear and exhilaration coursing through him. He was playing a dangerous game, but he knew he had to keep pushing forward.

"We can't stop there," he continued, his words gaining momentum. "We need to infiltrate more, the police, the politicians. Have them in our pocket. Control things from the shadows."

The bosses were silent for a moment, the weight of Simon's words hanging in the air. Then, slowly, they began to nod.

"You're thinking like a true player, Simon," the leader said, his voice filled with approval. "Keep this up, and you'll go far in this business."

Simon felt a rush of pride, tempered by the icy realisation of what he was becoming. He was no longer just a pawn in their game. He was a strategist, a mastermind.

And he knew there was no turning back.

The woman leaned forward, her eyes glinting in the dim light. "Speaking of business, let's talk about our little venture into people smuggling."

Simon's heart skipped a beat. He'd heard whispers of this before. He had hoped Detective Donovan would have taken the bait to bargain with him on his last arrest, but that didn't work out that well. He listened intently.

"We've got a sweet setup," she continued, her voice low and conspiratorial. "Bring them in through Felixstowe, hidden in shipping containers. From there, we distribute them across the country. Cheap labour, sex trade, you name it."

Simon's stomach churned. The scale of it—the sheer ruthlessness—was beyond anything he'd ever imagined.

The leader chimed in, his voice filled with perverse pride. "We've got contacts in border control and immigration. They look the other way, for a price."

Simon's mind raced. The implications were staggering. This wasn't just a criminal enterprise. This was a vast network of corruption and exploitation.

"How do you keep them in line?" he asked, almost afraid to hear the answer.

The bosses exchanged a dark look. "Fear," the woman said simply. "They know what happens if they try to run or talk. We make examples of the ones who step out of line."

Simon's blood ran cold. The casual cruelty, the utter lack of humanity. It was chilling.

He forced himself to nod, to maintain his composure. "Smart," he said, his voice sounding hollow to his own ears. "Fear is a powerful motivator."

Inside, his heart was pounding, his mind reeling. What had he gotten himself into? This wasn't just a criminal underworld. This was a realm of pure evil, where human life was just another commodity to be bought and sold.

He looked around the table, at the faces of the men and women who held the fate of so many in their hands. And he realised, with a sinking feeling, that he was now one of them.

The bosses leaned forward, their eyes glinting in the dim light. "Remember, Simon," the leader said, his voice a low growl, "you're part of this now. There's no turning back. No second thoughts."

Simon met their gaze, his jaw clenched. "I understand."

"Do you?" The woman's voice was sharp, cutting through the tense silence. "Because if you don't…if you even think about betraying us—" She let the threat hang in the air, unspoken but undeniable.

Simon's heart hammered in his chest, but he refused to look away. "I know what I signed up for."

"Good." The leader sat back, a cold smile playing on his lips. "Because we have big plans, Simon. And you're going to help us make them happen."

Simon nodded, his mind continued to race, He was in too deep now, his fate inextricably tied to these ruthless criminals. But even as fear coiled in his gut, a flicker of determination sparked to life.

He rose from the booth, his movements deliberate, controlled. "I won't let you down."

The bosses watched him, their expressions unreadable. "See that you don't."

"We will be in touch," the leader remarked, gesturing for Simon to leave.

Simon turned and walked away, his footsteps echoing in the empty bar. The weight of his choices pressed down on him, the gravity of his situation threatening to crush him.

But he couldn't afford to falter now. He had to be strong to play the game. Because in this world, weakness meant death.

As he stepped out into the night, the cool air hit his face, a stark contrast to the suffocating atmosphere of the meeting. Simon inhaled deeply, trying to clear his head. He was scared, the fear taking hold of him, making him throw up in the alleyway.

He had a role to play now, a path to follow. And he would do whatever it took to survive, to come out on top.

Even if it meant descending into the darkest depths of his own soul.

Simon walked through the shadowy streets of Birmingham, his mind reeling from the encounter with the top dogs. The city's pulse thrummed around him, oblivious to the dark undercurrents that now governed his life. He made his way to the train station, his steps heavy with the burden of his new reality.

As he boarded the train to Kidderminster, Simon slumped into a seat, his eyes staring blankly out the window. The rhythmic clatter of the wheels against the tracks filled his ears, a mocking accompaniment to his troubled thoughts.

Unbidden, memories of Jimi flooded his mind. Years of friendship, laughter and shared struggles are now tainted by the bitter sting of betrayal. Simon clenched his fists. Anger and hurt were warring within him.

How could Jimi have done this? How could he have turned on him, after everything they'd been through?

The pain of losing his only true friend cut deep, a wound that refused to heal. Simon's hands shook, his knuckles turning white with the force of his grip.

He had trusted Jimi and confided in him. And now, that trust lay shattered, as broken as the life he had once known.

The train sped on, carrying Simon further from Birmingham, but the weight of his choices followed him like a relentless shadow. He closed his eyes, trying to shut out the world, but there was no escape from the demons that now haunted him.

As the train pulled into Kidderminster station, Simon stood, his body feeling older than his years. He stepped onto the platform, the cool night air a stark reminder of the chill that had settled in his heart.

He walked through the quiet streets, each step a reminder of the path he had chosen. A path that would lead him deeper into the heart of darkness, into a world where loyalty was a commodity to be bought and sold.

And as he disappeared into the night, Simon knew that there was no turning back. He was a part of the inner sanctum now, bound by the chains of his own desperation.

A prisoner of his own making.

The train rattled beneath Simon's feet as he made his way back to Kidderminster, his mind still reeling from the chilling encounter with the top dogs. He stared out the window, watching the city lights blur into a kaleidoscope of colours, a stark contrast to the darkness that now enveloped his soul.

His thoughts drifted to Jimi, his friend for many years. The one who had betrayed him, who had given his name up to the police. The pain of losing his only friend cut deeper than any knife, a wound that festered with each passing moment.

Simon clenched his fists, his knuckles turning white. How could Jimi have done this to him? After all, they had been through together, all the secrets they had shared, all the times they had each other's backs.

"Loyalty," Simon muttered under his breath, the word tasting bitter on his tongue. "What a fucking joke."

He thought back to their last conversation, just days before his arrest. Jimi had seemed on edge, his eyes darting nervously, his words stumbling over each other.

"Listen, mate," Jimi had said, his voice trembling. "I need to tell you something. I've gotten myself into some trouble, and I don't know what to do."

Simon had brushed it off and told Jimi they would figure it out together like they always did. But now, he realised, that had been the moment Jimi had chosen to save himself, to throw Simon to the wolves.

The train pulled into Kidderminster station, jolting Simon from his thoughts. He stood up, his legs heavy, his heart even heavier.

As he stepped onto the platform, Simon knew that the old him—the one who had trusted; who had believed in friendship and loyalty—was gone forever. In his place, stood a man forged in the flames of betrayal, tempered by the cold reality of the underworld.

He walked into the night, his footsteps echoing on the empty streets, a lonely figure in a world where trust was a liability.

The only person he could count on was himself.

Chapter 45: The Docks

Donovan's M3 rolled to a stop at the edge of Felixstowe docks, gravel crunching under its weight. He killed the engine, the silence thunderous after the roar. Sea air—briny and cold—rushed in as he opened the door, mingling with adrenaline that surged through his veins.

"Officer Donovan," a voice cut through the darkness.

"Here," his response was crisp, eyes already scanning the cluster of black-clad figures ahead.

"Welcome to the fold," said a sturdy officer with a nod, stepping forward, badge catching a glint from the dock lights.

"Thanks." Donovan's hand clasped the other man's briefly: a warrior's greeting.

"Listen up," the team leader commanded, a circle of operatives tightening around him.

"Team, this is DI Donovan. He is here as an observer and will help us out as a remote pair of hands. He has a history with this crime group so he will be invaluable to us."

"Our window is tight."

"Understood." Donovan's voice was a low thrum, matching the energy that vibrated among them.

"Your eyes, Donovan. That's what we need." The leader's gaze pinned him like a blade. "You watch, you report. Precision is key."

"Got it." His reply was terse, mind already racing through scenarios.

"Speed," another officer interjected, "we take them down before they even blink."

"Speed," Donovan echoed, the word etched into his purpose.

"Alright, let's move out." The leader's command sliced the tension, sending them into a synchronised rhythm of stealth and readiness.

Donovan's pulse hammered, a drumbeat syncing with the hushed footsteps of his companions as they fanned out across the docks. The operation had begun.

Donovan scaled the steel lattice of a towering crane; his movements deliberate and silent. The vantage point—a narrow catwalk high above the docks—afforded him an unobstructed view of the operation's theatre. Below, containers loomed like giants in a concrete jungle; their corrugated bodies casting long shadows under the moon's pale gaze.

He crouched, steadying his breathing, the cold metal beneath him a stark reminder of the night's gravity. Eyes narrowed, Donovan scanned left to right, right to left, the expanse below a chessboard of potential threats and hidden dangers.

"Delta One, in position," he whispered into the comms, his voice barely louder than the wind that whipped around him.

"Copy, Delta One," came the terse reply, crackling with static.

Below, guards meandered along their designated paths, batons twirling idly in their hands, unsuspecting pawns in a game that had already begun. Their laughter floated up, punctuating the silence, evidence of ease. A false sense of security. Donovan's eyes followed their every move, analysing gaits, and predicting patterns.

"Two targets near the north gate. Casual," he reported, fingers tight on the binoculars that brought the scene into sharp relief.

"Roger, keep us updated," the team leader's focused voice returned.

Through the lens, Donovan watched as one guard paused—a lit cigarette dancing between his lips—the ember a beacon of nonchalance. The second leaned against the cool metal of a container, gaze lost to the sea.

"Stay alert," Donovan muttered to himself, the mantra a tether to the mission at hand.

His heart thrummed a steady beat, each pulse echoing the seconds slipping by. Time was narrowing the window of opportunity. The tension was a living thing, coiling tighter within him, ready to spring.

"Movement," he breathed out as a third figure emerged from the shadows, joining the duo. "Adjustment in patrol pattern. Watch your six."

"Confirmed, adjusting approach," the response was immediate, operatives below shifting like ghosts, unseen but ever-present.

The night air carried the tang of salt and metal, the sensory cocktail of the docks painting a picture even without sight. But Donovan's focus remained laser-etched on the task, the weight of his responsibility grounding him more firmly to his perch.

"Any moment now," he whispered, more to himself than the team, anticipation of a live wire under his skin.

"Standby, Delta One." The command was firm, readiness palpable even through the static.

"Standing by," Donovan affirmed, his body coiled for the signal that would unleash the storm.

The nod was subtle, almost imperceptible, but to Donovan, it rang out like a starting gun. In the space of a heartbeat, the stillness shattered.

"Go."

Muscles tensed and released with military precision as officers surged forward. They were shadows become substance, each step calculated, each breath measured.

"Left side, clear." The voice crackled in his earpiece, a lifeline threading through the chaos.

Donovan's pulse hammered in his throat, adrenaline surging like electricity through his veins. He watched, wide-eyed as the first guard crumpled, an officer's arm coiling around him in a silent, practised takedown.

"Right secure," another whisper, another ghost neutralised without sound or struggle.

His vantage point afforded him a panoramic view of the orchestrated assault. Officers moved in fluid unison. A ballet of violence, so finely tuned, it could have been choreographed.

"Centre down. Area contained."

Donovan exhaled, not realising he'd been holding his breath, his focus never wavering from the scene below. Each guard was met with swift incapacitation—a blur of motion, then stillness.

"Delta One, all threats neutralised."

"Copy that." His response was automatic, his gaze locked on the efficiency below him.

Training had turned these officers into machines of precision, their every move a testament to hours upon hours honed in the art of silent subjugation.

"Perimeter secure," came the final call, a signal that the operation had reached its next critical phase.

But Donovan's attention lingered on the fallen guards, the ease of their defeat both a relief and a warning of the dangers they faced. It was over, for now, yet his heart continued its relentless cadence, ready for whatever came next.

The last guard hit the ground with a thud, his arms secured behind him. Donovan's gaze snapped to the container. Cold metal, silent but for the faint creaks and groans of its structure settling. He knew the weight of what it held, the stifling darkness inside where hope turned desperate.

___ " ___

"Move," he muttered to himself, his feet carrying him to join the group crowding around the padlock.

"Clear out, I've got this," one officer said, the heavy bolt cutters in his hands catching a glint of moonlight.

Donovan stepped back, watching as jaws of steel bit into the lock. The silence was dense, packed with the unspoken thoughts of every man and woman present.

"Come on—" another officer whispered, a mixture of urgency and dread in his voice.

Snap. The lock gave way, clattering onto the concrete. A collective breath held. Hands in black gloves scrambled at the container's lever, muscles straining, faces set in lines of determination.

"Easy," Donovan cautioned, his voice barely above a whisper, eyes fixed on the door, knowing that whatever lay beyond was about to change everything.

"Ready?" the team leader's question hung in the air, met by a series of terse nods.

"Go."

The door creaked open…an inch…two inches—a reluctant reveal. Anticipation crackled through Donovan like static, every nerve ending firing, every sense heightened. He braced for impact, not the physical kind, but the emotional onslaught of reality rushing forth from the shadows of the container.

The door groaned fully open, and a stench rolled out, thick as fog. Donovan recoiled, his hand instinctively rising to shield his nose. The acrid smell of human misery clawed at his senses, the air ripe with the waste of confinement.

"Jesus," he breathed, the word slipping through his fingers.

Inside, dim light revealed huddled shapes. Bodies—too many to count—pressed into corners, limbs intertwined in a grotesque tapestry of survival. Eyes blinked against the sudden intrusion, wide and unseeing in the glare of flashlights that sliced through the gloom.

"Help us," a voice cracked from the darkness, its plea slicing the heavy silence.

Donovan's gaze locked on a young man leaning against the metal wall; his face gaunt, eyes large pools reflecting terror and the faint flicker of hope. Another figure stirred, a woman clutching a tattered shawl around her shoulders, her expression etched with the weariness of a thousand sleepless nights.

"Be calm, we're here to help," Donovan announced, voice steady despite the chaos churning inside him.

His words were a lifeline thrown into turbulent waters, eyes meeting those of the victims, silently promising salvation.

"Stay back," an officer ordered, stepping forward. "Give them space."

One by one, they stirred, movements sluggish. Disbelief etched onto every face as they edged towards the promise of freedom. Hope battled despair in their expressions, each glance a silent story of the journey that had brought them here, to this moment of rescue.

"Water…please—" another voice croaked, weak but urgent.

"Get the medics!" Donovan barked over his shoulder to an officer behind him, his training surging to the forefront, pushing aside the raw emotions threatening to overwhelm him.

"Right away." The response was swift, the team was already in motion.

Donovan watched, heart hammering, as the first of the trafficked souls stumbled free, their liberation unfolding before his eyes. He stood firm like a sentinel amid the turmoil, the gravity of their suffering anchoring him to the spot. This was why he'd joined the force—to make a difference, to be the barrier between order and chaos.

"Easy, easy," he murmured, more to himself than to the emerging figures, the scene unfolding like a slow-motion sequence from a nightmare turned reality.

Each breath they took was a gasp for life, each step a victory over their captors.

"Got you," he whispered, as the first person stepped into his view, a connection forged in the shared intensity of the moment.

"Safe now," he assured, though the words felt inadequate against the backdrop of what these people endured.

But it was a start—a vow that this was the end of their torment and the beginning of something new, something hopeful.

"Move, move!" the command cut through the heavy air, sharp and urgent.

Officers swarmed around the container like a well-oiled machine, their hands deftly working to unshackle the weary prisoners. Donovan's gaze followed every motion, every freed limb. He felt his jaw clench in time with the clicks of unlocked cuffs, the metallic sounds echoing the beat of his racing heart.

"Thank you," a weak voice uttered, its timbre laced with relief.

"Keep walking, head out into the fresh air," an officer directed, her tone gentle yet authoritative.

One by one, they emerged into the cool night, faces upturned to the open sky as if seeing it for the first time. Donovan watched a young woman pause at the threshold, her eyes brimming with tears that reflected the moon's soft glow. A staggered breath escaped the man's lips, a silent thank you that needed no translation.

"Let's give them some space," Donovan said, stepping back, his role as an observer never clearer.

He scanned each face, committing them to memory. These were the faces of resilience, the human spirit triumphant over unspeakable darkness.

"Good work," he muttered under his breath to an officer passing by, the praise feeling trivial but necessary.

"Couldn't have done it without the intel you gave to us, Donovan," she replied, a smile breaking through the tension.

As the last of the victims shuffled past, Donovan's mix of emotions forged into something tangible—a renewed sense of purpose. Relief washed over him like a cleansing tide, and anger simmered below the surface, fuelling a fiery determination. This was more than a successful sting; this was a promise to those who'd suffered—never again, not on his watch.

"Alright, let's secure the area!" His voice carried the weight of authority, of a man ready for whatever fight lay ahead.

As the last lock clicked open and the night reclaimed its silence, Donovan felt a shift beneath his feet. The ground was no longer just concrete and metal—the dock had transformed into a battleground of justice. He took in the scene, the officers' movements settling into routine checks, their radios crackling with confirmations of safety.

"Perimeter secured," one officer announced, voice steady over the radio.

Donovan leaned against a stack of shipping containers, the cool metal grounding him. He watched as medical personnel tended to the victims, wrapping them in blankets, and offering water and solace. Each small act chipped away at the colossal edifice of the OCG's cruelty.

"Hey," an officer called out, his hand resting on Donovan's shoulder. "You, okay?"

"Better than okay," Donovan replied, his gaze unwavering from the unfolding care. "We did good tonight."

"More than good," the officer agreed, nodding towards the victims. "They have a chance now because of this."

"Because of us," Donovan corrected quietly.

His fingers curled into fists, the skin across his knuckles tightening. This was personal. A fire lit within him by every story he'd uncovered and every lead he'd chased down.

The chaos around them dissipated, replaced by ordered activity. It was a lull that allowed Donovan's thoughts to race ahead—beyond tonight, and beyond the flickering blue lights and the sombre faces. There was still work to be done, an organisation to dismantle piece by piece until nothing remained.

"Once we process the evidence, it's only a matter of time," said another officer, joining the conversation, her eyes alight with the same fervour Donovan felt.

"Time isn't on their side anymore," Donovan stated flatly, his voice carrying the weight of certainty. "We've got them on the ropes."

"Damn right we do," she replied, clapping him on the back before moving off to join the others.

Donovan watched her go, the symphony of the docks filling the spaces between his thoughts. The distant sound of waves against the hulls, the murmur of voices, the shuffle of footsteps—it all culminated into a singular moment of clarity.

He turned his attention back to the container, now empty of its human cargo. It stood like a hollowed monument to the lives it had once held captive. Tonight, they had struck a significant blow against the OCG, but it wasn't enough. Not yet.

"Next time," Donovan whispered to himself, his jaw setting firm, "we take them all down."

There was no room for doubt or hesitation. The OCG had thrived in the shadows for too long, believing themselves untouchable. He could almost taste the victory, bitter and sweet as it lingered on the horizon.

"Let's wrap this up!" Donovan commanded, his voice rising above the ambient noise. Every action from here on out was a step closer to the endgame.

"Copy that," came the reply, a chorus of determination echoing through the ranks.

This was more than a single victory; it was a turning point. And Donovan was ready to lead the charge, to chase down the final threads until the tapestry of crime unravelled completely.

The docks buzzed with the aftermath. Donovan's pulse thrummed in his temples, each beat a hammer striking steel, forging resolve. His eyes scanned the horizon where night bled into dawn, a canvas of purples and oranges painting the beginning of the end for the OCG.

"Report," he barked into the radio.

"Containers secured, suspects detained," crackled a voice at the other end. "Waiting on your signal."

"Maintain position. Eyes sharp." Donovan clipped the radio to his belt, senses honed like a blade.

Intelligence had been right, their net tight. Yet this was merely the outer layer of an intricate web woven by the OCG.

He strode toward the makeshift command post, a flurry of activity orbiting him. Officers hunched over screens, fingers dancing across keyboards, collating evidence that would seal the fate of those at the top.

"Status?" Donovan demanded, approaching the lead analyst.

"Decryption in progress. We're close, very close," she replied without looking up, the glow of the computer illuminating her determined face.

"Time is not our ally," he urged with the weight of urgency in his tone.

"Understood."

Donovan turned away, a silent storm brewing within. The pieces were aligning, and the picture was almost complete. With every shred of evidence, they chipped away at the fortress the OCG had built around themselves.

"Boss?"

He glanced back, meeting the gaze of his second-in-command Jacobs, who approached with a brisk step.

"Perimeter is clear. No leaks. And the press is none the wiser."

"Good. Keep it that way," Donovan's reply was curt.

Leaks would not be tolerated; not when they were this close.

"Anything else?" Jacobs probed, reading the tension in Donovan's posture.

"Keep the team on standby. This isn't over. Not by a long shot." Every muscle in Donovan's body was coiled, ready to spring into action at the slightest provocation.

"Copy that. They're prepped and waiting for the green light."

"Once we've broken their code, we hit them hard and fast. No mercy," Donovan stated, his eyes flinty.

"Roger that." Jacobs nodded, a silent acknowledgement of the stakes at hand.

"Let's move out. Time to end this," Donovan said, stepping out from under the canopy of the command post.

The air was sharp with the tang of sea salt and diesel as he marched toward the armoured vehicle, his shadow long on the concrete. This was it—the calm before the final onslaught. The OCG's days were numbered, and Donovan felt the gravity of the moment settle on his shoulders like a mantle.

He slid into the vehicle, the door slamming shut with a definitive thud. A symphony of clicks signalled the readiness of his team, a unit forged in the fires of countless operations.

"Drive," he ordered, his gaze fixing on the rearview mirror where the docks slowly receded from view.

"Where to, Sir?" the driver asked, the engine's growl punctuating the question.

"Headquarters. We regroup, then we bring down the hammer."

"Understood." The tyres squealed against the asphalt as the vehicle surged forward.

Donovan leaned back, steeling himself for what was to come. The final confrontation loomed, a beast in the shadows, but he was no longer the hunted. He was the hunter, and his aim was true.

"Justice is coming," he muttered to himself, the words a vow etched in stone.

And Donovan was ready. Ready to face the beast head-on.

Chapter 46: Who Wins?

Donovan leaned against the wall; arms crossed. His eyes scanned the room, taking in the tense faces of his team.

"Right," he said, his voice cutting through the murmur. "Let's get to it."

"We had a great win down at the docks but, now, it's time to end this, to bring the OCG and its leadership to justice."

CI Grace stepped forward, her face grim. "The diamonds we recovered alone are worth millions. Untraceable. Perfect for their operations."

"And the names?" Amy asked, her pen poised over her notebook.

Donovan scowled. "A bloody who is who of corruption. Goes all the way to the top."

The room fell silent. The implications hung heavy in the air.

"What about the chief super?" Amy asked, her voice low.

Donovan met her gaze. "We do our job. No exceptions."

He pushed off the wall, pacing the room. "We've got one shot at this. Once we hand it over, it's out of our hands. We need to make sure every *i* is dotted and every *t* is crossed."

Amy nodded. "I'll double-check the evidence logs."

"Good," Donovan said. "Jane, I want you to compile a detailed report on the financial connections. Follow the money."

PC Jane nodded, already pulling out her laptop.

"The rest of you, start preparing for the handover. We'll need to coordinate with multiple agencies. It's going to be a logistical nightmare."

As the team dispersed, Donovan felt a familiar tension building in his shoulders. He caught Amy's eye and jerked his head towards the door. She followed him into the hallway.

"What is it?" she asked, her voice low.

Donovan ran a hand through his hair. "Something doesn't feel right. This is too big, too clean. We're missing something."

Amy frowned. "You think there's more to it?"

"I think we need to be careful. Very careful."

A sharp knock interrupted them. DC Thompson poked his head around the door, face pale. "Sir, you need to see this."

Donovan and Amy exchanged glances before following Thompson back into the incident room. The team had gathered around a computer screen, faces tense.

"What is it?" Donovan demanded.

CI Grace stepped aside, revealing a grainy CCTV image. "This just came in. It's from last night, near Witley Court."

Donovan leaned in, squinting at the screen. His blood ran cold.

"That's Simon," he said, voice tight. "What the hell is he doing there?"

Amy peered over his shoulder. "Isn't he supposed to be on remand?"

Donovan speaks up, "It appears that someone released him without notifying us. Do we have any information on his current whereabouts? Can we locate and retrieve him?"

Donovan's eyes narrowed. "Get me everything on Simon's release. Now."

The team sprang into action, fingers flying over keyboards, phones pressed to ears. Amy disappeared, returning minutes later with a stack of files.

"Sir," she said, voice tight. "Simon's release papers. Signed by Judge Hargrove, yesterday morning."

Donovan snatched the file, scanning it quickly. "Insufficient evidence? Bullshit. We had him dead to rights."

CI Grace leaned in. "Hargrove. He is on the list from the memory stick."

The room fell silent, the implications sinking in.

"Right. We move. Now. Before they can clean house," Donovan insists.

He turned to the team. "Amy, take two officers. Go to Simon's last known address. Jane, you're with me."

Donovan and PC Jane raced through the town's streets, sirens blaring in his unmarked car. The late afternoon sun glinted off windshields, momentarily blinding them as they weaved through traffic. Donovan's hands were tight on the steering wheel.

"Any word from Amy?" he asked, eyes never leaving the road.

PC Jane shook her head, phone pressed to her ear. "Nothing yet. Wait—" She listened intently. "Simon's flat was empty. Looks like he cleared out in a hurry."

Donovan cursed under his breath. "Where would he go?"

As if in answer, the radio crackled to life:

"All units, be advised. Suspect Simon Franklin…spotted at Kidderminster station. Approach with caution. Suspect is considered armed and dangerous."

Donovan spun the wheel, tyres screeching as they changed direction. "Tell Amy to meet us there. We can't let him slip away."

They tore through the streets, weaving through traffic with practised precision. Donovan's mind raced, piecing together the puzzle. Simon's unexpected release, the diamonds, the list of names—the OCG had power but were damaged from the previous night's raids.

As they approached Kidderminster station, Donovan spotted Amy's car pulling in from the opposite direction. He screeched to a halt, leaping out before the engine had fully stopped.

"Any sign?" he barked.

Amy shook her head, eyes scanning the crowded platform. "Nothing yet. But the 3:15 to London leaves in five minutes."

Donovan nodded, his training kicking in. "Jane, cover the north exit. Amy, take the south. I'll sweep the platforms."

They split up, moving swiftly through the bustling station. Donovan's eyes darted from face to face, searching for Simon's familiar features. The air was thick with the smell of diesel. An announcement echoed overhead, nearly drowned out by the rumble of approaching trains.

He pushed through a group of tourists, muttering apologies. A flash of movement caught his eye; a man in a dark jacket, head down, moving too quickly. Donovan's pulse quickened.

"Possible visual," he murmured into his radio. "Platform 2, heading north."

The suspect glanced over his shoulder, eyes widening as they met Donovan's. In that instant, Donovan knew.

"Simon!" Donovan shouted, breaking into a sprint.

Simon bolted, shoving passengers aside as he raced down the platform. Donovan pursued, his longer stride eating up the distance between them. The train whistle blew, and doors began to close.

"Stop! Police!" Donovan bellowed.

Simon leapt, trying to squeeze through the narrowing gap. Donovan lunged, tackling him just as the doors slammed shut. They hit the platform hard, rolling in a tangle of limbs.

Simon fought like a cornered animal, landing a solid punch to Donovan's chin. Stars exploded in Donovan's vision, but his training took over. He twisted, using Simon's momentum against him, and slammed him face-first into the concrete.

"Stay down!" Donovan growled, wrenching Simon's arms behind his back.

The platform erupted into chaos. Passengers scattered, shouts and screams filling the air. Donovan kept Simon pinned, his knee pressed firmly into the man's back. Simon writhed and cursed, but Donovan's grip was iron.

"It's over, Simon," Donovan growled, his breath coming in sharp bursts. "Four murders. Did you really think you'd get away with it?"

Simon's struggles weakened; his forehead pressed against the cold concrete. "You don't understand," he wheezed. "They'll kill me if I talk."

Donovan joked, "The OCG is finished. We have more than enough evidence to bring them down and they're not causing any more harm."

Amy appeared, shouldering her way through the gawking crowd. Her eyes widened at the sight of Simon, then narrowed with determination. She pulled out her handcuffs, the metal glinting in the harsh station lights.

"Simon Franklin," she said, her voice steady and official, "you're under arrest."

Donovan hauled Simon to his feet, keeping a firm grip on his arms. The crowd parted as they made their way off the platform, a sea of wide eyes and whispered conversations. Amy led the way, her posture rigid, eyes scanning for any potential problems.

They emerged into the weak afternoon sunlight, the air thick with diesel fumes and the metallic tang of the railway. Simon stumbled, whether, from exhaustion or a last attempt at escape, Donovan couldn't tell. He tightened his grip, feeling the man's rapid pulse beneath his fingers.

"Watch your head," Donovan said gruffly as he manoeuvre Simon into the back of the police car. The door slammed shut with a satisfying thunk.

Amy slid into the driver's seat. The radio crackled with updates and requests for information. Donovan ignored it.

"Bring him back to the station, complete the legal procedures, and put him in a cell. He won't be able to escape this time," Donovan states firmly.

―― " ――

Six months passed in a blur of paperwork, interrogations, and court appearances. Summer faded to winter, the station windows frosting over as Donovan and his team worked tirelessly to build their cases. Spring bloomed, and then summer scorched the pavement outside. Through it all, Donovan pushed forward, driven by the promise of justice.

But as the months wore on, a creeping unease settled in his gut. Whispers and half-truths. Deals made in shadowy corners. The gears of justice grinding far too slowly for his liking.

It was a sweltering August afternoon when CI Grace called him into her office. Donovan knew something was wrong the moment he saw her face.

"Close the door," she said, her voice low.

Donovan complied, then turned to face her. "What is it?"

CI Grace sighed, pushing a file across her desk. "It's not good, Donovan. MI5 has...intervened."

He flipped open the file, scanning the contents. His face darkened with each page.

"This can't be right," he growled. "Half these names are still walking free. Hargrove. Blackwood. Even bloody Carmichael."

Grace nodded, her expression grim. "MI5 claims they're more valuable as assets. Using them for leverage, they say."

Donovan slammed the file shut. "Leverage? They're criminals, not bloody chess pieces!"

He paced the small office. Nearly a year of exhaustion and frustration boiled over. Outside, the world had moved on. But inside these walls, the cases had not.

Donovan stormed out of CI Grace's office, slamming the door behind him. The office fell silent, all eyes turning to him. He ignored them, marching straight to his desk and grabbing his jacket.

"Sir?" Amy called after him. "Where are you going?"

"Out," he growled, not slowing his stride.

The summer heat hit him like a wall as he exited the station. Donovan walked aimlessly, his mind churning. A year's worth of work, of late nights and missed weekends with Jess. Of promises to victims' families. All for what?

He found himself at the River Stour. Its water is sluggish and brown in the August heat. Donovan leaned against the railing, watching a family of ducks paddle by.

His phone buzzed. Amy.

"Yeah?" he answered, his voice gruff.

"Sir, you need to come back,"

Amy's voice was tense. "There's been a development. Simon is talking."

Donovan straightened, suddenly alert. "What's he saying?"

"I can't discuss it over the phone. Just get back here. Now."

The line went dead. Donovan was already moving, pushing through the crowded streets. His mind raced. Simon had been silent for months, refusing to implicate anyone higher up the chain. What had changed?

He burst into the station, ignoring the startled looks from his colleagues. Amy was waiting by the interview rooms, her face pale.

"What is it?" Donovan demanded.

Amy glanced around, then lowered her voice, "He is naming names. Big ones. People we didn't even know were involved."

Donovan expresses surprise, saying, "I never would have thought he had access to that kind of information."

Donovan's pulse quickened. "Why now?"

"Someone tried to kill him in prison last night. He is scared"

Amy hesitated, then continued, "He is scared, and he has realised his so-called friends have abandoned him. He is facing four life sentences, Donovan No deals, no immunity. But we've offered him protection—his own cell in a secure wing."

Donovan nodded, his mind racing. "Let's hear what he has to say."

They entered the interview room. Simon sat hunched at the table, his face pale and drawn. Dark bruises bloomed across his cheekbone, a stark reminder of the previous night's attempt on his life.

"Simon," Donovan said, taking a seat across from him. "I hear you're ready to talk."

Simon's eyes darted around the room as if expecting shadows to leap from the corners. "They tried to kill me," he whispered. "In my own cell. I thought…I thought I was untouchable."

Donovan leaned forward, his voice low and urgent. "You're safe now, Simon. Tell us what you know."

Simon took a shaky breath, his fingers drumming nervously on the table. "It goes deeper than you think. The diamonds, the ledgers—they're just the tip of the iceberg."

Simon's words tumbled out in a frantic rush as if he feared being silenced at any moment. He spoke of offshore accounts hidden in the Cayman Islands, of blackmail material stored in underground vaults, of secret meetings in abandoned warehouses.

Simon's voice dropped to a hoarse whisper, "The chief super…he is not just involved. He is one of those at the centre of it all."

Donovan and Amy exchanged glances, their faces taut with shock.

"Go on," Donovan urged, his pen poised over his notebook.

Donovan spoke up with a frustrated tone. "We are aware of his involvement, but we have been struggling to gather enough evidence to incriminate him."

Simon's words poured out in a torrent. He spoke of midnight meetings in abandoned warehouses; of encrypted messages passed through burner phones; of vast sums of money flowing through a labyrinth of shell companies. The chief superintendent, it seemed, had been orchestrating a complex web of corruption for years.

"There's a safe," Simon said, his eyes darting nervously around the room. "In his office. Behind the painting of the old police station. The combination—" He closed his eyes, brow furrowed in concentration. "4-18-7-22."

Simon's voice dropped to a whisper, "Inside, there's a red leather-bound ledger. Every transaction, every bribe, every dirty deal—it's all in there. Names, dates…amounts. He was meticulous."

Donovan poses the question, "How can we be sure that this is all accurate?"

Simon confidently replies, "After I was released, I performed one final job for them. During my meeting in his office, he personally gave me instructions and I observed everything carefully…memorising the combination."

Donovan leaned forward, his heart racing. "And you've seen this ledger?"

Simon nodded, his eyes haunted. "I saw it. He opened the safe right in front of me and pulled out that red book. It was like he was showing off, you know? Flaunting his power."

Simon's voice dropped to a whisper. "There was a section at the back, handwritten. Blackmail material, I think. Things that would make your skin crawl. He has got half the area in his pocket, and the other is half too scared to breathe."

Donovan and Amy exchanged glances. The weight of this information settled heavily on them.

As the interview came to a close, Simon's lips pressed into a thin line, his gaze unfocused and sombre. He is escorted back to prison, knowing that he will spend the rest of his days behind bars, but secure from reprisals after his deal was made.

Chapter 47: Chief Super

Donovan's boots thumped in measured cadence across the polished floor of the Birmingham police HQ. The rhythm was a silent drumroll, each step echoing through the sterile lobby. Amy matched his pace, her eyes scanning their surroundings with a quiet intensity that belied the storm brewing beneath.

At the reception, Donovan leaned forward. "Detective Inspector Temple and Detective Sergent Campbell," he stated, voice low, devoid of the niceties usually afforded to colleagues.

The receptionist, a woman with red-framed glasses perched on her nose, glanced at them briefly before tapping on her computer. No questions asked. They were familiar faces, no need for explanations. She buzzed them through.

Metal detectors hummed as they stepped through. X-ray machines swallowed their belongings, spitting them out on the other side like a silent judgment. Donovan retrieved his badge and clipped it back onto his belt without breaking stride.

"Stay sharp," he murmured to Amy, though he knew he didn't need to remind her.

Her nod was quick, almost imperceptible.

They turned a corner, the chief superintendent's door in sight. Donovan's knuckles grazed the wood, three firm raps. He felt the weight of the moment settle on his shoulders, a mantle he wore all too often.

"Come in," boomed a voice from inside, laced with the false security of ignorance.

The door swung open, revealing the chief superintendent, ensconced behind his grand desk. He looked up, the lines on his face etching deeper as he smiled.

"Donovan, Amy. What can I do for you?"

"Sorry, to drop in unannounced," Donovan said, stepping inside with deliberate slowness.

Amy followed, closing the door with a soft click that resounded like a cell door sliding shut.

"Unannounced visits often bring interesting news," Chief Superintendent replied, leaning back in his chair. The leather groaned under his weight.

"Indeed," Donovan acknowledged, his gaze locking onto the man who had orchestrated more than just police operations.

"Chief Superintendent, you're under arrest," Donovan declared, the words slicing through the tension like a blade.

The chief superintendent's smile faltered, disbelief etching his features. "This is preposterous," he spat out, rising to his feet with an indignation that failed to mask his alarm. "You can't be serious."

"Deadly serious," Donovan replied, his tone ice as he held the man's gaze.

The air between them crackled with unspoken accusations and denials.

"Your involvement with the OCG ends today," Donovan continued, one hand resting on the cuffs at his belt.

"Accusations require evidence, Detective," Chief Superintendent countered, his voice now a low growl of defiance. "I've dedicated my life to this force!"

"Which made it all the easier to hide in plain sight," Donovan shot back.

The room felt smaller, the walls witness to the tense standoff.

Amy stood by the door, silent, her presence a steady pressure. No need for words. Their shared resolve was spoken in the set of her stance, and the readiness in her facial expression.

"Your dedication was nothing but a cover," Donovan pressed, watching as Chief's composure began to unravel, and strands of control slipped away.

"Arrest me and you'll regret it," Chief Superintendent warned, his threat hanging hollow in the charged atmosphere.

"I will have you up on charges for this," Chief Super insisted.

"Regrets are for those who have a choice," Donovan said.

And with that, he stepped forward, ready to expose the rot at the heart of the institution he swore to protect.

Donovan's gaze flickered briefly to the window, the cityscape beyond a blur of steel and shadow. The image sparked—the Docks; the stench of brine mixed with fear, faces of the trafficked haunted and hollow. He swallowed hard, the memory sharp as glass in his throat. Resolve hardened—this was for them.

"Look at this," Amy's voice cut through the silence, low and urgent.

He turned. Her eyes were fixed on a framed picture on the wall, a photograph of the headquarters, oddly out of place amidst the chief superintendent's commendations and accolades. Donovan stepped closer, squinting at the edges where dust had not settled—an anomaly in the otherwise meticulous office.

"Out of the way," he muttered, fingers probing the frame, feeling for the telltale click of a mechanism.

A soft snap, and the picture swung open like a door long waiting to be unlocked.

"Gotcha," Donovan breathed, peering into the dark recess behind it.

Donovan's fingers danced over the keypad, a staccato rhythm that belied his pounding heart. Amy hovered close, her breath quick and shallow, eyes darting between Donovan and the chief superintendent who stood with arms folded, a façade of composure.

"Simon better be right," Donovan muttered under his breath, each button press echoing in the tense silence.

"Trust him," Amy whispered back, her hand gripping the butt of her service weapon as if ready to draw.

The final digit entered, and they held their breath—a click so soft it barely stirred the air. The safe's door swung open, betraying its secrets with reluctant creaks. Donovan exhaled, a ghost of a victory smile crossing his face.

"Jackpot."

Inside, nestled among stacks of cash and glinting trinkets, lay the prize—a red leather-bound journal. Its cover was embossed with an intricate pattern, giving nothing away from the darkness inscribed within its pages.

"Here." Donovan handed the journal to Amy, his hands unexpectedly steady.

"Let me see that!" Chief protested, straining against the invisible chains of their authority.

"Shut it," Donovan spat, without turning.

Amy turned page after page, each revealing another piece of the puzzle: names, dates, places—all weaving a tapestry of corruption and power. The scent of leather mixed with the musk of hidden truths held close to the chest, now laid bare for the world to see.

"Blackmail," she said, voice low but laced with disgust.

"Enough evidence to bury them," Donovan replied, his voice equally grim.

Shadows from the blinds striped his face, hinting at the bars that awaited their suspect. His pulse thrummed in his temples, the gravity of their discovery anchoring him in the moment.

"Got you, you bastard," he breathed, not to the chief, but to the ghosts of the docks, to justice itself.

Donovan's fingers flicked through the pages, each one a revelation. Codes. Meetings. Payoffs. His eyes darted across the ink, committing names and numbers to memory—evidence that would dismantle the OCG from its rotten core. He could almost hear the empire crumbling.

"Those are lies!" Chief's voice was a desperate claw, trying to snag on anything that might save him.

"Truth hurts," Donovan shot back, snapping the journal shut with a sound that echoed finality.

He locked eyes with the chief superintendent; a man he once respected, now nothing more than a criminal in a tailored suit.

"Turn around." His command was steel wrapped in velvet, non-negotiable.

"Listen, Donovan, you're making a mistake—"

"Hands behind your back." Donovan wasn't listening.

He was already moving forward, cuffs in hand, the weight of justice heavy in his grip.

"Let's move," Amy said, their signal to end this charade.

Chief Superintendent's protests fizzled into silence as the metal clicked shut, a symphony to Donovan's ears. With each ratchet, another chain of corruption was broken.

"Let's walk," Donovan intoned, voice devoid of triumph. It wasn't a victory he felt but a grim satisfaction. The war against the OCG was far from over. But today, they had won an important battle.

Through the open plan offices of police HQ, Donovan led the way. Amy at his side, and the chief superintendent between them—handcuffed. The rhythm of their footsteps was a drumbeat of impending justice. Eyes lifted from screens; whispers grew into murmurs. Officers stood in disbelief as the procession passed.

"Isn't that—" someone began but fell silent.

"Keep moving," Donovan barked, his voice slicing through the thick air of shock.

Chief Superintendent's head was held high, but his eyes betrayed him; darting around like a cornered animal. With every step, his façade of control crumbled, leaving a trail of shattered illusions behind them.

"Clear a path," Amy commanded, her presence unyielding.

The sea of desks parted, uniformed bodies stepping aside, some with respect, others with a grim sense of satisfaction.

The elevator dinged its arrival, and they stepped inside. The doors closed on the last vestiges of normalcy in the HQ.

―― " ――

In the courtroom, the air was stagnant with anticipation. Donovan watched as Chief Superintendent—now defendant—stood rigid before the judge. The once-immaculate uniform hung heavy on his frame, badges of honour tarnished by the weight of his crimes.

The judge's words rained down like a death sentence, his voice cold and unfeeling as he delivered the final blow. "Guilty," he thundered, slamming his gavel with a resounding bang. "Life imprisonment without parole, you abused your position and now you must pay."

The weight of the sentence hit hard, sinking in like an impenetrable wall around him. There was no escape, no hope, only a lifetime behind bars to face the consequences of his actions.

A collective exhale filled the room, a sound made up of relief and disbelief. Scribbling pens paused, capturing the moment for posterity.

"Order!" The gavel struck, its echo marking the end of an era of corruption.

"Justice served," Amy whispered, her voice barely audible amid the shuffle of legal papers and the subdued chatter of a gallery grappling with reality.

Donovan breathed a sigh of relief, and the lines around his eyes etched a bit deeper today. As Chief Superintendent was led away, there was no gloating, no smile of vindication. There was only the resolute stride of a man who knew the fight was far from over.

The courtroom dissolved into a blur as Donovan turned on his heel and stepped into the corridor. The click of his shoes against the polished floor paced out the rhythm of a job well done. He leaned against the cool wall, feeling the solidity against his back. His heart still thrummed with adrenaline, but it was different now—tempered by accomplishment.

"Never thought I'd see the day," Donovan murmured to himself, more an affirmation than a statement.

Amy approached, her nod subtle but meaningful. "We did it, Donovan."

"Did we?" His eyes met hers, sharp and searching. "Or did we just start?"

"Both," she replied, understanding the weight behind his words.

They were soldiers in suits, fighting battles within these walls that had ripple effects far beyond.

"Justice," he said, the word tasting foreign yet familiar. "It's not just a verdict. It's a promise we keep."

"Every time," Amy's agreement was steadfast.

He pushed off from the wall, his reflection in the glass trophy case across the hall showing a man changed—not just by this case but—by a lifetime of them. Each one left a mark, each mark a story.

"Next steps?" Her voice was ready, poised for action.

"Clean up," he said decisively. "The rats will be scurrying now."

"Then let's hunt." There was no hesitation in her stride as they walked together, side by side.

"Until every last one is caught." The resolve in Donovan's tone matched his pace—relentless and unwavering.

"Until then," Amy confirmed.

They exited the courthouse, stepping out into the city that never rested, much like the fight they waged—a fight against shadows, against crime woven into the fabric of society. But today, the fabric had torn, and light had seeped through.

Donovan felt it, that sense of beginning anew. Justice had been served, yet the taste only steeled his appetite for righteousness. He would chase the dawn if it meant another dark corner illuminated, another victory for those who couldn't fight.

"Let's get to work," he said, and the city answered back with its ceaseless hum, a backdrop to the unending battle he was ready to face again.

The courthouse doors swung shut behind them, the clamour of the city swallowing their exit. Donovan's eyes scanned the horizon; steel and glass piercing the sky, a jungle of structures harbouring secrets.

"The vault," he uttered, his voice cutting through the hum of traffic.

"Already on it." Amy's fingers danced over her phone, alerting backup, her other hand signalling a black sedan kerbside.

"Every informant. Every lead."

"Every shadow."

The car door slammed, sealing them in a cocoon of urgency.

"Review the journal," Donovan commanded, flipping open the red leather cover.

Lines of info bled across the pages. Names. Dates. Transactions.

"Anything we missed?" Her eyes never left the road, weaving through cars like a thread through the fabric.

"Patterns. Connections." His finger traced a labyrinth of corruption, each entry a step deeper into the underworld.

"Here," he tapped a name that repeated like a sinister refrain. "Focus on this one."

"Got it."

Buildings blurred past, the cityscape a smudged painting under the sweep of streetlights. The car prowled the streets, a predator amidst prey.

"Pressure," he said, his gaze hardening. "We apply pressure until they crumble."

"Like always," she responded, her voice edged with steel.

"Checkpoints ahead." Blue lights flashed, and barricades were erected with swift precision.

Exiting the vehicle, they returned to their home base. It was time to gather the team and brief them on the upcoming raid on the Vault, now that they had confirmation from the journal that this was where the nest of vipers lived.

"Let's finish this." Donovan's voice barely rose above a whisper, but it carried the weight of finality.

"Until it's done," Amy affirmed, her hand resting on her holster.

They gathered around a large table, huddled in close as they meticulously planned the raid. Each detail was carefully considered and discussed, leaving nothing to chance, no stone upturned. The room was filled with tense energy.

Every member sat with a map spread out before them, their fingers tracing over it as they strategised. Not a single detail would be overlooked or underestimated. It was clear that this raid was of utmost importance, and they were fully prepared to see it through to success.

Chapter 48: The Syndicate

The Birmingham night clung to Donovan's coat as he led his team down the dampened streets. Streetlights cast long shadows around 'The Vault' bar, the neon sign flickering with a hesitating glow. He checked his watch: 23:07. Late enough for a cloak of darkness, early enough for witnesses.

"Stay sharp," he murmured, hand resting on the cool steel beneath his jacket.

His eyes darted from face to face, lingering on any lingerer who dared hold his gaze too long.

"Copy that," Amy replied, voice low, fingers brushing against the butt of her gun.

They reached the entrance. The door creaked open, a sliver of raucous laughter escaping into the night before being snuffed out by the closing gap. Inside, the scent of stale beer and sweat wrapped around them. Conversations stuttered. Eyes twitched in their direction.

"Fan out," Donovan instructed, his voice barely above a whisper but carrying the weight of command.

He stepped into the dim interior, the change from cold air to warm almost suffocating. The bar was a jungle of glances and murmurs. Patrons huddled over drinks, their whispers like the rustling of leaves just before a storm. Donovan's gut tightened and a silent alarm bell thrummed against his ribs.

"Something is not right," he said, catching Castle's eye.

She nodded, hand discreetly hovering near her holster as she sidled up to the bar, blending in with the crowd.

"Watch the exits," Donovan signalled to the rest of his team.

Their nods were minute, imperceptible to anyone not looking for them.

The bartender met Donovan's approach with a practised smile. However, his eyes flitted nervously to the corner where a cluster of bulky men stood watchful; their suits a size too small for the muscle they strained to contain.

"Can I get you something?" the bartender asked, his voice steady despite the tension that hummed through it.

"Info is what I'm after," Donovan answered, presenting his badge with a sleight-of-hand quickness. "About them."

The bartender's eyes flicked toward the corner, then back, a silent conversation passing between them.

"Can't help you," he said, but his Adam's apple betrayed him with a nervous bob.

Donovan didn't press further; he'd gotten all he needed. He slipped away from the bar, melting into the background noise. Every step was measured, and every breath was calculated. His team was a network of silent communication, each member aware of the other's positions.

"Ready when you are," he whispered into the comms, his thumb caressing the safety of his gun.

"Ready," came the echoed affirmations.

The air hung heavy with anticipation, charged with an electricity that buzzed louder than the neon signs outside. Donovan's heart thrummed a drumbeat in his chest, steady and ready for the dance to begin.

The first shot cracked through the din, a single, sharp disruption that preluded chaos. Glasses shattered. Brandy bled across the bar top. Patrons hit the floor, scrambling under tables as the guards surrounding *The Syndicate* leaders snapped to attention, their hands already drawing weapons.

"Contact!" Donovan barked, the word a trigger in itself.

His team, a well-oiled machine of discipline and precision, fanned out. They slid into cover, behind pillars and overturned chairs, their firearms speaking in staccato bursts. The return fire was immediate, bullets zipping close enough to singe the air, embedding themselves into wood and plaster with lethal intent.

"Left flank!" Donovan called out, sighting down his barrel at a guard trying to manoeuvre for a better angle.

His finger squeezed the trigger; the reaction was clinical, detached.

"Got him," came the clipped response over the comms.

The smell of gunpowder clawed at his nostrils, a pungent reminder of the immediacy of danger. Tables splintered under the onslaught, shards of wood joining the symphony of destruction that played out in *The Vault*.

"Covering fire," he ordered, shifting position to provide a clear line for his second-in-command, Amy to advance.

Their movements were synchronised, each step calculated amidst the anarchy.

"Advancing," she confirmed; her silhouette was a ghost flitting between beams of light and shadow.

"Watch your back," Donovan warned, catching movement from the corner of his eye.

"Clear," she replied a heartbeat later, the threat neutralised.

The gunfire dwindled, a crescendo falling away to reveal the gasps and murmurs of the bystanders caught in the crossfire. Donovan's ears rang with the residual echoes of the battle, but his focus never wavered from the mission at hand.

Donovan's breaths came hard and fast, mirroring the rhythm of his pounding heart. He ducked low, weaving through a hail of bullets, his gaze locked onto the guards' shifting positions.

"On three," he barked into the comm, veins throbbing with adrenaline.

"Two," his partner counted down, voice steady despite the chaos.

"Three." The word was a grenade, propelling them into orchestrated havoc.

They fired in unison, bullets tearing through air and flesh. Donovan's world narrowed to the space between heartbeats, each shot an extension of his will.

Commands flew between breaths, terse and absolute, "Push!"

"Pushing!" his team echoed and their movements a blur of tactical precision.

A guard crumpled, and another staggered back. Donovan advanced, his gun an unwavering beacon amidst the storm. Screams and gunfire melded into a grotesque symphony, yet his focus remained sharp as shattered glass beneath his boots.

"Corner clear!"

"Stairs secured!" reports punctuated the gunfire, signs of relentless progress.

The opposition's fire slackened, their numbers dwindling under the assault. Donovan pressed on, the taste of victory bitter with cordite. Each takedown a step closer to silence, to the end they all sought.

"Last one!" A shout cut through, tinged with triumph.

Donovan rounded on the final guard, the man's eyes wide with the dawning of defeat. A single shot rang out—a punctuation mark at the end of the sentence that was this battle.

Silence crashed down like a wave, leaving only the ragged inhales of survivors and the soft moans of the wounded. Donovan stood amid the stillness;

gun lowered but senses alert. His team's eyes met his—a wordless exchange—confirming their solidarity and success.

"Area secure," he finally declared, the weight of the moment settling over them like dust.

Donovan's gaze swept the bar, a predator's scan for hidden dangers. Empty shells crunched underfoot as he stepped over debris, his team maintaining a tight formation behind him. The dim light glinted off his pistol, still drawn, still ready.

"Check them," he barked, nodding toward the huddled figures of *The Syndicate's* leaders.

His voice was granite, echoing slightly in the sudden quiet.

"Clear here," came the curt reply from Jenkins, who patted down one of the men with methodical precision.

"Nothing on this one," said Mortimer, his hands swift and sure.

"Perimeter is secure," added Thompson, eyes never ceasing their vigil.

Donovan nodded, holstering his weapon with a click that seemed to reverberate through the newfound silence. He surveyed his team—each one alert, unscathed, their breathing steady despite the adrenaline that still charged the air.

"Good. Let's move." His command cut across any lingering tension, and they moved as one, a unit forged in the fires of countless skirmishes.

———— " ————

The courtroom was a stark contrast to the chaos of *The Vault*. Here—order ruled—the law's gravity palpable in the sombre wood panelling, the stern faces of the jury, and the silent gallery at Birmingham's high court.

"Stand," the bailiff intoned a word that brought the four accused to their feet.

Donovan watched from the back, his presence a shadow among shadows.

The dock held them—four men—once untouchable—now prisoners of their own making. Defiance warred with fear in their eyes, a dance of emotions played out in the flicker of lights above.

"State your names," Judge demanded, his voice slicing through the silence like a blade.

"Anthony Reddington."

"Paul Sanchez."

"Viktor Bains."

"Kwame Adomako."

Each name fell like a hammer, forging the final links in the chains that would bind them. Donovan's whole body tightened gradually—a silent witness to the weight of justice being served.

The judge's gavel was a gunshot in the silence, its echo a harbinger of verdicts to come. Donovan's heart didn't flutter; it was steady. Like a metronome to the months spent unravelling the Syndicate's web. He leaned against the cool marble pillar at the back of the courtroom, arms folded, the observer now, not the hunter.

"Members of the jury, have you reached a verdict that you all can agree upon?" The words were mere formality in the charged air.

"We have, Your Honour."

A collective breath held, then released in whispers as the foreman stood, a slip of paper—a fate—clutched in his hand.

"Please, read the verdict," the judge ordered.

The foreman's voice was clear, unequivocal. "We find the defendants guilty on count 1; the manufacturing and supply of Class A narcotics, count 2; the laundering of his majesties currency of the realm. Count 3; the smuggling of people across the UK's borders."

"Guilty." The word resonated, bouncing off polished wood and hardened criminals alike.

"Thank you, jury, for your service." The judge's nod was solemn respect, then his attention pivoted to the condemned. "This court will not tolerate the flagrant disregard for life and law that you have exhibited."

Donovan watched as the Syndicate leaders swayed, their façades cracking. Paul's dark eyes flitted about, seeking an escape that wasn't there. Anthony's lips pressed into a line, the reality dawning like a slow poison. Viktor's broad shoulders slumped, defeat wearing him down. Kwame's gaze dropped; the ground suddenly fascinated.

"Sentencing will proceed." The judge's voice left no room for hope.

"Anthony Reddington, Paul Sanchez, Viktor Bains, Kwame Adomako," he began, each name punctuated with the finality of a coffin nail. "You will each serve multiple life sentences without the possibility of parole."

The courtroom erupted, cries of surprise, disbelief, relief and anguish mingling in the air. Donovan remained still, his eyes tracing the arc of justice's long, often invisible, arm.

"Order!" The judge's command sliced through the chaos, "Take them down."

As officers ushered the broken men away, Donovan allowed the ghost of a smile. Justice had been served, cold and unyielding. And somewhere in the city's vibrant buzz, life went on, a little safer now.

The courtroom hum quieted to a murmur. Donovan's gaze cut across the space, finding Chief Inspector Victoria Grace. Her nod was slight, imperceptible to anyone not looking for it. The message was clear: *they'd done it*.

"Ma'am," he mouthed silently.

"Detective Donovan," she returned, her eyes echoing months of toil now settled in the gravity of victory.

He leaned back against the wooden bench, the creaking sound a testament to the weight he carried all this time. Now lifted. The air felt different—lighter, almost electric with the pulse of justice.

Victory had a scent, like the sharp tang after a rainstorm. It cleansed.

His fingers tapped a rhythm on his thigh. Muscle memory from countless nights working, waiting for the break that would bring them here. To this moment. Each tap is a reminder of the chase, the pursuit of something greater than themselves.

"Adjourned," the judge declared, breaking Donovan's reverie.

Chairs scraped. Voices rose in crescendo. Donovan remained seated, his thoughts racing even as the room emptied. Faces flashed in his mind's eye: victims, witnesses, the relentless team. Each one a stitch in the tapestry of their triumph.

"Drink?" CI Grace's voice cut through his contemplation.

Donovan considered, then nodded once. "Yeah, why not."

They stood together, moving against the flow of bodies streaming towards the exit. His steps were measured, the pace deliberate. Outside these walls, the world continued its spin, but within, time seemed to stand witness to their resolve.

As the last person left, Donovan paused at the threshold. He turned, taking in the empty benches, the silent gavel, and the echo of the ghost's past. This hall, once filled with the spectre of violence and greed, now held only the whisper of justice served.

"Come on, Donovan." CI Grace's voice pulled him forward.

"Right behind you," he replied, stepping into the corridor.

He knew the journey wasn't over. There were more monsters to chase, and more darkness to bring into the light. But tonight, they rested. Tonight, they remembered why they fought so hard.

Justice had prevailed, if only for a moment. And that was enough. For now.

Jimi got placed in a witness protection program, but tragedy strikes when—later that year—he is shot and killed during a botched drug deal. Some may see it as poetic justice.

Donovan and Amy are honoured with police commendation awards for their bravery and contributions to the operations at Witley Court and Drakelow Tunnels. Their names will forever be associated with taking down one of the most notorious criminal organisations seen in this country.

Chapter 49: Epilogue

Jess gasped, her eyes wide. "Donovan, I—"

He held his breath, heart pounding. Toby sat beside him, tail wagging.

"Yes!" Jess exclaimed, throwing her arms around Donovan's neck.

He stood, lifting her off her feet in a tight embrace. Their laughter echoed across the river.

Toby barked, joining the celebration.

They settled on a weathered wooden bench overlooking the river, fingers intertwined. Toby flopped at their feet, content.

"I can't believe it," Jess said, admiring the ring.

Sunlight glinted off the diamond, casting tiny rainbows on her skin.

Donovan squeezed her hand. "Believe it."

"Where did you get the ring? It's gorgeous," Jess inquired.

"I got it at that cute little shop you always love browsing through, Designs by Kim Johnson. They have all those unique candles and knick-knacks," Donovan responded.

They sat in comfortable silence, watching the sun dip lower, painting the sky in vibrant oranges and pinks. The river mirrored the colours, shimmering like liquid fire.

"So, the Lake District," Donovan mused. "Any specific plans?"

Jess' eyes lit up. "Hiking, definitely. Maybe we could do Scafell Pike?"

"Ambitious. I like it."

"And a boat tour on Windermere. Oh! And we must visit that little tea shop in Ambleside—you know, the one with those incredible scones," Jess gushed, her excitement palpable.

Donovan nodded, a smile tugging at his lips. "Sounds perfect. We could also check out Beatrix Potter's house. I know you've always wanted to see it."

"Oh yes!" Jess clapped her hands together. "And maybe we could do some stargazing? I've heard the night sky in the Lake District is incredible."

"We'll have to pack a telescope. I can borrow one from one of the team," Donovan promised. He leaned back, stretching his arm across the bench behind Jess. "You know, I can't remember the last time I had a proper break."

Jess leaned into him, her head resting on his shoulder. "Me" And a boat tour of Windermere.

"Let's celebrate," Donovan said suddenly, standing up. "Come on."

He took Jess' hand, and they set off down the riverside path, Toby trotting beside them. The evening air was cool and fragrant with wildflowers. They rounded a bend, the old stone bridge coming into view.

"Where are we going?" Jess asked, laughing.

"You'll see."

They crossed the bridge, footsteps echoing on the worn cobblestones. The town square bustled with early evening activity. Donovan led them to Hargrove's Bakery; a quaint shop with a red-striped awning.

A bell tinkled as they entered. The aroma of fresh bread enveloped them.

"Two lovebirds!" old Mr Hargrove called from behind the counter. "What can I get you?"

"Two slices of that cherry Bakewell, please," Donovan said, grinning. "And a small sourdough."

Mr Hargrove's eyes twinkled. "Special occasion?"

Jess held up her hand, the ring catching the light. "We just got engaged!"

"Well, I'll be!" Mr Hargrove exclaimed. "Congratulations! The loaf is on the house."

They left the bakery, the warm bread nestled in a brown paper bag. Donovan led them down a narrow cobblestone alley, past the old clock tower, and towards the museum.

The pond behind the museum was a hidden gem, known mostly to locals. Weeping willows drooped over the water's edge, their leaves dancing on the surface. A family of mallards glided across the pond, leaving ripples in their wake.

Donovan and Jess settled on a weathered wooden bench near the water's edge. Toby sprawled at their feet, his tail thumping softly against the grass. The evening light filtered through the willow branches, casting dappled shadows across the pond's surface.

Jess tore off a piece of the still-warm sourdough, its yeasty aroma mingling with the scent of water lilies. She tossed it gently towards the ducks, who quacked excitedly and paddled closer.

"Look at that one," Donovan chuckled, pointing to a small duckling lagging behind the others. "Bit of an underdog, isn't he?"

Jess smiled, breaking off another piece of bread. "He just needs a little encouragement."

She tossed the morsel directly to the duckling, who snatched it up.

Donovan laughs as he reflects on his journey from being an underdog to becoming a hero, all grown up and about to get married.

"I have to pinch myself to make sure this is real."

Jess leaned into Donovan, her warmth a stark contrast to the cooling evening air.

"It's real," she whispered, squeezing his hand. "We're real."

They sat in companionable silence, watching the ducks glide across the pond's mirrored surface. The sky deepened to a rich indigo, the first stars peeking through the fading light. A gentle breeze rustled the willow leaves, their whispers a soothing lullaby.

Donovan broke off a piece of the cherry Bakewell, the sweet almond scent mingling with the earthy aroma of the pond. He offered it to Jess, who took a bite closing her eyes in delight. A smudge of cherry jam lingered on her lower lip, and Donovan leaned in to kiss it away.

Toby's ears perked up, his head swivelling towards the museum. A faint melody drifted through the air, growing louder. The annual summer concert was starting, the orchestra tuning up in the courtyard behind the old brick building.

Donovan stood, offering his hand to Jess. "Shall we?"

They strolled hand-in-hand around the pond, Toby padding alongside. The music swelled, a lilting waltz that seemed to make the fireflies dance in the gathering twilight. As they rounded the corner, the old lawn came into view, strings of fairy lights crisscrossing overhead like a canopy of stars in the pergola.

Couples swayed, their shadows stretching long in the soft glow. Without a word, Donovan pulled Jess close; one hand on her waist, the other clasping hers.

"May I have the pleasure of this dance?" Donovan asked, extending his hand towards her.

The couple swayed and spun under the starry sky, lost in each other's embrace. The warm breeze carried the sweet scent of blooming flowers and the sound of laughter from nearby festivities. Their feet moved effortlessly to the music, creating a perfect harmony with each step. As they danced into the evening, their hearts overflowed with joy and love, making this a day that would be forever etched in their memories.

As they danced, the world seemed to fade away. The music swelled, wrapping around them like a cocoon. Jess' hair caught the moonlight, shimmering like spun gold. Donovan's eyes never left hers, drinking in every detail of this perfect moment.

Toby sat nearby, his tail thumping rhythmically against the grass. He watched his humans with adoring eyes, sensing their happiness.

The song ended, but they kept swaying. Donovan pulled Jess closer, breathing in her familiar scent of lavender and honey.

"I love you," he murmured into her hair.

"I love you too," she whispered back, her voice thick with emotion.

——— " ———

Simon's prison cell is small and dark, with gray concrete walls and a rusted metal toilet in the corner. He can see the other inmates through the bars, their faces hardened and filled with malice. The guards march by, their eyes constantly scanning for any signs of trouble in this maximum-security hell hole.

The bars on the cell windows glint in the harsh fluorescent lights, a constant reminder of his confinement.

The other inmates sneer and glare at him, their expressions contorted with deep-seated hatred. Their eyes burned with malice, and their lips curled into disdainful smirks, revealing crooked, yellowed teeth. The air thick with animosity, as if their collective resentment had materialized into something almost tangible.

The dank smell of mold and unwashed bodies fills the air together with the pungent stench of sweat and fear, the sharp odour of bleach used to clean the floors, the faint whiff of drugs being passed around.

The metal bars of his cell were cold to the touch, sending shivers down his spine every time he grasped them. The hard, uncomfortable cot he slept on offered no relief for his aching body.

Simon's days in prison are a never-ending cycle of fear and anguish. Every moment is spent in a state of constant paranoia, his mind a prison within a prison.

The weight of his past crimes hung heavy on his shoulders, a reminder of the darkness that consumed him. Even in the safety of his cell, he could not escape the haunting memories and the constant threat of retaliation from those he had wronged. And as the years pass, Simon's once youthful face will become etched with lines of regret and remorse, a physical manifestation of the prison that held him captive for the life sentence he now served.

——— " ———

Jimi dropped out of witness protection and spent his years navigating the shadowy underworld, working for small-time gangs, constantly hustling to make ends meet. The dimly lit alleys and the whispered deals were his familiar haunts.

On a grim and ominous day, amid the shadows of a secluded city corner, he found himself ensnared in a minor drug trade that spiralled into chaos. Suddenly, with a ferocious and savage thrust, a blade tore into his flesh, ending his life in a storm of violence. His murderer slipped away into the engulfing darkness, disappearing like a ghost, never to be captured or even seen again.

At his funeral, there was an eerie silence, the absence of mourners stark against the grey, overcast sky. Not a single soul was there to shed a tear for the man who had lived and died in the shadows. His body was buried in a pauper's grave.